Stephen Lloyd Jones's debut novel, *The String Diaries*, was a BBC Radio 2 Book Club selection, a Kindle Editor's Pick, and was translated into nine languages. *The Silenced* is his fourth novel, and his first two novels have both been optioned for television. His passions are strong coffee, telling stories and spending time in the mountains. He lives with his wife, their three young sons and a lunatic dog.

Praise for Stephen Lloyd Jones:

'Jones's tale of a people struggling for survival is as emotionally compelling as it is frightening' *Kirkus Reviews*

'Will keep you awake late into the night' *SFX*

'A rich story that has the detail and precision of a scholastic study thrust upon the suspense and visual grandeur of a cinematic thriller' Brooke Wylie, *Examiner.com*

'Original, richly imagined and powerfully told' *Guardian*

'So gripping you'll want to read late into the night; so terrifying you shouldn't' Simon Mayo, Radio 2 Book Club

'*The String Diaries* is edge-of-your-seat-turn-on-all-the-lights-lock-the-doors-and-cancel-all-appointments brilliant' *Bookbag*

'A page turner . . . a sophisticated horror story that induces elemental terror' *New York Daily News*

'Jones ⬚ , turning over h ⬚ dealer' *Enterta* ⬚

By Stephen Lloyd Jones and available from Headline

The String Diaries
Written in the Blood
The Disciple
The Silenced

# THE
# SILENCED

## STEPHEN LLOYD JONES

HEADLINE

First published in Great Britain in 2018 by
HEADLINE PUBLISHING GROUP

1

Cataloguing in Publication Data is available from the British Library

ISBN 978 1 4722 2892 5

Typeset in Bembo by Avon DataSet Ltd, Bidford-on-Avon, Warwickshire

Printed and bound by CPI Group (UK) Ltd, Croydon, CR0 4YY

HEADLINE PUBLISHING GROUP
An Hachette UK Company
Carmelite House
50 Victoria Embankment
London EC4Y 0DZ

www.headline.co.uk
www.hachette.co.uk

This book is dedicated to Kevin Jones.

Not only an awesome little brother but
a top-notch, unpaid IT helpdesk.

# ONE

**M**allory wouldn't return to the bathroom because that's where the dead man was, but she did need to wash off his blood – it clung to her skin like opera gloves worn to the elbow. She could smell it, rich and thick; in the surrounding darkness it dripped to the hallway floorboards with a steady *pt-pt-pt* in time with her heart.

She wanted to turn on a light. Daren't. The dead man wouldn't have done that, and he might have an accomplice outside. Watching the house.

If she couldn't use the bathroom to clean herself up, that left either the master bedroom's en suite or the ground-floor kitchen. From the landing, the staircase was a black void that promised to yield more horror; she would not descend into it so wholly unprepared.

Raising her hands – feeling the dead man's blood run from her forearms – Mallory tiptoed along the hall. Her every move left evidence; an incriminating trail for those who wished to exploit it. Between her bare toes the blood was already congealing.

Outside the bedroom, she leaned against the doorframe and felt herself teeter on the edge of consciousness. The darkness around her head throbbed, populated by the cruellest demons her imagination could conjure.

Was most of this blood her own? Could the dead man have inflicted more damage than she'd first realised? Perhaps the adrenalin fizzing through her arteries smothered the pain of mortal injuries.

Now, another thought surfaced: had she *really* killed him back there? Perhaps she was mistaken about that too. Perhaps he'd climbed up from the bathroom floor and was silently stalking her across the landing while she lingered here, ignorant of the danger.

Mallory turned, expecting the shadows to produce a monster. A lick of warm air touched her skin and she clenched her teeth, certain, now, that her assailant stood mere inches away. Her heart was a bird beating broken wings against her ribs. So loud in this silence. So fragile.

She tensed in the doorway, holding herself erect, terrified that by moving she would give away her position and feel the wet kiss of a blade, or the bone-shattering impact of a hammer.

Another press of air lifted fronds of hair from her face. Abruptly, she recalled the window she had found at the back of the house, open to the night.

Of course. *That* was the source of the breeze. The man in the bathroom was dead. No question.

Slipping into her bedroom, Mallory saw a narrow avenue of moonlight running across the floor. When she padded through it to the bed, someone stepped out of the wall in front of her, then vanished.

A scream lodged like a beetle in her throat. Yet when she plunged backwards through the ribbon of light, she discovered that the intruder was simply her own reflection, cast from the cheval mirror beside the dressing table. The moon's lambent shine had bleached her of all colour. Her forearms glistened, oily black. The front of her nightdress was slick. Somewhere, in the ghostly face hovering above the neckline, she recognised herself. Not the eyes, though. *They* appeared irredeemably lost. Two white spheres, swollen with awful knowledge:

*I killed a man.*

Yes. And if she were to survive this, she would have to kill again.

Her gown lay on the bed. She picked it up, using it as a towel to scrub the dead man from her skin. His blood was gummier now, like curdled egg yolks clinging to the fine hairs of her forearms. Once she'd taken off the worst of it, she stepped towards the en suite.

Hesitated.

There were no windows in there. No hope of escape should a second intruder arrive to finish the work of the first. She could lock the door, but it would last seconds against a determined assault.

Inside, Mallory heard the echoing drip of water.

Moving to the sink, she felt for the taps and spun them. Water spattered, then gushed. She scooped up cold handfuls, rinsed her arms clean. Beneath her feet, the tiles grew slippery.

Stripping off her blood-sodden nightdress, Mallory tossed it into the shower. She placed a hand on her belly and slid her fingers across it, checking for lacerations, bruising or swelling. She touched her chest, her throat, her face.

Unmarked.

Working fast in the darkness, she washed the blood from her torso and feet. The sound of water plinking onto the tiles was a score of miniature clocks, all slowing. Time: running down, running out. Abandoning the sink, Mallory retreated to the bedroom. There, in a slim wedge of moonlight, she paused and listened.

Again, that soft breeze feathered her skin, teasing it into goosebumps. It carried upon it myriad competing scents. From outside, the subtle astringency of London's streets, pollen-rich and laden with summer humidity. Far closer, the abattoir tang of the dead man, overlaid with her own sour sweat.

Against the far wall stood a chest of drawers. Mallory went to it. She dressed quickly – jeans, T-shirt, hoodie – and slipped her feet into Nike running shoes.

The clothes helped. Made her feel more in control.

From the dresser she retrieved her mobile phone and checked it. No missed calls or texts. No emails waiting in her inbox.

No warnings, then. No last-minute appeals for her to flee. These days, though, what allies did she have left to help her? Except Sal, of course. But perhaps Sal was already dead.

The phone had under half its battery available. How lax, in hindsight, she had grown. How careless. But spend too long in any one place and watchfulness would deteriorate; over time, the hard edges of paranoia grew as smooth as tide-tumbled stones.

From the dresser's drawer she grabbed a clutch of passports, driving licences and credit cards, and filled her pockets.

Outside, the night wind blew, knocking the branches of an ash tree against the window. The sound was like the clatter of knucklebones across a tombstone, and it drew a shiver from Mallory that she struggled to control.

*I killed a man.*

From here, there was no path back to the way things had been. On the first floor of this Clapham townhouse, her world had irrevocably changed.

There remained the slim possibility that tonight's attack had been random, that the man in her bathroom had been an opportunist – a burglar, or a rapist. But even if that *were* true it still meant that this house, in which she'd found sanctuary these last few years, was her home no longer.

No point fooling herself. In her gut, she knew that he had been Vasi. Knew, too, that despite her lapses, she'd been careful not to draw attention during her time in London. She was a ghost, here; a shadow. Which left only a single explanation for her unmasking, this one far too shocking to contemplate.

Beside the bed stood a wooden cabinet. Mallory pulled open the top drawer, rummaging through layers of folded underwear until her fingers touched another credit card-sized ID. She pulled it out, angled it towards the window. Saw the rainbow glint of a hologram. Of all the IDs she possessed, this was the only one not to feature her image.

The moonlight was insufficient to illuminate the boy's face, but she felt his eyes on her even so. Felt, too, a cold serpent of nausea uncoil in her gut. She wanted to drop the card back into the cabinet and slam the door shut on it, but in her fingers it seemed to radiate a power all of its own; before she quite knew what she was doing, she slid it into the back pocket of her jeans.

Immediately, her nausea cleared. Her breathing accelerated. Adrenalin smothered uncertainty.

From under the bed, Mallory dragged out a rucksack. Packed inside was a change of clothes, a sleeping bag and bivvy, four days' worth of rations, batteries, medical supplies and other equipment she might need. Everything else she had acquired during her twenty-four years – a few items of furniture, a small collection of art and curios – would be lost.

As Mallory slid her arms into the rucksack's straps, she thought she heard something, deeper inside the house. She stopped, breath trapped in her lungs.

Listened.

According to the masonry stone set above the front entrance, the building dated from 1844. On summer nights like this, as the day's heat dissipated into a cloudless sky, it grumbled around its foundations like an embittered old man. Floorboards creaked; pipework rattled and thumped; sash windows moaned in their frames.

Mallory had not heard anything like that, and yet she could not recall exactly what she *had* heard. Perhaps her subconscious had begun to weave menace from the tattered threads of her composure.

She stepped into the hallway, one hand raised before her. Here, the darkness was absolute. Her heart thumped so fiercely that she felt its echoes in her throat, her wrists. Treading softly on the old floorboards, Mallory edged along the hall. On her right – although she couldn't see it – ran the balustrade overlooking the stairs. She reached for the handrail and used it to guide her, fearing, as she progressed, that she would touch the hand of a second intruder approaching from the opposite direction. The thought made her skin prickle.

Silent, she walked past the guest bedroom. When her knuckles knocked against the newel cap at the corner of the landing, she halted.

To her right, three stairs descended to a quarter-landing. From there, the main flight led down to the unlit ground floor. Directly ahead, invisible in the darkness, a single step dropped into the passage that served the first-floor bathroom and the box room above the kitchen. The smell of blood was stronger here, so heavy that it clung to the back of her throat like a spoor.

Mallory tilted her head. Interrogated the darkness.

If she turned right, taking the main stairs, she could be outside within a minute, but would forego the emergency cash she kept hidden in the box room. Although she'd retrieved her credit cards, if her suspicions about this attack proved correct she would need all the money she could get. That slim fold of banknotes might mark the difference between evasion and capture; life and death.

But the box room also contained the forced-open window through which the dead man had entered.

*Don't think about that.*

*Do this last thing. Then get out.*

Nudging forwards, feeling with her foot for the edge of the step, Mallory descended into the passage. She kept close to the wall, minimising the chance of a loose tread betraying her position.

Night air pressed against her cheeks. Did she detect another scent on it now? One that hadn't been there before?

She wanted to close her eyes. Didn't. Extended her right arm instead. Gently she swabbed it left and right, hoping to give herself the earliest possible warning should someone emerge in front of her.

Behind, from the direction of the master bedroom, came a sound like an expelled breath. Mallory jerked around, biting back a cry. When she heard it a second time, she recognised it for what it was: the bedroom door whispering gently across the carpet.

Wind. Nothing more.

She turned back to the passageway. Another two paces would put the mouth of the upper stairs at her back. The prospect filled her stomach with acid, but an assailant ascending from the ground floor would be at a disadvantage, however fleeting. She could use the passage as cover should she need it; she knew the layout of this house better than anyone.

Another step. Now, the darkness surrendered to a soup of charcoal-greys. On her right the bathroom doorway emerged, a hard rectangle of black.

Mallory had vowed not to venture inside again, and yet to leave the bathroom unexplored while she continued to the back of the house would ignore all of Sal's advice.

The door hung open in mocking invitation. Through it rolled the manifold smells of death: not just blood and meat but urine too; the dead man, despite his passing, continued to violate her home.

Worse, however hard Mallory peered into the darkness, she could not see him lying there. The thought from earlier returned: had she really killed him? She could smell him readily enough, could recall the thickening gush of his blood. He had spouted like a slaughterhouse calf, and yet the human body was as resilient as the spirit; it accepted death reluctantly. If she intended to retrieve her cache of money from the box room, she could not leave the question of his fate unanswered.

From here, the merest illumination would betray her position. To do this, she would have to work blind.

Jaw set, Mallory pushed against the bathroom door. It squealed as it opened fully, tearing the silence. She cringed, readying herself for movement. When no attack came, she allowed the breath to trickle from her lungs and took another.

Three-quarters of the way through its arc, the bathroom door bumped against something solid.

She listened.

Took a tentative step forwards.

The air in here was still. She could no longer hear the knucklebone tap of the ash tree's branches, the thump of Victorian pipework or the pop of attic timbers.

Was she alone in the bathroom? No. She couldn't be. The door had bumped up against an obstacle that could only have been the dead man's legs.

Straining her ears, Mallory lowered herself into a crouch. A corpse was rarely entirely silent, especially one so recently dead; pockets of air escaped from settling lungs; small muscles − for a while, at least − spasmed and twitched; the stomach produced gas.

Around her, sepulchre-like quiet.

Slowly, excruciatingly, Mallory reached out. She clenched her teeth, determined not to scream if her hand met empty air, determined not to scream if it didn't. The chance that the man had survived her *kard*'s upward thrust was minimal − there had been so much blood − but she'd heard of stranger things. The possibility existed, however remote.

Her fingers touched fabric. Beneath it, she felt the firm curve of a calf, horribly warm. Trying not to gag, Mallory walked her fingers up the dead man's leg. When she reached his waist she encountered the stickiness of congealing blood. Maintaining her crouch, she shuffled closer. The floor was tacky beneath her feet. Her trainers smacked like chewed gum when she lifted them. She felt for his hand and found it.

It was warm and dry, so brutishly large that it could have completely enveloped her own. The fingers opened like the lobes of a carnivorous plant when she touched them. They were blunt-tipped, calloused, the nails bitten and jagged. She searched for the pulse-point at his wrist and lingered there, feeling for signs of life.

No insectile tick of pumped blood.

His arteries were silent.

Mallory suppressed a sob. This man – this Vasi assassin – had sought her out, had broken into her home with the intention of killing her. She felt no remorse for what she had done, but in taking his life she had lost something intangible, had created a void inside herself – a black burrow of emptiness – and for that she felt the profoundest sorrow, because if circumstances forced her to kill again, that emptiness would doubtless expand; over time, it would extinguish her as reliably as a bullet or blade.

The window blind was down, but a little moonlight leaked through the slats, enough to see the dull glimmer of the *kard*'s ivory handle. It stood up straight like a grave marker, immutable in the shadows.

*I killed a man.*

The air inside the bathroom had spoiled; Mallory's throat burned with the ammonia stench of urine. She pivoted on her feet, rubber soles crackling in coagulated blood. Careful to prevent the rucksack overbalancing her, she rose from the floor and stepped back into the passage.

Here, the night breeze still flowed. A few streets away she heard the rumble of London traffic; beyond it, the faint clatter of a train. So strange to think that out there life continued as normal.

In one of the neighbouring gardens, a fox screamed.

Fists clenched, Mallory crept along the passage. The box room had already spawned one horror this evening. No reason to believe it couldn't spawn more. A second intruder would be warier, more attuned to danger, more prepared for sudden violence. She should have retrieved her *kard* when she had the chance, but the thought of wrenching it from the dead man's throat had made her light-headed with revulsion. She could venture downstairs, arm herself with one of the weapons she kept there, return for the money. But instinct told her that right now speed was more important than caution.

Outside, the fox screamed again. From some distance away came an answering cry.

Padding along the passage, Mallory reached the box room. Moonlight, falling through the open sash window, had painted it silver. Either side of the sill, the floor-length curtains billowed like the sails of a schooner.

Cupboard in one corner; shelving unit along the far wall; a few woven seagrass baskets on the floor. Nowhere for an intruder to hide – which meant that unless someone had crept up the main staircase behind her, the building's first floor was clear.

Ducking down, careful to conceal herself from anyone watching outside, Mallory went to the shelves by the far wall. Finding a stack of old board games, she prised the lid off one and removed the board. Beneath, among the cards and counters, lay a fold of banknotes secured with a metal clip. As she shoved it into a pocket she heard something behind her, and wheeled around so fast that her rucksack thumped the shelf, knocking the board games to the floor in a shower of chits and bits. When a cardboard lid bounced off her leg, she nearly yelled.

No one leapt at her. No one plunged a blade into her belly or slashed at her throat. She wondered if the sound had come from the house itself. Perhaps there had been no sound at all.

Mallory moved to the door, and from there to the passage. Plum darkness greeted her. Steadily, she edged into it. She passed the bathroom without slowing, her stomach flopping at the rich odours wafting out.

On her left, the staircase beckoned like an open coffin. After a moment's hesitation she began to descend. It was cooler here; the air held a mausoleum chill.

Reaching the bottom of the flight, Mallory stepped into the ground-floor hall. The parquet floor near the front entrance glowed amber: illumination from streetlamps shining through the fanlight. When the wind pressed the branches of the ash tree outside, the light flickered and moved as if it transmitted images from a twirling zoetrope.

Opposite her stood the living-room entrance. Turning right would take her to the rear of the house, towards the kitchen and the study. Of those two rooms she chose the latter, padding across the hall and slipping inside. Earlier, she'd drawn the floor-length curtains. Like all the drapes in the house, they were lined with blackout material. When she shut the door behind her, total darkness returned. Here, for the first time, she dared to use a little light. Retrieving her smartphone, she activated its torch and shone the beam around the room.

Heavy oak furniture. Leather-upholstered chairs. No sign of disturbance.

Opposite stood a Regency-period display case with leaded glass panels. Mallory went to it and opened the doors. From its rows of books she selected just two, the first handwritten by her great-grandfather, the second an out-of-print work by a Balliol College scholar. From a desk drawer she took a spring-loaded stiletto.

Now, the decision. Did she leave the house from the back or the front? The dead man had entered through the box room above the kitchen. If an accomplice was watching outside, where was the most likely place he would station himself? Towards the rear, where he could monitor the initial breach? Or at the front, where he could cut off any escape attempt?

Over the last few years, Mallory had allowed the back garden to grow wild. In the far wall, a padlocked cast-iron gate opened into an unlit alley. It offered her the best route off the property undetected, but if she was intercepted there, the outcome would be quick, brutal and likely without a single witness.

The building's front entrance, by contrast, looked onto a well-lit street regularly populated – even at this time of night – with dog-walkers and those returning from late appointments in the city. Anyone monitoring the house would have to do so from one of the vehicles parked nose-to-tail along the pavement. If Mallory was fast enough, she might be able to escape before her assailant managed to get out of his car. She was weighed down with a rucksack, but she knew these streets and she trusted her speed.

In the end, with both options so tightly balanced, she made her decision based on the location of her Nissan. She never parked it in the street outside her home – one of the lessons from Sal she *hadn't* ignored. Right now the car was waiting in Montgomery Row, a sycamore-lined avenue just around the corner.

Mallory checked her pockets: car keys; IDs; credit cards; money. Reflexively she tightened the straps of her pack. Looked around the room one last time.

Over the fireplace hung a painting of the Library of Celsus at Ephesus in western Turkey. Sal had given it to her at their parting, and it pained her to surrender it. Likewise, the long-necked *bağlama* in the corner that she'd never quite learned to play. There were other instruments, too: a Turkish *cura mey*, beautifully carved; a hide-covered *davul*; even a twenty-six-string *qanun*, with which she'd had a little more success.

None of these items she would see again. Nor this magnificent old house, in which she'd lived, for a while, in safety and obscurity. Nobody here knew her. Nobody bothered her. Her name appeared on none of the mail that was delivered. Nor on the building's deeds. Once she left, ownership would revert to those who had endowed it; her mark on the place would disappear.

Time to go.

Clutching the stiletto, its blade still retracted, Mallory switched off the phone's torch. Then she inched open the study door and stepped into the hall.

With a glance towards the kitchen – not that she could make out anything in the inkwell of darkness back there – she padded to the front entrance.

The door was solid oak, seven feet in height. A brass letter box offered her the option of scouting her route, but opening it would alert anyone watching outside. It might make the difference between a successful escape and a fatal interception.

Was there anything she had forgotten? The Nissan's keys were in her right-hand pocket. She had the two books from the study.

That was it.

Reaching for the deadbolt, she carefully drew it back.

Breathe in. Breathe out.

Somewhere, a few streets away, a car alarm began to wail. Moments later, a dog started barking.

Mallory counted. One. Two. Three.

Snapping up the latch, she swung the door wide. Beyond it, concrete steps descended to a narrow courtyard enclosed by railings. Blocking her path to the street stood a man wearing a black motorcycle helmet, leather jacket and boots.

His visor was down, masking his features. Such was the menace that rolled off him that he seemed to Mallory not a man at all, but a monster woven from the darkest threads of the night.

Biting back a cry, she backtracked into the hall, grabbed the front door and slammed it. Before it could close fully, the stranger charged from the other side.

The door rebounded, striking Mallory in the chest. Her trainers squealed as she tried to recover her balance, but her feet couldn't move fast enough to compensate. In sickening slow-motion she toppled backwards, and as the parquet floor rose up to meet her the door crashed all the way open, its latch gouging a fat chunk of plaster from the wall.

Silhouetted in the doorway, the black-clad rider stood almost the height of the transom. He strode forwards, buckled boots ringing on the hallway floor. Without a word he closed the door behind him, sealing the two of them inside.

# Two

Obadiah Macintosh stood outside the back door of the West Penwith Animal Sanctuary, listening to the wind as he smoked a hand-rolled cigarette laced with crumbled buds of purple kush.

On nights such as this, a few miles north of Sennen Cove near the tip of Land's End, it was easy to imagine that he was the last human on earth. Above, the sky was cloudless: so vast and black that it commanded the eye. This deep into Cornwall's most sparsely populated peninsula, no glow rose up from the farmland further east. No light was cast from solitary vehicles travelling the night, or from what scattered buildings existed. Nothing sought to compete with that celestial tapestry twinkling overhead. The Milky Way was a smoky mist, feathering the heavens all the way from Perseus to Scorpius.

Minutes earlier, standing beside the exercise yard's perimeter fence, Obe had watched a waxen dish of moon set over the Atlantic. Inside the sanctuary, the dogs had fallen temporarily silent. From their kennels they had no direct view of the ocean, but they seemed to sense the change regardless. While countless myths had sprung up about the moon's effect on animal behaviour, Obe knew that among the hearsay lay truths that no one fully grasped. While he could not read the minds of the animals in his care, he remained convinced that out here, on this lonely stretch of peninsula, they seemed particularly attuned to the moon's changing state.

The West Penwith sanctuary occupied the site of a former dairy farm that had long ago fallen into disuse. Of the original house, only three stone walls and a fireplace remained. These days its surrounding pastures served as grazing land for the charity's equine residents – six Dartmoor Hill ponies and a dapple-grey Belgian Warmblood. The centre itself had been built on a patch of flattened land where the old feed sheds had stood. Initially a collection of prefabricated huts, subsequent funding from a national body had enabled the installation of a more permanent timber-built structure. It would win no awards for architecture, but the animals it housed were cared for no less passionately as a result.

Founded by Lynette Burgess, a retired Penzance hotelier, WPAS had been running for seven years, staffed almost exclusively by volunteers. As Lynette's only paid employee, Obe worked the night shift alone. He did not abhor the company of others – in fact he often craved it – but unless he was stoned or otherwise intoxicated, prolonged exposure to strangers, or even close associates, gave him headaches that only long periods of isolation could cure. Lynette had seemed to understand his condition without a word needing to be said. In repayment of her trust, he worked hard, rarely took holidays, and looked after the animals as best he could. Right now, it was time he checked on them.

As well as the horses overnighting in the stables, currently the centre was home to eighteen dogs, sixteen cats, three Nigerian dwarf goats, two Argenté de Champagne rabbits and a particularly vociferous ccara llama. Only one of those creatures had not been rescued from cruelty or abandonment – Lynette had purchased the llama, named Carlos Santiago, on a whim two years earlier. To everyone's surprise he'd turned out to be an excellent night watchman, within a few days of arriving appointing himself guardian of the Nigerian dwarf goats. Twice so far he had foiled the predations of a local fox, raising the alarm with a cry like a badly oiled hinge.

Taking a last drag, venting smoke into the night air, Obe stubbed out the roll-up and ducked back into the office. Earlier, he'd switched off the desk lamp so as not to lure moths into the building. The darkness smelled of lemon detergent and dog. It was to the dogs that he went now.

The office opened into the main reception space. The lights were off here too, the only illumination coming from the corridor that branched off it. There, a row of ceiling spots glowed on their lowest setting. Opposite the reception desk, reams of fresh printer paper stood beside a recent delivery of food, a pallet of bleach, and black bin liners filled with donated items: dog beds, cage scratchers, newspapers and toys. Later, it would be Obe's job to tidy everything away. It was a task he enjoyed, repetitive enough to soothe the chaos inside his head.

Crossing the room, he stepped into the corridor.

Here, doors with large inset windows accessed the laundry room, the intake room and the clinic. At the far end stood the entrances to the indoor dog kennels and the cattery. Between them was the food storage room, which also contained the dishwashing facility and grooming tub.

Outside, wind sawed at the rafters. Even in midsummer it rolled off the Atlantic with a fierceness that could knock a man flat. Along this part of the peninsula, few trees managed to gain a foothold. Below the fenced exercise yards, heather-felted headlands offered granite bedrock as sacrifice to the pounding sea.

Further south lay Sennen Cove, a community of a few hundred that had grown up beside a sandy crescent beach popular with surfers. On the hill above its tiny lifeboat station, Obe rented a one-bedroom flat. He'd lived there three years, ever since moving to Cornwall at seventeen and abandoning everyone from whom he'd needed to escape. Although the village attracted tourists during the summer, his working hours meant that their paths rarely crossed. Thanks to the job, he rarely saw other human beings at all – except Lynette, and those WPAS volunteers he met during shift handovers.

He loved people, but couldn't be around them.

He loved animals, and could.

At night, he kept the kennel lights on low, so that the dogs could sleep without fear. The eighteen units were split into two rows of nine, served by a narrow central aisle. Each epoxy-floored kennel contained a dog bed, a waste box, a drainage grate, a water bowl and a scattering of toys. The chain-link doors were partially screened, offering a little privacy from the facing pens.

Obe pushed through the entrance door and stopped in his tracks.

At this time of night, he would usually find a few animals – especially the newest arrivals – pacing about. Those he would feed a treat and offer a little physical attention, but the vast majority would be dozing.

Not now.

Of the eighteen dogs currently housed, there were six Staffordshire bull terriers, four Jack Russells, three Border collies, two German shepherds, a lab retriever, a poodle and Yoda. No one knew the particular mix of breeds that had come together to create Yoda. Perhaps, at one time or another, all of them. He was a large dog: muscular, ferocious and border-line feral. On his head, a patch of skin the size of a fist was bald of fur. He slobbered, growled and – with the exception of Obe – savaged anyone who tried to offer him affection.

Right now, in behaviour, Yoda was indistinguishable from any of the pedigrees with whom he shared these kennels; because every one of the centre's eighteen dogs stood at the door to its pen, flanks trembling.

They pointed their heads towards Obe, and in their eyes he saw the same silent unease.

'What is it?' he asked, surprised to hear the catch in his voice. 'What's wrong?'

Outside, beneath the black dome of night, a soughing wind rolled off the sea and raked its fingers through the heather.

# THREE

No time to think. Instinct took over.

Before the front door had even completed its arc, Mallory was worming her arms free of the rucksack's straps. The street-lamp glow, admitted through the fanlight, cast an orange halo around the stranger's crash helmet. When he dived forward, gauntleted hands outstretched, she rolled free just in time. He thumped down onto her pack, and for a vital second seemed to think he had her, ramming his fist into its side. On her back beside him, Mallory lifted her legs and pivoted ninety degrees. She kicked out her feet, connecting with his helmet and slamming it against the wall. Chunks of plaster exploded across the floor.

Unfazed, he reached out and clawed her ankle.

She screamed. Booted his hand away. Drew up her foot and delivered a second kick, this time to his unprotected side. He exhaled with a grunt, twisting away from her. Mallory slithered onto her stomach, pushed herself up. Before she could gain any traction, the stranger whipped out an arm and scooped her legs from under her. She crashed down once again, her spring-loaded stiletto skittering away, her knees smacking the parquet floor with a sound like two gunshots. The pain was stunning, so intense that she felt sure the bones had shattered. Blind from tears, she dragged herself forwards. One arm, then another. Teeth clenched. Desperate.

Behind her, the helmet-clad stranger grabbed her calf. She tried to shake him. Couldn't. A moment later he grabbed her other foot.

Mallory yanked back her leg, leaving him with an empty Nike. This time, when she drove back her heel, she connected with something solid. He let go of her calf and she heard him scrabble to his feet. Ignoring the pain in her knees, she staggered up.

No words between them. No curses or threats. None of the hate-filled vitriol she might have expected. Instead, just the horror-movie shriek of rubber soles on hardwood and the urgent suck of their breathing.

So intimate, this. Such a horribly choreographed dance.

Mallory found her feet first. She saw her knife three feet away and lunged towards it, but when the man shoved her in the back she overbalanced, striking her head against the wall.

White sparks before her eyes. A sickening dizziness.

*If you pass out, you die.*

She felt herself fall. Took the impact on her chest. The air burst from her lungs and she barely managed to roll onto her back before he was on her.

No breath to scream. No energy to fight. She raised her hands to ward him off but his weight was colossal. This close, she could smell him; a sour cocktail of sweat, testosterone and murderous intent. She tried to get her hands over his chinstrap, fingers searching for somewhere vulnerable. All she could see was the smooth black dome of his crash helmet, circled with amber fire.

It reared back.

Mallory knew what was coming. Instead of protecting her face, she tried to gouge his throat. He was too fast, bringing down his head like a sledgehammer. The front of the helmet crunched into her nose. Every nerve in her face shrieked. Her vision disintegrated. The rider's smooth black visage dissolved into silvery slivers. Blood flooded Mallory's mouth.

A gauntleted hand clutched her throat, pinning her to the floor.

Would he strangle her now? Open her up? Strew her insides around the house, as an example to others who might choose the same path?

Under his weight, she could no longer move. In such pain, she could barely figure out what was happening. Her head rang, a tuneless pealing.

With his spare hand, he began to fumble with something. A soft black shape fell to the floor beside her head. She saw blunt fingers, and in her confusion thought momentarily that he had unscrewed his hand and cast it aside. It wasn't a hand, though. Something like it.

A glove.

Yes.

Why remove it? Maybe he needed his fingers for a weapon. Nauseous, she wondered what he was planning. Sal had told her to expect a violent death if the Vasi caught her. She wondered how much pain she could withstand before she died. His hand was at her waist, now. With his knee he forced open her legs. His fingers found the hem of her T-shirt and delved underneath. For the first time she heard the rasp of his breathing. From under the helmet rolled the stench of spiced meat, recently consumed.

That he would attempt to violate her before killing her was so grotesquely ironic that she could hardly believe it, but in her weakened state she would not be able to resist. When he found the button to her jeans and popped it open she cried out in anger, spitting a mouthful of blood at his visor.

His grip around her throat tightened, cutting off her air.

Mallory closed her eyes.

After dying here tonight, her body would lie undiscovered for weeks. Perhaps months. She would leave no impression on the world she departed. No one – with the possible exception of Sal – would mourn her passing. Once her remains were incinerated, it would be as if she had never existed.

The thought angered her. Enlivened her.

Feigning surrender, Mallory dropped her hands to the stranger's waist, hoping to discover a weapon – a holstered pistol or a blade. Instead she found a loop of steel chain connected to his belt hoop by a carabiner clip. As he shifted his weight and grabbed the seat of her jeans, she tugged on the chain. A set of keys spilled to the floor.

Sal had taught her how to turn them into a makeshift knuckleduster. She closed her fist, pushing the individual keys through the gaps between her fingers.

Mallory tried to take a breath. Couldn't. Instead, she drew back her arm. During the struggle, the stranger's leather jacket had ridden up, exposing bare skin. Summoning her remaining strength, she rammed her fist into his side. The keys punched through flesh, grating against the bones of his ribs. He folded up like a spider, and before she wormed out from under him she ripped the keys free and buried them in him a second time.

This time he roared inside his helmet. Baring her teeth, Mallory twisted the keys like a corkscrew, tearing him open, inflicting as much damage as possible.

He swung his fist, ploughing it into the side of her skull.

Her head snapped sideways. Tramlines of orange light bisected and converged. The ringing between her ears mutated into a bass drone.

Somewhere in front of her, a black shadow reared up, crowned by an amber-glazed dome.

Mallory knew that if his fist connected again it was all over – she couldn't shrug off another blow like that. Bucking her hips, straining every muscle in her back, stomach and thighs, she somehow managed to topple him.

Released, she rolled onto her front. Felt fresh blood pulse from her nose. She got her hands beneath her. Scrabbled up.

Her trainer squealed. Her other foot – clad in only a running sock – skidded and slipped.

Finding her footing, she saw a chink of reflected light near the skirting board: her spring-loaded stiletto, its blade still retracted.

She lunged towards it.

Behind her came a violent thrashing of limbs: as if the shadows harboured not a man but something spawned from a nightmare.

Mallory's vision jittered. Kaleidoscopic patterns erupted before her eyes.

Fingers snatched at her foot. Too close.

She ignored the knife. No time. Better to gain some distance. She knew this house. He didn't.

Resolute, she surged forwards.

Kitchen in front. Stairs to her right. To her left, the console table on which sat the house phone, a table lamp, various other clutter. As she raced past she snagged the nearest leg and dragged it away from the wall. Heard her pursuer crash into it.

Wood splintered. Glass shattered. The table burst apart, its drawers ejecting their contents across the floor: pens, paperclips, matchbooks, fuses, coins. Ahead of the tide, Mallory slammed through the kitchen door.

Overhead, moonlight fell through three large skylights, painting the room in silver. Beneath a hanging pot rack stood a central island; by the French windows, a breakfast table and four rattan chairs.

Nowhere to hide.

Find a weapon instead.

Mallory slid around the island. Ripped open a drawer. Hunted for a knife. Couldn't find one.

The kitchen door smashed open. The motorcyclist appeared, one hand pressed to his side, his shoulders so broad that they almost blocked the doorway. His visor was a mirror the colour of obsidian. He gathered the darkness to him, distilling it into malice.

Mallory backed away. Put the island fully between them. If

he caught her here she was dead. She saw, in the way he held himself, that he knew it too.

She feinted left, hoping to fool him. No good. Reaching behind him, he closed the kitchen door. Then he edged closer. Put his hands to the work surface.

She could hear the hiss of his breathing; and in it, his bloodlust.

An empty saucepan stood on the island's halogen hob. Mallory snatched it up and flung it. Watched it career off his helmet and clatter to the floor.

He nodded, and even though she couldn't see his expression, she sensed his mockery. It ignited a rage in her so incandescent that her fear boiled away.

On the counter to her right was a kettle, a coffee maker and three ceramic jars. She grabbed the kettle from its base unit and hurled it. Followed it with one of the jars, then another. The missiles rained off him with the efficacy of pebbles thrown against a tank.

When Mallory picked up the coffee maker, he vaulted onto the central island and she screamed, dropping the machine and skating around him towards the door. He pivoted on his knees, snapped out a hand and grabbed a fistful of her hair, dragging her over. As her spine slammed the countertop, she knocked him off balance and he plunged backwards off the island, one arm tangling in the hanging rack and tearing it loose from its mountings.

Mallory ricocheted to the floor, copper pots crashing around her. The pain in her back was extraordinary, radiating out from her kidneys like tines of lightning. When her lungs emptied of breath, she struggled to take another. Choking, gagging, she rolled over and tried to crawl forwards. Refused to surrender her life easily, even if death, now, was inevitable.

She pushed upwards. One knee, then another. But she couldn't move fast enough to save herself. Her chest was empty. Her diaphragm was convulsing. Desperate, she hinged her jaw wide. Heard a squealing in her throat. Managed the merest sip of air.

Just as she found her feet she caught movement to her right. Her executioner rounded the island, gauntleted hand outstretched. Somehow she avoided him, tripping towards the door. Her fingers closed around the handle but they were slippery with blood. As she tried to get a grip, he charged her from behind. She screamed, yanked open the door. A moment later she was through.

No chance of reaching the front entrance before he caught her. No time to snatch up the knife she had lost. Mallory crashed through the wreckage of the console table and jinked right into the living room, slamming the door.

Pitch-black in here. No light from moon or street. She raced to the fireplace, spread her hands across the flue. Touched the *kampilan* longsword that hung there and unhooked it from its mount. Behind her, the living room door crashed open. She couldn't see her attacker but she could sense him.

In a single fluid action she unsheathed the sword. The blade sang as it came free. From the doorway she heard a triumphant snarl. Half a second later, she thrust the *kampilan* into the gaping darkness.

Its spiked tip encountered brief resistance. Then the handle jerked free of her fingers.

She did not hear the weapon fall.

A silence descended, so complete that she could almost imagine she was alone. Had she found him with the sword? Or had he ripped it from her grip?

She sidestepped, hoping to fool him should he come at her again. She could hear his breathing: a dry panting, like the sound of a hound deprived of water. Behind her stood the couch. Beside it, an aluminium floor lamp. Mallory reached out, touched cold metal.

Slowly she slid her hand up its stem. She found the switch, hesitated. If he'd disarmed her as she feared – if he stood before her, now, with the *kampilan*'s blade reversed – she was dead.

Her eyes smarted. Her mouth tasted sour. Something felt wrong with her face. Nothing she could do about that now. She was out of ideas. Used up.

Swallowing, lifting her chin in defiance of what she might find, Mallory switched on the light.

# Four

Two miles from Land's End, on one of the peninsula's exposed headlands, Obadiah Macintosh stood inside the West Penwith Animal Sanctuary and felt the hairs on his forearms lift as though compelled by static.

Never in his three years working here had he seen animal behaviour like this. Each dog stood at the door of its kennel, flanks shivering, ears pricked. Not a single one barked or growled or whined. They watched him in unison, every eye showing white.

After a few seconds, the silence was broken by the sound of urine splashing against the epoxy floor. Obe saw that the culprit was Sandy, one of the German shepherds. Sandy hadn't even lifted his leg against the kennel wall. Instead, urine spattered from him in fits and starts, soaking his undercoat.

'This some kind of Friday-night prank?' Obe asked. 'Did Yoda put you up to it?'

His forced joviality surprised him. He wasn't one to mask his emotions, especially not around animals, but neither was he used to the unease that had seized him since stepping inside this room. He went to the nearest cage door and squatted down opposite Rico, one of the Border collies. Rico tracked Obe's movements with his eyes, but the rest of his body remained rigid, as if a low current of electricity had magnetised him to the floor.

Abruptly, as if a switch had been pulled, the dog appeared to recover. He padded forwards, put his muzzle to the chain-link and licked Obe's fingers.

'What was all that about, eh?'

Looking around, he saw that the other dogs had restored themselves. A few retreated to their beds and lay down. Others paced back and forth, their eyes still tracking him.

Rising, he went to Yoda's kennel. The dog leaped up, resting his paws against the mesh. On hind legs, he was nearly as tall as Obe. The bald patch on his scalp gleamed pink. Loops of drool hung from his lips. He yawned, chuffed. Canted his head and whined.

'What's got you all so freaked, big guy?' Obe asked. 'The moon? Is that it?'

Yoda made a sound, deep in his throat.

Obe nodded. 'Want to hear some trivia? Did you know that the Greek moon goddess was called Selene? That the Romans called her Luna?'

Yoda cast his head backwards over his shoulder, before returning his attention to the boy.

'Yeah, course you did. What about that film – *Moon*? Did you ever see that?'

The dog pawed the chain-link.

'No? You really should. Sam Rockwell and Kevin Spacey. Directed by David Bowie's son. Really creepy. Really cool.'

Yoda licked his lips, knocking loose a string of saliva that spattered to the floor.

'So you want to tell me what this is about?'

In the low light, the animal's eyes were dark, full of intelligence.

Obe had been blessed with many gifts, but reading the minds of the creatures in his care was not one of them. As he watched, Yoda angled his head towards the kennel's rear wall and issued a low whine.

Outside, from the stables on the far side of the paddock, one of the horses began to scream.

# FIVE

The light dazzled Mallory at first, made her head throb. For a while her surroundings remained bleached of all definition. Finally – from coruscating vortices of colour – details seeped into being and grew firm. The room coalesced.

At its heart stood her black-clad attacker. His crash helmet was turned towards her, but even the glare from the floor lamp's bulb failed to penetrate his dark visor. He was a blank face, an automaton, albeit one that was mortally wounded.

The *kampilan* had pierced him a few inches above the waist, punching out somewhere near his left kidney. Dark blood rolled along the metal blade towards the tip, where it dripped to the floor with a quickening pace.

Mallory stepped backwards, forgetting that the couch stood behind her. When the backs of her legs knocked into it, she sat down with a gasp.

The stranger muttered something inside his helmet, guttural and half-formed. Following it came a word: 'Şeytan.'

Mallory spoke enough Turkish to know what he had called her: *devil*.

'Then why try to fuck me?' she asked. Her tone betrayed no fear; only disgust.

The longsword she'd used was a Maguindanao tribal weapon, forged on the Philippine island of Mindanao. The wooden hilt was rattan-wrapped, hand-carved in the traditional *ukkil* fashion. From the crossguard to the spiked tip, its blade measured thirty inches. Most of that had penetrated her attacker's torso, leaving a foot or so of clean metal.

The stranger lifted his gauntleted hand. He took a step towards the couch. '*Fahişe*,' he growled.

Another word she knew: *whore*.

Keeping her eyes on him, she picked up a cushion from the couch, using it to blot her lips. 'You made quite a mess of my face,' she said. 'I think my nose is broken.'

Her breath was beginning to return. For the first time she found she could think. Carefully, she rose to her feet.

Silence, now, except the urgent patter of blood dripping from the *kampilan*'s tip. The sword hilt quivered and twitched, as if its blade amplified the man's heartbeat from deep inside his body.

Such horrific intimacy they had shared. Still she hadn't see his face. She scowled, shook her head. 'It's over,' she said. 'We both know what they'll do with you.'

The energy seemed to go out of him. He stooped to one knee. Dropped his head.

Mallory skirted around him, walking from the room and closing the door. In the hallway, she dared to turn on a light.

The evidence of their earlier struggle greeted her: the pulverised console table, the parquet floor awash with coins and clutter. She recovered her knife, slipping it into a pocket. Found her lost trainer and pulled it on. Near the stairs, she picked up her rucksack and slung her arms through the straps.

At the front door, Mallory paused. She put her hand to the latch and took a last look at the building that had served, these last few years, as her sanctuary. '*Huzur*,' she whispered.

*Peace.*

If not for her, for whoever lived here next.

She unlocked the door and cracked it open. Screwed up her eyes and peered out. No one stood on the flagstones. The courtyard's black railings glimmered as if the paint were still wet.

Mallory slipped outside, sheltering for a moment in the covered porch. It was cooler here; when a breeze touched her forehead, she realised how heavily she was sweating.

Her priorities now were twofold: find the car and escape; work out how the Vasi had found her. She had an inkling, and it wouldn't take long to confirm. But if her suspicions were correct—

Her scalp contracted.

Better not think about that. Not yet.

It was a three-minute sprint to her car. Every second seemed to stretch out. The windows of each house and apartment harboured eyes. When a vehicle rolled by, she hid using whatever cover she could find.

Turning into Montgomery Row, she blipped the remote unlock on her keys. Up ahead, the Nissan's hazards flashed. The street appeared deserted; no one on the pavement; few lights in the Georgian townhouses lining it.

Mallory opened the car door and slung her rucksack onto the passenger seat. She climbed in, started the engine and watched the fuel needle as it climbed. It stopped just short of the quarter point, giving her a range of less than one hundred miles. Another unwelcome reminder of her negligence. She baulked at the thought of Sal's reaction if she survived long enough to tell him.

Still, for her next immediate task, she wouldn't need a full tank.

# SIX

Obe did not hesitate. The moment he heard the horse's distress he dived into the corridor, trainers squealing on the epoxy floor.

Behind him, Yoda begin to bark. *Frantic* sounds: part challenge, part fear. The German shepherds joined him. Then, all the remaining dogs. Outside, the screaming intensified.

From silence to mayhem in a matter of seconds – the peninsula's silence pierced by the frenzied baying and shrieking of what seemed like every sanctuary-homed animal in West Penwith. He could even hear Carlos Santiago, the ccara llama, adding his voice to the din.

Sprinting down the corridor – passing the laundry room, the intake room, the clinic – Obe burst into the unlit reception. The main window offered a view all the way to the ridge that hid the single-lane public road. Right now, the hill was a black hump against the paler blanket of night.

He saw no movement out there. No loose horses or predators.

The dogs' barking intensified.

Obe grabbed a torch from the reception desk. When he pushed open the entrance door, a motion-activated light over the porch snapped on, dazzling him.

Cursing, screwing up his eyes, he peered across the

courtyard. Something like this had occurred during the Perseid meteor shower the previous year, but back then the dogs had howled, not barked, and the horses had seemed not to notice at all.

Whatever this was, Obe knew that no astronomical event would explain it. *How* he knew that, he could not have said; but he felt, instinctively, that while the cause might be something just as unusual, its origin was far closer.

Moving beyond the security light's perimeter, he wondered if he should have paused to arm himself before stepping outside. The intake room contained a catch pole made from heavy-duty aluminium. It could double as a makeshift weapon.

But against what, or whom?

While a fox's scent might be enough to excite the dogs, it wouldn't usually bother the horses. Out here, the air smelled of sea salt, manure and summer heat. Obe detected no trace of smoke, nor any other odour that might offer a clue to the animals' panic.

Reports of big cats roaming the Cornish countryside regularly appeared on the news. And although many of the sightings were pure fantasy, enough half-eaten calves had been discovered on these hills to lend credence to the possibility.

Switching on his torch, Obe ran towards the stables. As the circle of light bobbed ahead of him, the sharp lines of the building began to emerge. Timber-framed, roofed by corrugated iron, it comprised ten individual stalls, a hay barn at one end and a tack room at the other. The upper halves of seven stall doors were open to the night, indicating those with tenants.

A post-and-rail fence enclosed the paddock. Reaching the gate, Obe vaulted over, landing on gravel. When he swabbed his torch across the stables, he saw all six ponies peering out of their stalls.

The opening to Orion's – the Belgian Warmblood – was dark. From inside came frenzied screaming, accompanied by the thunderous impact of hooves against wood. It sounded as if the horse was trying to kick a hole through the rear wall.

Fearful that the animal would injure himself, knowing the consequences if he broke his leg or hip, Obe unlocked the stable door and swung it open. He stepped aside just as Orion bolted into the paddock. The horse see-sawed, back legs kicking out in tandem before he found his stride. He charged towards the perimeter fence, feinted left and galloped to the far corner.

Obe resisted the temptation to track him with the torch, fearing that the harsh white light would cause further distress. Switching it off, he watched Orion complete a lap of the paddock. The horse ran for another minute, sweat coursing from his flanks, before pulling up. He lowered his head, flung it high. Nickered softly.

Keeping his movements slow and deliberate, Obe approached. Orion had been at the sanctuary six months, placed here by a national charity after being discovered in squalid conditions on a Devonshire farm. With infinite patience, Lynette had nursed him back to health, but the horse had never fully recovered his trust of humans, and likely never would.

As Obe drew closer he began to talk: gentle assurances, soothing sounds. When Orion's eyes rolled, he slowed his movements further. Gradually, the gap between them closed. Finally he placed his hand on the animal's flank. He felt Orion's chest expanding and contracting, noticing the heat the horse radiated, but he could see no signs of injury: no scratches, bite marks or other wounds. He smelled no blood.

'What happened, eh?' he asked. 'What's got you so spooked?'

Orion watched, flicking out his mane.

'Did you smell a fox? Is that it? Something bigger than a fox?'

The animal whickered. He came closer, nudging his nose against Obe's shoulder.

'Well, you're safe now, I think. Let me check your stall, though. See what I can find.'

He glanced across the paddock to the black oblong of darkness that framed the frightened creature's stall.

Removing his hand from Orion's flank, Obe trudged towards it.

# SEVEN

Mallory found a twenty-four-hour pharmacy across the river on the Old Brompton Road near Earl's Court. Even at this hour, this part of London was busy. A stream of traffic ebbed and flowed. Lorries cluttered the pavements, unloading goods to the many small shops and restaurants that served the rows of red-brick apartment buildings. Taking a risk, she parked in a no-loading bay and hurried across the street.

Inside the pharmacy, the air was sharp with disinfectant. Fluorescent strips lit the aisles so brightly that they made Mallory's head throb. A man of Middle-Eastern appearance, with a liver-spotted bald head and a thick salt-and-pepper moustache, stood behind the counter. Over a red turtleneck he wore several gold chains. From somewhere, she heard Anatolian music playing, a *Türkü* singer lamenting a son lost in war.

In the pregnancy and fertility section, Mallory picked up two Clearblue Early Detection pregnancy tests and carried them to the counter. The pharmacist scanned them without comment. A security camera bolted to the ceiling observed the transaction go through. She'd seen two others on the street outside.

No telling how much time she had before the carnage in Clapham was discovered. It would not take long to trace her vehicle, nor the route she had taken since. The credit card, although registered to a different name, couldn't be used again. 'Please,' she said. 'Do you have a toilet I could use?'

The pharmacist stared at her, unblinking, and she wondered whether he'd understood. His eyes strayed to the pregnancy kits and he shook his head. 'Toilet not for customers.'

Mallory glanced outside. From here she could see her illegally parked Nissan. So far it hadn't generated any attention.

She must look awful: eyes swollen; nostrils crusted with blood. In the last half an hour she'd killed a man and brutalised another: perhaps her face communicated that.

Returning her attention to the man behind the counter, she took a gamble. '*Lütfen, efendim.*'

He flinched, and she saw she'd correctly guessed his nationality. She didn't know a huge amount of Turkish, but she knew how to plead.

The pharmacist glanced through the plate-glass windows at the people rushing by on the street. Taking a sharp breath, he raised a Formica-topped section of counter, jerking his finger at the dimly lit passageway behind him. 'Go. First door on right. No drugs. *Anladın mı?*'

Mallory nodded; she understood. '*Teşekkürler.*' She stepped onto the raised platform and slid past him. The passage was piled with cardboard boxes waiting to be unpacked. Halfway down it she found a tiny washroom. Inside, the toilet and basin took up almost all the space. After locking the door, she broke open one of the Clearblue kits from its packaging. Pulling down her jeans and underwear, she perched on the toilet seat and scanned the instructions. She'd never done this before. Until three weeks ago she'd been a virgin.

Removing the cap, she held the wand between her legs. Her body was so high on adrenalin that at first she couldn't urinate. Finally, her bladder released. Six seconds later, the tip of the wand turned pink. Balancing it on the basin, she dressed, flushed the toilet and washed her hands.

The wand's plastic handle featured two windows. If the test

was valid, a vertical line would appear in the control window. If she was pregnant, a second line would bisect the result window. Three minutes for an answer, during which time she would hardly be able to breathe.

Mallory glanced around the cubicle. She was horribly confined in here, blind to whatever was happening outside. Blind, too, to what was happening inside her body.

It was a few days until her next period. According to the instructions, that meant the accuracy of the test result would be around ninety-six per cent. Had that one night three weeks ago in Plymouth damned her? She'd heard that the Vasi could track her should she fall pregnant. Is that how they'd found her?

Gripping the basin, she examined herself more closely in the mirror. She really did look like shit – hardly surprising that the pharmacist was reluctant to let her back here. She cleaned her nostrils of dried blood, washed her face and dried herself with a hand towel.

In the wand's control window, a vertical line appeared.

What to do if the second window showed positive? Mallory filled her cheeks, puffed them out, ran her tongue around her teeth. She couldn't bring a baby into this world; she probably wouldn't even survive long enough to deliver it. Sal had tried to train her for this eventuality, but she'd vehemently resisted his attempts.

If the test confirmed her suspicions, she was living on a timer. Nowhere safe. Nowhere to hide. Not until she dealt with this disaster in the only way that was humane.

She looked at her watch. One minute left. From outside came a shriek of brakes. Moments later, a car horn blared.

Had they found her? Surely not. No one could have followed her trail that fast. She picked up the wand, clutched it in both hands. Willed the second window to remain clear. Closed her eyes and prayed.

*I know I've been a screw-up. But you can't let this happen to me, you can't. It was one time. One. It won't happen again, I swear it.*

*Give me another chance. Don't burn me for a single night's excess.*

The test window shimmered. Was that a line? No. Too faint.

Mallory swallowed, shook her head.

But the line was darker now, the edges beginning to thicken.

She was pregnant.

She had to get out of here.

'*Merhamet,*' she whispered, but if the Vasi caught her again, they would show no mercy; they would take her life and the one growing inside her as casually as if they crushed two locusts beneath their heels.

Tossing the wand into the waste bin, slipping the second test kit into her pocket, Mallory unlocked the washroom door and stepped back into the passage. The pharmacist stood at the far end, his arms folded.

'OK?' he asked.

She nodded. Walked towards him. Asked herself what she would do if he attacked her. The thought was ridiculous – an example of just how shaken the events of the last hour had left her. '*Teşekkür ederim,*' she said, thanking him.

'*Bir şey değil,*' he responded. *You are welcome.* He tilted his head, the gold chains at his throat glinting. 'You get your wish?'

It took Mallory a moment to work out his meaning. When she opened her mouth to reply, her eyes filled with tears. Pushing past him, muttering apologies, she fled out onto the street.

# EIGHT

Aylah İncesu piloted her Lexus through South London's clogged streets, not quite willing to believe that of all nights, this could be the one to change her fate.

As her attention switched between the car's in-built satnav and the view ahead, Joremi fed her a steady stream of audio through the dashboard speakers.

So long she had prepared for this moment. So many years of searching, of sacrifice. And now, thanks to the recklessness of others, all that was at risk. Hidden in the glovebox was a suppressor-equipped Beretta, but she wouldn't use it – not unless absolutely necessary. Under the passenger seat lay her favoured weapon: a double-edged *qama* known to some as the Cossack dagger. Three blood gutters ran the length of its blade. In appearance it resembled a Roman *gladius*, designed both to stab and to slash. Aylah had practised with it so often that she felt sensations through its steel almost as keenly as through her own fingertips. So many times she had imagined using it on the one they now hunted, thrusting it into the girl's womb and destroying her ability to create chaos.

Ahead, a black cab slowed and pulled into the kerb, blocking the street. Aylah bumped her Lexus up onto the pavement to avoid it, slamming her palm against the horn.

'Where are you?' Joremi asked.

'Minutes away. Is it secure?'

'It's a pretty anonymous location. Doesn't seem to have attracted any attention.'

'Neighbours?'

He paused, and in the brief silence Aylah sensed his rancour in having to deal with her. It made her head thump with tension. 'Nothing to worry about,' he said.

Aylah slowed for a junction, accelerated when she saw that it was clear. 'Is he alive?'

'Korec? Just about.'

She nodded. 'Will he live?'

Another pause. 'There's a chance, but I wouldn't say it's great. That Arayıcı bitch of yours ran him through with some kind of antique sword.'

Biting down on her retort, Aylah changed tack. 'A *kampilan*, I'll bet.'

'Say again?'

'Does it have a split pommel?'

'Yes,' Joremi replied. 'Decorated like a gaping mouth. Ugly-looking thing.'

'I'm surprised she left it. That weapon belonged to her grandfather.'

'Perhaps she didn't want to kill Korec by removing it.'

Aylah wrenched the car into a side street, barely slowing. 'Then you're underestimating her. Mallory didn't care either way. She was hurrying, that's all. Knew we'd be on her if she hesitated. She killed one man and left another dying. Don't mistake efficiency for compassion.'

She ended the call before Joremi could respond, slowing the car and glancing through the side windows. Smart Victorian townhouses, dressed in pale limestone, lined the street. 'Well, well,' she muttered. 'You dragged yourself up, didn't you, *orospu*? Just how did you afford one of these?'

Luxury saloons and SUVs were parked nose-to-tail along the pavement. Aylah almost reached the end of the street before she found a space. She killed the engine and sat for a moment in silence, before retrieving her *qama* and running her thumb along the blade. As usual, the sharp kiss of pain was a tonic to her anxiety. Calmed, she tucked the weapon back under the passenger seat and climbed out. With her thumb clamped between her lips, tongue teasing the edges of the wound, she doubled back towards Mallory's hastily abandoned townhouse.

Joremi opened the front door before Aylah had a chance to knock. He was a lean-muscled man, a decade older than herself. When he offered her a pair of blue polythene overshoes, she refused them.

'How's Manco taking it?' he asked, stepping inside.

'By the time he finds out, we'll have this contained.'

'You mean he doesn't know?'

'You go to Manco with solutions or you find yourself with more problems. I'll tell him the moment we've cleaned up this mess. It's why we're on the clock here.'

Pieces of a smashed console table littered the hallway. On the parquet floor she saw wet streaks of blood, cut into curious patterns by twisting feet. 'Hers?'

'No way of telling. Not unless we—'

'Well, you could fucking ask Korec. He tried to rape her. Didn't he?'

Aylah glanced up, and realised that the thought had not even occurred to him. Despite her enmity towards the girl she'd come here to find, the knowledge of what Korec had attempted revolted her. 'Animal,' she spat, her attention on the bloody mural. 'All of you. Utter animals.'

Her mobile rang. She checked the display and saw that it was Teke. 'What've you got?'

'A vehicle,' he told her. 'White Nissan Juke. Looks like she—'

'I don't need you to regurgitate whatever crap you dredged from the DVLA. The girl is smart, Teke. She won't have—'

'I'm not regurgitating anything. This comes from area

CCTV. It nabbed a few stills before she drove off.'

'Registration number?'

'I've sent details to your phone.'

'Send me the stills, too. I want to see what our little *fahişe* looks like after all this time. Have you got someone monitoring ANPR?'

'You betcha.'

'So where'd she go?'

'After taking out your guys she headed north-west. Crossed the river into Chelsea, stopped at a pharmacy somewhere in Earl's Court.' Aylah heard the click of key strokes. 'Old Brompton Road, to be exact. After that she drove east, back across the river via Vauxhall Bridge.'

'How'd you know about the pharmacy?'

'We got a hit on a credit-card transaction. The Kahveci Pharmacy. It's a twenty-four-hour place. Card was registered to the same Clapham address. Pretty sloppy.'

'It was a one-off. She knows we'll be tracking her. How much did she spend?'

'Twenty-one pounds ninety-eight.'

Aylah flinched at that. Blew out air through her lips. 'My God. She didn't even know.'

A pause on the line. 'You want me to speak to the pharmacist? See what she bought? Maybe we're in luck, and Korec or Levitan injured her before she escaped.'

'I know what she bought. Things aren't priced at something ninety-eight. Mallory made two purchases. Divide that figure by two and you're looking at the price of a home pregnancy kit.'

'Bit of a leap.'

'So get someone to verify it. You'll see I'm right.'

'Why two?'

'She won't have believed the first, won't have accepted it.'

In the smeared blood trails on the hallway floor, Aylah saw the perfect imprint of a trainer. Lifting her leg, she hovered her booted foot above it. It made an almost perfect match. 'And I thought I was having a bad day.'

'You're saying she didn't know she was pregnant?'

'I guarantee it. When did she last ping a camera?'

'About ten minutes ago.'

'Where this time?'

'Still in Vauxhall. Hold on and I'll give you the exact street.'

'She's stopped again,' Aylah said.

'Seems so. Any idea what she might be doing?'

The lights were on in the ground-floor hall, but the upper floor remained dark. A breeze rolled down the stairs, carrying upon it the organic stench of death. 'Mallory's first instinct will be to abort,' Aylah said. 'Let's hope she doesn't manage that before we find her.'

In the hallway, Joremi looked up sharply.

On the phone, Teke said, 'Don't we *want* her to abort?'

'Yes. But on our terms, not hers. If she manages to get rid of it in the next forty-eight hours, all the electronic tracking in the world isn't going to help us. She'll go to ground, tough it out, and that'll be that until the next time she spreads her legs. Not even I'll be able to find her.'

'OK, I have the location. Albert Embankment, SE1, north of the junction behind the MI6 building. One street back from the Thames, right beside the railway lines.'

'I know that place,' Aylah said. 'It's swarming with CCTV.'

'I'm accessing what I can.'

'She's either visiting one of the apartments blocks, or one of the drinking holes under the arches.'

'Funny time to be grabbing a cocktail.'

'She'd be meeting someone. Soon as you have the location, send in whoever's closest. People we can *trust*. In the meantime, circulate the photograph. I want everyone to see it.' Again, Aylah glanced at the blood trails drying on the parquet floor. 'I'd prefer to take her alive, but it's not vital.'

'Understood.'

'Oh, and Teke?'

'What?'

'Korec and Levitan – they weren't my guys. Manco pushed them on me, and then they ignored their instructions. This isn't my screw-up. That isn't going to be the narrative.'

Aylah hung up. She turned to Joremi, disliking the way the man was studying her. 'Take me to Levitan.'

He frowned, gesturing towards a door along the hall. 'Don't you want to see Korec?'

'I want to see things in the order they happened.'

'Korec's in a bad way. I—'

'Did you forget who's in *charge*, Joremi?'

His face darkened, but he lacked the balls for a confrontation. Eyes averted, he walked to the stairs and began to climb.

Aylah followed him to the first floor. At a quarter landing near the top they came to an antique display case. Behind leaded glass doors she saw a collection of İznik pottery that looked as if it might date to the sixteenth century. For such ancient pieces, the colours – turquoise, olive and Manganese violet – were vivid and beautiful.

'They're hers,' Aylah said. 'Once we're done here, get someone to gather them up.'

He nodded.

'I want them destroyed.'

'Fine. You want to see Levitan?'

'I can smell him already.'

'Yeah. Even in death the guy's pretty obnoxious.' Joremi turned from the display case. 'He's through here.'

The bathroom had been decorated to reflect the building's period. Toile de Jouy wallpaper featured blue-inked pastoral scenes on a background of soft grey. A claw-footed roll-top stood beneath the window, opposite a chain-pull lavatory. A marble-topped vanity cabinet was cluttered with a messy collection of cosmetics. Beneath it lay Levitan.

The man had died in a vast pool of his own blood. One of

his arms pointed up at the elbow, fingers curled into claws. His eyes bulged, as if he'd glimpsed something in the moment of his death that appalled him.

'He soiled himself,' Aylah said.

'Probably after he died.'

'We'll give him the benefit of the doubt on that. What do we know from Korec?'

'Not much. There's a room at the back of the house, above the kitchen. Levitan got in through there. Korec was waiting in the car out front. When Levitan didn't reappear, he went to investigate. Caught the girl as she was leaving.'

'By which point she'd already done this.'

Joremi glanced down at the corpse. 'That's the likeliest sequence.'

Aylah slammed her fist against the doorframe. 'They had *orders*! Keep watch, stay out of sight, wait for me to arrive. What were they thinking?'

'Perhaps they were trying to impress you.'

She stared at the ivory-handled *kard* lodged in Levitan's ruined throat; his bib of congealed blood; his sightless expression of horror. 'I'm not impressed.'

Joremi shifted his weight. 'Korec's downstairs,' he reminded her. 'I know he screwed up, but the guy's going to—'

'We'll *deal* with Korec. Right now he's not my priority. This place needs to be scrubbed and burned in an hour. In the meantime there may be something here to give us an edge. If so, I intend to find it.' She stepped over Levitan's corpse, careful not to tread in blood. Her curiosity winning out, she bent over the cosmetics table and investigated the bottles. 'Huh.'

'What is it?'

There were far too many parallels to her own tastes for comfort. Aylah averted her eyes from a flacon of Guerlain Shalimar perfume and focused her attention on Joremi. 'Show me where she slept.'

He led her along the hall to the master bedroom at the front of the house. In the en suite, beads of rose-coloured water clung to the porcelain basin. 'Mallory came back here after killing Levitan,' she said. 'Washed off his blood.'

Joremi craned his head for a look. 'Can't fault her for that.'

'All this time searching, and she was right here in Europe.'

'We don't know how long. She could have moved in last week.'

'Use your eyes,' Aylah snapped. 'This place has been *lived* in. She even had time to set up that İznik collection. She had a life here, Joremi. Or something resembling one.'

He nodded. 'It's a big two-fingers to Manco, isn't it?'

'It's a big two fingers to us all.' She gazed around the room. The sheets on the mahogany sleigh bed had the subtle sheen of Charmeuse silk. The fabric was pure white, hand-painted with plum blossoms and tiny exotic birds. 'You enjoy your little luxuries, don't you, *orospu*?' Recalling the cluttered cosmetics table in the bathroom, she tried in vain to dodge the thought that intruded: *What other traits do we share?*

In one corner stood a huge wardrobe, its doors ajar. 'You searched it?' she asked.

'Not yet. I was going through her study when you arrived.'

'She has a study?'

'Downstairs.'

Aylah went to the wardrobe, examining the clothes hanging up inside; functional but good quality, mostly androgynous. She saw only one dress: midi-length in cream open-weave lace, embroidered with satin-stitched poppies. When Aylah put her hand to the fabric, it released the last traces of a floral fragrance. She checked the label but didn't recognise the designer. 'This is a one-thousand-pound dress. Where did she get the money for it?'

Joremi grunted. 'Where did she get the money for this place?'

It was a pertinent question. What remained of the old Arayıcı network was clearly not as diminished as Aylah had assumed. *Someone* had financed this safe house; and they'd doubtless intended to support Mallory in her pregnancy when the time came.

'We're done here,' she said, glancing up. 'Show me the study.'

'But . . . Korec,' the man protested. 'I'm telling you, Aylah, if we don't get him to a—'

She lifted her chin, giving him the full benefit of her gaze. 'The *study*.'

# NINE

In the paddock of the West Penwith Animal Sanctuary, Orion's stall was a black void that smelled faintly of clean straw. Obe edged towards it. If a fox or some other small predator had got inside, it was unlikely to have hung around. Even if one of Cornwall's semi-mythical big cats had tried to attack Orion, remaining inside an enclosed space with a panicking horse would have been suicidal. Perhaps he would find the twisted carcass of such a beast laid out on the straw, but he doubted it.

He'd smoked a few buds this evening. Usually, he restricted his habit for when he was going to be around people, and needed something to slow his reaching mind. Yet all night he'd been feeling restless, as if he balanced on the brink of a revelation. Might there be a connection? Could his curious mood, and the unusual events playing out, be somehow connected? Past experience suggested it was possible.

Then again, perhaps he was just stoned.

Going to the open stable door, standing at its threshold, Obe raised his torch.

Black shadows flitted to the stall's far corners. In the ice-white light he saw a layer of straw covering the floor. An overturned water bucket lay in one corner. Dozens of pale indentations marked the back wall where Orion's hooves had cut into the wood.

There was no dead fox. No puma. No sleek black panther lying prone. Obe adjusted the angle of his torch, picking out the steel bars of the hatch to the adjoining stall. Into the light wandered Pixie, one of the Dartmoor Hill ponies. She rolled a glossy eye towards him. Tossed her head.

'It's me,' Obe muttered, placating her. 'Just wanted to see what all the fuss is about. Seems like Orion got himself worked up over nothing.'

Despite his reassuring words, the darkness at his back felt increasingly uncomfortable. He wanted to turn around, and for exactly that reason forced himself to remain still. How long could this place remain a refuge for him if he started to fear the night?

The dogs had stopped barking. Had that just happened, or had they been quiet for a while? He'd been so focused on the horses that he had ceased to think about the animals back in the centre. He wondered if he should call Lynette, or possibly Giles Mattock, one of the charity's trustees. But what benefit could there be in dragging either of them out of here in the middle of the night? And what would he tell them if he did? That the dogs had been barking? That one of the horses had been spooked? Perhaps, in their concern for him, they'd stop him working out here all alone. The thought of *that* was intolerable.

Switching off his torch, he put his back to the empty stall and faced the night. Nothing flew at him from the darkness. Nothing lunged for his legs or throat. He crossed the paddock, climbed the gate and went to the neighbouring enclosure. He could see the silhouetted goat house. Carlos Santiago grazed nearby. The animal raised its head, jaw working reflexively.

'Nothing fazes you, eh, Carlos?'

The llama made a soft humming sound.

Nodding, Obe turned away. The wind shuddered in his ears. Out to sea he could see the distant lights of fishing trawlers and tankers. From here, they offered the only evidence that he shared the planet with other human beings.

Then, as the wind slackened, he thought he heard something from beyond the ridge – the hollow clatter of an engine.

The sound faded as quickly as it had appeared, replaced by the wind's steady sawing; and had it not been for the unusual behaviour he had witnessed in the animals, he would have dismissed it. The single-lane road on the far side of the ridge connected some of the coast's old tin mines and a handful of farms, but apart from that all it offered was a way of accessing the main road a mile to the east. Never, at this time of night, had he heard vehicles travelling along it. The tin mines had been closed for decades, and none of the local farmers would have much reason to be out on public roads.

It could be Lynette, driving over to visit him. Sometimes, especially if she'd been forced to turn away an animal, she didn't sleep well. He'd be sitting in the office, so deep inside a comic or graphic novel that he wouldn't notice her car, and when she barrelled through the door he'd leap out of his chair and eject whatever he was reading across the room, much to her amusement. She'd bring coffee, and usually something baked: shortbread, perhaps, or Welsh cakes. Lynette understood his difficulties around people, and she always added a little cannabis to those treats. They'd eat and drink and talk, and as the Atlantic wind railed against the windows, Obe would believe that here, on Cornwall's westerly peninsula, he'd found his nirvana.

It couldn't be Lynette. His boss drove a petrol-fuelled Impreza estate, but the sound he had heard on the road, muffled by the hump of land that shielded it, had been the throaty rattle of a diesel. Not a small engine, either. Larger than two-litre. Possibly three.

His stomach lightened, a sensation he hadn't experienced in three years of living here. Shaking his head, scolding himself, he traipsed back towards the main building. 'You've muddled your head with smoke,' he muttered. 'No reason to be rolling joints at this time of night, especially when you're alone. Serves you right if you start hearing things. Wouldn't be surprised if you imagined the thing with the dogs, too. *And* Orion.'

Except that he hadn't imagined the thing with the dogs. And, despite his self-rebuke, he couldn't help noticing that his pace across the gravelled courtyard was a little faster than he would have liked.

If he re-entered the building by the main entrance, he'd trigger the security light. Clenching his teeth, he changed direction and headed for the narrow office door around the side. Westwards, a cloudbank was rolling in from the Atlantic. Already it had obscured a quarter of the visible constellations. Soon the entire sky would be dark.

Inside the office, Obe fetched a pair of binoculars and moved to the window. No barking, still, from any of the dogs in their kennels. Never before had they reverted to silence so soon after being roused.

Lifting the glasses to his face, he aimed them towards the ridge at the site's easternmost boundary. He found the point where land met sky, panning the binoculars until he saw the shallow indentation where the track bisected the summit.

Although no trees grew on this part of the peninsula, its slopes were dense with gorse and heather. Plenty of places for someone to hide, should they wish.

Obe blinked, dismayed by the thought. For a moment the view wobbled out of focus. He gripped the glasses tighter, and then he caught it – brief, elusive, but unmistakable: the greyish fug of exhaust fumes lifting into the night. They vanished like a wisp of expelled breath, but he knew what he had seen. For a moment he did not know how to feel; relief that his sanity hadn't unravelled, or concern that someone was out there, at this hour, and had chosen not to announce themselves.

As he watched, a man's dark shape appeared on the ridge. The stranger remained visible for a second at most before vanishing into the undergrowth.

Obe lowered the binoculars. Tried to think through the implications. He raised the glasses back to his eyes just in time to see a second man dart across the ridgeline, partially silhouetted against the clear night sky. In his hands he carried a hunting rifle, complete with what looked like an infrared scope.

Obe shrank from the window. He breathed deep, tried to clear his head. The deer-stalking season didn't start for two months; likewise, the season for most game birds. The intruders could be lamping for rabbits, but it was unlikely. The land, here, was privately owned, and well signposted from the road.

Even as Obe considered these explanations, instinct told him the real reason these men had appeared in West Penwith; because in the three years he had lived on this peninsula only one thing had happened of note, occurring just three weeks earlier, eighty-five miles away in Plymouth.

They were here because of the girl.

The girl he had tried to forget, and knew he would not see again.

As Obe processed that, he realised something else, just as clearly: if he remained here much longer, the men would find him; and when they did, they would kill him.

# TEN

The Red Sun in Vauxhall seemed unsure of whether it was a restaurant, a nightclub or a low-grade brothel. Sitting at a booth, poking at a strawberry daiquiri, Mallory wondered if the place was trying to be all three. She'd been told of the establishment by the man who had settled her in London, but until tonight she'd never visited.

It was a labyrinthine place, far deeper than it seemed from outside. The music was loud but badly distorted; a thump of bass accompanied by a muffled braying that might have been a woman singing. Gaudy paper lanterns hung from the ceiling. Wall hangings decorated with gold foil depicted Asian women in various stages of undress. A long mirrored bar dominated one side, stocked with every conceivable brand of whisky, absinthe and brandy. The air smelled of peanut oil, spilled beer and sweat.

In one corner, a Chinese girl in hot pants and bikini top gyrated against a pole. She held the attention of barely any of the Red Sun's clientele – who were, Mallory saw, almost exclusively male. A few harried-looking women ferried drinks and bowls of dim sum to packed tables. One or two others, their faces heavily painted, engaged punters in conversation wearing smiles that never reached their eyes. Every so often they cast looks of snake-like enquiry in Mallory's direction.

She glanced at her watch. Nearly midnight. An hour since the ambush at her Clapham townhouse; twenty minutes since she'd taken the pregnancy test that had confirmed her worst fears.

Had the carnage a few miles south been discovered? Probably. Soon she would have to dump the Nissan. For much of the next seventy-two hours – depending on the outcome of her meeting at the Red Sun – she would rely on taxis, checking into hotels for snatched periods of rest whenever possible.

A man appeared beside her booth. Chinese, mid-thirties, shaven head. His eyes, beneath hooded lids, looked like chips of coal in the low light. 'This way, please.'

Mallory stood up too fast. 'Where're we going?'

'You came to see Mr Lin.' Without further comment, he turned and threaded his way between the tables. Mallory hurried to catch up, ignoring the looks – both hostile and solicitous – that she raised from those seated nearby.

Along the back wall, a carpeted staircase climbed to the first floor. She followed her host as he ascended. Up here the lights were even lower, the music less intrusive. Inside a row of booths, partially concealed behind sets of red curtains, she saw glimmers of bare flesh. Around a large table a group of Asian men played poker, the baize stacked with chips, folds of foreign currency and red cartons of Chunghwa cigarettes.

The air smelled odd, and not just from the fug of tobacco smoke. There was a nauseating sweetness to it reminiscent of spoiled poultry.

The man led her past the gaming table and the curtained booths, and into a narrow corridor. He passed two closed doors and stopped at a third, at which he raised his hand and knocked.

Mallory heard no acknowledgement, but a moment later he ushered her inside.

It was one of the strangest rooms she had seen. A floor-to-ceiling cage stretched the length of one wall, filled with tiny chirping birds. They appeared to be canaries, their plumage yellow or bright orange. In the centre of the room stood four red leather sofas around a square coffee table. On an ironwork pedestal perched an African Grey parrot. Beside it, feeding the bird berries from a small dish, stood Mr Lin.

He was older than Mallory had expected. His eyes were lined and pouched – so absent of warmth when he looked at her that she found it difficult to hold his gaze.

'His name is Chaofeng,' Lin said. 'Named for one of the nine sons of the dragon. After I became enlightened, I realised that keeping birds in captivity is an indefensible cruelty, but Chaofeng has been with me thirty years. To release him now would be to pass a death sentence. The canaries, likewise, would suffer similar fates.'

'Enlightened?' Mallory asked. It seemed a strange choice of words for an old man who had chosen to surround himself with drugs and prostitution.

'Man is not a fool for a hundred years,' Lin said. He smiled, and she saw that his front teeth were missing. 'Your references check out. Your request, however, is a little unusual, considering that what you seek is available readily from other sources.'

'I don't have time to wait.'

'Ah.' The old man placed the dish of berries onto the coffee table, blinked. 'Modern life.'

Mallory could feel the bass of the music downstairs, transmitted through the floorboards into her feet. 'Do you have what I'm after?'

'No,' he said. 'I do not.'

Before, Lin's face had seemed empty of emotion, but now his expression flattened so completely that he appeared lifeless; a mannequin masquerading as human. 'When I arrived here from Tianjin, thirty years ago next month, I brought a wife, a son and three *heihaizi* – that vile label for those born outside the one-child policy. What you seek is hateful to me. Abhorrent.'

Listening to him, Mallory suddenly felt so tired – so frightened and alone – that she wanted to close her eyes and slump down onto the floor. 'Please, Mr Lin. I hope you didn't allow me to come all the way here just to lect—'

'When I became enlightened,' he continued, 'I understood that we all choose our own path. I will not provide what you require, but I will send you to a man who can.'

She straightened, opening her mouth to thank him, but he held up a hand.

'All choices have a consequence,' he said. 'Do not offer gratitude. I ask that you never return, nor attempt to contact me again.'

Lin took a folded slip of paper from his pocket and crossed the room to where she stood. Instead of handing it to her directly, he laid it on the arm of the nearest leather sofa. 'A name,' he said. 'And the address where you can find him. He is not an honourable man, but I am sure you are prepared for that.'

Grimacing, Mallory picked up the paper. The fact that Lin had avoided skin contact bothered her more than she might have imagined. 'Is he expecting me?'

'Of course.'

Picking up the bowl of fresh berries, Lin returned to the African Grey. As Mallory walked from the room, he announced, in a voice just loud enough for her to hear: 'The spectators see more of the game than the players.'

She glanced over her shoulder, but already he had switched his focus to the bird. Closing her fist around the scrap of paper, she abandoned the Red Sun for her car.

# ELEVEN

Inside the West Penwith Animal Sanctuary, a short distance from where the Atlantic surf pounded the peninsula's rocks, Obadiah Macintosh sheltered beneath the main reception window. Caught in the turmoil of current events, thoughts of the girl bloomed inside his head.

Mallory, that was her name. In truth, it was about the only thing he remembered of her. If he closed his eyes, he could not picture her face. Nor could he hear her voice if he tried to recall it. She was a feeling, nothing more; a wisp of memory, stubbornly opaque.

At most, a few seconds had passed since he'd spotted the men outside. Even if they sprinted down here to intercept him, it would take them at least a minute to reach the main building. Longer, if they attempted to remain concealed. Of course, armed with at least one rifle and night sight between them, they could ruin his evening without even descending from the ridge.

Obe screwed up his face. The men had *already* ruined his evening. Perhaps even his entire week.

He took a breath, focused. He could decipher the girl's connection to this later. Right now, he needed to act. Energised, refusing to give in to fear, he scrambled away from the window. The office door faced east, the direction from which the strangers had appeared. If he tried to leave that way, they would almost certainly see him; and although the building's main entrance pointed north, the motion-activated security light over the porch would betray him the moment he slipped outside.

Obe stepped into the darkened WPAS reception. Using the low light spilling from the corridor to navigate, he wheeled a swivel chair from the desk to the far wall. Then he climbed onto the seat, putting his face level with the fuse box.

Thanks to the three years he had spent maintaining this building, he knew the electrical system better than anyone. Flipping the lid, he felt for the main breaker and worked along from there. The interior lights were controlled by two separate circuits, each protected by a six-amp trip. One served the kennels, the cattery and the rooms branching from the service corridor. The other served the main reception and the office. That one also fed the security light over the porch. With his thumb, he located the switch and snapped it down.

Immediately, the four ceiling spots glowing in the corridor went dark.

Obe jumped down from the chair. He grabbed his jacket, slipped it on and checked the pockets: tobacco tin, wallet, keys. No phone. He'd never owned one.

Going to the glass-panelled entrance door, he peered outside. From here he could see the stables and surrounding paddock, and the field where Carlos Santiago guarded the goats. Beyond that, the land fell away steeply before the next headland rose up behind it. Further north, the Atlantic was an oily expanse, interspersed by the white lines of incoming breakers.

Holding his breath, Obe opened the main reception door.

Above his head the security light remained dark. He found a fire extinguisher, propped open the door and retreated inside.

Perhaps twenty seconds had now passed since he'd spotted the men up on the ridge. He had around forty remaining before they reached him. Perhaps longer, if they chose caution over speed.

Turning his back, Obe crossed the reception and stepped into the darkened corridor. Feeling his way by touch, he passed the intake room, the laundry room and the clinic. He opened the door to the kennels, propping it with a mop. Here, controlled by a different circuit, the overhead lights still burned on their lowest setting.

The dogs displayed none of the bizarre behaviour from earlier. Most were lying down near the entrances to their units. Only Yoda was prowling about. He jumped up when he saw Obe, resting his forelegs against the chain-link. Opening his mouth, displaying speckled gums and a fearsome set of canines, he licked his lips and sneezed.

'You ever see *Butch Cassidy and the Sundance Kid*?'

Yoda growled, deep in his throat.

'Paul Newman and Robert Redford. End of the movie, they're holed up in this building, unaware they've been surrounded by what seems like half the Bolivian army.'

In the adjoining kennel, Sandy the German shepherd climbed to his feet, ears pricked. A moment later, across the aisle, Milo – the second German shepherd – sat up straight. The dogs rolled their heads towards the corridor, began to pant.

Obe nodded. 'They're coming. *I* know that, because I saw them. But the wind's blowing in off the sea tonight. No way you can smell them from here. No way you can see them, either. You want to let me in on the trick?'

Sandy's lips peeled back from his teeth. He growled. Milo joined him.

'I'm being selfish here, I'll admit,' Obe told them. 'But if I'm honest, I think I might need your help. I know this place – these hills, this stretch of coast – better than most. But I don't know how to fight. And while your doggy radar seems to be firing on all four, until I sleep off this weed my spidey sense is pretty much kaput.'

He approached Sandy's door and drew back the bolt. 'I won't lie. This might be a one-way ticket. I've no idea what's happening here.' Turning towards Milo's kennel, he released the bolt on that one too. Then he swung both doors wide.

Hackles raised, the dogs trotted into the aisle, their tails held stiffly behind them. They paused at the entrance to the service corridor, ears angled forwards.

Finally, Obe turned to Yoda's cage. 'Well, buddy,' he said. 'This is probably *adiós*. You're an odd fish, it has to be said, but I do love you. If this is anyone's gig, it's yours.'

Leaning forward, he opened the mesh door and stood back. Yoda considered him with bloodshot eyes, head twisted as if he were trying to communicate a thought. His jaw tensed. Then, with a snarl, he burst from his kennel, nails scratching for purchase on the epoxy floor. He raced past the two German shepherds and bolted down the corridor into darkness. Sandy and Milo stared after him. Growling with excitement, they followed.

Outside, Carlos Santiago began to bellow.

Obe slipped into the corridor. He opened the door to the food storage room and felt for the shelf where Lynette kept the knife used for opening food sacks.

Never in his life had he intentionally inflicted pain; and despite the seriousness of his situation, he knew that if the opportunity arose he would not take it. He had a different reason for taking the knife. When his fingers touched the handle, he snatched it up. Outside, Carlos Santiago's warning cries grew more agitated. With the alarm raised, the men would doubtless move faster.

Dropping the knife into his pocket, Obe stole back across the corridor. He let himself into the clinic and closed the door. Black ink pooled on the glass doors of wall cabinets. He stepped around the examination table, paused at the room's west-facing window and looked out. From here, in a series of bluffs, the peninsula dropped all the way down to the sea.

Well over a minute had passed since he'd spotted the men. Plenty of time for them to reach the main building, should that be their intention. Twenty seconds, give or take, since he'd released the dogs. At the speed they could move, assuming that the trespassers had remained on the ridge, they should—

Somewhere outside, a man yelled in anger and pain.

Obe listened. He couldn't pinpoint the exact location of the cry, but it had originated on the far side of the building. Too close to come from the ridge.

He heard another shout. Possibly the same man, possibly another. Obe opened the window. Atlantic wind tried to press him back, but he slung one leg over the sill. He hesitated there, glancing over his shoulder.

For three years this place had been a sanctuary not just for the rescued animals in its care but for him. It had offered him a purpose – had allowed him to contribute to society despite his inability to interact with it.

Looking around the room, he felt sure that this was the last time he would see it, that his relationship with Lynette, and the other volunteers of West Penwith, had come to an end. His chest grew tight with the knowledge, but it was a sweet ache; never would he surrender to despondency. The world was filled with too much beauty to allow fear or misfortune to overshadow it. As always in his life, endings signified new beginnings.

Into his head swelled an image of the girl. This time he saw her not as an impressionistic smudge, but in startling clarity. He gasped, transfixed, for in her face he glimpsed something he sensed was of vital importance.

Mallory.

A face. A name. A feeling.

Outside, the brutal report of a rifle clattered off the surrounding hills. Obadiah Macintosh, with hope in his heart and determination in his blood, dropped lightly from the window to the grass.

# TWELVE

Retracing her steps past the display of İznik pottery she had ordered destroyed, Aylah İncesu followed Joremi down the stairs to the Clapham townhouse's ground floor.

The man paused outside the living room, opening his mouth as if to say something, but when he caught Aylah's expression he seemed to think better of it. Silent, he led her to the study.

The room faced north, into a walled garden that had been allowed to grow wild. Heavy oak furniture dominated, the largest piece a Regency-period display case. A leather-topped desk stood in front of the window. On the floor lay a *halı* of breathtaking beauty, hand-knotted in rich maroon silk.

Every Anatolian *halı* relayed a unique story that its creator wanted to impart. Aylah crouched down beside this one and studied it. Immediately she spotted the repeated triangle motif that warded off the evil eye. She saw, also, the symbol of Cybele, the Phrygian mother goddess who represented fertility and transformation, and the double-headed axe that signified the duality of life and death. She noticed motifs reminiscent of loss, and others that indicated resistance in the face of aggression. Along with the oft-repeated triangle, she saw further stylised wards against evil: cockerels, parrots, amulets and dogs.

It was as sharp an insight into the girl's psyche as she could have wished to find; and what it showed was a deeply conflicted individual who would resist to her last breath.

The *halı* seemed to have been specially commissioned, but it looked far older than the girl's twenty-four years. When Aylah dropped to her knees and put her nose to the threads she discovered that it smelled old too.

'Don't ask,' she muttered, noticing Joremi's expression.

'You want me to destroy the rug too?'

Aylah thought about that. Earlier, she'd intended to dent the girl's spirit by desecrating her most valued possessions. Now, after reading the *halı*'s motifs, she saw that such a strategy would backfire. 'No, but we'll take it with us,' she told him. 'The pottery, too.'

'We're still smashing it?'

'Not any more.' At the display case, she gave the books a cursory glance. Most of them were works of non-fiction: Middle-Eastern history; philosophy; art. Nothing to pique her interest. Turning back to Joremi, she said, 'Take me to Korec.'

The living room was a grand space, its high ceiling enhanced by elaborate stucco. A bronze and crystal chandelier cast a diffuse light on the period furniture beneath. Two walnut-framed armchairs stood either side of the fireplace; in the bay window sat a three-seater Chesterfield in maroon leather.

In such elegant surroundings, the blood that had saturated the pale carpet appeared even more grotesque. Korec lay on his side in the middle of it, pierced through his lower abdomen by a *kampilan*. A good fifteen inches of the blade had emerged from his back, a red lump of meat caught in its spiked tip. The pommel's grinning gilt mouth seemed to mock Aylah as she considered it, communicating a challenge direct from the weapon's owner: *Look what I did, and how easily I did it. Look what I could do to you, if you come close enough.*

The sight enraged her: not just what the girl had done, but what Korec, in his foolishness, had *allowed* her to do.

He still wore his motorcycle helmet. The visor was down,

its surface crusted with dull-looking stains. For a moment, as Aylah contemplated him, she wondered if he'd died already, bleeding out while she'd investigated the rest of the house. But then, pendulous, his crash helmet swung towards her. His gauntleted hand trembled, then lifted.

'You're a disgrace,' she told him. 'You and Levitan both.'

Korec's lungs filled. He shuddered, twitched.

'Shall I get him into the car?' Joremi asked.

Irritated, Aylah waved the interruption away. 'You thought you knew better, didn't you, Korec? Thought you knew how to handle her.' Disgusted, she shook her head. 'Joremi, here, suggested that you ignored my instructions because you wanted to impress me, but I don't believe that, and I'm certain that he doesn't. You just couldn't stomach the thought of taking orders from an Arayıcı turncoat. It wasn't me you wanted to impress, was it? It was Saul Manco.'

She gestured at the *kampilan*'s grinning mouth, and the lake of blood that had spread from beneath him. 'Do you think this impresses anyone, Korec? Do you think Levitan – lying dead beside a toilet with his throat torn out – impresses anyone? Do you think that *rape* impresses anyone?'

That glossy black dome continued to measure her.

'Do you think this might be exactly the kind of thing that happens when you ignore your instructions and try to put your cock inside the target instead of killing her – instead of staying out of sight and *watching the house like you were told*?'

Korec made a choking sound, deep in his throat. '*Merhamet*,' he croaked, the word muffled inside his helmet.

'Oh, you want *mercy* now?'

'Aylah . . .' Joremi began.

She held up her hand, finger and thumb pinched together, daring him to interrupt her again. Her phone starting buzzing. '*Bok*,' she spat. Moving to the sofa, she saw immediately that the caller was Teke. 'What've you got?'

'Good news. We picked her up going into a—'

'Alive? Has anyone else—'

'Whoa, slow down,' he said. 'Let me speak. We got her on CCTV, that's all. Two cameras on Albert Embankment, just north of the train station. She went into one of the clubs there, just before midnight: place called the Red Sun. Stayed ten minutes and came out alone.'

'Was she carrying anything?'

'Nope.'

'What do we know about it?'

'Strip club, whorehouse, late-night drinking den – not really sure and probably all three. Got a mainly Asian clientele, licence in the name of a Joseph Lin. We weren't made to feel welcome. Pretty sure they thought we were police.'

'Where did she go after?'

'Straight back across the river, through Hammersmith all the way to Chiswick. Then onto the North Circular. Last time she pinged a camera was in Ealing, ten minutes ago.'

'She's stopped again.'

'Maybe, but that's not central London. There're plenty of routes out that avoid ANPR.'

'Has she made any attempt to avoid them so far?'

'No, but—'

'She's there, Teke. I'm telling you. We just need to figure out what she's doing.'

'I'm checking all the area CCTV, but it's a little patchier around there. Plus we're having to pull in major favours to access it.'

'Stay on the line,' Aylah said. 'Let me think this through.' She took the phone from her ear and paced the carpet, careful to avoid the bloody mess Korec had created.

*What are you thinking, Mallory? What's your plan?*

She recalled the motifs woven into the *halı*. Thought of everything she'd learned about the girl, everything she remembered.

*You didn't know about the worm in your belly. That's why you stopped at the pharmacy to confirm it. What went through your head when you saw the result? What did you feel?*

Aylah went to the sofa. She closed her eyes and bowed her head. How often had the girl sat in exactly this spot, legs tucked beneath her as she flicked through one of the books from the study's library?

Had she entertained friends here? Unlikely. Nothing in this house suggested a life enjoyed in the company of others.

*How lonely you must have been. How incomplete.*

*Something else that we share.*

Aylah scowled, angered that such a subversive thought had intruded. Reflexively she lifted her thumb to her lips and used her teeth to prise open the self-inflicted wound. Blood flooded her mouth, accompanied by a bright sting of pain.

*You didn't know you were pregnant. You didn't intend to fall pregnant. You're far from a natural mother, which means your first instinct is to abort. If you'd had any intention of keeping it, you'd have gone to ground the moment you saw the result. But you didn't, did you? Instead you went to the Red Sun.*

Aylah opened her eyes. The leering mouth of the *kampilan*'s pommel greeted her, quivering as Korec breathed. She stood, fished in her pocket and took out a white silk handkerchief.

*You arrive alone. You leave alone. And empty-handed.*

Stepping forwards, Aylah draped the white square of silk over the *kampilan*'s hilt, covering the mouth. Again, Korec swung his head towards her. In response, she touched a finger to her lips.

*What was so important about the Red Sun? Why journey halfway across London to get there?*

Eyes fixed on Korec's visor, she placed her hand over the handkerchief, carefully wrapping her fingers around the grip.

'Aylah?' Joremi said, lurching away from the wall. The man's eyes were huge.

*Who were you meeting there, Mallory? What were you buying?*

Korec raised his gauntleted fingers, attempted to bat her

hand away. He presented such a pathetic sight that Aylah almost felt pity. Almost.

Softly, she shook her head.

*The pregnancy test is positive.*

*You go to the Red Sun. You arrive alone. You leave alone. And empty-handed.*

The *kampilan* trembled in her grip, as if the blade transmitted the man's faltering heartbeat directly into her palm. She enjoyed the feeling of power it offered. 'You're a stain, Korec,' she whispered.

*You go to the Red Sun.*

*You arrive alone. You leave alone. And empty-handed.*

*The trip isn't wasted, even so. Because you've played this game a long time. And you rarely make a wrong move.*

*But you know something, Mallory? Neither do I.*

Absently – her focus on the girl and not the man – she moved the *kampilan*'s hilt left and right, as if she were toasting a marshmallow over a log fire. Impaled, powerless, Korec squirmed. Kicked out his legs.

*You arrive alone. You leave alone. And empty-handed. The trip isn't wasted, even so.*

*Because.*

*Because-because-because . . .*

With as much strength as she could muster, Aylah ripped the blade free of Korec's abdomen, twisting her wrist and opening him up. As a flood of dark blood spilled out of him, he squealed like an abattoir pig. His arms thrashed, striking the fireplace and scattering andirons, pokers and bellows. His spine arched. The heels of his motorcycle boots slid across the soaked carpet.

Aylah could feel his hatred, his impotent rage. She wished she could see his eyes. Such a pity that his visor was closed.

'Information,' she said. 'So simple.'

Finally, the muscles in Korec's spine relaxed. He groaned once.

Then nothing.

*You arrive alone. You leave alone. And empty-handed.*

*The trip isn't wasted, even so.*

*Because now you have information. And what kind of information might you seek at the Red Sun if you're desperate for an abortion and have nowhere else to turn?*

Aylah lifted the phone to her ear. 'Still there?'

'I'm here,' Teke said. 'What happened? Thought I heard screaming.'

'Korec just died.'

'Oh. Shit.'

'Yeah, we're all crushed. Has Mallory tripped any more cameras?'

'Not since you've been on the line.'

'She won't, not for a while. Throw up a net around that part of Ealing. Use any un-pinged cameras to plot the perimeter. Flood the area with everyone you can find and get them looking for her car. Check every road, every alley. In the meantime, pull together a list of all the doctors in the vicinity, particularly any who've retired or have been struck off. Find out where they live and prioritise those locations. Do it all fast enough and we'll catch her.'

'You think she's arranged an abortion?'

'That's why she went to the Red Sun, Teke. To find a contact.'

'And you know all this how?'

'Because I'm smarter than you,' she replied, and hung up.

Aylah filled her lungs, so light-headed with adrenalin that she needed a moment to steady herself. When she turned to face Joremi, the man shrank away from her, his earlier antipathy spent.

'Looks like we got our lead,' she told him.

His eyes strayed to Korec's corpse. He nodded.

'I'm leaving. Get the rug and the pottery, take it all out to your car. I want this place burned to the ground. I don't mean some campfire blaze. Make sure you do a proper job. Ashes, nothing else.'

'It's a residential street,' he began.

Aylah took a step towards him. 'If your *conscience* is troubling you . . .'

Joremi held up his hands. 'Ashes, nothing else.'

'Call me when it's done.' She tossed the *kampilan* onto Korec's corpse and stuffed the handkerchief back into her pocket.

Out in the hall, she debated whether or not to call Saul Manco. The Vasi principal wouldn't remain ignorant of this fiasco for long. Better that the news came from her than one of her many detractors, but until she had a solution, she was loath to draw attention to what had happened. Although Korec and Levitan's failure wasn't her fault, the challenge to her authority was clear. Manco abided no weakness; and without his patronage, her own end would come soon enough.

Avoiding the detritus of the wrecked console table, Aylah was about to leave when she noticed something adhered to the floor, half concealed by a slick of blood. Crouching down, she picked it up.

It was a blue NHS donor card, registered in the girl's name. Beneath the familiar logo was a printed statement: *I want to help others to live after my death*. The card must have been dislodged during her struggle with Korec.

Mallory had ticked the box that donated all her organs and tissue. Aylah imagined, for a moment, her own constituent parts being separated by a surgeon's blade, thinking of the enormous relief such a dispersal might bring; bloody petals on the wind. She put out a hand to steady herself, feeling an eel-like slipperiness in her stomach. Allowing her mind to wander too freely was always a mistake.

Had she not been crouching down, she might have missed the second credit card-sized ID. This one, a glossy pink, had come to a rest in a vertical position flush with the hallway's skirting. Leaning forwards, she plucked it up.

It was a UK driving licence, but it wasn't registered to Mallory.

'Obadiah Macintosh,' Aylah whispered, and felt, as she spoke that name, a flicker behind her eyelids, as if a captive bird rustled papery wings inside her skull. Her fingertips, where they gripped the licence, grew cold. The sound of Joremi moving about in the neighbouring room faded from her ears. As she stared at the face in the photograph, that strange and half-forgotten region of her brain – the one that had so recently intuited Mallory's London location – began to throb.

*It's you, isn't it?*

*Obadiah Macintosh.*

*We're here because of you.*

He was an odd-looking boy. Arctic-blue eyes. Shaggy black hair in childish curls. In a way he reminded her of an actor she had once seen in a movie about a magic ring, although with less rounded features.

According to the date of birth on his licence, he was twenty years old.

*Why you, Obadiah? What was it she recognised in you?*

Aylah looked at the address: The Bailiwicks, Stone Chair Lane, Sennen Cove, Cornwall. The licence had been granted three years earlier: time enough for several changes of address, and yet the longer she considered the boy's face, the more convinced she became that she would find him in Sennen Cove.

Climbing to her feet, Aylah left the house for her car, where she connected her phone to the hands-free and dialled Teke. 'Got something else for you,' she told him.

'You're really stacking it up.'

'Find me everything you can on an Obadiah Macintosh.'

'Oba-what?'

'Obadiah.' She spelled it out. 'I've got his address and date of birth. I want everything else.'

'Let's start with those details.'

Switching on the overhead light, Aylah read directly from the licence. 'He may not be in Cornwall, but I've a strong hunch he is.'

'Why're we interested in him?'

'Because he's the father.'

Teke sucked in a breath. 'Are you sure?'

'Sure as I can be. If he's in Cornwall, we need to get a team down there tonight. Pull in every resource, use up every favour.'

'I'm on it. Are you at all concerned about how much noise we make?'

'Yes,' she said. 'But do it anyway.' And hung up.

Aylah tapped the phone against her teeth. Then, accessing her email browser, she found two new messages. The first, sent earlier that evening, contained Mallory's vehicle registration; its accompanying attachment showed a catalogue image of a white Nissan Juke.

The subject of the second message, sent minutes ago, was *CCTV SE1*. There were three attachments.

Aylah tapped the first, holding her breath as the file downloaded, until she found herself looking at a greyish image snapped from a few metres above street level. Caught in the centre was a female figure in jeans, trainers and hooded top, dark hair pulled into a loose ponytail. Her head was twisted away from the camera.

Aylah wondered briefly if that was deliberate – that Mallory sought to avoid what surveillance she could – but when she clicked on the second image she saw it wasn't the case, because this time the girl was far closer, and staring straight up at the camera.

Aylah spread her fingers, magnifying the image. The Turkish *halı* on the study floor in Clapham had warned her not to expect evidence of panic or fear; but it hadn't prepared her for this. Even in such low resolution, Mallory's eyes seemed to *burn*.

Years had passed since she'd last seen an image of the girl. In that time Mallory's jawline had sharpened and her cheeks had lost all traces of fat. The muscles in her legs and shoulders were taut and well-defined. Such a physique could only have been achieved through rigorous training; no wonder she had dispatched Levitan and Korec so efficiently.

'I'll find you, *orospu*,' Aylah whispered. 'And when I do I'll cut that filthy worm out of you myself.'

Even as she spoke, she sensed at her back a familiar rushing darkness, a vast locust cloud threatening to overtake her. Lifting her shoulders against it, she tried to forget what she had been and concentrate solely on what she must do.

Teke called her back fifteen minutes later. 'Obadiah Macintosh,' he said. 'That address seems to check out. He's not on the electoral roll, but utilities are registered in his name. I've got a linked bank account, plus a Netflix subscription and broadband. All of them current.'

'What's his bank balance?'

'No way of finding out.'

'Freeze the account.'

'No way of doing that either, Aylah. We can't just—'

'Ranee can. Give it to her. What else have you got?'

'Seems he works at some animal sanctuary in West Penwith. Nights, mostly.'

'How do you know that?'

'The charity's website has a blog. He writes most of the posts.'

'What else?'

'Not much. Seems a bit eccentric. Then again, he's got to be some kind of oddball to do a job like that.'

'Family?'

'Checking it out. Nothing yet.'

'I don't know that part of Cornwall.'

'It's about as far west as you can get. On the coast just above Land's End.'

'People *live* there?'

'Not many. This charity he works for – it's on the site of an old dairy farm right beside the sea.'

'Remote?'

'Looking at the satellite pictures, I doubt they have a Costa.'

'Good. Then it doesn't matter if we're a little obnoxious. I want him dead before sunrise.'

'On the case.'

'What about the girl?'

'No more sightings of her car, but we've a pretty decent lead. A Dr Fabian Pataki. Lives in Ealing, appeared in court a year ago, charged with using poison to cause a miscarriage. Seems he sold abortion drugs to an undercover reporter while trying to cover debts from his divorce. Case was thrown out, but a few months later the BMA struck him off. Something else interesting, too – according to the paper, the wife walked because of his weakness for young Chinese girls.' Teke paused. 'Which might connect him to the Red Sun.'

Aylah ran her tongue across her teeth. 'That's our man.'

'I've got people heading over now.'

'Give me the address.'

'Twenty Garfield Avenue. Just off Ealing Broadway.'

'I'll meet you there.'

'Where are you now?'

Aylah glanced at the satnav. 'About ten minutes away. Don't you dare kill her, Teke. Not till I get there.'

# Thirteen

Garfield Avenue served a row of modern red-brick apartment buildings opposite a ramshackle collection of 1960s maisonettes. While the apartments looked clean and well-maintained, the maisonettes had seen much better times: stained fascias; broken guttering; crumbling tarmac paths choked with weeds and rubbish.

Mallory parked two streets away, in a bay reserved for the tenants of an adjoining building. She locked the car and walked back towards Garfield Avenue. A fried chicken place stood on the corner. Inside, a few customers lingered at the counter. The junction stank of food waste wafting from three industrial bins.

Number twenty was the only maisonette without a number on the front door. It was also in the worst state of disrepair. Flakes of paint, pale in the moonlight, peeled from the woodwork like scabs from a wound. Rusting security bars enclosed the single ground-floor window. Beneath it, two green recycling tubs overflowed with glass bottles and pizza boxes.

Glancing over her shoulder, checking that the street was clear, Mallory walked up the path. Through narrow strips of privacy glass in the front door she glimpsed a shadowed staircase. She pressed the buzzer and heard it reverberate somewhere upstairs.

On the first-floor landing a light winked on. She heard

footsteps on the stairs, saw a black shape flowing down them. Through the distorting effect of the glass, its outline appeared to shift and swell.

Mallory removed her knife from her hoodie, shrugging down her cuff to conceal it. Right now she couldn't afford to trust anyone; certainly not a contact introduced to her by Mr Lin.

Inside the porch, a deadbolt drew back. A latch unlocked and the door swung open three inches, anchored by a taut security chain. Peering through the gap, wearing a dirty bath-robe, stood an overweight man in his late fifties. His face was soft and fleshy, gleaming with sweat. The thick fringe of hair around his balding head was greasy and unkempt.

'Dr Pataki?'

He blinked at her through large-framed tortoiseshell glasses. Then his gaze strayed to her right hand. Although her knife was hidden from view, he seemed to recognise the threat. He scowled, eyes narrowing. His attention returned to her face. 'You Anna?'

She nodded.

'That your real name?'

'No.'

'Good. I don't want to know your real name. Don't want to know anything about you.'

'That suits me fine.'

'Are you an addict?'

'No.'

'I don't deal with addicts. They lie, cheat. Make poor choices.'

Mallory glanced over her shoulder. The street was still quiet. 'I don't take drugs.'

'If you're a hack, this won't end well. I got caught once, not again. You met Lin?'

'Yeah. Just now.'

'He's not a guy you want to offend.'

'I'm not a journalist, Dr Pataki. I'm not going to sell you

out. I'm here, on my own, as agreed. And if we do this, in five minutes you'll never see me again.'

Pataki grunted. He jerked his chin towards her covered hand. 'What're you hiding?'

'Just a little protection.' She maintained eye contact, keeping her expression as passive as possible. 'It's been a difficult evening.'

Behind her, an engine clattered. She turned, saw a moped pull away from the chicken place and accelerate away. Across the street, two men walked along the pavement, swinging food containers in white carrier bags. One of them chugged from a can of orange Fanta.

'I don't know what kind of trouble you're in, My-Name-Isn't-Anna,' Pataki said. 'But if you think I'm letting you in here with a knife, or any other kind of weapon, you're deluded. Throw it on the mat. Then back off.'

Mallory stared. She wondered whether she had enough strength to kick the door and break the chain. Probably. But then what? She wanted Pataki to give her what she needed, not some cocktail of drugs designed to knock her out. She didn't fancy waking up in Lin's office, tied to a radiator.

Again she glanced behind her, shifting her weight on the balls of her feet. The two men with carrier bags crossed the street towards the maisonette, talking in loud voices. One of them tripped as he stepped onto the kerb. His friend brayed with laughter.

Gritting her teeth, Mallory tossed her knife onto Pataki's mat. The doctor slammed the door. Through the privacy glass, she saw him bend down and retrieve the weapon. He straightened, appeared to examine it. Then he unlocked the door and swung it wide. 'Get in here.'

She did as he asked. Pataki flicked on a light switch. Above them, a bulb in a cheap paper lantern winked on, revealing décor as shabby as it was old. Textured wallpaper, mould-blackened at the corners, peeled from the walls.

'Nice place,' she said.

'Yeah. It's a palace.' He nodded at the stairs. 'Go on up.'

The carpet sucked at her trainers like putty as she climbed. At the top she found a narrow landing. A second flight of stairs led to the unlit second floor.

'Kitchen,' Pataki said. 'First door on your right.'

Mallory glanced into the living room as she passed, relieved to find it unoccupied. While the décor up here was just as tired, it looked like the doctor had done his best to keep the place clean. The upholstered sofa and single armchair looked freshly vacuumed. The surface of a glass coffee table gleamed. A half-empty bottle of Talisker stood on it beside a cut-crystal glass. On a TV opposite the sofa, a frozen image lingered: three teenaged Asian girls in the midst of a pornographic act. A lead trailed to a laptop on the floor.

'Whatever,' Pataki muttered, noticing the direction of her gaze. 'We all like our kicks. You wouldn't be here if you didn't.'

This close, she could smell the booze on him, and the sweat rolling off his skin. Ignoring the comment, she walked into the kitchen. It was a bright space, lit by a harsh fluorescent strip. Unopened post cluttered the nearest work surface, but the others were spotless. Tucked by the door stood a pine breakfast table surrounded by chairs. Nearby, a floor fan performed lazy revolutions.

Pataki waved her to a seat. 'Shall we conclude the matter of payment?' he asked. He collapsed onto the chair opposite and his robe gaped open, revealing a dark-thatched belly and the tangled nest beneath it. He made no effort to cover himself.

'Mr Lin didn't specify a sum.'

'One thousand,' Pataki said. 'Cash.'

Mallory laughed. 'That's ridiculous. To think I'd even turn up here with that amount.'

The doctor gestured towards the door. 'Then let me be the first to say *adieu*.'

'I can get these drugs prescribed for free, in pretty much any clinic I choose to visit.'

'But you won't. Otherwise you wouldn't be here.'

'To save that much cash? You bet I would. Don't get greedy, doctor. I'm not the only one around here who seems a little desperate. Three hundred.'

'Huh.' He scratched his belly. 'Six hundred, or it's not worth my risk, especially not after Lin takes his cut. You're getting an out-of-hours consultation thrown in free of charge.'

'Yeah, and in such a stunning location.' Onto the table Mallory counted out four hundred pounds in fifty pound notes. 'That's all I can afford.'

The doctor lifted his chin, shrugged. 'No deal.'

Mallory stared at him a moment longer. Then, calmly picking up the money, she climbed to her feet. '*Adieu.*'

Pataki blinked. Abruptly, he collapsed in on himself. 'OK, OK, four hundred. *Jesus.* Just sit back down, will you?'

She complied, handing over the cash.

Outside, a car drove by far too fast, music thumping from its stereo.

Pataki tucked the money into his robe. 'A few questions.'

'Shoot.'

'Are you anaemic?'

'No.'

'Allergies?'

'No.'

'On any medication?'

'No.'

'Recreational drugs? Alcohol?'

'No to both.'

'Any history of heart problems in the family?'

Mallory shook her head. 'But it's kind of you to ask.'

'This isn't kindness, trust me. Getting caught selling this stuff is one thing. But if you drop dead from a haemorrhage, I'm in a whole different world of pain.'

'As I said, no history of heart problems.'

The doctor took off his glasses. He cleaned the lenses on his robe. 'When's your period due?'

'Any time now.'

'You missed the last one?'

No. But I'm three weeks pregnant. I took a Clearblue test that confirmed it.'

'Those things aren't always reliable.'

'This one was,' she insisted.

Pataki shrugged. 'It's your money. When did you last have sex?'

'Three weeks ago.'

'Uh-huh.' He stared at her. 'You know this is irreversible, right? No going back.'

'Of course.'

'Is the father aware of what you're doing?'

'Is that relevant?'

'Not to me, it isn't. Might be to him.'

'The father doesn't know. The father won't ever know.'

'Right,' Pataki said. He stood, wrapped the robe around his gorilla-hair chest and refastened the belt. 'You want a beer or something while you wait?'

'I'm good.'

He nodded, stared at her a moment longer. Then he slipped out of the room.

Mallory rubbed her neck and arched her back. The kitchen's fluorescent lighting was giving her a headache. Outside, another vehicle roared past. It slowed at the end of the street, brakes shrieking.

Twenty-four hours and all this would be over. Her life in London was at an end, but she was used to starting afresh. This time she'd choose somewhere with a slower pace of life – somewhere on the continent perhaps; a fishing village along the coast. For now, she was done with big cities.

She heard floorboards flexing above her head: Pataki moving

about. A few minutes later he reappeared. At the sink, he filled a glass tumbler with water and placed it down in front of her. Then he searched through one of the cupboards, returning to the table with two earthenware bowls, of the type used to serve olives or hummus.

Pataki slid one towards her. A large white pill rested inside it. 'That's mifepristone,' he told her. 'It blocks the progesterone your body needs to continue the pregnancy. Once you take it, your uterus will start shedding its lining and your cervix will soften.'

Mallory stared at the pill. Nodded.

The doctor pushed the second bowl towards her. It contained four hexagonal pills. 'That's misoprostol,' he said. 'It'll bring on the contractions. As you're only three weeks in, you can take them at the same time, or up to seventy-two hours later. There'll be bleeding, obviously. And some cramping. Do you have sanitary towels with you?'

'Yes.'

Pataki nodded, and she noticed a curious hunger in his expression. 'You haven't asked me about pain.'

'I think I deserve a little pain. Don't you?'

He shrugged. 'I'm no therapist. I can't even look after my own shit. You've got what you came for. Rest is up to you.'

Mallory stared at the drugs sitting in their earthenware bowls. An image bloomed inside her head: Obadiah Macintosh; his boyish face, his arctic-blue eyes. Scowling, she picked up the glass tumbler and filled her mouth with water. She scooped up the mifepristone from its bowl, pushed it between her lips and swallowed it down.

Pataki watched her. A bead of sweat cut loose from his forehead, trickled down his nose and dripped from the tip.

'Bravo,' he said.

# FOURTEEN

After climbing out of the window, Obe crept to the building's south-western corner. The wind harried him, throbbing in his ears and pressing at his back.

A few seconds had passed since the gunshot had bounced off the surrounding hills. He thought of Sandy and Milo, the German shepherds he had released from the kennels, and Yoda, the bad-tempered mongrel whose scarred and hairless scalp was testament to the cruelties others could inflict. Had the intruders just killed one of them? Obe cringed away from contemplating that.

Reaching the corner of the building, he ducked his head around it. The moon had set some minutes earlier, but so pure was the starlight overhead that it feathered the slopes with silver. Halfway up the track to the road beyond the ridge he saw commotion. Without the binoculars, he couldn't make out much detail, but it looked like a man wrestling with something. Nearby, a black shape lay on the grass. About the right size to be one of the dogs.

Obe's heart clenched. He wanted to shout out, call the surviving animals away, but in doing so he would give himself no possible chance to escape. Already his options were dwindling. From here, he couldn't reach the ridge without being seen; and on foot, he couldn't move fast enough to put safe distance between him and those who might follow, especially if they were armed. He could work his way down to the shoreline, but from there the paths north and south were blocked by vertical granite headlands. Even in full daylight they were unclimbable.

Reversing direction, Obe sprinted along the side of the building to the north-west corner. He leaned out, checking that the way was clear, then crept to the north-eastern edge. From here his view ran parallel to the front façade, extending to the fields and scattered outbuildings beyond. He could see the dark lump beside the track up to the ridge, but the man had gone. Obe squinted. Was that a single form lying inert? Or was it now two? So hard was he concentrating that he nearly missed the flicker of movement off to his right.

Despite the courtyard's covering of gravel, the figure moved without sound – a weightless shadow. Reaching the building's front entrance, it slipped inside.

Obe hadn't even realised he was holding his breath until he released it. If there was a time to run, it was now: the intruder's attention – for the next minute, at least – would be focused on searching the building.

Gritting his teeth, he broke from cover, sprinting across the courtyard. His trainers exploded off the gravel, scattering chips behind him. When he reached the grass, the urge to throw himself down was overwhelming but he fought against it, powering forward with as much speed as he could muster. He jinked left and right, hoping to throw off the aim of anyone who might be targeting him. From the kennels, he heard the dogs begin to bark.

He wouldn't risk a look back. Ahead the grass became patchier, the land rising at a gentle gradient to the lip of an ocean-facing bluff. If he ran too far, he'd topple straight over the edge.

Obe changed direction once more, swerving to the right and heading east. Forty yards away stood the paddock fence.

Following it, he reached the stable block and ducked out of sight.

The wind railed, drowning the dogs' cries. He wondered if it had masked the sound of his flight across the courtyard. Recovering his breath, he crept along the stables' back wall. Peered around it.

Orion, the Belgian Warmblood, stood at the paddock's far end, munching grass. He seemed a different horse to the one that had tried to kick free of his stall. Obe scanned the surrounding landscape. He made a clicking sound at the back of his throat.

Orion lifted his head. The horse remained motionless for a few seconds. Then he lost interest and continued to graze.

Obe clicked his tongue again. This time, Orion swung his head all the way around. He whickered softly.

'Come on, pal. Don't leave me hanging.'

The horse flicked out his mane. Whickered again.

'How about if I toss in a sack of oats?' Obe hissed. 'Apples, too. Granny Smiths, your favourite.'

Orion turned to face him. After a moment's hesitation, he walked to the fence. Obe reached out, taking a fistful of mane. Using a fence post to steady himself, he climbed onto the horse's back.

Unused to the feel of a rider without a saddle, Orion tossed his head and kicked out, but Obe bent low and reassured him. 'You're an old dude, I know that. But you're much stronger than you think you are. Trust me.'

He straightened, gripping the mane with both hands. 'OK, I'll admit it. That's a quote from *All-Star Superman* – the scene with the goth girl on the ledge – but it's still relevant, I think.' Using his knees, he turned the horse to face the ridge. 'I don't know if you ever jumped a fence, or even if you know how. Either way, we're about to find out.'

Obe kicked his heels.

Orion might be old, but he was responsive too. With a jerk

of his hind legs and a sudden lengthening of his neck, he surged forwards. The ground thumped beneath his hooves. Obe tried to move in tandem, but without the benefit of saddle or stirrups the ride was a painful one. Ahead, the boundary fence loomed into view. The topmost wire ran a good five feet above the ground.

The paddock's surface became a dark blur. Despite his fear, Obe began to grin. He had no idea if Orion would even see the fence, let alone attempt it. Even if they made it over, without a saddle his chances of remaining seated were slim. Ahead, the obstacle looked even taller than it had been, an impossible barrier rising up to deny them. From the main building, he heard a shout and tucked down his head in anticipation of a shot.

The fence rushed closer. Ten metres. Three. Obe closed his eyes. Bunched his shoulders. Bellowed, from the pit of his chest: '*Now!*'

Beneath him, Orion's muscles tensed. Released.

The pounding of hooves ceased. Up they went.

The horse was airborne for mere fractions of a second, but to Obe it felt like a moment snipped from time and forever frozen. He felt Orion's neck press against his chest. Sensed the fierce thump of his heart. At the zenith of their arc, he leaned backwards as far as he could, bracing himself for impact.

Orion's forelegs slammed into the dirt on the other side of the fence, sending a shockwave of pain through Obe's spine. They'd taken the fence too fast, and now their momentum was far too great. He felt himself topple forwards. Felt the horse's rump lift up behind him. His best hope was to hit the ground cleanly and pray that the animal's weight didn't come down on top of him. His fists tightened around Orion's mane, knowing that it wouldn't save him. Not unless the horse got its feet back beneath it – which, somehow, it did.

One moment Obe was sailing forwards with nothing to obstruct him. The next, as Orion recovered his balance, he was jostled back into position. The horse's hooves beat a frenzied tattoo upon the earth. So much adrenalin had flooded Obe's system that a yell born of sheer relief burst free of him, but before he'd even had a chance to recover his breath, a black shape swam out of the darkness ahead. It coalesced into the form of man, with feet planted and one arm outstretched.

The stranger's features were little more than two dark holes framed by a pale smudge. Obe could not see what he brandished: whether a gun, a knife or some other weapon. His instinct was to veer away but he fought against it, turning his hips towards the danger and pointing his head the same way. Whatever gods of horsemanship were watching seemed pleased, because Orion realigned himself at once, galloping towards the man without pause.

Standing his ground, the stranger adjusted something on the device he held.

In Obe's ears was roaring wind, pounding hooves. Beneath him he smelled grass and damp earth, tuned by his adrenalin to a startling richness. Again he felt the urge to yell out a challenge to the destructive forces that had slunk onto this wild peninsula he loved so much. He recalled the prone mound of fur that was very likely one of the dogs in his care: Sandy, Milo or Yoda. Just as distressing was the knowledge of his complicity. Aware of the danger, he was as responsible as the hand that dealt the blow.

As if attuned to his rider's thoughts, Orion bore down on the stranger with all the fire of a medieval warhorse. As they closed the last few yards, the man fired whatever device he was aiming.

Obe heard no percussive discharge of gunpowder, saw no incendiary flash. The weapon made a dry snap – a sound like a plastic ruler striking a table. The front of it glittered and something shot towards him, silvery and sleek. A moment later – as if a deviant puppeteer had seized control of his limbs, commanding his movements with strings of blue lightning – every muscle in his body contracted.

The pain was like nothing he had previously experienced, so intense that he barely noticed himself tumbling from the horse's back. Or the broken ground, rushing up.

# FIFTEEN

Crossing London to the Ealing address Teke had given her, Aylah İncesu tripped five speed cameras and nearly hit two pedestrians. To shave a few minutes from her journey time, she would have readily bounced the pedestrians off the Lexus's bonnet, but in the end such carnage would have been unnecessary, because when she pulled onto Garfield Avenue the assembled team had not yet gone inside.

Aylah drove past number twenty – the maisonette where Dr Fabian Pataki lived – without slowing. At a first-floor window she saw fluorescent light seeping around the edges of a roller blind, and felt a curious ticking sensation inside her head, as if an insect had crawled beneath her lid and was working its way around her sclera. It made her blink, shudder. She shook her head to dispel it.

*Is that you,* orospu?

*Because if it is, time's running out.*

At the end of the street, a fried chicken place was serving its last customers. Aylah turned right, parked the Lexus and dialled Teke. 'Where are you?'

'Red van,' he said. 'East end of the avenue.'

'Which way is east?'

'You see the takeaway? Opposite end. Where are you?'

'Road behind it. Who else is here?'

'You'll see a black Audi A8 three houses along from number twenty. Guys inside are Chevry and Washienko.'

'I don't recognise the names.'

'No – they're Caleb's branch.'

Aylah's jaw clenched so tightly that she almost cracked a molar. '*Caleb* knows about this?'

'Amount of noise we've been making, he was bound to hear something. I thought we might as well use his guys. It could look a little better on us, if we're seen to be playing nice.' A pause on the line. 'Sorry.'

'No. It was the right thing to do. Given the chance, Caleb's sure to try and paint me in the worst possible light.'

Historically, Caleb Klein had operated as second-in-command to Saul Manco, the Vasi principal; over the last five years, thanks to a steady chain of successes, Aylah had usurped him. 'Who else is here?'

'Two of our own. Elias Hunt and Talaal Safi. There's a private road that loops around the back of the maisonettes. It's a potential escape route. I've got them stationed at each end.'

'Good. If this is the endgame, we need to keep it discreet.'

'That's what I thought. We can snatch our target when she comes out, and once—'

'No. I won't risk that.' Aylah peered through the windscreen, counting the number of lighted windows in the nearby apartment blocks. 'I said discreet. That means off the street.'

'Well, Chevry and Washienko can get inside without making a fuss. Neighbours shouldn't notice a thing.'

'Have you set up a shared line?'

'It's live.'

'OK, call me back on it.'

'Before you go . . .' Teke began.

'What is it?'

He hesitated. 'Did it draw you? Pataki's place?'

The question caught her off-guard, made her stiffen. Teke was the only Vasi she'd encountered who seemed remotely capable of ignoring her Arayıcı blood; his sudden reference to her ancestry – and her innate ability, just like all Arayıcı, to track her pregnant kinsfolk – was as unwelcome as it was unnerving. She stared out of the window, watching the low black form of a cat slink across the street towards the bins outside the fried chicken place. 'It doesn't work that quickly,' she told him. 'I only begin to sense them at all once they fall pregnant, and they need to stay put for quite some time before I can get a fix.'

'Hence Clapham,' he said.

'Hence Clapham.'

For a moment, neither of them spoke. She heard Teke's breathing; wondered, as she listened, if his face was creased in distaste; wondered how she'd feel if that were true.

'OK,' he told her. 'Hang up and I'll dial you into the party.'

Aylah ended the call and screwed in an ear bud. Almost immediately, her mobile began to vibrate. 'This is Aylah.'

'Teke. Let's do a roll-call.'

'Elias Hunt,' said a voice.

'Talaal Safi,' said another.

'Aylah, this is David Washienko. I'm here with Guy Chevry.' The man's voice was syrupy, gloating. 'Teke tells me this is a clean-up job, celebrity target. If you'd notified us sooner, maybe we could've—'

'I heard you can get inside without a fuss,' she snapped. 'Is that true?'

'Guaranteed.'

'Hunt, Safi. Do you have eyes on the house?'

Both men responded with affirmations.

Aylah leaned over the passenger seat and retrieved her *qama*. Holding the blade steady, she sliced into her thumb, reopening the wound from earlier. This time the steel cut deeper, the pain brighter. When she lifted her thumb to the light, she saw the fleshy pad had parted like a set of red lips. A fat trickle of blood rolled towards her palm. Aylah licked it off. When its metallic tang spread across her taste buds, her breathing slowed. She climbed from the Lexus, holding the weapon flush against her leg.

Although the skies overhead were clear, London's streets had retained much of the day's heat. Such was the humidity that in the amber pools of light cast from the streetlamps it appeared as if millions of fireflies were dancing.

Aylah could smell the stench of rotting food from the bins outside the takeaway; Dr Pataki, it seemed, had fallen upon hard times.

Rounding the corner onto Garfield Avenue, she saw the black cat from earlier streak out from beneath one of the waste bins and vanish into a hedge. Animals often chose to flee when she drew too close, especially cats. As a girl, she'd believed the phenomenon was due to her Arayıcı blood. In adulthood, she'd observed that her Vasi counterparts could trigger the same effect.

Aylah felt blood seep from her thumb, wetting the *qama*'s hilt. When she thought of how long she had prepared for this moment, she could hardly take a breath. The girl had come here seeking an easy end to her pregnancy. She would end up receiving so much more.

Ahead, Aylah identified the Audi A8 occupied by Chevry and Washienko. A streetlamp bounced light off the windscreen, rendering the occupants invisible.

Her heel scraped the pavement. She cursed, lifted her feet. Tightened her grip on the *qama*. Wished that she'd kept a pair of running shoes in the boot of her car.

On the second floor of number twenty, a light came on. A few moments later, it winked out.

Aylah crossed the street. In her ear she heard the hiss of an open line. 'Everyone ready?'

A chorus of agreement.

'OK. Chevry and Washienko, do your stuff on the door. Don't go upstairs until I'm there.'

'Where are you?'

'Coming up on you now.'

'Just so you know,' Washienko said, 'I'm the good-looking one. Guy's the dwarf.'

Aylah scowled, infuriated by his flippancy. She stepped onto the pavement in time to see the Audi's passenger door swing open. A squat, thickset stranger climbed out. From the passenger side a taller man appeared. Together they walked up the path to number twenty and crouched in front of Dr Pataki's front door. A few moments later it swung wide.

Washienko and Chevry slipped into the darkened porch. Aylah crossed the threshold behind them and closed the door. She watched each man produce a suppressor-equipped pistol.

Voices drifted down the stairs from the first floor. Older male; younger female; a disjointed conversation.

Aylah licked her teeth. So close, now. Although most of the Vasi still resented her involvement, tonight she would justify Manco's faith in her. Killing the girl would prove her loyalty beyond doubt, making her untouchable. The mere thought made her skin tingle.

Chevry and Washienko, as silent as stalking wolves, began to ascend.

Upstairs, the conversation halted, then resumed.

Chevry reached the top of the flight. He peeled off left, covering the staircase to the second floor. Washienko stepped onto the landing. Peering around him, Aylah saw one closed door, another slightly ajar.

The disjointed conversation tailed off. She heard someone sobbing.

Washienko paused, head cocked. Then he moved towards the partially open door, blocking her view. Pushing lightly against it, he stepped inside. Aylah trapped her breath, bracing herself for action. The girl had killed once tonight. She'd be expecting further violence – would likely have prepared for it.

Abruptly, Washienko surged out of the room he'd

investigated, kicked open the door opposite and burst inside. Aylah followed close behind. The semi-darkness disoriented her; for a vital half-second she was blind. She heard a shout, followed by a crash. As her surroundings coalesced, there came a panicked cry, then a barked command from Washienko.

On the floor, beside a glass coffee table, cowered a man in a white bathrobe. His robe was unbelted, exposing a hair-matted belly. Around him lay the shards of a smashed whisky bottle. Blood flowed from his hand.

On the wall, a flickering TV painted the doctor's skin in shades of blue. Aylah glanced at the screen and saw a scene that appalled her: two teenage Asian girls, directed by an older man, were torturing a third.

'This is entrapment!' Pataki shouted, clutching his injured hand to his chest. 'You can't just burst in here unannounced!'

Behind him, the sobbing on the TV graduated into a wail. For a moment, as Aylah watched, the image seemed to blur. The tortured girl's face became her own, and suddenly it was *her* cry she was hearing, in a scene from long ago.

*Dripping water. Whispering voices. An excrement-streaked cage.*

Shaking her head to dismiss it, she glanced over at Washienko. 'Turn that shit off.'

The man grabbed a remote from the sofa and killed the set, but on a laptop beside the coffee table the scene continued to play. Chevry came into the room, flicking on the overhead lights. 'Upstairs is clear,' he said.

Distracted by the tinny sounds of torment issuing from the laptop's speakers, Aylah took a moment to digest his words. Incensed, she strode across the room and kicked the laptop against the wall, destroying it.

'Jesus. Christ!' Pataki yelled. 'You can't do that. What the—'

'Dr Fabian Pataki?'

'Of course I am,' the man snapped. For the first time, he seemed to notice her *qama*, and the firearms carried by her Vasi associates. In a quieter voice, and one that was far less confrontational, he added: 'Question is, who are you?'

*Dripping water. Whispering voices. An excrement-streaked cage.*

*The unbearable expectation of pain.*

Aylah pushed the memory away. 'I'm someone whose life I *guarantee* you'll want to make as easy as possible.'

Pataki blinked, and all the indignation seemed to flow out of him. 'Did Joseph send you?'

She tilted her head, unsure of his meaning. Then it clicked: the proprietor of the Red Sun had been a Joseph Lin. She raised the *qama* until its tip was level with his eyes. 'The girl,' she said. 'Don't lie to me, Doctor. Don't waste my time and try to fob me off. Mallory. She was here. Earlier tonight. Wasn't she?'

Pataki held her gaze for only a moment. 'She didn't call herself that.'

'What did she want?'

'I'm pretty sure you know exactly what she—' He caught himself, took a steadying breath. 'She wanted drugs that would help her to miscarry.'

'And?'

'I prescribed her mifepristone and misoprostol.'

'You prescribed?'

Pataki scowled. An artery pulsed in his neck. 'Sold, then.'

'When did she leave?'

'Five minutes ago? Ten? I haven't exactly been keeping count. Can I get up now? I think my hand needs—'

'Where did she go?'

'Well, let's see. I've a hunch she was considering Ayia Napa.' The doctor rolled his eyes. 'How the hell should I know?'

Striding forward, Aylah punched him hard across the jaw. Spluttering, Pataki tumbled backwards. Adjusting her earpiece, she said: 'Teke, we missed her.'

'I know. Her car just pinged ANPR.'

'Where?'

'A4020, Uxbridge Road. West of your location, right outside Ealing Hospital.'

'What's she doing at the hospital?'

'No idea.'

Aylah glanced over at Pataki. 'Did you poison her?'

With the sleeve of his gown, the doctor blotted blood from his nose. 'That's ridiculous. They're legitimate drugs. If she's having a bad reaction . . .' He shrugged. 'I didn't *ask* for this.'

Aylah worked her thumb against the *qama*'s hilt, releasing an energising flash of sensation. 'Teke?'

'I'm here.'

'We're so close I can taste her. Take Safi and Hunt to the hospital. I'll squeeze what I can out of Pataki, then I'll join you.'

From the floor of his living room, the doctor listened with a grimace.

# Sixteen

Half a mile from Garfield Avenue, Mallory gripped the Nissan's steering wheel and tried to concentrate on the road. She hadn't anticipated the emotions that had swelled in her since swallowing the mifepristone, nor the feeling of utter hopelessness that had enveloped her since leaving the maisonette.

Never in her life had she encountered a man so ideologically impoverished as Dr Fabian Pataki. Even compared to the Vasi fanatics hunting her he seemed monstrous. She recalled his face as he watched her ingest the drug. A bead of sweat had rolled down his forehead and dripped from his nose. '*Bravo*,' he'd said, as if he wished to compliment her act of destruction. He'd smiled too, a slow reveal of crooked teeth. Even worse, she'd paid him: four hundred pounds, a sum she would miss in the coming days. Earlier this evening she'd had a plan and now she had . . . what, exactly? In the space of two hours she'd lost everything she'd built; and the decision she'd taken back at Pataki's place had likely damned her. The entire Vasi network would be scouring London. If she didn't recover quickly, they would find her soon enough.

Her throat burned. Her stomach clenched, a greasy knot. The lights of oncoming traffic pierced her like needles inserted directly into her brain.

Was she getting a migraine? Some kind of reaction? She'd never experienced anything like this. The streetlamps strung orange necklaces across her vision. When the Nissan veered to the right she overcompensated, nearly losing the wheels from beneath her.

*Get hold of yourself. You made this choice. Live with it.*

Mallory leaned forwards in her seat. Blinked away the tracers. Pressed down on the accelerator and watched the needle begin to rise. Buildings blurred past either side. Oncoming traffic shot by with a flash and a roar.

Ahead she saw a sign for Ealing Hospital. She sped past, knuckling away tears. A stone bridge lifted the road over a river. Then the hospital complex loomed up on the left, a long grey structure with a stark tower rising behind it. Even this late, the car park was full. She saw three ambulances parked head to tail. Paramedics stood on the kerbside, engaged in chatter.

*All of this is happening because of you. Because of your mistakes. And now you have to stand by them. Make the best of things that you can.*

Ahead, the road widened and passed beneath a metal-framed bridge. A few hundred yards further on, she spotted a lay-by and pulled over. Switching off the engine, killing the headlights, she unbuckled her belt and rested her head on the steering wheel.

An articulated lorry blasted past, rocking the Nissan on its suspension. A waspy two-stroke moped trailed in its wake.

Mallory tasted bile in the back of her throat. She swallowed it down and tried to think. Unbidden, an image of Obadiah Macintosh bloomed in her mind. She snapped her eyes open, sat up straight. She didn't want to even *think* about him right now. But although she had no desire to see the boy again, she knew, with sudden conviction, that she must. Leaning forwards, she fished in her jeans for his driving licence. Inexplicable, really, that she had stolen it. Had she intuited, even back then, the consequences of their encounter?

Her fingers, instead of sliding into her back pocket, touched a hanging flap of denim where the pocket had been.

Mallory frowned. Lifting her buttocks, she felt around on the seat beneath her. Alarmed, she bent forwards and searched the footwell. When she didn't find anything on her first sweep, she switched on the interior light, but it didn't pick up the pink glint of a driving licence; nor could she find it in the door cavity, or the passenger seat footwell, or anywhere else she looked.

Frantic, she emptied her front pockets, producing a fistful of credit cards and IDs, but when she cycled through them not one revealed the boy's face. She tried to visualise the text that had appeared on the licence. Failed. She remembered his date of birth: the month and the year, at least. But what she needed, vitally, was his address. From their conversation that night, she knew that he lived in Cornwall. There had been something about animals, too.

It wasn't enough.

Distressed, she slammed the steering wheel.

*Damn it, Mallory. Think!*

But so much of that night remained shrouded in shadow.

A black Audi shot past, far too fast. She watched its tail lights recede into the darkness. The longer she stayed in London, the greater the danger.

*And the only lead you have is Cornwall.*

Mallory twisted the keys in the ignition, found first gear. She accelerated, heading west.

# SEVENTEEN

The pain was a thorn in Obe's veins, an unbearable tightness in every one of his muscles, as if his body were trying to brace itself against the weight of a stone monolith. He couldn't work out what was happening; couldn't do anything at all.

And then – as suddenly as it had seized him – the paralysis lifted and the pain vanished. He heard the thump of Orion's hooves on the sod and saw the ridge up ahead, tilting at a crazy angle.

Too late, Obe realised that he was falling. With his knees he tried to grip onto Orion's flanks, but he'd slid so far over the animal's right side that he had no leverage. When he tightened his fists around the horse's mane he discovered he no longer held it.

The horizon flipped. The ground rushed up. Obe put out a hand to save himself, heard the dry snap of bone. An instant later he punched the earth with his shoulder, rolling twice before slamming the ground chest-first, so forcefully that every ounce of his breath exploded from his lungs.

Riderless, Orion galloped into the night.

The pain hit. Worse, in some ways, than that which had unseated him. He dared not look at his arm – knew that a bright shard of bone had thrust out through the flesh. The thought made his stomach clench. He felt himself vomit into the soil.

Purged, Obe tried to get a breath, but even though he managed to fill his lungs they seemed unable to process the air. He couldn't see what was happening behind him; guessed that the sights of a rifle were lining up on his skull.

Somehow he rolled onto his side. Another white-hot bolt of agony exploded in his arm when he cradled it, but he felt no protrusion through his jacket, and realised that the bone, although splintered, had not cut through his skin.

The stranger stood nearby, winding in whatever electronic projectile he had fired. After slipping it into his jacket he came closer, his boots stopping inches from Obe's face.

'Obadiah Macintosh,' he said.

The man's cheeks were cratered with old acne scars. He wore an expression of curiosity laced with disgust, as if he observed an organism in a Petri dish: a malignant bacteria, or a fungal growth. 'Why'd you run?'

Running his tongue around his teeth, Obe spat out a mouthful of soil. 'Why'd you kill one of my dogs?'

'I didn't.'

'Your friend, then.'

'He was bitten.'

'Which dog?'

The man shrugged. 'The dead one.'

Obe barked a laugh: pure disbelief. He'd heard of such callousness, but he'd rarely witnessed it first-hand. 'What did he look like?'

'Covered in blood. Guts hanging out. Like he was having a bad day.'

'I didn't mean—'

'I don't give a shit about the dog. We're not here to donate. We didn't come out here to see puppies.' The pockmarked stranger paused, glanced back towards the main building. 'You ever put animals to sleep in there?'

'Not if we can help it. Not unless they're too sick to recover.'

'What do you use?'

Obe stared, unsure of where he was being led. He felt a curious lightness inside his head. Thought he might pass out.

'Pentobarbital, probably,' the man mused. 'Given intravenously. You can inject pentobarbital straight into the heart, although I believe most vets shy away from that. They say it's painful, cruel. Either way, they'll usually supply a little sedative beforehand: ketamine, maybe, or acepromazine. You recognise the names of those chemicals, Obadiah? You come across any of that stuff?'

'No.'

The stranger leaned closer. 'Sure about that? It'd be entirely natural to lie, and I could hardly blame you, but it really won't do you much good. My colleague discharged his firearm earlier and that was unfortunate, but all the way out here, under these vast and magnificent skies, it's so laid-back and lonely that I can't imagine any of the locals will care. There's plenty of time for us to get to know each other.'

'We don't keep any drugs like the ones you mentioned on site,' Obe said.

The stranger canted his head. 'Is that right? If so, it's a shame. I don't like to inflict suffering if I can possibly help it. We must act humanely, or we cease to be human. I firmly believe that.' He came forwards, crouching down opposite. 'Thing is, Obadiah, there's an impurity in you. A form of sickness, if you like. I know you know what I'm talking about. It's not your fault, this burden that you're carrying, and I don't believe for one second that you're malicious with it, that you intend to do anyone harm.' With a smirk he gestured towards the sanctuary's main building. 'You rescue abandoned *animals*, for God's sake. How cute is that? Not even ones we can eat, either. Old dogs and horses. *Cats* and shit. But you're dangerous, my friend, even if you don't realise it. Tell me. What did she get from you?'

Obe knew at once to whom his interrogator referred, but he

tilted his head, feigning ignorance. 'What did who get?'

The stranger sighed. Slowly, he rose off his haunches. Lifting one boot, he placed it on Obe's broken arm and steadily applied pressure.

The pain was a nail in his flesh and a scream inside his head, so sharp and sick that he almost cracked a tooth. He tried to worm backwards, couldn't. The pressure increased – his bones felt like shards of glass, crunching and sliding. Even when the man removed his foot, the pain still shrieked.

'I hate doing that stuff. *Hate* it. But I need answers, Obadiah, and I need them tonight.' Again, the stranger glanced towards the rescue centre, from which lights now blazed. 'I want to help you. I don't want you to suffer like this. Give me something. Just a crumb. Let's start with the girl.'

Obe gasped for breath. 'What about her?'

'See? That's better already. We're collaborating – *helping* one another.' He grinned, cocked a finger. 'Being humane.'

'I know hardly anything about her.'

'Oh, I'm pretty sure you don't. In fact, I guarantee it. But let's start with the easy stuff. When did you meet?'

'Three weeks ago.'

'Where?'

'Plymouth.'

'Go on.'

'There was a sci-fi convention. Comic books and stuff.'

'Uh-huh. And you met her at this convention?'

Obe shook his head. 'Afterwards. At a bar.'

'This is good, Obadiah. This is exactly what I need to hear.' The stranger's smile faded and his eyes grew flat. 'She recognised something in you. Didn't she? Saw something different. I need to know what it was.'

'I don't know what you mean.'

'Right. So, let's try this a different way. How old are you, Obadiah?'

'Twenty.'

'And you seem like a charismatic guy. I'm no homosexual, but I'd take a punt that women find you attractive. Yet you've tucked yourself away on this lonely little hump of rock, with no company except for a few mangy old strays.' He gestured around him. 'I mean, it's lovely, all this. But what are you *doing* out here, Obadiah? Who are you *hiding* from?'

Obe clutched his broken arm closer to his chest. *People like you*, he thought about saying. But it wouldn't have been true. Until tonight, he hadn't known that people as bad as this existed. 'Who are you?' he croaked. 'Who was she?'

From his pocket, the stranger pulled out a couple of plastic ties. 'They're good questions, Obadiah – complex and existential – but I could never do them justice. I need to know what you gave her, and then, if we really can't find any pentobarbital back there, we're going to have to figure out some other way of euthanising you.'

In his ears, Obe could hear distant surf. When he rested his head against the ground he saw stars glittering above. In the last hour, his world had changed so immeasurably that he no longer recognised it.

The man came forward with the plastic ties, his smile apologetic. 'They'll chafe a little,' he said. 'But not too badly if you don't struggle.' As he reached for Obe's wrist, something furred and black exploded out of the night. It slammed into the stranger, pitching him across the grass. In the commotion, Obe recognised a gleam of pink scalp. A moment later he saw Yoda clamp his jaws around a flailing arm.

The dog found his feet first, bracing his forelegs. Snarling and growling, he shook his head left and right. The stranger's light jacket offered him no protection from those teeth. He screamed, rolled onto his back and kicked out. Yoda was too fast, twisting out of range and dragging his victim around in a circle.

Blood flowed black in the starlight.

'Get it off!' the man screamed. '*Get it off me!*'

Obe rose into a sitting position, then stood. Orion waited some distance away, restlessly tossing his mane. But even if he managed to calm the horse, he'd never seat himself with only one arm.

The top of the ridge stood a few hundred metres to the east. Up there, parked in a dilapidated cow shed, was his Datsun. The car was a relic, donated by a fellow volunteer, so notoriously unreliable that he'd never even tested it on the dirt track down the hill. He trusted it well enough along the flatter roads past the summit, but he doubted that he'd reach it in time – not with the stranger's accomplice still at large. Obe was still debating his options when something incredible happened, something he would remember for whatever span of life he had remaining.

Orion tucked his forelegs beneath him, knelt on the grass and lowered himself onto his stomach. He switched his tail, shook out his mane.

Obe did not understand what was happening here, but he'd witnessed enough unusual events in his short life not to question them when they occurred. Going to the horse, muttering soft sounds of reassurance, he leaned his body against Orion's flank and eased a leg across his back. 'OK, dude,' he muttered. 'Better take this steady.'

Behind him came sounds of violence. Snarls of excitement, shouts of pain.

Gently, Orion rose from the soil. When Obe nudged him with his heels and the horse trotted forwards, the jolt of movement through his forearm was so excruciating he had to bite back a cry. The animal seemed to sense his distress, deliberately choosing a path across the softest ground.

Injured, Obe found it difficult to balance at first, but as he concentrated on the feel of Orion moving beneath him he began to adjust his position in anticipation. Some distance away, the stranger and the dog thrashed in the starlight.

Far sooner than he had expected, Obe arrived at the top of

the ridge. He recalled how starkly the two men had been silhouetted when he'd spotted them up here earlier. Leaning forwards, he urged Orion into a canter. Just as they crossed the summit, the air beside his left ear unzipped with a pressurised crack. An instant later, the report of a high-powered rifle crashed around the hills.

Teeth clenched so firmly that he thought they might fuse together, Obe rode down into sheltered scrubland, putting the West Penwith Animal Sanctuary, and the men who'd come to kill him, at his back.

Orion whickered.

'I know,' he said, easing the horse back into a more manageable trot. But they were empty words: it seemed he knew nothing at all.

The clouds sliding in from the Atlantic now covered two-thirds of the sky. It felt as if a shade was being drawn across his old life, but he refused to let the thought depress him. Despite the horrors of the last hour, the earth still brimmed with wonder.

Within a minute he reached the old cow shed. This side of the ridge, the darkness was far deeper, but his eyes were keen enough to spot the black Range Rover that stood beside his Datsun.

Without prompting, Orion walked to a patch of grass and knelt. Obe slipped off, rubbing the horse's cheek. 'You're a miracle,' he whispered. 'I never doubted it.'

He went over to the Range Rover. From his pocket he retrieved the knife he'd taken from the rescue centre. Circling the 4x4, he punctured each tyre, releasing the air with a whoosh. Obe took out his car keys and was about to step inside the cow shed when something hit him from behind.

The impact knocked him flat, and the flash of agony through his forearm almost knocked him unconscious, but when he recovered his balance he forgot the pain entirely because Yoda was standing there, big wet tongue lolling from his mouth like a rag.

Kneeling in the dirt, crying out with relief, Obe submitted himself to a licking. 'You dirty, stinky, delicious old mutt,' he said. 'You good boy. You *brave* boy.' Standing up, he threw open the Datsun's door. 'In you get.'

The dog obeyed without hesitation, leaping onto the passenger seat. Obe climbed in after him and started the engine. With his good hand, he found reverse and backed out of the shed. Fumbling once more with the gearstick, he accelerated up the track towards the main road.

Through the rear-view mirror he saw Orion, silhouetted against the sky. The horse watched the departing Datsun for a while, then dropped his head to the grass.

Obe adjusted the mirror, angling it down until his view of what lay behind him disappeared. He switched on the headlights, peered through the windscreen. Wondered what lay ahead.

# EIGHTEEN

On the first floor of the Ealing maisonette, Aylah İncesu sat at the kitchen table opposite a tightly bound Dr Fabian Pataki. On the table between them lay her bloodstained *qama*. The blood was her own. She hadn't started on Pataki yet. Every few moments the torture scene she'd seen on his TV slid back into her head, triggering memories she wanted to forget.

*Dripping water. Whispering voices. An excrement-streaked cage.*
*The unbearable expectation of pain.*

Washienko lounged in the doorway, reading the blurb from a pornographic Blu-ray sleeve. Chevry stood at the kitchen counter, searching through the overhead cupboards.

'If I could just explain something,' Pataki began. His face was pale, his skin greasy with sweat. He fell silent when Aylah shook her head.

Taking her thumb from her mouth, she leaned forwards. 'I want to see what you gave Mallory.'

With a twitch of his shoulder, the doctor indicated his restraints. 'If you'd allow me to—'

Again, Aylah shook her head. 'Tell us where to find it.'

'In the bathroom,' he said. 'Inside the cistern. There's an air-tight box at the bottom, a brick over the top to weigh it down.'

Aylah glanced at Washienko, clicking her fingers to get his attention.

He looked up from the Blu-ray sleeve, his expression pensive. 'This is making me horny,' he said. 'Queasy, but horny. Do you think that's weird?' Switching his attention to the doctor, he asked, 'Do *you* think that's weird?'

'The box,' Aylah snapped. 'From the cistern. Now.'

Smirking, Washienko dropped the sleeve and disappeared into the hall.

'Don't break the seal while it's underwater,' Pataki shouted. His eyes darted back to Aylah, apologetic. 'There's stuff in there worth a fortune.'

'We'll bear it in mind.'

At the counter, Chevry extricated himself from a cupboard, holding what looked like a tub of instant coffee. 'Is this decaf?'

Pataki nodded.

'Have you got non-decaf?'

'Beans are in the fridge. You'll have to grind them.'

Chevry opened the fridge. He took out the beans, sighed. 'Nothing's ever easy, is it?'

A minute later Washienko returned from the bathroom, his right arm dripping with water. In front of Aylah he placed a plastic box, complete with a rubber seal. 'If we're going to party,' he told her, 'I should give you fair warning – when I get high, I get crazy munchies. *Crazy.* Tell her, Guy.'

Chevry closed the fridge. 'It's true,' he said. 'He does. But the worst thing – he just doesn't shut up. Talks a lot of shit. Really tedious stuff.'

Washienko turned out his bottom lip. 'I'm a pretty tedious guy.'

Aylah clenched her teeth, knowing that a show of irritation would simply encourage him. When she prised the lid off Pataki's box, rows of orange plastic pill boxes confronted her. Each of them bore a handwritten sticker.

'You're looking for mifepristone and misoprostol,' the doctor said.

It took her a few moments to find the bottles. 'She took both?'

Pataki shook his head. 'Just the mifepristone. She was going to take the misoprostol later. I expect she wanted to get away from you first – find somewhere private where she could miscarry.'

'She mentioned us?'

'Not directly.'

'So what makes you think she wanted to get away from us?'

'I would.'

Aylah grunted. 'How quickly does the mifepristone take effect?'

'Pretty much immediately.'

'Does it work on its own?'

'It's best to take it with—'

She shot him a warning look. 'Does it work on its own?'

'Yes. Misoprostol – the other drug – just brings on the contractions. Sort of like pulling a toilet chain.'

Aylah stared at him. With some effort, she kept her face passive. 'Did she say where she was going?'

'No.'

'Did she pay you?'

'Yes.'

'How much?'

'Two . . . one hundred.'

'Two . . . one hundred? Think carefully. I won't ask you again.'

Pataki swallowed. He glanced down at the *qama*. Then he looked past Aylah to Washienko and Chevry. The men had gathered to her like wolves drawn to a kill. 'OK, OK, *four* hundred,' he blurted. 'Jesus! It's in a cup. On the window sill.'

Washienko retrieved the money. He counted it out, then tucked the fold into his back pocket.

'Great,' Pataki muttered. 'Thanks for robbing me.'

'Like I said,' the man replied. 'I'm a pretty tedious guy.'

Aylah tried to ignore him. 'Did she say anything about the father?'

The doctor shook his head. Then: 'Actually, yeah, she did. Just a throwaway comment – that he didn't know what she was doing, and that he never would.'

Aylah thought about that. 'One final question, if you don't object.'

'Shoot.'

'Do you think this a legitimate way to make money?'

He stared at her for a while, before snorting derisively. 'Ask me again once you've met my wife.'

She waited a beat, then nodded. 'I think we're done here. We've probably broken at least twenty different laws by bursting in and questioning you like this.'

Pataki scowled. 'I'm hardly going to say anything. Just untie me before you go. And please don't come back.'

'We won't be coming back,' she replied. 'And you definitely won't be saying anything.'

The doctor studied her. For the first time, he seemed to grasp the full gravity of his situation. 'Now wait a second—'

Aylah leaned forwards, curling her fingers around the *qama*.

'There's more to tell.'

She shook her head. 'I don't think there is. Not really. I'm sure you'd like us to believe that, but I have no time to waste on a—'

'I swear it,' Pataki said. 'I give you my word.'

'Really? And how much is that worth?'

'Maybe not much, but you'll want to hear this. And if I help you out, if I show you that I've—'

Aylah climbed to her feet, hefted the *qama*.

'She's still *pregnant*,' the doctor blurted.

# NINETEEN

Slumped in the passenger seat, head against the rest, Mallory watched dark Surrey countryside roll past the window. From her elevated position, the lights of oncoming vehicles didn't dazzle her as much as they had, but the pain behind her eyes still stung. Her stomach gripped and rolled.

The last few hours had thrown her into the depths of a crisis from which she was still fighting to recover. She had lost her home; lost, too, nearly all the securities that had framed her existence.

It had never been a life. Not really. And now even that had gone. All she owned in the world was the rucksack between her feet, and the balance on whatever credit cards she still dared to use.

Abandoning the Nissan had been the hardest decision so far, but she had ridden her luck with it long enough. She had to assume that by now the carnage in Clapham had been discovered, and that the Vasi had marshalled their full resources in their hunt for her. Hopefully, some opportunistic car thief was leading them on a futile chase across London.

After dumping the Nissan half a mile from Ealing Hospital, Mallory had walked into Southall, skirting a wide path around any CCTV. Over the course of ten minutes she flagged down three black cabs, but none were willing to ferry her as far out of

London as she needed to go. Finally, intercepting an Uber in the midst of a drop-off, she persuaded the driver to take her fare. Half an hour later he dropped her at Fleet Services on the M3, a few miles east of Basingstoke. The thirty-mile trip made another dent in her cash reserves, but she judged the cost worthwhile. At Fleet, she found the HGV park and toured the assembled lorries until she happened across Joos Lagerweij, a forty-nine-year-old trucker from Enschede in Holland.

Joos was sitting in his Volvo cab with the door open, smoking a cigarillo and watching a DVD. The man wore cowboy boots, a leather bolo tie and – despite the heat – a rabbit-felt Stetson in a dark chocolate shade. He struck up a conversation the moment she approached, pausing the Clint Eastwood movie playing on his dash-mounted screen.

There was a gold wedding band on his ring finger, and Mallory saw photographs of children fixed to the cab's interior, around bunting in the style of the Confederate flag. On the passenger seat lay a fringed suede waistcoat with silver studwork and black bone beads.

Joos had stopped in Fleet en route from a shipyard in Rotterdam, from which he was hauling thirty tons of parts intended for a Falmouth boat builder. He was delighted with the prospect of a little company. He offered her a cigarillo, which she declined, and invited her to hop up inside the cab while he finished his coffee. Removing the waistcoat from the passenger seat, he draped it on the bunk behind him with the care one might show to a priceless cultural artefact. 'It's custom-made,' he told her. 'I had it shipped from Colorado. All the seams are hand-stitched. There's a Native American tailor there, seventy-six years old. You send him your measurements and he gets straight to work.'

'It's beautiful.'

Joos nodded, his eyes sparkling. 'I haven't made it to America yet. But one day, God willing, if I haul enough crap. What do you say?' He slapped his thigh to emphasise his point, and for the first time all night, Mallory found herself smiling.

A few minutes later they joined the motorway, heading south-west. Joos swapped the Clint Eastwood movie for a country music CD. As the singer reminisced about a dog he'd once owned, Joos offered an accompaniment in heavily accented English.

Beside him, Mallory studied the Volvo's in-built satnav. If they drove without a break, they should reach Falmouth in a little over four hours. But while that was the end of the road for Joos, she still had no idea of her final destination. 'Do you have any paracetamol?' she asked.

Joos paused in his singing. His face fell, as if it pained him beyond measure to be found wanting. 'I'm sorry,' he told her. 'I don't believe so. But I can offer you coffee. The caffeine might help.' He pointed behind him, indicating a six-cup machine that she hadn't noticed until now. 'If you lift the bunk, you can get at the fridge. Ground coffee's in there. Milk, too.' Joos waggled his eyebrows. 'Columbian beans. Very good.'

Mallory thanked him. It was such a relief to busy herself with a task as mundane as brewing coffee that for a while she lost herself in it. She filled the machine's reservoir and found herself a mug. 'Want one?'

Joos shook his head. 'I already drank five cups. Any more and I'll be pissing like a Texan Quarter Horse.' He glanced over and winked.

She loved him for that, felt such a powerful sense of connection that her vision swam. Moments of kinship had been so fleeting in her life that they always took her off-guard. Her tears weren't lost on Joos. The man didn't say anything, but he skipped through the song about the dead dog, finding instead an ode to daytime drinking. It was an up-tempo track, and he thumped the steering wheel heartily in time.

Settled in the passenger seat with a coffee, wearing Joos's Aviators to shield her eyes from oncoming traffic, Mallory replayed her encounter with Obadiah Macintosh, searching for clues.

Three weeks ago she'd taken herself across London to Little Venice, north of Paddington, where she'd sat outside a café and sketched the narrowboats on Regent's Canal. As a child she'd been a half-decent artist, and lately she'd been trying to improve her skills: perhaps, in hindsight, she'd intuited that her time was running down and hoped to leave something behind, even something as short-lived as a pad filled with sketches.

Back at Paddington, acting on impulse, she bought a ticket for the next train to leave the station. Once a week for the last six months, the urge to travel – at random times and to random places – had grown in her. Four hours later she found herself in Plymouth, standing on the cobbled waterfront as the setting sun turned the sea to gold.

She watched a couple walking hand in hand, and they seemed so happy in each other's company, so carefree and complete, that she suddenly needed to get drunk. In a bar opposite the marina she ordered a mojito, swiftly followed by three more.

Had she met Obe then, or in one of the many other bars she'd stumbled into afterwards? It hardly mattered. What *did* matter was the conversation they'd shared – the snippets he'd revealed about himself before the alcohol in her blood called time on her memories.

He'd been in Plymouth for a science fiction convention, some geeky thing where fans dressed up as their favourite super-heroes; the bar had been awash with bright capes and spandex. Obe hadn't taken things that far, but he'd been weighed down with weird-looking merchandise. She remembered a mug with tentacles sprouting from it; comic books sealed in protective plastic; weird dice; weird clothing; weird games. He had talked animatedly, excitedly, deflecting her various attempts at ridicule with back-handed compliments or self-deprecating jokes.

And then there had been the sayings. A saying for this, a

saying for that; until her head had rung with them. *Love your neighbour, even if he plays a trombone*, he told her, in response to a barb about his fellow attendees. *Eagles may soar, but weasels don't get sucked into jet engines.* She didn't even know what that one had meant, and yet she couldn't forget it.

His eyes were bright with whatever he'd been smoking; and every time he ordered a beer he tipped into it a double tequila shot. He should have frustrated her, and he did. He should have irritated the hell out of her, and he did that too. But for reasons unfathomable, she'd found it impossible to turn away from him. It had been, even by recent standards, the oddest night of her life.

Mallory lurched forwards in her seat, nearly spilling coffee into her lap.

*Surfing*, that was one of the things he had talked about. In fact, he'd practically eulogised about it.

'You OK?' Joos asked, glancing across at her.

She nodded, taking a sip of her drink and hoping the caffeine would deliver a kick to her brain.

Surfing.

And the sea.

And the place he went when he wanted to think.

He lived on the coast. Close enough, he had said, to feel sand beneath his toes within a minute of leaving his door. It wasn't one of the busier Cornish tourist destinations like St Ives or Penzance. His home patch was quieter, more remote.

Mallory closed her eyes, wishing that she could remember the address printed on his licence, but even if she managed to recall the name of his town, her chances of bumping into him as she wandered the streets were slim.

He led a cloistered life, she remembered that; not only living in isolation but working in isolation too. Perhaps that was the reason she'd been so drawn to him; for all their differences, they endured the same self-inflicted solitude.

Beside her, Joos said, 'You hungry? Want something to eat?'

Earlier, the thought of food would have made her retch. Now, she found she was ravenous. 'What've you got?'

'How about a cheeseburger? Microwaved, but still pretty good. Or there's nachos, a whole bag of 'em. Sour cream and salsa in the fridge. Even got some habanero moose jerky, if that gets your taste buds bouncing.'

Mallory settled for the nachos and dip. 'Do you have a roadmap I could look at?'

Joos gestured behind him. 'Cupboard above the bunk.'

She popped her seatbelt and crawled into the back, rummaging around until she found a road atlas of the British Isles. Back in her seat, she balanced a double-page spread of Cornwall's south-western peninsula across her knees.

'King Arthur,' she muttered. 'Knights of the Round Table.' Glancing through the windscreen, she wondered why that thought had entered her head.

# TWENTY

Tied to a chair in the first-floor kitchen of his Ealing maisonette, Dr Fabian Pataki talked – entirely appropriately – like a man in immediate fear of losing his life. Pearls of sweat rolled down his face. Even the lenses of his glasses looked wet.

'She seemed so self-assured,' he said. 'So certain of what she had to do. She never even asked me about pain, and they always want to know about that. The way she was talking, she actually seemed to *welcome* the prospect of a little pain, as if she viewed it as some kind of penance.'

Beneath the table, Aylah curled her bleeding thumb into her fist, resisting the temptation to reopen the wound. 'Go on.'

'I explained the consequences of each drug – what it would do, how quickly it would take effect. She drank some water and swallowed the mifepristone down, but she decided to take the misoprostol later. Once that's ingested, the contractions come on pretty quick. I'm guessing that if she knew you were after her—'

'Get to the point,' Aylah said.

'After taking the mifepristone, she must have sat in that chair for about five seconds without saying anything. Then she leaped up and shot over to the sink. Stuck two fingers down her throat and tried to make herself sick.'

Aylah's heart began to thud inside her chest. 'Did she succeed?'

'Not at first. She started shouting, all kinds of crazy shit. Then she grabbed a salt shaker from the cupboard, dumped a load of it into her water glass, stirred the whole thing up and drank it down. She vomited pretty much immediately after that.'

'This salt shaker?' Washienko asked, plucking one from the counter.

'That's it.'

Aylah stared. If the doctor was telling the truth, it was the best news she could have received. Only while Mallory remained pregnant could she intuit the girl's location. After Korec and Levitan's insubordination in Clapham, only a certified kill would reassert her dominance. 'If you're lying . . .' she began.

Pataki thrust his chin towards the sink. 'She must have vomited her entire dinner down it. Unscrew the U-bend if you don't believe me.'

She glanced over at Washienko. 'Check it out.'

The man jerked away from her. 'I'm seriously bad with puke,' he said. Pointing at Chevry, he added, 'There's your guy.'

Chevry frowned. 'Oh, come on,' he said, gesturing at the doctor. 'It's his sink.'

'Do it,' Aylah hissed.

The man leaned over the plughole and screwed up his face. 'Certainly smells of puke.'

'Check the U-bend.'

Muttering, Chevry opened the cupboard beneath the sink. On hands and knees he unscrewed the pipe, recoiling in disgust when the contents leaked over his fingers. Moving fast, he poured what remained onto the drainer. 'Ah, fucking gross.'

'Told you,' the doctor said.

'Do you see a pill?' Aylah asked.

'This is messed up.'

'Do you see a *pill*?'

Grimacing, Chevry leaned closer. 'Just pasta, mainly. Least I'm guessing it's pasta. Few vegetables, too, but . . .' He hesitated. 'Wait a minute. Yeah. There it is. Just like the one he showed us.'

'I hope this means we're friends now,' Pataki said.

Aylah sucked her teeth. Before she could respond, her mobile phone buzzed: Teke again.

'The hospital was a red herring,' he told her. 'She's pinged another camera a little further west. I'm guessing she's heading for the M25.'

'She is.'

'How do you know that?'

'Turns out Mallory wouldn't take her medicine. That's good news for us. It means we're not totally screwed if you lose her on ANPR.'

'Any idea where she's going?'

'She's running to him, Teke. I'm convinced of it. If I'm right, she'll pick up the M3 or A30. Both head south-west.'

'Do we still want to intercept?'

'Uh-uh. The focus, now, is on Cornwall.'

'That's already been arranged.'

'Good. Mallory's got a five-hour trip ahead of her. We need to have neutralised Obadiah before she arrives. I've done what I can in London. I want to be down there too – as fast as possible.'

'I'm on it.' He paused. 'Aylah?'

'What?'

'Manco left me a message.'

Thinking of the Vasi principal, Aylah felt an unpleasant tightness in her stomach, but there was still time to rescue this before she faced him. Ending the call, she picked up her *qama*. 'Returning to your point, Doctor,' she said, 'I'm afraid you couldn't be more wrong. We're not friends, you and I. We're nothing of the sort.'

Pataki's face sagged, as if he recognised his death in her expression. 'What do you mean?' he croaked. 'What's going on?'

She angled the weapon's blade, watching the way the fluorescent light played across its surface.

'Aylah?'

Turning, she found Chevry at her side.

He wore a look of intense interest. 'What do we do with him?'

'This man's an abortionist,' she replied, returning her attention to the doctor. 'He kills indiscriminately, takes innocent life before its inevitable corruption – before, even, it's had the opportunity to inflict suffering.' Aylah paused, raised an eyebrow. 'What could be purer than that? I'm hard-pressed to think of a more practical application of Vasi doctrine. Just imagine where we'd be if we had a few thousand more like him.'

So far, Fabian Pataki had been holding his breath. Now, sensing a reprieve, he slumped forwards against his restraints.

Seeing his relief, recalling the torture scene that had been playing when she'd arrived, Aylah's mind swam with fractured memories.

*Dripping water. Whispering voices. An excrement-streaked cage.*

*The unbearable expectation of pain.*

*A bowl filled with rotten food. Another brimming with filthy water. A dog collar around her neck, connected to a length of heavy chain. More an animal, now, than a human being; a receptacle for humiliation and pain.*

*And out of that, a light; Saul Manco's alligator eyes; his steady, patient voice:*

*'There's a way to end this, Aylah, if only you'll open your eyes. A way to end your torment, a way to end all the world's torment. Would you like me to tell you about it? Would you like me to show you the true path towards silence?'*

Aylah blinked away the memory. 'The problem with Dr Pataki,' she continued, changing her focus to Chevry, 'is that there's no grand vision influencing his choices. His actions are guided not by sagacity but by depravity. He's a parasite, a leech; one of the worst.'

Dismayed, Pataki raised his head. 'That's not true.'

'Even if our work wasn't secret, even if the doctor convinced us that he'd keep silent about events here tonight, it would be our *duty* to put an end to him.'

Chevry stepped towards the table. His expression had changed indelibly. He twisted his fingers together, licked his lips. 'If we're really going to kill him,' he said, 'would you consider giving me the task?'

Aylah blinked. Turning fully in her chair, she examined the man more closely. 'You?'

He nodded, eyes bright, and in that moment she saw that his earlier irreverence, his banter with Washienko, had been nothing but a façade. Now, with the mask removed, she glimpsed something infinitely darker, far more interesting and exploitable.

'I'm Vasi,' he told her. 'I've dedicated my life to ridding the world of Arayıcı influence. But these days there are precious few of them left to kill.' His nostrils flared. 'Pretty soon you'll be the last one.'

Careful to keep her expression neutral, Aylah said, 'That's a fact that should please you.'

'It does, of course it does. I just . . .' He treated Pataki to a contemplative look. 'Until now, I've never taken a life. And let's face it – even when we catch up with the girl, it's pretty clear that you've reserved honours on that one.'

'Our good doctor here isn't Arayıcı.'

'But he might be the next best thing. I just . . . I wanted to do it once, you know? Take a life. Snuff it out and see how it felt. Understand the . . .' He stopped, shrugged.

Glancing across the table at Pataki, Aylah asked, 'How would you do it?'

Now, Chevry made a sound in his throat that was almost sexual. 'I could shoot him. We brought along suppressors. It'd be quiet.'

She shook her head. 'You know how much attention a

shooting homicide gets. Even beating him to death would cause us problems, and I'm not burning down another house, not tonight.' She strummed her fingers on the table. 'We have a little time until Teke arranges my transport so I'm happy to indulge you, but if you want to do this, you need to make it look like an accident. Either that or a suicide.'

Chevry licked his lips. When his eyes lit upon the tub of pills Washienko had retrieved from the cistern, he made that odd sound in his throat once more.

# TWENTY-ONE

Obadiah Macintosh sat with his back to the dunes and his eyes on the sea, watching the incoming surf break apart like so much smashed porcelain. The sun had just risen in the east, a copper smudge in a lavender nest of cloud. This early, both air and water seemed silken, mercurial.

Apart from the dog, Obe was alone on the beach. If this was to be his last hour, he couldn't have imagined one more perfect.

The men from the sanctuary would doubtless be hunting him. In truth, he should have fled inland, but the pull towards the ocean had been irresistible. For a while, at least, they would likely concentrate their efforts on the main roads leading away from the peninsula: the A30 east, through Crows-an-Wra; the road north towards St Just; the south-eastern route via Trevescan and Boleigh.

In the movies he had watched, and the comics he had read, men like those he had encountered used numerous techniques to locate a target. They could turn a mobile phone against its owner, use satellites and drones to monitor victims in real time. Obe's phone couldn't betray him, because he'd never owned one; craning his neck, he peered up into the sky. Was he being watched from up there? He didn't think that satellite imaging was of sufficient resolution to capture a human face; but on the off-chance that it was, he raised his uninjured arm and waved.

Of more concern, if they were using satellites, was his car. A human face might be difficult to pick out, but a vehicle was a much larger target, and around here there were so few cars that his Datsun could be quickly identified. He had abandoned it before first light, parking it inside a partially collapsed ranger's hut, but no orbiting electronic eyes would be restricted to the visible spectrum alone; thanks to infrared, they could keep watch just as easily in the hours of darkness. If they'd tuned in prior to the attack, they already knew his location, which meant he had no chance whatsoever of evading capture.

Hours had passed since he'd last smoked anything – already he could feel the effects of his abstinence building like a dull pressure behind his eyes – but right now, whatever the short-term discomfort, he could not afford to dull his senses. Instead, he broke out his rolling tin and fashioned a thin cigarette. Rarely did he use tobacco without weed, but as he took a drag and vented smoke into the sky, the gentle hit of nicotine helped to corral his thoughts.

Those thoughts, inevitably, turned to the girl: who she was; where she had gone; what trouble she had brought him – or, just as likely, what trouble he had brought her in return.

'Mallory,' he said.

Speaking her name seemed to enliven it, investing it with power. Obe shivered, said her name again, and when he glanced down he saw that he had scratched it in the sand, using a driftwood stick as a marker.

His skin contracted into goosebumps.

Beside him, Yoda yawned. Sneezed.

Obe stared across the beach, to the milk sea crowned by pale sky. 'If in doubt, paddle out,' he said. Then he turned to the dog. 'Right?'

Yoda growled, averted his head.

'I mean, those could be some of my last waves out there. Am I going to sit here watching them until those guys pick me up?'

The wind was blowing offshore, the high tide rolling perfect barrels towards the beach. Each wave seemed a gift, a perfect construct – aquamarine at the face, copper-tinged at the lip, holding its form in slow-motion splendour before breaking apart in a thunderous celebration of spray.

So much beauty in this world. Obe was grateful that in his twenty years he had experienced such a surfeit. He had known good people and bad, but the scales that weighed humanity's worth were not balanced equally: there was far more love out there than hate. And while, thanks to his condition, he had sequestered himself more than he might have liked, his limited interactions with others had felt even more valuable as a result, his experiences of everyday human kindness and companionship distilled. Surrendering to those who spread violence and hate – allowing even the smallest measure of their darkness to pollute him – would be a betrayal of all the grace he had known. If this was to be his last day, he would live it without fear and without regret.

Well, one regret, perhaps.

The girl.

But that was OK.

'You think I can surf with a broken arm?' he asked.

Yoda continued to ignore him, as if the dog had intuited his intentions and did not wish to encourage them.

Obe looked at his arm. Before abandoning the Datsun, he'd snapped off a piece of the fascia and used it as a splint, fixing it with cotton strips torn from an old T-shirt. In the boot, he'd found a packet of co-codamol and had tossed down a couple of pills. His board had been strapped to the roof rack, his wetsuit laid out on the passenger seat. He'd carried both down here with him, along with a rucksack filled with the rest of his scavenged possessions: the spare clothes he'd kept in the car, a bottle of Lucozade, a block of surf wax and a tattered copy of *Y: The Last Man*.

'*I* think I can,' he told the dog. 'But there's no way I can get my arm into my wetsuit wearing a splint, and that water's *cold*.'

He still had the knife he'd used to puncture the 4x4's tyres. Leaning over the suit, he cut off the right arm just below the shoulder seam. Then he stripped off his clothes and struggled into it.

The dog watched in disgust.

With his good hand, he tethered his leash and picked up his board. Already, his heart was racing. His lungs filled with Atlantic air. Traipsing across the sand to the water's edge, Obe went surfing.

# TWENTY-TWO

With thirty tons of boat parts rumbling along behind them, Mallory and Joos Lagerweij reached Cornwall around four hours after leaving Fleet. Joos's destination was Falmouth, but he wasn't due in the town until late morning, and once he learned of her intended location he insisted on driving her all the way there. It was an act of superlative kindness, and she found herself humbled by it; embarrassed. Twice she tried to refuse his offer, but Joos would hear nothing of her protests. Nor did he want to waste what time they had remaining by listening to repeated expressions of gratitude.

Mallory settled, instead, for making him breakfast. She brewed another pot of coffee and toasted four slices of bread, which she spread with butter and jam. Afterwards, she wound down her window and let the early morning air revive her. She'd gone a whole night without sleep. Her eyes were gritty and her head pulsed with the vestiges of her earlier headache. She'd have to rest soon; she couldn't afford mistakes caused by exhaustion.

The rising sun was a split yolk in the wing mirror, promising a day of clear skies and unrelenting heat. In such good company, with such a sight behind her, it was difficult to believe that the events she'd escaped had really occurred.

*You killed a man.*

Yes. And if she'd shied from the task, he would have killed her instead. She felt no remorse for what she had done, but she did feel revulsion, sadness. She had asked for none of this; had earned the attentions of the Vasi by the simple virtue of her ancestry.

Across her knees lay the road atlas, open at the spread that showed West Penwith. Earlier, she'd traced her finger around the coastline, checking every one of its villages and hamlets. When she came to Sennen Cove, less than a mile north of Land's End, she recognised it as the place Obadiah Macintosh had mentioned. The map did not name the handful of roads it depicted, but when she borrowed Joos's mobile phone and investigated them on Google Maps, she found Stone Chair Lane and recalled it from the boy's driving licence.

She would track him down, discover the essential information she needed and disappear as quickly as she had arrived. He had no place in her plans after that: the future looked difficult enough without a Kusurlu — if her suspicions about him were correct — to slow her down.

Beside her, Joos Lagerweij wound down his window and lit a cigarillo. The smell of it was sharp — acrid but not unpleasant. 'I still haven't figured it out,' he said.

'Figured out what?'

'Whether you're running away from someone, or running to them.'

Mallory grunted. 'What makes you think it's either?'

'It's always one.'

'Maybe not.'

He shrugged, took another drag.

'Which do *you* think it is?'

'Me? Ha! I don't know. Even asking you about this stuff goes against one of the main rules I live by. I'm just curious. Too curious for my own good.' He curled his bottom lip. 'Ah, hell. It's more than that. I guess I'm concerned.'

'Concerned?'

'Worried. About you. Worried that you'll be all right.'

'Me?' She looked at him, surprised. 'You don't even know me.'

Joos glanced over. 'So?'

She held his eyes for only a moment before looking away. 'Tell me your rule.'

'Huh?'

'The rule you mentioned. The one you live by.'

'Oh, that.'

'What is it?'

Joos flicked ash into the tray. 'Never miss a good opportunity to shut up.'

Not long after, they turned off the A30 onto a meandering road that wound towards the sea. The water sparkled with morning sunlight. Its scent bloomed in her nose, briny and green.

From Joos's phone, Mallory had learned that Sennen Cove was a small community of around two hundred, although that number swelled during summer months. At its south-western edge, where the sandy bay surrendered to a rocky promontory, a stone-built breakwater protected a fishing fleet that comprised a handful of boats dragged up onto a slipway. A Tamar-class lifeboat operated out of the station beside it. Extending in a crescent to the north, the wide strip of Whitesand Bay emerged from gently sloping headlands tufted with beachgrass.

Joos's lorry was too large for the road along the waterfront, but he insisted on navigating it even so. Mallory squinted through her side window, examining the slate-roofed dwellings that receded up the hill. She wondered which of them Obe called home.

At last they reached the lifeboat station. In the adjoining car park, Joos turned his rig around. The air brakes hissed, bleeding off water vapour.

'Guess this is it,' he said.

Mallory nodded. She peered outside: at the gulls wheeling overhead, the foaming sea. 'Guess so.'

'You have money?'

She nodded.

'Know where you're going?'

'Sure.'

'Food?'

'Some.'

He rummaged behind him. 'Here. Take this.'

She looked at what he proffered – a pack of habanero moose jerky. 'Really. I don't—'

'Take it,' he said, and in the end she stuffed it into her rucksack just to placate him.

Joos took off his Stetson, running his hand around the crown. 'This design,' he said. 'It's what they call a pinch-front crease. Finest rabbit felt, too. Made in Texas, same process they've been using since 1865.' He looked over at her. 'Few things you need to know about a hat like this. First, you never leave it anywhere upside down. They say your luck drains out of it that way. Second: never put it on your bed. Don't ask me the reasoning for that, but I've never done it, and it's served me pretty well. Hopefully it'll serve you just as faithfully.'

Mallory opened her mouth. 'Uh-uh,' she said. 'I can't take that.'

'Hat like this,' Joos continued, 'it tells you when it needs to move on – when it's found someone new, someone who needs a little of its luck.'

She raised an eyebrow. 'It's told you that about me?'

He nodded, solemn. Then, gently, he placed it on her head. 'Look after it,' he said, 'and it'll look after you.'

For a moment, Mallory couldn't think of anything to say. 'You're an unusual man, Joos Lagerweij.'

He indicated the photographs tacked amongst the bunting. 'I'm just doing what Mrs Lagerweij would expect of me. Key ingredient for a happy marriage is doing what's expected. I've got another pearl of cowboy wisdom for you, if you'll hear it.'

She smiled. Nodded.

'Don't go in if you don't know the way out.'

Mallory laughed. 'That's pretty good advice. Not sure if I can follow it, though.'

Surprising herself, she put a hand on his shoulder, and realised, as she did it, that aside from her liaison with Obadiah Macintosh it was the first time she'd touched another human being in three years. Again, she looked out of the window, at the ranks of slate-roofed buildings arrayed up the hill.

*Don't go in if you don't know the way out.*

Picking up her rucksack, shrugging her arms into the straps, Mallory opened the door and jumped down onto the tarmac.

'See you around, cowboy,' she said.

# TWENTY-THREE

A Bell Jet Ranger dropped Aylah İncesu on a patch of scrubland near the Mayon Old Coastguard Lookout, west of Sennen Cove, just before dawn. Her arrival was hardly subtle – the urgent shrill of the helicopter's turbine had likely awakened most, if not all, of the community's residents – but by flying here instead of driving she had shaved four hours off the journey time, guaranteeing that she reached the village far in advance of her quarry.

During the flight she had received a disturbing report from Teke that Obadiah Macintosh had evaded the team sent to apprehend him at the animal sanctuary. Aylah knew the calibre of the men involved, which made their failure even less understandable. Worse, they had now forfeited the element of surprise.

It was another reason Aylah worried little about her very public arrival. She wanted the boy to feel pressure, to see the extent of the resources aligned against him. Already, the main roads off the peninsula were being monitored. As more manpower flooded the area, Aylah would methodically tighten the noose. In the meantime, she intended to discover as much about him as possible.

The two men assigned to the sanctuary – Ali Irmak and Nik Pavri – were waiting when she emerged from the Jet Ranger.

Both men wore angry expressions. Pavri was nursing a badly bitten forearm. 'Your deviant knew we were coming,' he said.

'That's impossible.'

His eyes narrowed. 'I'm telling you. Shithead set his dogs on us. I've probably been infected with some kind of canine syphilis. He slashed our tyres on his way out, too. Stopped us from following.'

'Your car's still there?'

'Clean-up team's getting it towed, but we had to hike cross-country to get here. Took us ninety minutes.' Irmak turned and spat on the ground. 'What are we meant to do now?'

'Can you handle a little breaking and entering?'

'Obadiah's place?'

She nodded.

'No chance he'll go back there now.'

'No, but the girl might be on her way here, and there's a chance she'll go straight to his flat. Even if she doesn't, I need to get a better feel for our target.'

'What makes you think she's coming?'

'A hunch.'

'Is that all?'

'Are you questioning *me*?' she asked. 'After your frankly startling performance at the sanctuary? Is *that* what's happening here?'

The man ran his tongue across his front teeth, scowled. 'I heard Manco is on his way. He needs to know this wasn't our fault. That somehow your freak was forewarned.'

Aylah caught the unease in his expression. She tried to ignore the worm of fear coiling in her own gut. The Vasi principal's low tolerance of failure was widely known.

The Bailiwicks turned out to be a two-storey block comprising ten one- and two-bedroom units. The communal entrance, carpeted in functional grey nylon worn down in places to its rubberised backing, opened into a lightless lobby. Concrete steps led to the first floor and the door to Obadiah Macintosh's flat. Beneath it, a coconut-fibre mat bore the legend: *SCRUFFY NERF HERDERS WELCOME.*

Nik Pavri stooped down and busied himself with the lock, jimmying it open and swinging the door wide.

A life-sized cardboard cut-out of Hulk Hogan guarded the entrance hall. Above it, a Spiderman lampshade enclosed the ceiling bulb. When Aylah entered the living room, the breath rushed out of her. She turned slowly in disbelief. 'What *is* this?' she asked. 'What kind of nut are we dealing with here?'

Irmak looked around, whistling low.

'Wow,' Pavri said.

Into an area of floor space no larger than twelve square metres, Obadiah Macintosh had crammed a lifetime's collection of comic books and B-movie merchandise. Perhaps several lifetimes. A linen-backed poster dating from the 1950s dominated one wall. It depicted a giant red-headed female clad in a white bikini top and shorts stepping across an American freeway. Between her feet, terrified drivers fled from hastily abandoned vehicles. Large red letters proclaimed the movie's title: *ATTACK OF THE 50 FT. WOMAN.*

Other walls featured posters for similarly outlandish productions: *Crack in the World*; *It Came From Beneath the Sea*; *Plan 9 From Outer Space*; *The Day the Earth Caught Fire*. In one corner stood a half-sized Tardis; stepping out of it, a red-eyed robotic skeleton the height of a three-year-old child. A glass-fronted display case contained plastic figures from the *Buffy the Vampire Slayer* TV series, a collection of 1970s Smurfs and a set of Lego *Ghostbusters* characters.

The middle shelf was empty save for a single velvet-lined box that held what looked like the cylindrical handle of some futuristic weapon.

'A Master Replica,' Irmak said. 'Nice.' Going to the display case, he opened the door and picked it up. 'This is Luke Skywalker's. The one he built after losing Anakin's at Cloud

City.' Experimentally swiping the air, he added, 'You know, I'm actually starting to hate this guy a little less.'

Aylah glanced over at Pavri. 'Any idea what he's talking about?'

'The green lightsaber,' he replied. 'From *Return of the Jedi*.'

On the floor beneath the TV, amid a mass of cables, lay five different games consoles. Nearby, the shelves of two bookcases bowed with the weight of their brightly decorated tomes. Along the window she saw a row of rubber zombie masks beside a red, white and blue shield decorated with a white star.

'Even if he wasn't Kusurlu,' Aylah muttered, 'I'd still want him dead.' She went to the sofa and sat in front of a coffee table from which a blackened face and a pair of hands appeared to be escaping.

When her phone rang, she answered straight away. 'What've you got?'

'Bad news,' Teke said. 'Manco will be with you in a few hours. 'You're to stay exactly where you are until he arrives.'

'*Bok.*'

'Sorry.'

She shook her head. 'It was inevitable. Anything new on our targets?'

'Nothing on the girl since she pinged that camera near Southall. But if you're right about her intentions, she'll be with you any time from seven.'

'Two hours,' Aylah said, glancing at her watch. 'What about the boy?'

'That's where it gets strange. Other than the bank account and the Netflix ID, Obadiah Macintosh is a ghost. He appeared in Sennen Cove four years ago. Before that, there's no shred of history.'

'National Insurance number?'

'Doesn't exist.'

'What about his job?'

'There's no tax record. They must pay him cash.'

'Who runs the charity?'

'Woman called Lynette Burgess. Retired hotelier.'

'Send me her address.'

'Done. You find anything interesting at the flat?'

Aylah looked around her. Irmak was standing at the display case, fiddling with one of the action figures. 'More like bizarre. Seems like we're hunting the world's biggest nerd.' She paused. 'I think I need you to come down here.'

'I'm working on it.'

'Keep me updated,' she replied, and hung up.

Beside the sofa sat a large cardboard box. Aylah tore off the lid, revealing a row of clear-plastic cases. She pulled one out and examined it. 'This just gets weirder. Anyone know what I'm looking at?'

Irmak glanced over. 'It's a comic.'

'I can see that. Is it from Chernobyl? Why's it vacuum-packed in plastic?'

'It's been slabbed, that's all.'

'Slabbed?'

'Encased. To protect it.'

'From what?'

'Anything. Water damage, sticky fingers, greasy teenagers. The number on the top shows its grading. That one's a nine point eight, which is near mint.' Irmak paused. Then his mouth fell open. 'Is that *The New Mutants* issue ninety-eight? Because if it is, it's worth—'

Aylah flung it at him before he could finish his sentence.

Saul Manco arrived just before seven. A Chrysler Grand Voyager pulled up outside and Caleb Klein climbed out of the driver's seat. Aylah stiffened; aware, immediately, that any attempt at damage limitation had just grown far harder. In the last few years she'd replaced Caleb as Manco's deputy. His contempt for her was personal, his desire to see her unseated common knowledge.

He walked around the vehicle and opened the side door, from which the Vasi principal emerged.

For a man approaching his seventieth year, Saul Manco still looked like he could bench press his own body weight. His steel-coloured hair, swept back from his forehead into a ponytail that flowed down his back, revealed a stark widow's peak. Beneath it, the man's alligator eyes blinked rarely and missed nothing. He walked with the same cane he had carried since she'd first known him: a shaft of blackthorn topped by a handle of carved horn. He flicked it out before him as if he were furious with the world and sought to punish it.

Aylah shivered when she saw him, feeling a tightness in her muscles; memories of humiliation and pain. Raising her thumb to her lips, she ran her teeth along the wound her *qama* had opened. In their years together, Manco had elicited from her every conceivable emotion. She'd hated him at first, had even tried to kill him once or twice; and yet when he'd finally broken through her defences and forced her to hear his message, she'd found herself awestruck.

*'There's a way to end this, Aylah, if only you'll open your eyes. A way to end your torment, a way to end all the world's torment. Would you like me to tell you about it? Would you like me to show you the true path towards silence?'*

She'd been so filled with terror, with grief, with confusion. Saul Manco had promised to take it all away.

*After violence, silence.*

'You might want to put that down,' Aylah said, directing her comment to Ali Irmak. When he glanced out of the window he dropped the action figure onto the coffee table.

A toilet flushed in the bathroom and Pavri appeared, rolling a bandage around his forearm. 'What's up?'

'Manco,' Irmak replied, looking a little sick. 'Remember what I told you. We explain it exactly as it happened. No spin. Anything but the truth and he'll know.'

Moments later, Saul Manco swept into the room. He came

to a halt, chin thrust forward, and rapped the tip of his cane against the floor. In that single action he seemed to draw electricity from the air. Aylah felt the hairs on her arms rise.

At first, her old mentor chose not to make eye contact. His attention drifted around the room, observing the display cases, the bookshelves, the posters on the wall. His voice, when he spoke, was like sandpaper. 'Who, here, has overall command?'

Aylah pushed back her shoulders. 'I do.'

Manco nodded. Finally he turned and examined her. This close, his eyes were spheres of broken glass. After a minute's scrutiny, his attention shifted once again. 'And you are?'

'Ali Irmak.'

'And you?'

'Nik Pavri, sir.'

'The pair tasked with intercepting our young Kusurlu. You must be hungry after your long night of fucking things up.'

Irmak flinched. 'Sir, it's not as—'

'There's a café down the street. Find Caleb and buy him some breakfast. We'll discuss your performance later.'

Silent, the two men filed out. Once the front door had snicked shut, the Vasi principal stepped forward and slapped Aylah's face with the back of his hand, so hard that one of his knuckles tore her lip.

Blood flooded her mouth. She swallowed it, her vision blurring.

'Stand up straight,' Manco said.

With her tongue, Aylah probed her gashed lip. She raised her head, hands fisted. Immediately he struck her again, this time sending her to her knees. The room swayed. She saw the blackthorn cane lift from the carpet, and closed her eyes at what was coming.

'Do you know why?' he asked.

'Because I failed.'

'We all fail, Aylah. But when we *conceal* our failures, we deceive.'

With a hiss, the blackthorn shaft descended.

The pain was a snake egg hatching in her flesh. It radiated out from her kidneys, wicking the strength from her limbs. She fell forwards, mashing her chin against the floor.

'Sit,' Manco said. 'Recover your breath.'

Aylah obeyed, crawling to the couch. She could hear her heartbeat in her ears; so loud that it frightened her.

A small breakfast table stood in the corner. Manco plucked an action figure from its surface, turning it over in his hands. 'When one of my predecessors – several hundred years before you were born – first chose to use enlightened Arayıcı to hunt out the propagators of Kusurlu corruption, his critics decried him.'

As Aylah listened, the memory of an earlier time intruded.

*Dripping water. Whispering voices. An excrement-streaked cage.*

*A bowl filled with rotten food. Another brimming with filthy water. A dog collar around her neck, connected to a length of heavy chain. More an animal, now, than a human being; a receptacle for humiliation and pain.*

Recoiling from the memory of her own enlightenment, she focused instead on the steady throb of her injuries.

'When I chose you to continue that work,' Manco continued, 'there were those among the Vasi that decried *me*.'

'I can believe it.'

'I'd be most disappointed if you proved them right.'

Aylah felt a fresh pulse of blood leak down her chin from her split lip. She took out her handkerchief and blotted it away.

'Tell me what happened.'

'She's pregnant, Saul.'

'I know that. We all know it.'

'She ran.'

'You found her hideaway?'

'Yes.'

'Yet you didn't apprehend her.'

'Because of those—' Aylah began, then fell silent.

'No recriminations,' he said. 'Speak freely.'

She took a breath. 'Levitan and Korec. They were meant to stay out of sight, keep watch until I arrived.'

'They didn't?'

'Levitan broke in through a back bedroom. We found his corpse in the bathroom. Single knife wound to the throat.'

Manco opened his mouth a fraction, displaying his pointed yellowed teeth. 'And Korec?'

'He tried to grab her on her way out. There was a fight. She wounded him before escaping.'

'And then,' said her mentor, 'you executed him.'

'He compromised himself. And me.'

Carefully, Manco stood the action figure on the table. 'The moment you discovered what had happened, you should have contacted me.'

It was hard to look at him without swallowing. 'I know.'

'Instead, you tried to rescue the situation before I learned of it.'

A bolus of saliva clung to the back of her throat. She locked her teeth together, tried to ignore it.

'You compromised yourself,' he continued. 'And me.'

'I can fix this, Saul. I can fix everything.'

For long seconds, he remained silent. Aylah heard a ticking that she thought must be a muscle in her jaw, until she traced the source to a Wonder Woman clock by the TV.

'This boy,' Manco said. 'He has a sickness. If we don't put an end to her, she'll spread it like an infection.'

'I won't fail twice.'

'I want you to work with Caleb. *Help* one another.'

'I will.'

'What's your plan?'

Aylah rose from the sofa. She moved to the window and looked at the ocean. 'She's on her way here, I'm convinced of it. The boy might have eluded Irmak and Pavri, but he can't get out by road. We've got all the major routes pinned down, and we're bringing in resources from other places.' Through the window, she watched an articulated lorry with Dutch plates make its way along Sennen's main street. 'Teke's digging up everything he can about his history.'

'How old is he?'

'Twenty.'

'And this is where he lives?'

'Yes.'

'Alone?'

She looked around. 'I'd assume so. Wouldn't you?'

Outside, the articulated lorry reached the car park beside the lifeboat station. Gunning its engine, it began to turn around.

'Once, when I was a boy,' Manco said, 'I saw at the cinema a black-and-white feature called *The Crawling Hand*.'

Aylah listened, her eyes still on the lorry. Its driver – a middle-aged man wearing a chocolate-brown Stetson – completed the turn and idled his vehicle at the kerb.

'*The Crawling Hand* starred Peter Breck and Allison Hayes,' Manco said. 'After an American spacecraft crash-lands on Earth, a boy discovers one of the astronauts' severed hands in the wreckage. A while later, various locals are found strangled to death. No prizes for guessing the culprit. The hand nearly gets away with it, too. Except that right at the end it's eaten by a hungry cat.'

Outside, diesel fumes plumed from the lorry's twin exhausts. Steadily it rolled away from the kerb.

'*The Crawling Hand* was one of the worst examples of film-making the world had ever seen, but it kept me awake for a solid week after watching it.'

Turning from the window, Aylah stared at her mentor.

'Obadiah Macintosh,' Manco said, gazing at the B-movie posters that hung from the walls, 'would have loved that fucking picture.'

# TWENTY-FOUR

Getting out beyond the breaking waves proved trickier than Obe had anticipated, but by matching his progress to the lulls between sets, he soon found himself in deeper water. There he lingered, trailing his splinted arm and waiting for the co-codamol he had swallowed to take full effect.

At low tide, the receding sea united Whitesand Bay into a single mile-long strip, but right now its crescent was divided, forming the individual beaches of Gwynver and Sennen. North along the coast, Obe saw the rocky headland of Cape Cornwall and its old tin mine chimney, along with the twin rocks of the Brisons a mile offshore. South-west, the unmanned Longships lighthouse rose from the mass of Carn Bras.

The ocean slopped through the hole he'd cut in his suit, washing out the warmer water his body had created, but he could feel the sun heating up the neoprene. By noon, the day would be scorching. Yoda, guarding Obe's small pile of belongings, watched from the dunes.

At the peak of high tide, the surf at Gwynver sometimes flattened out. Right now, though, it was overhead, the waves maintaining their shape in long, clean builds before they burst into whitewater close to shore. As the sun climbed higher, the ocean turned a glorious emerald. And then, just as Obe was paddling into position, something magical happened: a pod of bottlenose dolphins appeared.

They were ten in number, snailing through the water from the north-east with sunlight winking off their skins. Within moments he found himself encircled. They held their faces upright, mouths split wide in trademark grins, clicking and whistling and shrieking.

'What is it?' Obe asked. 'What're you telling me?'

He felt a dolphin swim beneath his board. Another breached the surface a few yards away, showering him in water.

'Oh, you just want to play?'

But even as he spoke, he realised that he was witnessing something far more unusual. Despite the dolphins' demeanour, there appeared an unsettling unity of purpose to their behaviour, as if they knew something that he did not, and wished to communicate it. Three more breached, forming a barrier between him and the beach. A fourth surfaced on his right, so close that it nudged against him, and yet so gentle that it hardly raised a wash.

During his years in Sennen Cove, he'd seen plenty of dolphins, basking sharks and seals. Several times, in the past, he'd been the subject of their curiosity. But never like this. The dolphin beside him made a series of rapid-fire clicks and squeals. Reaching out with his good arm, Obe rubbed one of its pectoral fins. 'You're a talkative little dude, aren't you?'

Opening its mouth wide, the dolphin issued a few last clicks before ducking beneath the waves. It breached a few yards away, landing on its back in a flat explosion of spray. Moments later, the circle of bobbing heads broke up and the snailing resumed, the entire pod heading south-west towards Carn Bras.

Heartened by his encounter, although mystified by it, Obe kicked towards the spot where the waves were breaking. He allowed the first few to roll beneath him, tracking the point at which they rapidly began to build. The combination of cold water and co-codamol had dulled the pain in his arm. He hoped it would be enough.

The third wave was his. Positioning himself at a slight angle to the shore, he paddled as hard as he could. The water began to trough, the wave behind him rising into a steep green wall. With his back arched, and his splinted arm braced, he curled his toes and popped up onto his feet.

Immediately a lightning strike of pain raced up his arm to his shoulder. Somehow he managed to roll his hips and keep his balance, pivoting the board so it lay perpendicular to the wave's face. With a climbing wall of water at his back, with the rails of his board cutting sharp white lines, Obe lifted his head and howled.

He heard the roar of water in his ears, felt the raw energies of sea and moon pushing him onwards. So joyous was the experience that he lost himself utterly in it, piloting his board through instinct borne from years of chasing surf.

Moments later, rolling off the beach in undulating currents, the presence of another struck him

*—the-boy-the-boy-die-he's-going-to-die-going-to-DIE-IN-THE-WATER-OBADIAH-GOING-TO-DROWN-GOING-TO—*

with the force of a hammer. The words spooled around a gruesome knot of emotions: wretchedness; paranoia; rage. They unleashed a monstrous pain inside his head, so calamitous that it felt as if his skull had been cracked against a pan and his brain tipped, sizzling, into boiling oil.

Behind him, the wall of marbled water climbed higher and began to barrel, propelling him even harder across its face. Unbalanced, crippled by the assault on his senses, Obe tried to pull out, turning over the back of the wave, but his attempt was too sluggish, too late. As the nose of his board pearled into foaming surf, he dived headfirst into a white maelstrom. Then, at the worst possible moment, the wave he'd been riding unleashed its full power, punching him down, tearing the makeshift splint from his arm and filling his head with screams.

His ankle leash tightened and abruptly snapped, and now the agony in his splintered bones was so great that it forced the air from his lungs. He didn't know how deep he'd plunged. Didn't know if he faced up or down. The sea rolled and dragged him. Against such a force he was powerless, his nerves awash with the barbed-wire tang of pain. The pressure in his ears was immense, a tuneless roaring. The water seemed darker, blacker, colder; in its clutches he rolled again.

Somewhere beneath him he perceived a greyness, a lighter patch in the surrounding murk. He kicked his legs, moving away from it, until he realised that the glimmer he had spotted was the surface, and in his confusion he was swimming deeper.

Cradling his broken arm, Obe propelled himself up. He broke the surface just in time to meet another wave bearing down on him, this one a true monster. He had no time to fill his lungs before it broke, punching him so deep that the roaring in his ears became a pressurised slab of silence. Out of strength, out of air, he drifted with his head canted back, at the mercy of whatever gods observed him.

Despite the knowledge that he was drowning, Obe felt no panic, no bitterness at the sea's lack of mercy; nothing, in fact, except a fleeting sense of regret. If only the throb of his broken bones would fade and the ache inside his chest diminish, he was sure he could feel peace. His morning had been filled with such extraordinary beauty that its memory would be the last thing to leave him. He wondered if the dolphins had sensed the dangers into which he swam, and had formed a circle to dissuade him.

That ache in his lungs blossomed, now, washing away all thought. He felt his throat relax, last defence against the water pushing into his lungs, but before he could surrender fully to it, fire exploded once again in his arm. Behind his eyes he saw white flashes of magnesium intensity. His body swung around, a sudden anchor against the tide. Abruptly the white flashes became blue sky, and he was coughing, choking, and still drowning, and the pain in his arm was of such ferocity that he would have bellowed in defiance had his lungs retained any air. As another wave washed over him, flushing his suit and foaming cold around his ears, he realised that he was above the surf, not beneath it, and the reason his legs were dragging in the sand and his arm felt like it had been twisted off at the elbow was because he was being pulled from the sea, towed firmly from its grasp, and when at last his chest filled with air and he managed to focus, he saw that his rescuer, surprisingly, had been . . .

'. . . a cowboy,' Obe spluttered.

As an expression of gratitude it was somewhat lacking in elegance. The girl stared down at him, the morning sun haloed around her head. It lent her the appearance of an angel, albeit one wearing a chocolate-coloured Stetson and a look of unalloyed rage.

'You *idiot*,' she hissed. 'What the hell were you doing?'

He blinked, trying to formulate an answer, but she was holding his forearm with a grip strong enough to throttle a gorilla; the pain was a blister in his brain. 'Please,' he croaked. 'Hurts.'

She frowned. 'Where?'

'Arm. Broken.'

Abruptly, Mallory released him and he tumbled into the surf. With a conspicuous lack of tenderness, she grabbed him under the armpits and hauled him up. Together they retreated from the water.

Obe sat down on the hard-packed sand, but before he had a chance to catch his breath, something slammed him from behind, pitching him onto his face. Abruptly his world shrank to the dimensions of a coarse pink tongue, bracketed by appalling canine breath.

'Mallory,' he said, and shook his head, wondering if he was concussed. Opening his mouth, he tried again. 'Dog.'

As a second attempt, it didn't sound much better. Pushing himself into a sitting position, he shielded his broken arm from Yoda's attentions. 'OK, buddy,' he murmured. 'It's good to see you. Yeah, it is.'

Displaying a playfulness at odds with his usual character, Yoda rolled on his back and pawed the air, soliciting a belly rub.

'That thing belong to you?' Mallory asked.

Obe looked up at her. 'No. Yeah. Well, maybe.'

'Maybe?'

'It's . . . kind of . . . I don't know.'

'You don't know if it's your dog?'

He swallowed, examined her more closely. She looked different to how he remembered. Only her eyes, flashing with cold intensity, matched his memories. Her skin was a little darker, her features a little sharper: angular nose; wide mouth; lips so downturned that they seemed incapable of forming any expression except a scowl. Those eyes drew him in: watchful, predatory, and utterly lacking in warmth. They appeared swollen, as if she'd recently been in a fight.

'What the hell are you looking at?' she snapped.

'Sorry.' Further down the beach he saw his board, rolling in the surf like a waterlogged corpse. 'I should probably get that,' he said. But when he tried to stand, he collapsed back onto one elbow.

Mallory swore, marching away from him across the sand, cowboy hat tipped back on her head. Even in his exhaustion, Obe couldn't help noticing the way her jeans accentuated the hard muscles of her legs; there was a fluidity to her movements that was easy to appreciate. She waded into the surf, heedless of the cold water as it surged around her calves. Snatching up the surfboard's leash, she turned back towards the beach. When she caught the focus of his gaze, her scowl intensified.

'Uh-oh,' Obe muttered. Beside him, Yoda buried his head.

Mallory towed the board out of the sea and dragged it over to where he lay. She dropped it down and stood over him, hands balled into fists. 'You think I won't break your other arm if you stare at me like that again?'

He felt colour rising on his cheeks. 'I didn't mean to—'

'Listen to me, dickhead. Concentrate on what I'm saying, answer my questions, and then I can leave you to whatever para-Olympic event you're trying so desperately hard to recreate.'

He nodded, unable to process her rage. 'I'm sorry,' he said. 'I just . . .' He swallowed. 'I wasn't expecting to see you again.'

'Believe me, I'm not here out of choice.'

'It's good. To see you, I mean.' He blinked, took a breath. Tried to work out why his sentences sounded like they'd been composed for him by a Furby. 'What I'm trying to say is that I'm glad you came.'

She stared at him, her face unreadable. Obe struggled to hold her gaze. The last effects of the purple kush he had smoked had all but worn off; the familiar pain of sensory overload was welling once more inside his head. He felt a sudden spike of fire behind his right eye and flinched away from it.

Mallory watched, her scowl lessening by half a degree. 'Your arm. You said it was broken.'

He clenched his teeth, nodded.

'In the sea?'

'It was already broken. It's why I had to cut the sleeve off my suit.'

She frowned. 'You went out there, in those waves, with a broken arm?'

'I thought it'd . . . you know . . . be OK.'

'You thought it'd be OK. When did you break it?'

'Last night.'

Now, her expression turned incredulous. 'Last *night*?'

'Well, I took some co-codamol. It's pretty strong.'

'If I hadn't showed up,' she told him, 'you would've drowned.'

He shrugged. 'Death keeps no calendar.'

'Oh, really? "Death keeps no calendar"?' She placed her balled fists on her hips. 'What is that? Some kind of happy-hippy surfer bullshit?'

'It's just a saying.'

'You don't care about dying?'

'I don't fear it.'

As if sensing that Mallory's words might spill over into violence, Yoda rose onto all fours and trotted up the beach, his tail slung low.

'How'd you find me?' Obe asked.

She sucked in a breath, trapping it in her lungs before releasing it. Then she dropped to the sand and folded her legs beneath her. 'Something you mentioned. That night.' At her mention of the evening they had shared she looked away, addressing her words to the sea. 'The place where you went when you needed to think. A beach. I couldn't remember its name but I did remember it had something to do with King Arthur.'

'Gwynver Beach,' Obe replied. 'From Guinevere, Arthur's Queen. That's a pretty big leap.'

'Not really. I had your address. The name of the village, at least. This is the nearest beach to Sennen Cove that matched.'

'But I never gave you my address. I mean, I would've done, if you'd asked, but the next morning, when I woke, you'd already—'

'I stole your driving licence,' she said. Her eyes swung around to regard him, and she lifted her chin.

'Right.' Obe blinked. He ran a hand through his wet hair, feeling like he'd tumbled into the strangest conversation of his life. 'Can I ask why?'

'At the time, no idea. Looking back . . . maybe I knew, even then.'

'Knew what?'

Mallory ignored the question, raising her knees and clasping her arms around them. 'Why you, Obadiah? That's what I want to know. Why did I seek you out? What's special about *you*?'

'Obe,' he said. 'I prefer Obe, if that's OK.'

The intensity of her gaze was so fierce that he felt his skin growing hot, as if he held his face too close to the embers of a beach barbecue.

'What's special about you?' she repeated.

An emerald wave, copper-tinged, broke so close to the beach that it raced up the sand and covered their legs. As the water drained back into the sea, Mallory continued to stare at him.

'We should head up to the dunes,' he told her.

'What's special about you?'

The pain behind his right eye was back, making him wince. 'There's nothing special about me.'

'That night,' Mallory pressed. 'Three weeks ago. You didn't strike me as dishonest.'

'I'm not.'

'An oddball, perhaps. A loner, maybe even a loser. But not a liar.'

'Well,' he said. And when he tried to follow that with something meaningful, he found that he could not.

'What's special about you? What're you hiding?'

Pain, again, behind his eyes. Scrunching up his face, he tried to ignore it. 'I don't know what you're talking about.'

'Yes,' she insisted. 'You do. Something that sets you apart. Something that makes you different. Something that brings you all the way out here to a place like this and keeps you here.'

Obe gazed across the sand. He saw Yoda, up in the dunes, urinating against a clump of beachgrass. 'You think I need a reason to live in a place like this?'

'That's not what I meant. You know that's not what I meant.'

'Tell me about the men.'

'Men?'

Obe angled his face back towards her. 'The men from last night,' he said. 'The men who killed one of my dogs, and tried to kill me too.'

# TWENTY-FIVE

Sitting on the hard sand of Gwynver Beach, with soaked jeans and legs burning from the cold of the sea, Mallory stared at the boy she hadn't expected to meet again and tried to digest his words.

Although she had kept Joos Lagerweij's Stetson, she had returned the man's Aviators. In the east, the morning sun was a white fireball that scratched her eyes like a nail. She'd gone twenty-four hours without sleep – no way she could maintain this pace much longer. But as Obe recounted the attack at the animal sanctuary, Mallory realised that her situation was even more desperate than she had feared, and that her chances of navigating a successful outcome were far slimmer than she had hoped. Watching him as he talked, she wondered what madness had overtaken her that night in Plymouth, three weeks ago. He was good-looking enough, in a boyish kind of way, but he possessed none of the qualities she usually found attractive.

'And then,' Obe said, 'just as Orion and I were—'

'Orion?'

'One of the horses. I didn't have a chance to saddle him but he's pretty easy to handle – that is, until I was hit by one of your Men in Black. At the time I thought it was some kind of ray gun, that I was in the middle of a Lowell Cunningham story.'

Mallory raised an eyebrow.

'Oh,' Obe said. 'He's a comic book writer. *Jack Ooze? Alien Nation?*' He shrugged. 'It's not important. I guess the guy used a Taser on me. Man, I wasn't prepared for just how much those things *hurt*.' His eyes, as he said that, appeared to shine more with excitement than fear.

'This isn't a comic book,' she said. 'You're not a superhero.'

He nodded. 'I know. Definitely not. Not even close.'

'So what happened to Orion?'

'I left him back there. We rode up to the old cow shed where I keep my car, and that's when I found their 4x4. I slashed their tyres and vamoosed.'

'You slashed their tyres?'

Obe grimaced. 'Well, they *were* trying to kill me.'

'Where's your car now?'

'Hidden, about a mile away.' He tilted his head, looked up into the sky. 'I just thought – you know, satellites.'

'Satellites?'

'Like . . . *Men in Black*.' Obe licked his lips. 'Or whatever this thing is.'

Mallory stared. 'Let me get this right. These guys killed one of your dogs, shot at you, broke your arm, tried to kill you. And the first thing you did after you managed to get away was come down to the beach and go surfing?'

'I didn't know how long I had left.'

'Not long, if you continue to act like a twelve-year-old fucking child.'

He flinched, as if she'd bitten him. 'Why are you so angry?'

'Because . . . because you're just so . . .' She flailed for words. Her head pulsed as she considered him.

'They wanted me because of you,' he said. 'Didn't they?'

'Not even close. What's special about you?'

'Nothing.'

'The truth.'

'I make good pizza,' he said. 'And I do a halfway decent Chewbacca impression. That's literally it.'

'Obe, if you don't start taking this seriously, you're going to get yourself killed. Worse, you're going to get me killed.'

'I *am* taking this seriously.' He climbed to his feet. With great care, he began to extract himself from his wetsuit. His body was more toned than she remembered. Beneath the suit he wore a pair of form-fitting shorts. 'I'm guessing that staying on this beach is a bad idea.'

Mallory stood up. 'That's the first sensible thing you've said.'

'Thanks,' he replied. 'Then I'd better get dressed. And figure out something for this arm.'

She followed him across the sand to where his rucksack lay beside a mound of clothes. Pulling on a T-shirt, Obe slipped his feet into battered trainers. 'What happens now?' he asked.

'First, we need to get off this peninsula. Then you need to tell me the truth. After that' – she shrugged – 'you go your way, I go mine.'

He stared. 'That's it?'

'You think I trekked all this way because I couldn't resist another deeply disappointing fuck?'

His face fell. 'No. I just . . .'

'I'll tell you something for free, Obe. You need to stop wearing every single emotion on your face like that.'

'That night,' he said. 'I don't remember you being this angry.'

'I don't want to talk about that night.'

'Why not?'

'It isn't relevant.'

'It isn't?'

'Not now.'

He said, 'I need to fix this arm.'

'Fix it later. We've got to get off this beach. If they came for you at the sanctuary last night, they'll be all over the coast by now.'

'There were only two of them.'

She laughed, hard. 'You think those two were the height of

our problems? By now they'll have flooded the area. They'll be watching the roads, watching the village. It's going to be virtually impossible to get out.'

'I can get us out.'

'You think?'

'Once I've gone back to my flat, picked up a few essentials, we can go down to the—'

Mallory shook her head. 'Uh-uh.'

'What?'

'You don't go home, Obe. They'll have people waiting there, guaranteed.'

'But what about my stuff?'

She gestured at his rucksack. 'That pretty much encompasses it.'

'I can't just walk away, abandon everything I own!'

'You've no choice.'

He stared at her, appalled. 'Dude, I've got a mint copy of *Fantastic Four* back there from 1961, signed by Stan Lee. And a slabbed first issue of *Walking Dead*. Then there's an entire boxful of—'

'You could have the entire collected works of Peppa Pig back there for all I give a shit,' she shouted. 'You go to your flat, they'll kill you. You need to get that fact into your comic-book-reading, cannabis-smoking, hipster-beatnik brain as quickly as you can, and deal with it. You are not a superhero. Nor are you a child. Your life is at risk – right here, right now. What you do once I'm gone is your decision but for the time being, considering that we're stuck with each other for at least the rest of the day, try to act like a fully functioning adult, don't piss me off too much, focus that tiny amoeba-like mind on making good decisions, and for fuck's sake – *fuck's* sake – don't call me dude.'

His cheeks, as she delivered her monologue, gradually filled with blood. She knew that she'd hurt his feelings, didn't care. Every minute she spent in his company solidified her poor opinion of him. He wouldn't survive this – he was spectacularly unequipped – and unless she unshackled herself fast she would doubtless share his fate. Her priority was to extract the information she needed and escape to a place where she could prepare for what was coming.

Averting her eyes, examining the coastline to the south, she wondered how much time she had left.

# TWENTY-SIX

Obe listened to her speak, screwing up his face against the pain inside his head. Her words of condemnation hadn't affected him; but her rage, and the bitterness that sloughed off her like a snake's shed skin, was as debilitating as Kryptonite. Never had he experienced so much negativity at such close quarters.

Had she been this *violent* the first time they met? He wished he could recall, but that day, in preparation for the crowds he expected to face, he had consumed so much cannabis that such details had hardly registered. From the fractured memories that *had* survived their encounter, he didn't think she'd done much talking. 'Do you think they're watching us right now?' he asked.

'Unlikely.'

'Why's that?'

'We're alive.'

He grunted a laugh. 'Who were they?'

'Bad people.'

Her voice changed when she said that. When he glanced over, he saw that her expression had changed, too. 'Did you travel here from London?'

She nodded.

'By car?'

'Hitch-hiked.'

'All the way?'

'All the way.'

'When did you last sleep?'

'I haven't.'

'You look baked.'

'I'm fine.'

'You said we can't get out by road.'

'I meant it. Were you serious when you said you could get us off the peninsula?'

He hooked a thumb towards Sennen Cove. 'It'd mean heading back in that direction a little. Can we risk it?'

'Not really.'

'We don't need to go in all high-key. There's a place, right on the other side of the bluff. We can take the coastal path.'

'If it's our only option, we'll have to try it.'

'Bomb diggity. But if we're going to do this, I need to know that you trust me.'

Mallory's scowl returned. 'What?'

Obe shrugged. 'Like you just said: we're stuck with each other. Maybe only for the next few hours, but still.' He paused. 'Total honesty, now: Do you trust me?'

'No.'

'OK, not total honesty. Can you at least *say* that you trust me?'

She narrowed her eyes. 'I trust you.'

Obe picked up his rucksack and carefully threaded his injured arm through one of the straps. He shrugged it onto his back and lifted his board from the sand, watching Yoda scrabble up. 'Let's go see Gollum.'

Mallory deflated a little at that. 'Gollum?'

'Trust me,' he said, and grinned.

Giovanni 'Gollum' Petrucelli lived in a stone-walled tin miner's cottage set back from the beach in a protected cleft of scrubland with westerly views of the ocean. A meandering track linked it to the road heading towards Crows-an-Wra.

No one answered the door when Obe knocked. From around the back he heard the hum of an electric planer, and led Mallory down a bramble-choked path to a brick-built garage at the rear. The side-door stood ajar, the single window thick with fibre-glass dust. Outside, a trio of grey-furred cats lazed in the morning sun. They gave Yoda a brief look of contempt before settling down to ignore him. Stepping around them, Obe ducked inside the garage.

Surrounded by shavings, Gollum stood in the centre of the poured-concrete floor, wearing a half-face respirator and a set of sleeveless brown overalls. Tribal tattoos robed his arms. His grey dreadlocks had been pulled into a loose ponytail. Around his neck hung a gold ring on a silver chain. When his eyes lit on Obe, they flared in recognition. The power-sander whined to a stop and he dropped it onto a workbench. Ripping the mask from his face, he released a six-inch-length of plaited beard that jutted from his chin like a lightning rod. 'Obi-Wan!' he bellowed, surging forward and enveloping his friend in a hug.

'Sméagol,' Obe countered, clenching his teeth against the wave of nausea that assaulted him.

Holding him at arm's length, Gollum studied Obe's face. 'Dude,' he said. 'You straight? You look like a carnival zombie. Like you traipsed through an ash cloud.'

Obe nodded, his right eyelid beginning to twitch. 'Standard brainfreeze.'

In the middle of the garage, a cherry-red surfboard lay across two wooden sawhorses. 'New commission,' Gollum said. 'From a guy who saw my work at the Nationals back in October.'

'Looks sick.'

'Will be if I finish it in time.' He produced a blunt from the pocket of his overalls. 'You want to medicate?'

'Maybe a little. But first I need to introduce a friend.'

Gollum looked past him to Mallory, his mouth falling open. 'Well, damn,' he said. 'Obi-Wan finally met a girl.'

'I guess he finally did,' she muttered.

'Permit me to say it, but he's not the only one who lucked out. You could live a thousand years and still have interesting shit to discover about Obadiah Macintosh.'

'No doubt.'

Gollum held her gaze a moment longer. Then he stuck the blunt between his teeth, lit it and passed it to Obe. 'Northern Lights,' he said. 'Home-grown batch. Should iron out the wrinkles.'

Obe took a hit. Almost immediately, he felt the tension in his head begin to subside. He took another drag, then passed it back to Gollum.

'All yours if you want it,' the man said.

'Can't afford to. Not right now.'

'Trouble?'

'How'd you guess?'

Gollum glanced at Mallory, then back at Obe. 'I don't see you for six months. You show up here, first thing in the morning, mystery girl at your side. That's some kind of trouble if my name isn't' – he shrugged – 'whatever.'

'Can you help us?'

'Man, you need to ask?'

'I'll be honest. Helping us might put you in danger.'

'Good. I need a little excitement in my life.' Gollum rubbed at one of his tattoos. 'What do you need?'

'I'll come to that,' Obe said. 'But first a question.'

'Hit me.'

'You ever use any of this stuff to make a cast?'

'A cast for what?'

He indicated his injured arm. 'Broken bone.'

'Ah, shit. You take a dive?'

'Off a horse.'

'A *horse*?' Gollum looked past Obe to Mallory. 'See? Interesting shit.'

'Do you think you could figure something out?'

'Dude, I'll fashion you something so gnarlatious you'll want to break your other arm just to get a double serving of awesome.'

He was true to his word: within ten minutes, Obe sported a fibreglass cast sealed with the same cherry-red resin used on the surfboard. Afterwards, Gollum led them into the house, parking them at the kitchen table while the resin cured. 'I'll whip up some pancakes,' he told them. 'You look like you need some breakfast.'

While Gollum found a treat for Yoda and busied himself at the stove, Obe stole a sideways glance at Mallory. The girl was staring through the window at the ocean, on which a shoal of sun-forged silverfish now glittered. The hard lines of her mouth had softened somewhat, but her eyes, rimed with red, retained the same cold intensity. During their walk to the cottage he had tried to extract from her an explanation for the attack at the sanctuary, but she'd revealed little, choosing to repeat what he already knew: bad people were hunting them, and the longer they dwelled on the peninsula, the greater their risk of discovery.

'Don't,' she said quietly, her eyes still on the sea.

'Don't what?'

'Don't look at me like that. Don't try to figure me out. Because you won't.'

Gollum came to the table and set down a plate piled with pancakes. He fetched a bowl of chopped bananas, another of chopped pecans and half a dozen bottles of maple syrup. 'You gotta experiment to find the one you like,' he told Mallory. 'Me, I prefer a rich syrup with a nice amber glow.' He tapped the cap on one of the bottles. 'You pretty much can't go wrong with Bobo's Mountain Sugar.'

Obe grabbed an empty plate and dug in. Mallory joined him. Their host sat opposite, talking all the while of the commission he was working on, as well as his plans for boards he'd yet to shape. Every so often a grey-furred cat wandered in through the back door and Gollum picked it up for a stroke or offered it a little food. 'So,' he said, once they'd finished eating. 'You going to cut me in? Tell me what you need?'

Obe flexed his fingers inside his new cast. 'We need you to get us out of West Penwith.'

'That all?'

'Without being seen. And without using any of the roads off the peninsula. And today. This morning, in fact.'

Gollum thought for a moment. Then he shrugged. 'Cool.'

# TWENTY-SEVEN

Inside Obadiah Macintosh's cramped first-floor flat, surrounded by comic books and sci-fi memorabilia, Aylah İncesu searched for clues that would reveal something of the boy's identity, and where he might go next.

In the living room she tore posters from the walls and yanked every one of his comics from the shelves, flicking through their pages for hidden documents, photographs or letters.

She found nothing to help her. Worse, as she skimmed through the thousands of brightly illustrated pages she found it impossible to shield herself from the messages those stories tried to impart. Obadiah's tastes were not just infantile but subversive. The fiction he consumed offered false hope, odious platitudes, portraying examples of human behaviour that were patently misleading. The more Aylah read, the angrier she grew, until she could barely concentrate for thoughts of killing him.

After finding nothing of importance on the shelves, she ransacked his Blu-ray collection and pulled up the living-room carpet to expose the wooden boards beneath.

In the bedroom, she discovered the apparatus of recreational drug use: a glass bong filled with fetid brown water; a butt-clogged ashtray; lighters; matches; papers. She dragged his clothes from the wardrobe, searched through the pockets of board shorts and hoodies. Right at the back, beneath a pile of old wetsuits, she found a metal tea chest and hauled it out. When she opened the lid and saw a stack of loose-leafed papers she thought she'd struck gold, but closer inspection revealed they were merely the boy's own crude efforts at comic-book art. Among them were scores of handwritten scripts, their contents even more hateful than the professionally produced works in the living room.

The boy recognised human weakness, and many of humanity's flaws, but he lacked the courage to accept the obvious conclusion. He hunted for light in the darkest corners, and searched for hope where none could be found. The more Aylah read, the more she wanted to slice off Obadiah Macintosh's fingers, rip out his tongue by its root, and prevent him from creating any more of this delusory, contemptible filth. By the time she had worked her way to the bottom of the chest she was shaking with emotion, consumed by a desire for violence. She fed the flames of her outrage by tearing into pieces every one of the boy's hand-printed pages, and when she walked from the room she left in her wake a trail of confetti-like scraps.

*After violence, silence.*

The bathroom surrendered nothing of interest. The kitchen was similarly bereft of clues. While she searched its last nooks, Saul Manco filled a kettle and prepared a cafetière. 'At least the boy buys good coffee,' he told her. 'For that, if nothing else, he deserves a quick death.'

After what she'd read, Aylah had no intention of delivering Obadiah anything but the most excruciating suffering, but she didn't say anything. Returning to the living room, she saw the cardboard box filled with slabbed single-issue comics. Squatting down, she hauled one out: *Conan the Barbarian #1*, from October 1971. With her *qama,* she pierced the plastic, plunging the blade through the comic and out the other side. Using fingers and teeth, she tore open the package and dragged out the butchered pages. They yielded nothing but crudely drawn fight sequences and scantily clad women. Aylah flung the tattered remains across the room.

Next, she pierced *The House of Secrets #92* from July 1971. Shredded paper, like the powdery remains of crushed moth wings, fell from her fingers. Finding nothing of interest, Aylah moved onto *The Walking Dead #1* from October 2003. Inside that comic she found much to like, including a faded photograph tucked between the pages. It showed a young boy sitting in a water-filled paddling pool. The child looked about four years old. It was, quite clearly, Obadiah Macintosh.

Excited by her find, Aylah punctured a copy of *New Mutants #98*. That one was a dud, and in her disappointment she tore the comic to pieces. A signed *Saul Trashcan #2* offered nothing. Neither did *Tales of Suspense #43,* from 1963, but inside a signed copy of *Deathstroke the Terminator* she discovered a folded slip of pink paper and opened it out. Across the top were two rows of text:

**FORM H3** *Regulation 4 (4) and 5 (5)* **MENTAL HEALTH ACT 1983**
**Sections 2, 3 and 4 – record of detention in hospital**

Below that, several fields had been completed in ink. Aylah's gaze fell to the first box, which indicated the name of the patient: *OBADIAH BLACK*.

'Found you,' she whispered. Quickly she phoned Teke, flinching at the burst of static when he answered.

'I'm airborne,' he explained.

'Got anything useful?'

'Maybe. We synched the girl's movements across the ANPR network with phones that were pinging masts in the same area at around the same time. Got quite a few hits, as you can imagine, but only one of them hasn't pinged since. Right now it's refusing all requests, which means it must be switched off. If it's hers, the moment she turns it on we'll have her. And we can hack its GPS to give us a location within a few feet.'

'That's *if* she switches it back on.'

'So far it's all we have. Unfortunately, Obadiah Macintosh is still a ghost. I've got nothing more than what I gave you earlier, which is literally—'

'Try Obadiah Black.'

'Say again?'

'I'm looking at a mental health sectioning report from February 2003, made on behalf of one Obadiah Black.'

'Where'd you find it?'

'Long story.'

'Which hospital?'

Aylah glanced down and saw that the paper was smudged with blood – the cut in her thumb had opened again. She read out the name of the institution, along with details of the two signatories. Then she stuck her thumb in her mouth and sucked it clean.

Outside, the residents of Sennen Cove were beginning to stir. Already, a few surfers were carrying boards across the sand. On the harbour's tiny slipway, a fisherman was loading crates onto an open-topped boat. 'Is the area secure?' she asked.

'There's not a road out that isn't being monitored.'

'Airports?'

'There's only one, at Land's End. They'll have no luck there.'

'Sea?'

'All the major ferry services are much further east. There's one in Penzance that serves the Scilly Isles, but they'd still have to break through our perimeter to reach it.'

'There's a harbour here,' Aylah said. 'Maybe a dozen small boats. I'll have Caleb's team put a watch on it, but get someone to grill the harbourmaster. See if you can get a list of local boat owners. I want to know who's coming in and out.'

'On it,' Teke said. 'Anything else?'

'Yeah. Find Guy Chevry, the guy I met at Pataki's place.

I don't want Washienko, but Chevry might have his uses. I'd like him down here, joining the search.'

Aylah hung up, walked to the window and watched a flock of gulls hovering on the wind. 'You'd better run, Mallory,' she whispered. 'Because I'm on your trail, and I'm catching up fast.'

Saul Manco appeared, handing her a cup of coffee. He gestured at the bloody print her thumb had left on the ceramic. 'Cutting yourself again?'

'Accident.' She took a sip of coffee, burning her tongue.

'Is she close?'

'Yes.'

'Are you sure?'

Aylah returned her gaze to the window.

Outside, the gulls screamed and swooped towards the earth.

# TWENTY-EIGHT

For seven long minutes, as the container in which she curled bumped and rattled around her, Mallory tried not to vomit. Through a slit in the plastic lid she could see a chink of blue sky. All she could smell was dead fish.

The stench clung so thickly to the back of her throat that she could barely breathe without gagging. The container was empty, but it wasn't dry; a generous slop of fish water rolled in its moulded gutters, soaking her clothes.

Earlier, Gollum had led them from his cottage to a rusting panel van. Into it he loaded two high-sided ice crates used for transporting fish. He suggested that they sit in the back of the van until he drove it onto the slipway to unload, but Mallory didn't want to risk it. 'You sure you'll be able to lift these things once we're inside?' she asked.

Gollum cocked his head. 'What are you – nine stone? Hundred and twenty pounds? I can bench two-fifty, no problem.'

'Swoon.'

He grinned, throwing her a wink. 'Pity you're leaving. I'm starting to like you.'

Hearing that, Mallory softened a little. 'Sorry. I'm grateful – really – but I haven't slept. When I get tired, I get snappy.'

'You like fish?'

'I *hate* fish.'

Gollum pulled the lid off a crate. 'Then you might want to rethink that gratitude.'

After sealing them inside separate containers, and with Yoda riding up front, he drove up the track to the main road and down through the village to the harbour. Mallory's crate skidded and bounced, slamming off walls and other pieces of gear. By the time they reached their destination, she felt like she'd been in a road accident.

The van tipped alarmingly as it reversed down the slipway. The rear doors banged open and Gollum lifted out her container. He dropped it into his boat, jarring her bones and knocking the wind from her lungs. Moments later Mallory heard Obe's container crash down beside hers, accompanied by a hiss of pain. She couldn't help smiling at that.

She heard the rasp and scrape of a chain, and felt the boat slide into the water. Soon, the briny scent of the ocean began to penetrate the stink of fish. Somewhere beneath her a diesel engine started up, its vibrations thrumming through the hull. The boat turned in a slow circle, then the engine note increased. Mallory heard the churn of water and the percussive slap of waves against the bow. She strained her ears for indications that something was wrong – sounds of pursuit, shouted instructions from the harbour wall – but nothing intruded over the steady knock of displaced water.

Her guts roiling as if she'd gorged on spoiled fish, she tried to ignore the litany of complaints her body raised. Her knees still throbbed from their impact with the parquet floor back in Clapham. Her nose felt swollen and sore.

Closing her eyes, she rested her head against her arm. For the first time in the eight hours since she'd discovered she was pregnant, her thoughts turned to the tiny seed of life growing inside her. She'd had no intention of keeping it. After leaving the pharmacy, her sole focus had been on a swift termination. She couldn't risk attending a clinic, so in desperation she'd used up an old favour, leading to her meeting with Joseph Lin at the Red Sun, and her visit to Dr Fabian Pataki's maisonette. The abortionist had sold her what she'd needed: a main course of mifepristone and a chaser of misoprostol.

If she'd kept the first drug down and taken the miso-prostol as instructed, she would have miscarried by now. But for reasons inexplicable, moments after swallowing the mifepristone she had made herself vomit the pill into Pataki's sink. She'd washed it into the drain and fled the man's house without a word.

Why?

She couldn't answer that.

*Really, Mallory? I think you can.*

But she wouldn't.

Not yet.

Her throat grew tight. Her eyes, still clenched shut, suddenly felt hot. Crammed into the ice crate, with her knees drawn up to her chest, Mallory suppressed a sob. She clenched her teeth, furious, but anger didn't help. Tears oozed from beneath her tightly squeezed lids.

*That's it. Because crying's going to help, isn't it? You had your chance. You could have walked away. But you chose this instead.*

She took a breath, forcing herself to surrender it slowly before taking another. For long minutes she concentrated on nothing else, until finally her diaphragm stopped convulsing and the tension in her throat waned.

The lid of her crate popped open a while later. Hot summer sunshine flooded in. Mallory blinked, temporarily blinded. She saw Gollum peering down at her, the stiff grey plait of his chin beard pointing like a way marker.

'Hot towel, ma'am?'

'If only,' she said, wrinkling her nose. 'I'd climb out, but I think my legs went to sleep.'

Grinning, he reached his hands under her, and as he lifted her out she caught herself thinking – just for a fleeting instant –

how good it felt to be held. Gollum smelled of tobacco smoke, surfboard resin and leather. Not entirely pleasant. Not entirely disagreeable. With greater gentleness than she'd expected, he deposited her onto the deck. 'Welcome aboard *The Heart of Gold*,' he said. 'Kind of a shit-heap, but she floats.'

The wooden-hulled boat, twenty-five feet in length with an open cockpit, looked at least forty years old. Empty lobster pots took up most of the deck space. A hydraulic unit near the bow had been installed to haul them from the sea floor. Overhead, a small flock of gulls kept pace. The hull knocked and slapped in a rhythm that was soothing, hypnotic.

West Penwith's rocky coastline slid by to starboard, the sea foaming white around its shattered granite stacks. Gollum clambered over the lobster pots to the front of the boat and began to roll himself a joint. Obe was already sitting aft, one hand on the tiller. Retrieving her Stetson, Mallory perched on the bench seat beside him.

'Never had you pegged as a cow girl,' he said.

'Long story.'

'You been crying?'

'Nope. Just not a fan of fish.' She adjusted the hat's brim. 'How's the arm?'

Obe lifted the cherry-red cast, allowing her to inspect it. 'Aches a bit, but a few more co-codamol took the edge off.'

'That's good.'

He smiled. 'Thanks.'

'For what?'

'Worrying about my arm.'

'I wasn't.'

'Caring, then.'

'I don't give a shit if your arms falls off, as long as it doesn't slow us down.'

'Well,' he said. 'I don't think it's going to fall off.'

'Whereabouts are we?'

'We headed north from Sennen. Followed the coastline

around. About another half-hour and we'll hit St Ives. We can moor up there or continue on to Portreath.'

'St Ives works. It's far enough away, I think.'

He nodded. 'So you want to tell me what's going on?'

Mallory hesitated. Then she tilted back her cowboy hat and examined him. Until now, she'd had no intention of divulging the truth, but she knew they'd reached an impasse, and she needed to move things on. 'I'm pregnant,' she said, and watched closely for his reaction.

Obe blinked.

Then he sat up straight. The colour leached from his face. His hand loosened on the tiller and the boat turned lazily towards the coast. 'You're what?'

'Pregnant. With child. I'm assuming you know what that means. I'm guessing there's been a comic book, at some time or another, that's spilled a few details on the science of it.'

Watching his slow, dumb, stoned reaction, she felt her anger beginning to build.

'Is it mine?' Obe asked. 'I mean, are you—'

Before he could finish his sentence, Mallory slapped him. Then, snarling, she drew back her fist and punched him full in the face.

Obe toppled back against the gunwales, ripping the tiller to full lock. The boat tipped violently to starboard. In the bow, Gollum crashed to the deck, striking his head against an empty pot.

Fearing they would capsize, Mallory grabbed the tiller and steadied their course. Once the boat had righted itself, she seized the front of Obe's T-shirt and hauled him back onto the seat. Already, his right cheek was swelling. A half-inch long cut dribbled blood.

'That was a stupid thing to say,' he told her.

Mallory shook her head. 'Not stupid. Rude.'

'Yeah. You're right. Rude, unpleasant, dickish. I'm sorry. Really.'

She refused to look at him. 'How's your face?'

'Trying to figure out what expression to wear, I guess.' He hesitated, and she knew that he was testing his words for potential offence. 'Is this why you came looking for me?'

'No, Obe. I just needed someone to value my comic book collection.'

'Sorry. Again. I'm playing catch-up here, and pretty badly, too.' He took a breath, exhaled through his teeth. 'We're pregnant.'

Appalled, she reared away from him. 'Uh-uh. None of *that* shit. *I'm* pregnant, Obe. There *is* no we.'

He nodded, chastened. 'Understood.'

'I came down here for one reason – to find out more about you. Then I'm gone.'

Obe touched his fingers to his cheek. They came away wet with blood. 'Are you keeping it?'

At that, her eyes filled with tears. She turned away so he couldn't see.

Gently, Obe placed his hand on the tiller beside her own. 'We'll get to St Ives,' he said. 'Find a B&B and grab a few hours' sleep. Then we'll talk about this. Work something out.'

Mallory nodded, blinking until her eyes were clear. She looked up to see Gollum clambering over the lobster pots towards her.

'You've got a decent right hook,' he said. 'But if you really want to hurt someone, you should go for the nose. Busted conk stings like a bitch.' He turned to Obe. 'Everything sweet between you two now?'

'Mallory's pregnant.'

Gollum laughed, the plait on his chin quivering. 'No shit.'

'You *knew*?'

'Dude, for someone so astute, you can be pretty blind.'

Mallory frowned. 'I'm not even showing. How could you possibly know?'

The man shrugged. 'I read auras. I know that sounds like

horseshit but I do. And yours is all kinds of intense. Red, orange, silver. You're like a firework on Guy Fawkes'.'

'Maybe I'm just very, very pissed off.'

Mallory rubbed her scuffed knuckles, and wished she knew what to do.

Gollum dropped them in St Ives thirty minutes later, motoring around the headland and up onto the sand at Harbour Beach. Shielded from the sea by long harbour walls, the water was far calmer than it had been back at Sennen Cove.

Wearing her pack, trainers grasped in one hand, Mallory slipped over the gunwales into surf up to her knees. She waited for Gollum to complete a complicated handshake with Obe before she addressed him. 'If anyone asks—'

'Never saw you,' he replied. 'Never even heard of you.'

She nodded. 'If you want to give us the best chance of making a clean break, take your time getting back.'

'It's a nice day. Maybe I'll go have a beer.' He reached into his pocket and pulled out a small brown card that featured a surfboard's silhouette. 'Here,' he said. 'My details. Just in case you ever need them.'

Once she'd pocketed it, Gollum held out his palm. Obligingly, Mallory slapped it. Then she began to wade ashore.

Obe appeared beside her, hefting his own rucksack. 'You said *us*.'

'What?'

'Back there. *If you want to give us the best chance.* That's what you said.'

She halted, ankle-deep in foaming surf. 'Me and the baby,' she replied. 'Not me and you.' Turning away, she marched up the beach.

At nearly eleven in the morning, St Ives was awash with tourists: families and couples wandering in and out of the shops lining the front, sunbathers staking their claims on the sand. Mallory climbed the steps to the wharf road, Obe trailing behind her. 'We need to find a room,' she told him. 'I'm asleep on my feet.'

'Gollum told me about this hotel. Old Victorian place up on the headland, a little out of town. Doesn't get much business these days because the landlady's a dragon and doesn't really advertise, but she does allow dogs.'

'Let's grab a taxi,' Mallory said.

# TWENTY-NINE

The Mên-an-Tol Hotel perched on the granite outcrop of Godrevy Head, pointing north-west towards the offshore lighthouse that marked the Stones reef. Faced with dark grey stone and crowned with steeply rising eaves, the building brooded like a sour old man.

'Looks nice,' Mallory remarked, after paying the taxi driver with cash. 'Sort of place you might come to commit suicide.'

Obe grinned, grateful for the banter, even if it was only sarcasm. 'At least it's remote. Kind of reminds me of a miniature Wayne Manor.'

'If that's a comic-book reference, it's lost on me.'

'Bruce Wayne's house,' he explained. Noting her blank look, he added, 'The Dark Knight?'

'Nope.'

'Batman.'

'Right.' Hefting her pack, Mallory climbed the steps.

The Mên-an-Tol's proprietor, Mrs Murdina Tremethyk, was almost exactly as Gollum had described. Bird-thin, bereft of warmth – as if a cold gruel seeped through her veins in place of blood – she entered their details into the ledger with a fountain pen that scratched so violently it nearly tore gashes in the paper.

Fetching a key, she led them up a cold staircase and along a lightless hall hung with the works of taxidermists whose talents were brutish and peculiar. The room itself was shadowed and cool, tall enough to escape the suffocating density of its Gothic furniture. The bed was dressed not with a duvet but an eiderdown embroidered with sun-faded birds and flowers.

'Breakfast finished two hours ago,' Mrs Tremethyk said, fixing Yoda with a glare. 'There'll be nothing now until the morning.'

'That's fine,' Obe told her. 'We're both so tired that we'll probably sleep straight through.'

'We've been travelling most of the night,' Mallory explained.

The woman sniffed at that. 'I'm on duty until midnight. Then I lock up. If you're out past then, you're out all night. No exceptions.' Pursing her lips, she retreated to the hall and closed the door.

Mallory threw down her rucksack and opened the window. A sea breeze rolled in, lifting the hair around her face. She filled her lungs, arching her spine and rolling her head.

Obe watched, until he realised with a lurch that he was staring again. 'Coffee?'

Leaning out of the window, she craned her neck. 'Coffee would be great.'

'What're you doing?'

'Looking for the fire escape.'

'Are you planning to start a fire?'

She pulled in her head. 'I'm planning on having a plan.'

He filled a kettle, opening sachets of coffee and milk while the water boiled. Mallory kicked off her trainers and stretched out on the bed. When he placed her cup on the side table, she said, 'There's some stuff I need to tell you. Stuff that's going to sound a little crazy. Stuff you probably won't believe.'

'You might be surprised at the kind of thing I'm willing to believe.'

Obe glanced over, and when he saw her hair feathered across the pillow, an image came to him of the night three weeks earlier: Mallory, lying on her side, her naked skin painted by moonlight, her dark eyes glimmering as she considered him.

He flinched from the image, retreating to a nearby chair.

She sat up on the bed, hugging her knees. 'What is it?'

'Nothing. Just a—'

*—way-he's-watching-me-with-those-eyes-remember-that-will-they-find-us-IF-HE-KNOWS-CAN'T-TRUST-HIM-HE'S-HIDING-WHAT–IS-HE-HIDING—*

A searing bolt of pain behind his right eye made him gasp. He dropped his coffee cup to the floor and clutched his head, teeth squealing together in his mouth.

Mallory swung her legs off the bed. 'What the hell, Obe?'

He held up his good hand, warding her off. So far, the northern lights he'd smoked at Gollum's place had dampened the chaos inside his head. Now, it seemed to be wearing off.

'Is it a migraine?'

*—JUST-MY-LUCK-FUCK-IS-WRONG-WITH-HIM-CAN'T-AFFORD-SHIT-LIKE-THIS-SHOULD-NEVER-HAVE-DONE-IT-TOO-LATE-NOW-FAR-TOO-LATE—*

He couldn't nod, couldn't do anything. Darkness pulsed at the edges of his vision.

'. . . always had them?'

Mallory's voice, coming as if from a tunnel.

Carefully, Obe sipped air. His skull felt like it was made from the world's thinnest glass; the slightest movement could fracture it. 'Yeah.'

'Around people?'

Slowly, he felt the pressure in his jaw begin to release. 'Since I was thirteen.'

'What if you smoke a joint? Will that help?'

'It numbs it,' he replied. 'But I shouldn't. Not right now. Besides – as you said, we need to talk.'

He saw that his hands were shaking. Saw that she noticed. He wondered if he was going to throw up, and what she would think of him if he did. Mallory went into the bathroom and returned with a towel, which she used to mop up the spilled coffee. He said, 'Tell me what you wanted to say.'

She hung the towel over a radiator. Then she sat on the bed, took a long breath and blew it out. 'First time I've had to do this.'

'Do what?'

'Explain this stuff. To someone who doesn't know.'

'Start at the beginning.'

'Just like that?'

'Truth has no answer.'

She rolled her eyes. 'Is that a superhero thing?'

'No. Just something I heard.'

'I'm so frigging tired, Obe.'

'You look cashed. Tell me,' he said. 'Some of it, at least. Then we can both get some sleep. Start with those men last night, back at the sanctuary. What do they want?'

Mallory picked up her coffee from the nightstand and took a sip. 'In the short term they want stagnation; an end to disruptive acts.'

'That's pretty opaque.'

'I'm leading you in gently.'

'Thanks,' Obe said. 'But you don't have to. Truth has no answer, remember? Tell me, Mallory. What do they want?'

'An ending,' she replied. 'To me, you, everyone. They despise humanity, hate what we've become. They think we've taken too many wrong turns to be righted, that we've forfeited our right to exist. Their priority, now, is a mass cleansing, allowing God – or nature – to start again.'

He felt something pulse inside his head, as if a blood vessel in his brain had swollen to the point of rupture. 'Are there many of them?'

'Too many.'

'Why are they hunting me? I mean, why me specifically?'

'Because you're a threat.'

He frowned, incredulous. 'How am *I* a threat?'

Placing one hand on her belly, Mallory scowled. 'Because of this.'

'Because of the pregnancy?'

'Because of the possibilities it represents.'

'I don't get it.'

'I know you don't. Perhaps if you were honest with me – perhaps if you started answering some of the questions I've been asking since I arrived – we could figure this out.' She shrugged. 'Maybe you have your reasons. I don't know. Right now, I'm too tired to care.'

'How did they find me?'

Wrapping her arms around her legs, she rested her forehead on her knees. 'I screwed up.'

'Meaning?'

'You're not the only one who escaped with your life last night.'

'They came for you too?'

'Back in London. Two of them. They broke into my place.' Mallory lifted her head. 'I killed one.'

Obe saw from her expression that it was true; saw, too, that she hadn't intended to share that. A coldness began to spread out from his core. He didn't know how to respond. Didn't know how to conduct a conversation with someone who had taken a life.

'You're going to judge me for it?' she asked.

He shook his head.

'It's written all over your face.'

'I wasn't there.'

'No. You weren't.'

Only a few feet of empty space separated them, but it could have been an ocean. 'Are you sure he's dead? I mean, maybe you—'

'I stabbed him in the throat,' she said, her voice going flat. 'Opened one of his arteries right up. There was so much blood you could've surfed in it.'

'Jesus.' Obe blinked. 'The other guy?'

'I stabbed him too.'

'He's not dead?'

'He might be by now.' Her expression hardened. 'He tried to rape me. Afterwards, if he'd succeeded, he would've killed me.'

Obe felt the blood drain from his head. 'How'd they find me?'

'I lost your driving licence. I guess someone must've found it. They'd have understood the significance, no question.'

A memory surfaced – the man who had intercepted him as he tried to escape: *Thing is, Obadiah, there's an impurity in you. A form of sickness, if you like. I know you know what I'm talking about.*

'This world you're in now,' Mallory said. 'It's like nothing you've known before. You can't get into the heads of these people. They're ruthless, fanatical. They don't care who dies because they want *everyone* dead.'

'The devil can cite scripture for his purpose,' Obe muttered.

Mallory nodded. Closed her eyes. 'Something like that.'

He studied her, concerned at what he saw. 'You look like something from *The Walking Dead*.'

'I can't imagine that's a compliment.'

'Not really. You should grab some sleep. I can take the floor if you want the bed.'

'We can share it,' she said. 'Doesn't matter to me.' Opening her eyes, dragging herself off the mattress, she picked up her rucksack and disappeared into the bathroom.

Moving slowly, lest he loose another firebolt inside his head, Obe went to the hotel door and turned the key. Retrieving his coffee cup, he filled it with bottled mineral water and gave Yoda a messy drink. Then he closed the window and drew the drapes.

*Perhaps if you were honest with me – perhaps if you started answering some of the questions I've been asking since I arrived – we could figure it out.*

Obe kicked off his trainers and lay down on the bed. His head throbbed. He tried to ignore it.

Inside the bathroom, Mallory stood at the sink and examined herself in the rust-spotted mirror. A blood-crusted cut ran across her brow. Her eyes looked like someone had thrown acid in them. She'd been awake for twenty-eight hours, but although she craved sleep, she needed to wash off the horrors of her long night and scrub herself clean. Carefully, she began to undress, folding her clothes and placing them on the floor.

Running the shower, she stepped in and pulled the curtain closed. The water was hot; soon, the air filled with steam. Afterwards, back in front of the mirror, she dried her hair and brushed out the tangles. From her rucksack she found a T-shirt and pulled it on. Once she managed a few hours of sleep, she'd glean from Obe what she needed. Then she'd cut him loose.

In fairness, he wasn't bad company. But she'd spent so little of her adult life around others that her yardstick was hardly reliable. His obsession with fictional worlds frustrated her, and she found his relentless optimism confounding. He possessed a childlike naivety that jarred her nerves, and a sense of wonder that seemed impervious to ridicule. She knew he wouldn't survive without her; but if she stayed with him much longer all three of them would die.

*Three.*

Mallory cringed, felt her fingers drop reflexively to her belly.

Her feelings about *that* were still too raw to process. After brushing her teeth, she opened the bathroom door and stepped back into the bedroom.

Obe had lain down on the bed, a vague shadow in the darkness. His splinted arm rested on his chest, the other tucked behind his head. Mallory tiptoed across the floor and climbed beneath the sheets.

She curled onto her side, facing away from him. 'There's a word, but it's meaningless,' she said, her voice low. 'At least until I've explained the rest. The word is Arayıcı. If you spoke Turkish, you'd recognise it. It means "Seeker", although – from what I've read – the Turks borrowed it from a far earlier language.

'The Arayıcı have had a presence in every culture since the beginnings of man, but they've done their best to remain hidden. Few of their origin texts survive, and those that do are fairly inaccurate – attempts to explain things that at the time appeared supernatural, even if they weren't. Still, if you went through them you'd find a common thread: throughout history, they've produced offspring whose impact on humanity has been profound.'

Mallory paused, allowing her words to sink in. 'But the Arayıcı don't get all the credit. Just as important are those, outside their own, that the Arayıcı sometimes choose as partners. Kusurlu, they're called. That's another Turkish word you might not know. It translates as "tainted", or "defective", although in this context the meaning isn't as negative. A kinder description would be "blessed", but I doubt many Kusurlu would agree, firstly because few of them are aware of what they are, and secondly because often they're victims of the very blessing that sets them apart.

'Put the two together and you get a child with the potential to change the world, or so they say. There've never been that many Arayıcı, and supposedly there've been even fewer Kusurlu – perhaps no more than a handful each generation. But humanity hasn't *needed* that many for the effects to be felt. When you think about how society advances, or how evolution works, it's not a linear process. It happens in fits and starts, unique individuals making huge, one-off contributions.'

She paused, surprised at how the darkness of their room

made it easier to talk. 'They say the beginnings of language was sparked by a single gene mutation in an early human, some eighty thousand years ago. Then there's the invention of writing – around five thousand years ago. It developed gradually, but still stemmed from a single source. In both cases, there's cause to believe the genesis was an Arayıcı-Kusurlu child.

'Even in more modern times – by which I mean the last few thousand years or so – if you investigated some of humanity's greatest contributors, you might uncover a similar heritage.'

Mallory heard the muted crash of waves a few hundred feet below the window. Somewhere, out to sea, came the distant horn of a container ship: two mournful blasts. 'I'm Arayıcı,' she said. 'I think you're Kusurlu. Which means that this child, if it lives . . .'

Holding herself still, she listened to the silence.

A minute passed. Still, Obe did not respond. Finally she turned onto her side and faced him. The boy's eyes were closed, his chest gently rising and falling.

Shaking her head, Mallory rolled onto her back.

She needed sleep. Within moments, she found it.

# THIRTY

When Mallory opened her eyes, she found that the clock had wound back twenty years and she was back in her old bedroom, in the house of love and horror: love, because of the cherished memories of family it still held; horror, because of the evil that had found her there.

The chalet stood on a slope high in the Trentino province of northern Italy. Stone-built and timber-roofed, it offered extraordinary views of the surrounding landscape. Behind it, a dense forest of sweet-smelling spruce climbed the flanks of the Dolomites. Now, in early winter, mountain snows felted the area in silence.

It was the first place Mallory had ever called home for a period longer than a few months. Right now, it smelled of lime juice and stewing meat, which meant it must be Saturday, the day her mother cooked *khoresh gheymeh*. Although her father, Matthais Gurvich, was of Jewish descent, he loved his wife's Iranian cuisine, and Laleh Gurvich loved to please him.

When Mallory came downstairs, she found him in his armchair beside the fire, a leather-bound copy of Homer's *Odyssey* open on his lap. He glanced up when she walked in, removing his spectacles. 'Little *pupik*,' he said. 'What've you got there?'

'It's a fairy door,' she told him, holding up a construction of wood and glue. 'I read about them in my book. If you place one against a tree, fairies visit you through it and grant you a wish.'

'And what is it you would wish for?'

'That we can live here for ever,' she said. 'And that we won't ever have to run.'

Her father polished his spectacles on a fold of his cardigan. He placed them back on his face and smiled. 'Then make sure you choose a fine tree. Remember to keep in sight of the house.'

'Yes, Abba.'

'Wear your coat, too.'

Grabbing it from its peg, Mallory pushed open the back door and raced down the steps to the garden. No fence contained it. Beyond her mother's chicken coops, closed up for winter, the snow-covered grass led right to the forest's edge. There, trunks of Norway spruce rose like the masts of ghost ships, their upper boughs crusted with white. Beneath, the earth lay dark and rich.

Careful to obey her father's warning, Mallory threaded her way between the trees. With the fairy door trapped beneath her arm, she sought out a suitable candidate, finding one twenty yards into the forest. It was a grand specimen; roots spread out from its base like the tentacles of some vast sea creature. Mallory knelt before it, a mulch of dead needles pressing through her leggings. Shivering, she positioned the fairy door. Then she closed her eyes and recited the words she'd memorised: '*Fairy friends, come to me, through this door upon this tree; grant my wish and you will see, a good companion I will be.*'

She counted back from one hundred to zero, trying to visualise the door rolling open. When she rose to her feet and opened her eyes, it looked just like she had left it. The book had warned her to expect that – fairies visited the human realm on their own terms and in their own time – but when she turned towards the chalet she gasped in surprise; because there, right beside her mother's chicken coops, stood a man she didn't recognise.

He was dressed entirely in black, which was odd. The book had suggested that fairies wore far brighter colours, their clothes sewn from rainbows and spider silk and morning dew. Yet if the newcomer wasn't a fairy or a forest sprite or any of the other denizens of these mountains, who was he? Except for old man Vecchi, they hadn't received a single visitor since moving to Trentino.

In the pockets of her coat were her mittens. Mallory pulled them on, flexing her fingers inside them. Ahead, leaning on a slim black cane, long hair flowing down his spine like a bolt of silver silk, the stranger stared at the chalet, breath spiralling in white gouts. Reaching into his overcoat, he produced a revolver.

Something cold and greasy hatched in Mallory's stomach.

She tried to take a forward step, but her boots felt as if some subterranean creature clutched their soles. She opened her mouth but her voice wouldn't come.

A gunshot clattered off the slopes, followed, inside the house, by a scream.

Mallory's lungs emptied of breath. When she tried to take another, she found she couldn't. For a moment she wondered if the bullet had whipped between the trees and struck her, but she was still on her feet. She'd seen from TV that people fell over when they got shot.

The chalet's back door banged open and Laleh Gurvich appeared, tripping down the steps to the garden. Over a ribbed white vest she wore a plaid work shirt, sleeves rolled to the elbow, hands dusted with flour. She ran across the snow-covered grass towards the trees, keening like a wild animal in distress; or, just maybe, a human being too overcome by terror to think.

Behind her, the back door banged open once again, revealing a second stranger. This one held a silver pistol. He raised it towards Mallory's mother and squeezed off five shots.

The valley echoed, whip-like cracks chased by rolling thunder. Three of the bullets missed their target, but one struck Laleh Gurvich between the shoulders. Her vest blossomed red, a perfect Valentine's carnation in the very centre of her chest. Moments later the fifth bullet slapped through her skull, jerking her around. She died in mid-air, twisting towards the snow like a broken ballerina.

Mallory's fingers flexed and unflexed. She shivered, wondering why she suddenly felt so cold, wondering whether the men would let her fetch a pillow and slip it beneath her mother's broken head.

She blinked. Flinched. Had such a foolish notion just hit her? She knew what was happening here: knew these were the people her parents had spent their lives trying to avoid.

Vasi.

Such a silly name. Such a pointless crusade. She had laughed when Abba had explained their twisted doctrine – not just their desire to end Arayıcı influence but to return all of humanity to the soil whence it had sprung.

And now they had killed her mother.

She watched the back door bang open a third time, releasing Matthais Gurvich. He was a man transformed, so unlike the father she had known that had it not been for his round Oxford spectacles she would not have recognised him. He was red and ragged, a blood-soaked spectre that launched from the upper step like a bat and tangled with the man who had shot his wife. They rolled together in the snow and Matthais came up on top, but instead of battering his quarry with his fists, as Mallory had expected, he raised his head and searched the forest. Within an instant his eyes lit upon her.

So much he communicated in that look, such expressions of love and regret.

Mallory was so consumed by it that she hardly noticed the man with the slim black cane lift his revolver and step out of cover. She raised a hand towards her father, as if somehow she could reach across the open ground that separated them and transport him away.

'*Run*,' he urged, his eyes fierce. Then the stranger pulled the trigger of his gun, and Matthais Gurvich fell lifeless into the snow.

Mallory still hadn't taken a breath. Less than a minute ago she'd been planting fairy doors and reciting children's rhymes, and in the intervening seconds she had lost both parents and sacrificed infancy for adulthood.

The man with the slim black cane turned on his heel. When he spotted the trail of small footprints leading across the snow to the forest's edge he lifted his head. His eyes met hers and he smiled, his teeth a row of yellow lanterns. Raising his cane, he pointed its silver tip towards her.

Moaning, Mallory turned and ran, kicking through the frozen mulch, which somehow became a tangled sheet, and found herself scrabbling up, up and out, her arms thrashing at her coverings, her throat clamped tight around a scream, the pale, bristled trunks of mountain spruce transforming into tall walls, shadowed dark and the looming lumps of hotel furniture.

Lurching upright in the bed, gasping as if she'd been submerged in a bath filled with ice, she burst free of the nightmare, clutching herself and sobbing like the nine-year-old girl she had once been.

# THIRTY-ONE

In Obadiah Macintosh's first-floor living room, Aylah İncesu sat among the shredded remains of rare comics and plastic packaging, considering her next move. Most of the boy's collection had not yielded additional information, but some of it had. Although her haul was mainly photographic, she'd discovered a few archived news articles that made her skin crawl as she read them.

Teke called back as she was puncturing the last of the slabbed comics. 'Obadiah Black,' he said. 'Aka Obadiah Macintosh.'

'What can you tell me?'

'We're talking about one messed-up individual. Or was, last time there was any record of him.'

'Hardly surprising,' she replied, 'when you consider his history.'

Teke exhaled explosively. 'Are you ahead of me again?'

'Always, but tell me what you've got.'

'Both parents dead, killed when he was twelve years old.'

'I just read the news article.'

'So I won't bore you with the details. No other family came forward afterwards, so the boy was placed into care. From there he had a pretty rough ride, although it's likely he was having problems long before that. Parents might've been covering them up. He was home-schooled, and the welfare visits were pretty sketchy. Looks like the family was virtually ignored. Once he was made ward of the state, things derailed fast. He had a protracted association with mental health services. They categorised him as tier four, which is as extreme as you can get. Bright enough kid, but just couldn't be around people.' Teke paused. 'Does this sound like classic Kusurlu to you? Because it sure as hell doesn't to me.'

'Me neither. But he sounds like just the kind of retarded mess *she'd* be drawn towards. What else have you got?'

'Right now, not much that's going to help. There's reams of material, but I'm still trawling through it. I just wanted you to have the headlines.' He grunted. 'Seems like you beat me to it.'

'It's still useful to have it confirmed. It'll take some doing, but see if you can access his medical records. Better still, hunt down any of the psychiatrists who treated him. If Mallory stays with this freak, he's going to be the weak link. Any little trigger, anything that gives us leverage, could be critical.'

'You'll hear it first.'

She climbed to her feet. Stretched. 'I'd better.'

'You sound exhausted.'

'No way. I'm wired.'

'Did you see Manco?'

'Briefly.'

Teke hesitated a fraction. 'Bad?'

'Tolerable.'

In the ensuing silence, someone rapped on Obadiah's front door. Aylah tensed. The house was being watched, so it couldn't be either of her targets. She picked up her *qama*, just to be safe. 'Gotta go. Someone's here.'

'Yeah, it's me,' Teke said. 'Open up.'

Aylah's heart kicked. She strode through the flat and tore open the door. 'Fucking comedian,' she told him. 'Get in here.'

Teke stepped past her. Six foot seven in height, he was so long-boned and frog-pale that had he thrown on a cloak he could have passed for Death. His eyes were unusually washed out, his features lumpen and irregular; but there was an intensity to him, and a deep reservoir of self-control, that was fascinating. 'Are we alone?' he asked.

Grabbing him by his belt, Aylah dragged him along the hall, barely making it to the living room before she pulled him down on top of her. 'I need you to hurt me,' she said, her voice shaky. 'Real pain.'

Afterwards, while Teke set up his laptop at Obadiah's breakfast table, Aylah retreated to the couch. Her body ached with the aftershocks of pleasure and pain. The sensation was all-consuming, dampening her thoughts and allowing her to drift. Knowing that he would alert her if there was a development, she closed her eyes and slept. When she woke, the sunlight streaming through the window had turned copper, and Teke was standing over her. 'Good news,' he said.

She rubbed her face, swinging her legs off the couch. Her spine felt like it had been beaten out of alignment with a hammer. 'What?'

'Remember the phone I told you about? The one we isolated from ANPR data?'

'The one that was switched off.'

'Somebody just switched it back on. Less than a minute later it dropped out again. It didn't make any calls or send any data, but it was long enough to get a GPS fix.'

'Where?'

'Place called Godrevy Head, about twenty miles north-east of here. Big lump of rock that sticks right out into the sea.'

'What's on it?'

'An old hotel. Place called the Mên-an-Tol.'

Aylah slipped on her boots. 'It's her. Guaranteed.'

'Why would she come all the way to Cornwall, then hole up somewhere twenty miles away?'

'We can ask her just before we kill her. Who do we have available?'

'That guy you asked for is waiting outside.'

'Chevry. Who else?'

'Depends if you want to take manpower off the roads. It's a solid lead, but it could be a ruse.'

Aylah hesitated. It was an important decision, and she didn't have long to make it. 'I need to see a map.'

Teke handed her a tablet. The screen showed a satellite image of Godrevy Head with the local roads overlaid. A glowing blue icon indicated the location of the activated phone. Aylah zoomed out. 'We could pull everyone back, set up another barrier between Lelant and Longrock,' she said, tracing her finger between the two points. 'That's only a five-mile stretch.'

'It's still much larger than the area we're covering now. And if you want to take reinforcements to the hotel, you'll stretch yourself even further.'

'It feels like the right thing to do.'

'Shouldn't you run this by Manco?'

'He wants to be kept informed, not micro-manage the detail.'

Outside, a white Range Rover Evoque was parked on yellow lines. Aylah swung open the passenger door and climbed in beside Guy Chevry. Once Teke had slid onto the back seat, Chevry accelerated away from the kerb.

'Know where you're going?' she asked.

'Some shithole hotel. Got the address programmed into the satnav.'

Aylah nodded, observing Chevry as he drove. Last night, at the Ealing maisonette, she had tasked him with making Dr Fabian Pataki's death look like an accident or suicide. Standing at the kitchen table, Chevry's eyes had fallen to the pill boxes retrieved from the cistern. He unscrewed all the caps and began to push their contents into Pataki's mouth. The man resisted at first, spitting and choking, but then Chevry began to talk, explaining in a quiet yet mellifluous tone exactly what he would do if the man failed to obey his wishes. Some of the tortures promised such indelible agony that even Aylah found herself tuning out. Pataki ingested perhaps three hundred different tablets before he lost consciousness. Afterwards, Chevry carried him into the living room and laid him on the sofa. He perched close, holding one wrist, and when he felt the last tick of the doctor's pulse, he sighed with a satisfaction that was almost sexual. Aylah couldn't decide if it was the most grotesque thing she had ever witnessed or the most alluring.

'How long?' she asked.

'Satnav says forty-two minutes.'

'I think you could do it in half that.'

Chevry shrugged. 'Let's find out.'

# THIRTY-TWO

Free of the dream's images but not its memories, Mallory slipped from the hotel bed and padded across the room to the bay window. When she eased aside the drapes, she saw that the sun had sunk below the horizon. The ocean had darkened so dramatically that the water looked like a slick of crude oil. North-west, the Godrevy lighthouse was a black finger pointing up at the oncoming night.

Behind her, Obe moaned in sleep. He lay beneath rumpled sheets, his face creased with anguish. Recalling her own dream, she wondered what demons stalked his.

Seeing her parents like that had triggered a profound sense of disquiet; years had passed since she'd relived their deaths so vividly. Now, she felt their loss all over again. It was a pinching grief, cruel and sharp; it pulled at her like an unravelling thread.

With Obe still muttering into his pillows, Mallory left the bay window for the bathroom, where she locked the door and turned on the light. Its brightness seared her. In the mirror over the sink she glimpsed a wraith and recoiled, mistaking her reflection for a vestige of the dream.

If anything, the snatched hours of sleep had accentuated her exhaustion. Her skin looked greasy, clammy. Her bloodshot eyes blinked out of dark hollows.

On the floor beside the sink lay her rucksack. Rummaging

through it, she retrieved the second pregnancy kit and carried it to the toilet. Tugging down her underwear, squatting on the seat, she forced out a thin stream of urine, holding the wand in the flow.

Back at the mirror, Mallory held the wraith's gaze and tried to think. Eighteen hours ago she'd had a plan, however crude: terminate the pregnancy; put as much distance as possible between herself and the Vasi; start again. She'd almost carried the first part through to fruition, but in Fabian Pataki's maisonette she'd been seized by . . . what exactly? Vomiting up the mifepristone had been an act of suicidal recklessness, one that made absolutely no sense. Living in isolation for so long, Mallory had believed her self-knowledge was matchless. How distressing to discover that she knew herself hardly at all.

Within a minute, a vertical line appeared in the pregnancy test's control window. Shortly afterwards, a line appeared in the larger result window.

Confirmation.

A few days before her period, the test wasn't infallible, but she knew.

She was pregnant. A Kusurlu life growing inside her, invested with matchless potential. But until she discovered the secret Obe was hiding, and the nature of the gift he had passed on, she had no idea what talents might manifest in the child, nor how to nurture them.

Last night, she'd felt unable to bring any kind of life into the world, let alone one as special as this. Now, she felt she had no choice.

Mucus ran from her nose. She tore off a strip of toilet paper and blotted it away.

Sharp spears of pain pricked her lower abdomen. Doubled over, she wondered if some of the poison she'd ingested at Pataki's place had remained inside her, and was finally beginning to eject the minuscule scrap of life from her womb. But she had seen the pill in the sink; it had been whole. Likely these cramps were simply a reaction to all she'd endured in the last twenty-four hours.

On impulse, she dug through her rucksack for her phone and switched it on. Suddenly, more than anything, she wanted to talk to Sal. She'd have to endure his analysis of how she'd handled herself, but she could bear that to hear a familiar voice.

Halfway through dialling his number she changed her mind, switching off the phone. The device was unregistered, and she could conceive of no way for the Vasi to link her to it. But if the pharmacy's security camera had recorded her voice, perhaps there were ways to sniff her out across the mobile phone network. Right now, she was so bone-tired that she was in danger of making mistakes. Better to contact Sal when her head was clear enough to think properly.

Opening the phone's case, she removed the battery. In the morning she would question Obe again. This time she wouldn't rest until she had the facts she needed. After that she would disappear.

Filling the sink, Mallory washed her face. Then she switched off the light and crept back into the bedroom. It was dark in here now; the last light had leached from the sky. From the floor she heard a chuff of expelled breath and the thump of Yoda's tail. 'Chill,' she muttered. She hadn't warmed to the dog – could hardly believe she was sharing a room with it. Reaching the bed, she crawled beneath the sheets.

'You had a nightmare,' Obe said.

She stiffened momentarily. 'Sounded like I wasn't the only one.'

'Kind of unsurprising, I guess.'

The silence stretched out, so charged that she could almost feel Obe's thoughts. How alien, this, to lie beside another human being, to feel their warmth and sense the ticking of their heart. Crazy to think that for many in the wider world this was a part of life so natural that it barely warranted a thought. Obe was so close that she could reach out and touch him if she wished; but they were separated, in this bed, by far more than physical distance.

'Arayıcı,' the boy muttered, and waited for her to respond.

Mallory's stomach muscles tensed. 'I didn't think you'd heard any of that. I thought you'd fallen asleep.'

'I did. At some point. But I remember that.'

'I shouldn't have said anything. Should have kept it to myself.'

'Why?'

'Because . . .' she began, and faltered.

*Because it makes no difference. Because after tonight, you won't see me again. Because even if I manage to survive what's coming, there's no way you're strong enough.*

Obe hissed through his teeth, twisting onto his side.

'What is it?'

'Just the arm,' he said.

'The co-codamol wore off?'

'Think so.'

'Should you take some more?'

'Probably. But I don't want to. I put enough crap into my body yesterday.'

*Me too*, she thought.

'Who are you, Mallory? What's happening here? I know you don't owe me anything, but surely you can tell me that much.'

'I told you who I am.'

'Arayıcı.'

She stared into the darkness, listening to the boy as he breathed. Propping herself up on one arm, trying to resist her body's call towards sleep, she said, 'It's not the only thing we've been called. In Judaism, and some sects of Christianity, they call us "Elioud".'

'That's a name I *have* heard of,' Obe said. 'It's from the Book of Enoch. The Elioud were the offspring of the Nephilim.'

'How'd you know that?'

'There was a comic book,' he replied. 'Not a great story, but pretty good on the lore. The Nephilim were meant to be fallen angels who went against God and bred with humans.'

Mallory snorted. 'I can't tell you much about God, Obe, but I'm pretty sure my ancestors didn't breed with angels, fallen or otherwise. If you ask me, those stories were trying to explain events that seemed supernatural or directed by God, even if they weren't.'

Obe was silent for a while. 'What kind of events?'

'The birth of gifted individuals,' Mallory replied, her hands sliding to her belly. 'Individuals who changed the world, and shaped humanity in extraordinary ways.'

Outside, a gust of Atlantic wind twined over the cliff, shaking the window in its frame.

'The Elioud were Pre-Noachian,' the boy said.

'I know.'

'You're telling me you can trace your ancestry back to a point before the Flood?'

Mallory closed her eyes. Immediately, she saw an image of her mother's bullet-smashed skull. 'Yes.'

'How old are you?' he asked.

'Me?' She laughed. 'How old are you?'

'You've seen my licence. I'm twenty.'

'Then I'm four years older. I might have a long ancestry, Obe, but so does everyone.'

'Not like yours.'

Again, the silence stretched between them, an unnavigable road. The fact that he seemed to accept her words so readily, without any trace of scepticism, bothered her greatly.

'Why me?' the boy said. 'I mean, everything you've just described. What's it have to do with me?'

'I think you're Kusurlu – the other half of the puzzle.' She felt a chill spread out from her chest like cold ink. 'I wouldn't have been drawn to you so powerfully if you weren't.'

Beside the bed, Yoda lurched to his feet. He padded across

the room, toenails clicking on the varnished floor. Moments later, Mallory heard him drinking from his cup.

'Back at the sanctuary,' Obe said. 'The guy who knocked me down. He said there was an impurity in me. A sickness.'

'He was wrong.'

'Was he?'

'Yes.'

With some effort, Obe turned himself onto his side, facing her in the darkness. 'Please, Mallory. Tell me what this is. Tell me what's happening here.'

His words were so earnest that she felt sudden empathy for him. For the first time she thought about how frightening his experience at the animal sanctuary must have been. She'd had a lifetime to prepare for this. Obe had had no time at all. The fact that he'd survived was a near miracle.

Opening her eyes, searching him out in the darkness, she said, 'That night, three weeks ago in Plymouth, and what we did. It's an event that might happen once in a hundred years or so.'

Obe remained silent for a while. 'You mean the sex?'

Mallory flinched, her skin prickling with heat. It was difficult, suddenly, to ignore how close they were, and what had occurred the last time they had shared a bed. 'I mean an encounter between Arayıcı and Kusurlu. What it *produces*. The few of us still alive thought this would never happen again. It's why I've been asking you to spell out what's different about you, ever since I found you on the beach. Because whatever it is you're hiding, Obe, it's likely to manifest ten times as strongly in this child.'

'I don't understand,' he whispered. 'I don't understand any of this.'

'Throughout history, the Arayıcı have been drawn to those with a gift – or an abnormality – that might have been a blessing if not for one fatal flaw.'

Across the room, Yoda finished drinking. The dog trotted to the window and slumped back down on the floor.

'Once, when I was a girl,' Mallory said, 'my parents took me to Kelebekler Vadisi. It's in south-western Turkey, a place sometimes known as the Valley of Butterflies. My father had a lifelong interest in lepidoptery. Every year during spring and early summer he'd take us to somewhere new, hunting for rare species. We came into Kelebekler Vadisi on a charter boat – it's the best way of reaching the valley. The water there was the bluest I'd ever seen, and the scenery was like something from the Jurassic – sheer canyon walls framing this flat expanse of green that became a white sand beach at the water's edge. We visited in spring, just in time for the hatching.

'I don't know who found it hanging from a branch, but I do remember us clustering around the chrysalis of a False Apollo. This particular guy was having all kinds of trouble breaking loose, but he didn't give up, wriggling and shaking and working his way out. Dad said his hindwings – they're the smaller set – were far larger than they should have been, and we could all see that they were far more striking.

'Just as he made it all the way out, he caught those wings on a sharp nub of his cocoon, tearing them to tatters. I couldn't breathe when I saw that. The poor thing didn't even seem aware of what had happened. He sat there for ages, drying his broken wings in the sun. Then, when he was finally ready, he cut loose from the branch, but instead of flying into the sky he spiralled straight down to the ground. Back then, it was the saddest thing I'd ever seen. I was only seven, and still pretty sentimental about that kind of stuff.'

She turned her head, wondering what kind of expression Obe wore. 'My mother pointed at the False Apollo twisting and flopping in the soil. "That, right there, is a Kusurlu." she said. "If he'd have lived, he'd have outshone all others with his beauty. But he wasn't ready for this world, and couldn't live within it. When you're older – if you live long enough, and if God is smiling on you – there's a chance, one day, that you'll uncover a creature like this."'

Mallory fell silent, thinking of her mother's face that day at Kelebekler Vadisi. Back then, it had been difficult to hear those words. Right now, it was difficult to repeat them.

'And help it to live?' Obe asked.

She heard the hope in his voice, and tried to ignore it. 'No.'

'Then what?'

'To pass on its gift before it dies.'

Abruptly, the mattress shifted. She heard the floorboards creak on the far side of the bed. 'I think,' Obe said, speaking through clenched teeth, 'I'm going to be sick.'

Before she could respond, he crashed across the room to the bathroom and slammed the door behind him. From inside she heard retching, so fierce and prolonged that she wouldn't have been surprised had he ruptured something.

A thought seized her. She could leave, right now – grab her stuff and get out before this situation grew any more difficult. He hadn't opened up to her so far. Why wait any longer? What difference would another few hours make, other than increasing the likelihood of the Vasi catching her?

Mallory slipped out of the bed and tiptoed across the room. She'd bagged her soiled clothes and left them in the bathroom, but she had a spare set, and money to buy more.

She heard Obe vomit again, then moan in discomfort. Crouching down, she unzipped her rucksack.

Something nudged her from behind and she nearly cried out, but it was only Yoda, pressing his nose into her spine. Shooing the dog away, she searched for her clothes. Inside the bathroom, the toilet flushed. The hotel's pipework rattled in concert.

Yoda nosed her again, harder this time, knocking her off balance. She fell forwards onto her knees, cursing as the impact woke her recent injuries.

The bathroom door opened. A triangle of white light illuminated her. Obe swayed in the doorway, a wad of tissues pressed to his mouth. He blinked. 'What're you doing?'

Mallory sat back on her haunches. 'Just checking my stuff.'

'Uh-huh.' He stumbled past her to the bed and burrowed beneath the covers. 'I've got to get some more sleep.'

She nodded, stood up, turned her attention to the dog.

Yoda stared back. He chuffed, licked his lips. After a few moments, he retreated to a corner of the room.

Zipping up her rucksack, Mallory placed it on a chair. Then she went into the bathroom and switched off the light.

By the time she slipped back into bed, Obe was already asleep.

*You could go now. It's not too late.*

Lying on her back, she stared at the ceiling, wondering what to do.

# THIRTY-THREE

Guy Chevry didn't quite beat Aylah's challenge of driving to Godrevy Head in twenty-one minutes but he was close, reaching the headland as the last light bled from the sky. A dusty single-lane road led them past a shuttered café and a surf school before it turned north, hugging the coast.

To the east, the land opened out: cultivated farmland surrendering to weathered scrub. To the west, the Atlantic Ocean cradled moonlight.

'Hotel's a few hundred yards up ahead,' Teke said from the back seat. 'You want to leave the car here? Go up there on foot?'

Aylah shook her head. 'It's not that late. We're just tourists looking for a place to stay.' On her lap lay her *qama*, its blade cleaned of blood. In the door recess was her suppressor-equipped Beretta M9A3. Chevry had brought his own pistol. Teke, too. Back in Clapham, Mallory might have avoided Korec and Levitan. She wouldn't avoid this.

They saw a wooden sign: *THE MÊN-AN-TOL HOTEL*. After fifty yards the road became a stony track pitted with holes, an unbroken centre-line of weeds bisecting it. They passed through an open gate into a gravelled courtyard. Only two vehicles stood there now: a dusty transit van that probably belonged to the hotel and an ancient Renault Five, sagging on its suspension.

Aylah flicked the front cabin's interior light to the off position, preferring not to be illuminated when the passenger door opened. 'I'll go inside with Chevry,' she told Teke. 'You stay here. There's every chance that Mallory's already moved on, but just in case she hasn't, I want someone waiting outside.'

'And if she comes out?'

'Grab her. And if you can't do that, kill her. Better that she's dead than we give her another opportunity to run. It's not just Manco watching us now. It's everyone.' She screwed a receiver into her ear, retrieved her Beretta and slipped it under her jacket. Then she opened the door and stepped out.

The hotel loomed up ahead, lights shining from its ground floor. The dining room and bar area were devoid of customers or staff. White cloths covered the tables, but no cutlery had been laid for breakfast.

The building's upper windows were dark.

Aylah climbed the steps and went inside. The entrance lobby, carpeted in faded tartan, was as deserted as the dining room. A reception desk stood at the far end. Behind it an archway opened into an unlit office. Beside the stairs leading to the first floor, a grandfather clock ticked. The air smelled strange and vaguely unpleasant: mothballs; boiled vegetables; dust. Somewhere, a TV played – a game show interspersed with audience laughter.

At the reception desk, Aylah saw the ledger lying open and read the slanted handwriting. Her heart began to thump. Only one room appeared to be occupied: two guests. Had Obadiah managed to break through her cordon and meet up with the girl? If so, finding them here – together – was the most extra-ordinary good fortune.

Before Aylah could alert Chevry, a bird-like woman swept through the shadowed archway. A pair of half-moon spectacles clung to her nose, the frames connected to a looping chain. When she saw Aylah examining the ledger, her eyes flared and her lips shrank from her teeth. '*I'll* take that,' she hissed, snatching it away. 'Can I *help*?'

Aylah reached into her back pocket and flashed an ID, one of many she had brought along for just such an encounter. 'You might want to rethink the attitude.'

The woman's glower intensified. 'Let me see that,' she said, plucking the ID from Aylah's fingers. Pushing the spectacles further up her nose, she scowled. 'This is a Metropolitan Police ID. What are you doing in Cornwall?'

'You're making enemies here that you really don't need,' Aylah said. 'What's your name?'

The woman drew herself up. 'Murdina Tremethyk.'

'You're the proprietor?'

'I own the place, yes.'

'How many guest rooms do you have here?'

'Twenty-six.'

'And how many of those are filled this evening?'

'You've seen the ledger.'

'Answer the question, please.'

The hotelier barely managed to keep her voice civil. 'Just one.'

'Describe them.'

'A young couple, early twenties. Somewhat alternative. They arrived late morning. Said they were tired from travelling all night. I showed them to their room and I haven't seen them since.'

'Did they go out?'

'Do I look psychic?'

Aylah stared. 'Do I have to arrest you for obstruction?'

Twin spots of colour appeared on the woman's cheeks. 'I haven't heard anyone come down. I'd assume they're still in their room.'

'The Renault outside. Is that theirs?'

'No. It's mine.'

'How did they get here?'

'In a private car.'

'A taxi?'

The woman lifted her chin. 'Do I need to be more precise?'

'That won't be necessary.' Aylah produced Obadiah Macintosh's driving licence and laid it on the counter. 'Is this one of them?'

Murdina Tremethyk examined it closely. Then she looked up, frowning. 'That's him. But this isn't the name he used.'

'They're in room twenty-four?'

'Yes.'

'Where is that exactly?'

'Second floor. On the left, towards the end of the hall.'

'Anything else you can tell me?'

'They had a dog with them. I don't know which breed.'

'Do you have any more guests arriving this evening?'

The woman shook her head.

'Any other staff on the premises?'

'Not tonight.'

'What about Mr Tremethyk?'

'Mr Tremethyk,' the woman said, 'lives elsewhere.'

'So right now, in this hotel, it's just us, the couple and the couple's dog.'

'I can see why you became a detective.'

Aylah turned to Chevry, nodded.

The man lifted his suppressor-equipped pistol and shot Murdina Tremethyk between the eyes. The gun made a sharp percussive crack as it discharged, but the sound didn't reverberate. It wouldn't reach the second floor.

The dead woman tumbled backwards, striking the rear wall before collapsing in the archway.

Aylah raised a section of the reception counter, retrieving Obadiah's licence from the carpet. From a pegboard she took a key for room twenty-four. Through her earpiece, she spoke to Teke: 'I don't know how, but it seems they hooked up. The hotelier identified the pair of them. Said they arrived this morning and haven't been seen since.'

'You think they're on site?'

'We're about to find out. Stay where you are, and stay alert. The hotelier's dead, which gives us some privacy.'

'Understood.'

Aylah turned to see Chevry crouching over Murdina Tremethyk, his fingers pressed to her wrist. 'You put a bullet in her brain,' she told him. 'There's no need to check.'

Slowly, the man rose to his feet. He looked forlorn, like a dog forced to relinquish a bone. Leading him to the staircase, Aylah began to ascend.

# THIRTY-FOUR

The first time Mallory woke inside the hotel suite, the faces of her dead parents accompanied her out of the dream. This time, when she opened her eyes, she encountered something almost as shocking: a man's face, bone-pale; slick with a sweat that smelled rotten, like the sweetness of an infected wound.

When she tried to reel away, a hand clamped down over her mouth.

'Don't,' the ghoul whispered. 'Not a sound.'

Mallory bared her teeth, preparing to bite, until an awareness reached her that the voice was Obe's. In the soft light cast from the night lamp, he looked like a corpse. The flesh on his face seemed baggy. His eyes appeared loose in their sockets. When she glanced past him to the floor she saw that he'd opened her rucksack and pulled out her clothes. Standing beside them was Yoda.

Carefully, Obe released his hand. 'Get up,' he said. 'Get dressed.'

Something in his tone made her comply without hesitation. Jumping out of bed, she slung on her jeans, stepped into trainers, pulled on her hoodie and zippered it. After throwing the cord of her Stetson over her head, she asked: 'What's happening?'

Obe, still perched on the edge of the bed, looked like he'd aged sixty years. With effort, he raised his head. 'Found us,' he muttered. 'Three of them.'

Mallory froze, one arm threaded through a strap of her rucksack. 'How'd you know that?'

'Killed . . . her.'

Obe swung his head around. His right eye was a mess of burst blood vessels. 'Think I . . . might pass out.'

Mallory went to the bed, taking him by the shoulders. 'Obe, look at me,' she demanded. 'How do you know they're here?'

'Shot her, I think. The . . . hungry one. Enjoyed it – *fed* off it. Gotta get out. Gotta get out *now*.'

Whatever Obe's eyes were seeing, Mallory knew she wouldn't find it inside this room. Something was happening here that she didn't understand. 'Are they close?'

'Coming up the stairs.'

'*Shit.*'

Mallory went to the door, hesitated. Retreated instead to the window. Raising the sash, she hung out her head. Saw, two storeys below, the plate-glass roof of a conservatory.

'Obe. Can you stand?'

'No.'

'You have to.'

'Leave,' he said. 'Now.'

Mallory stared at him. Knew that he was right. She had what she needed: had grasped, in the last minute, a little of what he had been trying to conceal.

Yoda stepped towards the door. The dog stood with his forelegs spread, ears flattened against his head. His thigh muscles trembled, wound to the limits of their tension.

Mallory lifted Obe's rucksack. Carried it to the bed. 'You're just giving *up*? What's wrong with you?'

'Can't focus,' he whispered. 'Can't see.'

He swayed, and she thought he might tumble to the floor.

Dropping the rucksack onto the mattress, she cupped his face in one hand. With the other, she slapped him.

Obe's head snapped to the left, rebounded. His eyes rolled in his head. Then he screwed up his face and stared past her. '*Look*.'

When Mallory glanced over her shoulder, the blood ran from her stomach.

In perfect, lubricated silence, the handle of the hotel door was turning.

On the first floor of the Mên-an-Tol Hotel, Aylah İncesu and Guy Chevry came upon a hallway decorated in shades of deep maroon. Yellow light bled from antique brass wall sconces. At the far end, two fake potted palms flanked the doors of a lift.

'Wait here,' Aylah said, going to the lift and calling it. When the doors rolled open, she dragged one of the palms halfway inside. Rejoining Chevry, she ascended to the second floor. Here, bizarre specimens of taxidermy hung from the walls: lump-faced deer; bulge-eyed foxes; game birds with missing tail feathers and clumps of down like chewed paper. A polished brass plaque read: *ROOMS 20–26*.

Aylah passed the first four rooms without pause: odd numbers on the right, even ones on the left. Room twenty-four waited a few yards away. She stepped past it and pressed herself to the wall. Waited as Chevry took up position.

Listened.

Did she hear movement inside the hotel room? Or was it merely the roar of blood in her ears? In the last few minutes so much adrenalin had flooded her system that it seemed like she'd cast off the shackles of gravity and could – if she wished – kick off from the floor and sail through the air like a samurai.

A soft bar of light bled from beneath the door. Aylah thought she caught the play of shadows across it. With the hotelier dead, and no other guests on site, she would have the time, and the requisite privacy, to visit horrors upon the girl for as long as she wished. A particularly brutal killing would send a clear message to those Vasi who wished to oust her. It might, in turn, bolster her current standing with Saul Manco.

Aylah wrapped her fingers around the door handle. Carefully she twisted it downwards, pleased that the moving metal parts didn't betray her with a sound. When she pushed forwards, the door moved a few millimetres before encountering the resistance of an engaged bolt.

Easing the handle back to its horizontal position, she retrieved the key she'd taken from the pegboard downstairs, but when she tried to slide it into the lock it bumped against an obstacle: another key.

Aylah's heart pounded so hard in her chest that she felt it as a pressure in her throat.

*They're inside.*

Retreating from the door, she indicated to Chevry what she wanted him to do. She lifted her Beretta, pointing its barrel at the ceiling. Then, filling her lungs, she gave the signal.

Chevry raised his right leg and slammed the heel of his boot against the door.

The wood splintered – a crack racing down it from top to bottom. He kicked it a second time, a third. With each blow he inflicted more damage, splinters and paint chips raining onto the carpet. On his seventh attempt the wood around the lock disintegrated and the door flew open.

Even before Chevry regained his balance, something streaked out of the room, sleek and low. Aylah leaped backwards, seized for an instant by the notion that they'd unleashed something ungodly; but almost immediately she saw that the culprit was a large dark-furred dog. The creature reached the staircase before she could squeeze off a shot, and by then her attention was elsewhere because Chevry, finding his balance, had charged inside the room.

Aylah followed, sweeping her Beretta left and right, telling herself not to lose control, fearing in the excitement that she would drill Mallory through the heart or the head, prematurely ending the pursuit that had consumed her for so long.

Dark wooden furniture. Rumpled bed covers. No boy. No girl.

For a moment, Aylah refused to accept what she saw.

The drapes were open. The sash window was closed. In the left wall a door opened into an unlit bathroom. She swept the interior with her weapon, then switched on the light.

White bath suite. Damp towels. Nothing on the sink except a slim bar of soap unshelled from its wrapping. On the floor, a rattan waste bin.

Aylah kicked it over.

It ricocheted off the bath and the packaging for a Clearblue pregnancy kit rolled out, along with a plastic wand. She snatched it up and saw, in the result window, what she already knew.

Aylah dropped it to the floor. Then, her fingers moving without conscious thought to direct them, she did something that appalled her; she touched her own belly, imagining how it would feel to sense the flicker of a life.

Shocked by her response, robbed of strength, she staggered forwards and nearly fell. The bathroom swam around her, a carousel of shadows.

*It could have been you.*

She tasted bile in her throat. Bit her own tongue and tasted blood.

A needle-like pain lanced her, so deep in her abdomen that it seemed to come directly from her womb. She bent double, clamping shut her lips against a cry. Saul Manco's voice rang in her head:

'*There's a way to end this, Aylah, if only you'll open your eyes. A way to end your torment, a way to end all the world's torment. Would you like me to tell you about it? Would you like me to show you the true path towards silence?*'

How she craved an end to torment. How she yearned for silence.

From the bedroom she heard the rattle of a sash window rolling up in its frame. Moments later came the dry snap of Chevry's suppressor-equipped pistol.

# THIRTY-FIVE

If Mallory exerted any more pressure through fingertips curled into a mortared seam above her, she knew that the pads would tear open. Her feet balanced on the window ledge of the room beside her own. She'd stepped across a three-foot gap to reach it.

Atlantic wind gusted over the sea cliffs and tried to tear her loose. Thirty feet below, the ground waited to greet her – but unless she reached the next ledge, her fall would be broken by an even deadlier obstacle: the hotel conservatory's glass roof. Ahead, Obe blocked her forward progress. At the speed he was moving, the wind would rip him off his perch long before he found safety.

She was amazed that he'd made it this far. A minute earlier she had thought him utterly incapable of movement, and yet somehow she'd managed to shock him out of whatever paralysis had gripped him. Pushing him out of the window had felt monstrously callous, but abandoning him to the Vasi would have been crueller.

Somehow, Obe had summoned the strength to climb onto the ledge; had found, too, the dexterity required to cross to the next window. But now his slow progress might kill them both.

'*Move*,' she hissed.

As if to punctuate her words, commotion broke out inside

the hotel – a sudden pounding, followed by a splintering of wood. Balancing on the ledge, she realised that the door to their room had been breached.

Obe swung his face towards her. She shook her head, urging him on with her eyes: *Go! Now! We're out of time!*

He slid along the ledge and stepped out into the abyss. Hampered by his cast, maintaining his balance was almost impossible, but somehow he managed it a second time, his foot finding the next ledge. Mallory swung onto the one he'd vacated, her fingertips snatching at the mortared seam above.

She glanced down, grateful that she'd bypassed the conservatory, but the hard ground looked no less threatening. Her rucksack lay on the grass where she'd tossed it; Obe's too.

Bolted to the corner of the building was the cast-iron fire escape she'd scouted earlier. The gap between it and the ledge on which Obe balanced was far greater than those he'd already traversed. Previously he'd bridged the space with a foot on each sill, but reaching the fire escape would require a leap into the darkness. Rust had spread across its railings like a fungus. Even if Obe leaped cleanly, if he caught a weakened strut and tore it loose, he would plummet thirty feet.

She saw him sizing it up, his face sallow with whatever sickness assailed him, and knew that he lacked the energy for a successful leap. When he threw her a look she clenched her jaw. Nodded.

Behind her, their hotel room's sash window rattled up inside its frame. Mallory glanced backwards, her foot nearly slipping on the sill. A stranger leaned out. His eyes found her and he grinned.

She twisted her head back towards Obe, but in the space of a breath he had vanished.

Mallory stopped thinking, stopped breathing. No time to do anything except trust her dexterity and hope that it didn't fail her.

Behind her she heard commotion – didn't waste time

investigating it. Ahead, a little lower than eye level, she saw a glint of something red, recognising it as Obe's cast. It looked like he had missed the railings for which he'd been aiming but had managed to entangle himself a few feet lower down. He stared up at her, one arm wrapped around a strut. '*Go!*'

Mallory didn't need encouragement. She ran along the window ledge, fingers sliding through the seam between the stones, abandoning caution for sheer speed. Even as her momentum carried her forwards, she felt her torso bow out from the building. By the time she reached the corner of the ledge she'd already started to topple, and when she pushed off with her feet, instead of leaping towards the fire escape she sailed out into darkness.

The wind was cold against her face as she plummeted. The ground was a black slab, rushing up. She saw a montage of snatched images: the motorcyclist pawing her; her eyes in the pharmacy mirror; the man who shot her father pointing his cane.

Out of those horrors, Obe's hand snatched at her. He lacked the strength to arrest her fall, but his momentary intervention swung her around. As her clothing whipped free of his grip, she slammed against the iron railings – so hard that the air was punched from her lungs – and somehow got a hold.

For a heartbeat she clung on, too winded to move. Above her, Obe wormed through a gap in the railings. Seconds later, sparks erupted like fireworks above her head and the entire structure reverberated. When she glanced back at the hotel, she saw the man at the window aiming a gun.

Even as Mallory twisted her body into the fire escape, the air exploded with orange light. Obe crashed past, his feet ringing off the cast-iron steps. Strange, how their roles seemed to have reversed. Pulling herself upright, she clattered after him.

Shouts from the hotel window, a confusion of different voices. More hollow bangs as bullets struck metal. Obe peeled out of the fire escape and stumbled across the grass, gathering up their rucksacks. A round smashed into the ground beside his foot. He jerked backwards as another tore into the soil where he'd been standing, then he rounded the corner. Mallory followed, yelling at him to watch his step, recalling that the garden was hemmed on two sides by the sheer cliffs of Godrevy Head.

Heeding her words, Obe chased the hotel's southern wall towards the front entrance, until out of the darkness loomed a man taller than any Mallory had seen.

He spotted Obe just before the boy slammed him with both rucksacks. Grunting in pain, he cartwheeled away, a spider-like contortion of limbs. As Mallory raced past the hotel, a black shape leaped from a ground-floor window and she cried out, switching direction, but when she heard its breathy exhalations she realised that it was Yoda, keeping pace on her left. Somehow, the mongrel had evaded their assailants and discovered an escape route.

Ahead, Obe jinked left, into the cover of the rhododendron bushes that surrounded the hotel. Mallory raced after him, twisting her head towards the car park. On the tarmac stood a white Range Rover Evoque that hadn't been there before. The sight made her guts twist like a snake. So confident were their Vasi pursuers that they hadn't even bothered to conceal themselves. She wondered how they'd found her. Wondered, too, how many more were out there. Had they already sealed off the headland? Probably. Her only hope was to discover a weak point in their perimeter.

To her right, something cracked off a rhododendron branch. The air cleaved in two. Not a suppressed weapon, that one. The night crashed with its report. Head ducked down, one hand protecting her eyes, Mallory chased after the boy who had saved her, his dog chasing at her heels.

How long they ran, she could not have said with any degree of certainty. From the hotel garden they zigzagged down a slope as dark as pitch. She ran with the crippling expectation that a bullet would strike her, and that the last thing she'd feel would be the front of her chest blowing out, or a piece of her skull caroming into the night. Her lungs grew tight and still she ran, marvelling at Obe's reserves of strength. Earlier he'd seemed on the verge of collapse, yet from somewhere he'd tapped a new reservoir of energy. And while Mallory ran unimpeded, Obe still carried both rucksacks. She heard his breath straining in his chest. Wondered how long he could keep up this pace.

Not long.

Some minutes later, after they pushed through a hedgerow into a wheat field, he threw himself down among the stalks and rolled onto his back. He raised a hand and pressed it to the side of his skull, closing his eyes tight. He still looked desperately sick.

Gathering her breath, Mallory crouched down in front of him. 'What is it?' she asked. 'What's wrong?'

Yoda wormed through the hedgerow and began to nose his face. Gently, Obe pushed the animal away. His mouth dropped open and he began to pant. 'They hate you,' he gasped.

'Yes.'

After a moment, he opened his eyes and looked at her. 'Not just you. Everyone.'

Mallory nodded. Snaked her arms around her belly. 'It's why they want to destroy us, destroy this. They hate what it represents.'

'What *does* it represent?'

'Hope,' she said. 'A future.' She looked back the way they'd come. 'How do we get out of here?'

'How should I know?'

'The same way you knew they were coming.'

Obe winced at that, as if a toxic memory had risen in his mind.

'Talk,' she said. 'Before it's too late.'

He lay back, his face pointed at the stars. When he spoke, his voice was husky. 'There are three of them back there. More on the way, but they won't get here for a while. We still have a chance.' Obe turned to face her, and when he saw her watching him he rolled onto his front and climbed to his feet.

'Can you walk?' she asked.

He nodded.

'Want me to carry your pack?'

He shook his head.

'Want to lead, or should I?'

Obe gazed across the field. Silent, he hefted his rucksack and began to cut a trail through the wheat. With the moon silvering the grain heads, Mallory followed.

After a while, all concept of time abandoned her. She would have been no more surprised to find that they had walked for a minute than an hour. They came to a fence and crossed into a neighbouring field, this one sown with barley. Halfway across it Obe changed direction, leading them diagonally until they reached a gate that opened onto a single-lane road. Some way along that they came to a boarded-up surf school. An ageing Citroën Saxo sat outside, its windows speckled with sand. Beyond the building, Mallory heard the steady crash of the sea.

Obe cupped his hands around the Saxo's window and peered inside.

'Are you kidding me?' Mallory asked. 'That thing looks like it was dumped here last century.'

Ignoring her, he retreated to the side of the road. She heard the sounds of retching. When he came back, he looked even paler. Gluey beads of sweat clung to his forehead. He was carrying a rock, which he used to smash the Saxo's window. Reaching in, he popped the door lock and swung it open.

'We don't have a key,' she told him.

Obe braced himself with one hand against the vehicle's frame and his cast against the driver's door. He took a few steadying breaths. Then, raising his right leg, he slammed his foot against the steering column. It took a few attempts before the plastic housing shattered. He swept the broken pieces from the footwell and climbed behind the wheel.

'You're telling me you can hotwire a car?' she asked. He glanced up, the moonlight glittering in his eyes, and she shook her head before he could speak. 'Let me guess. There was a comic.'

'Do you have a torch? I don't want to electrocute myself.'

Mallory shrugged off her pack. She pulled out a penlight and aimed its beam at the wires spilling from the lock.

Obe ducked down and inspected the cabling. 'This may take a while.'

'Have we got a while?'

'Maybe not.'

'Do you even vaguely know what you're doing?'

'This looks . . . there's more wires here than I expected.'

'Great.'

While he worked, Mallory listened for approaching vehicles. Wind gusted over the dunes of Godrevy Beach, soughing through the marram grass. In the light of her torch, Obe's fingers shook like an old man's. He looked exhausted; at the very end of his endurance.

Five minutes later, the Saxo's starter motor lurched and the engine turned over. The exhaust pipe rattled, belching out black smoke.

'You did it,' Mallory said.

Obe closed his eyes.

'Shift over,' she told him. 'Let me drive.'

Once Yoda had squirmed into the back, Mallory slammed the door. Squinting at the fuel gauge, she saw that the tank was half-full. Probably the first decent break they'd had. She glanced over at the passenger seat. Already, Obe was asleep. Whatever gift he'd tapped to lead them from the Vasi had drained him utterly. If they were to survive the next hour, she would have to step up. She'd saved his life at the beach, and he'd repaid the debt twice over: first by alerting her to the dangers at the hotel; second by arresting her fall from the window ledge. She still had no plans to stay with him longer than was necessary, but she would remain until he recovered his strength. She owed him that, at least.

It was an unusual thought, one that she would ponder frequently in the hours ahead. Releasing the handbrake, keeping the headlights extinguished, Mallory turned the car in a tight arc and accelerated.

# THIRTY-SIX

They drove.

After following the coastal road for a few miles in the direction of Portreath, Mallory joined up with the main A30 leading out of Cornwall. While she disliked using such a major route, she suspected that the Vasi would have committed most of their resources further west. The car would be reported stolen around sunrise at the earliest, which gave her at least eight hours before she had to abandon it – even longer if she managed to switch its plates.

Near the village of Indian Queens, she switched onto the A39, following the north-eastern coastline past Padstow, Tintagel and Bude. Soon after they crossed into Devon, skirting the southern boundary of Exmoor. There she stopped briefly, allowing Yoda to relieve himself before they joined the motorway. At one-thirty a.m., and the Citroën's fuel gauge sliding towards empty, she pulled into a twenty-four-hour garage outside Bristol.

With Obe still asleep beside her, Mallory grabbed her Stetson and pulled it down onto her head. She might fetch a few odd looks, but better that than being captured by a CCTV camera. The petrol station bristled with them: four monitored the pumps from the forecourt roof; two more filmed the tarmac outside the main entrance. Inside, there would doubtless be others.

After topping up the tank, she went inside and filled a basket with items – tinned beans, tinned tuna, dog food, bread, milk, bottled water and a huge slab of Galaxy. Before she rejoined the motorway she chugged water from one of the bottles and managed to give the dog a drink, too, an event that soaked both of them.

'We haven't got off to the best of starts,' she told him. 'But I'm willing to give it another shot if you are.' Yoda listened in silence as she delivered her offer, then turned his head to the rear window.

From Bristol Mallory crossed the Severn Bridge and drove for another hour until she reached the Brecon Beacons. Fleeing to the Welsh mountains had not been part of any particular plan, but she knew that their chances of survival – for the next few days, at least – hinged on finding somewhere far from cities, people and electronic eyes.

As the road began to climb, Mallory re-examined the events of the last twenty-four hours, trying to catch all the mistakes she had made. Losing Obe's driving licence had led the Vasi to the sanctuary where the boy worked, but what had led them to the Mên-an-Tol hotel?

Only when she replayed the night's events in detail did she recall her momentary lapse in the hotel bathroom, her sudden impulse to contact Sal. She'd switched on the phone for only a moment before changing her mind; but clearly it had been long enough.

Mallory swore, knuckles whitening on the steering wheel. She'd been exhausted, distraught – traumatised by the violence back in Clapham and consumed by the implications of what the Clearblue test had revealed – but that was no excuse, not after all the effort Sal had invested in preparing her.

Her stomach rolled. She'd eaten nothing since the pancakes at Gollum's. With her teeth she tore open the Galaxy bar and snapped off a chunk.

Ahead, the road narrowed, plunging into a forest of pointed

firs. Two miles in, Mallory saw an unpaved track veer off to the left and pulled onto it.

The Saxo bounced and thumped on its suspension, its headlights illuminating the trunks of close-growing trees. When Mallory spotted an even narrower path branching off the one they were following, she turned the car again, bumping it over the boulders that had pushed up through the soft earth. Parking between two huge Douglas firs, she switched off the engine and doused the lights.

For nearly five hours, the clatter of the Citroën's engine had been a constant companion. Now the mountain silence rushed in, so heavy and unexpected that it was a pressure in Mallory's ears and throat. Not a lick of wind stirred the trees. When she eased down the window, no hint of breeze feathered her skin.

Opening the car door, she let out the dog. Yoda trotted to the nearest trunk, urinating against it before commencing a busy interrogation of their camp.

Hauling her pack onto the seat, Mallory took out a tiny Primus stove, a camp kettle and a couple of fold-out pans. Joining the dog outside, she set up the stove on a patch of flat ground and lit the burner. While some beans were heating, she opened a tin of dog food. She'd never dealt with the stuff before, and wasn't prepared for how badly it stank. 'You *eat* this shit?'

Yoda ignored her, as if insulted by the question.

'Well, I don't have a bowl for you.'

She considered dumping the jellied mess straight onto the needles that littered the forest floor, but it made her queasy to think of him slopping it up, mulch and all. 'You better not have any diseases,' she muttered, squeezing the food into a spare fold-out pan.

Yoda ignored that comment too, but he didn't ignore the offering, guzzling it down with a sound like a rhinoceros wading through mud.

'You,' she said, turning away from the spectacle, 'are the

perfect example of why I never had a pet.' Despite her words, she found the process of tending to him strangely fulfilling. The discovery unsettled her; and when, as she considered it, her hands reached for her belly, she grew even more distressed.

Boiling some water, she made coffee from her small supply. Then she leaned against the car bonnet, canted back her head and gazed up at the night. Here, stars glittered with an intensity that she had never seen in the city.

Looking over her shoulder, Mallory saw that Obe was still asleep, his head angled so far towards the open window that his neck would doubtless be stiff when he woke.

Obadiah.

She knew almost as little about him now as she had done that night three weeks ago in Plymouth; and yet the few things she *had* learned were extraordinary. The world he inhabited seemed almost entirely fantastical. Were the comic books and science fiction movies surrogates for the family he hadn't mentioned, and from whom she suspected he was estranged? Mallory understood better than most the sense of futility that could develop when living in isolation of others. And yet Obe did not seem bitter or bruised by his experience. Neither did he share her cynicism or general misanthropy.

That, in itself, was remarkable enough; but it might just turn out to be one of the least extraordinary things about him. The fact that he had survived his encounter at the sanctuary, and had alerted her to the danger at the hotel, was startling. Even more curious was the *manner* in which he had survived, and the knowledge on which he had drawn to outsmart his pursuers.

She recalled his face, bone pale and grotesque with sweat, just prior to their discovery by the Vasi.

*Killed her*, he had whispered. *The hungry one. Enjoyed it* – fed *off it.*

Mallory grew cold at the memory. Obe could have heard the approach of their Range Rover, and his subconscious might have invented the rest. But there were other possibilities.

Usually, her scepticism would have rejected them without pause. Here, in the depths of this desolate Welsh forest, with moonlight silvering the treetops, it was somehow easier to consider them.

Whatever the explanation for his intuition, she was certain, now, that he was Kusurlu. Everything her parents had taught her, all the stories Sal had passed on, and everything she had read in the books written by her grandfather and the other Arayıcı before him, seemed to confirm it.

For the first time since Cornwall, Mallory's thoughts turned to the busy cluster of cells dividing and subdividing inside her womb. Too early, really, to call the unfolding chemical process a life, too early to *risk* calling it that. She wondered why she felt no protectiveness towards it, no warmth or concern. Had the long years of isolation drained her of what humanity she'd once possessed? She still didn't know why she'd vomited up the pill Pataki had given her. How easy it would have been to knock back the other drugs and wait for the inevitable.

Looking at her watch, she saw that it was past three a.m. Out here in these woods, the heat of the day had long since evaporated. The sun wouldn't rise for another hour and she was starting to shiver. Tossing the dregs of her coffee, she climbed back inside the Saxo. From her rucksack she grabbed her sleeping bag and draped it over her legs. Winding back the seat, she closed her eyes.

Mallory lay like that for over a minute. Then, swearing, she sat up straight, unzipped the bag and opened it out. She tucked one half around Obe before snuggling back down.

A minute later she sat up again. He still lay with his head at an awkward angle to the door. Mallory moved it into a more natural position. After a few seconds, it rolled back. She swore again, louder this time. Once more she readjusted him. Once more, his head rolled away from her and thumped against the door post. Grabbing a fistful of his hair, she yanked it back.

Obe's eyes shot open. He lurched upright, throwing off the

sleeping bag. 'What?' he shouted. 'What's happening?'

Mallory turned away from him, closing her eyes. 'Go to sleep.'

'I *was* asleep.' He was silent for a while. Then: 'What time is it?'

'Late,' she replied. 'Or early. Take your pick.'

'Where's Yoda?'

'This isn't a kennel. He's outside.'

'Where are we?'

'In a wood. On a mountain.'

'Which one?'

'Does it matter?' She rolled her eyes beneath their lids. 'The Black Mountain.'

'We're in Wales?'

'*Dix points.*'

Obe sucked in a breath. Mallory was already beginning to recognise the sounds he made when in pain. She heard him rummaging in his rucksack and, shortly afterwards, the rustle of a cigarette being rolled. Flint scratched against steel, and presently her nose caught the woozy stink of cannabis. She thought about telling him to get out of the car, but she was far too tired to care. The windows were down; she wasn't about to feign concern for the baby.

Beside her, Obe sighed out his smoke. The springs of his seat creaked, his heels scraping against the footwell as he stretched out. For five minutes he sat in silence. Finally, he said, 'Thanks for tucking me in.'

She bristled at that, wondering how he seemed to know, without any apparent effort, the surest way of irritating her. When she didn't respond, he asked, 'Do we have any food?'

'Some.'

'Anything we can give Yoda?'

'I already did.'

'You fed him?'

Mallory opened her eyes. She felt Obe's gaze and tried to ignore it. 'Pedigree in gravy with chicken,' she said. 'Smelled like dead guy in a tin.'

Obe laughed. 'I'll bet he jumped right into that.'

'Washed his face in it.'

She heard the crackle of burning weed and saw the glowing tip of his joint. He blew a deep cloud of smoke out of the window and she watched it drift into the forest. 'How much of that shit do you get through?'

Obe shrugged. 'Depends. If I'm alone, hardly any. If I'm going to be around people, a lot.'

'You're not worried about your health?'

'I *do* this for my health.'

'You know what I mean.'

He sent another ghost chasing through the trees. 'To be honest, I never expected to live long enough for it to be a problem.'

Hearing that, she glanced across at him. He looked calm, contemplative. 'Why not?'

'Death comes quickly in my family.'

She rolled that around in her head. 'Your parents. Are they—'

'We're not talking about them. Not yet,' he said, firmly but with no trace of anger.

'How did you know about the Vasi at the hotel?'

When he glanced over, his eyes were red-rimmed and stoned. 'Vasi?'

Mallory shook her head. 'We're talking about you now, remember? How did you know?'

Obe's eyes swung away. A heaviness seemed to settle upon him. 'People get in my head,' he told her. 'I don't want it. But they do.'

Overhead, the first faint traces of grey were leaching into the sky, a promise of the coming dawn. Mallory drew the flap of sleeping bag closer around her. 'What does that mean?' she asked.

Obe stubbed the butt of his joint against the wing mirror and flicked it into the forest. Crouching over his cigarette papers, he began to load one with the crumbled buds he produced from a metal tin. 'Exactly that.'

'You're a telepath?' she said, after a pause.

He snorted. 'Hardly.'

'Then what?'

Obe twisted the joint into shape, sealing it with his tongue. 'If I was a telepath, I'd be able to send you a thought.'

'You can't?'

He raised an eyebrow at her. 'What am I thinking?'

'I have no idea.'

'See?'

Now it was her turn to snort. 'What, then?'

Obe lit up and took a drag, screwing up his face at the harshness of the smoke. 'I never really explained it to anyone before,' he said. He flicked a glowing lump from the tip of the joint. It arced into the darkness, trailing sparks. 'Imagine, for a second, that people's brains are these big, leaky transmitters. Pumping out not just thoughts but emotions, too. Then, imagine you had a receiver inside your head that tapped into all that. Imagine you couldn't ever turn it off.'

He settled back in his seat and rolled his neck. 'I was seven when it started. My spidey-sense, I called it. Guess I was into comics, even back then. At the beginning it was actually pretty cool, and so subtle that I had some form of control. It involved . . . I don't know . . . *effort*. Like trying to do that Spock thing with your fingers, or rubbing your belly and patting your head. After a while it got easier. Then, too easy. By the time I was twelve . . . well, imagine being in a room full of strangers, all of them screaming their most intimate thoughts. Imagine being surrounded by thirty or forty different transistor radios, all of them with the volume cranked up so high that they're distorting, tossing out every single uncensored thought, emotion or desire their owner was experiencing.'

He grimaced. 'Imagine going to a shopping centre, or a school, or a football match, and those thirty or forty broadcasts swelling until there're two hundred of them. Or four hundred. A thousand. Imagine *experiencing* all those conflicting emotions – like some kind of mental osmosis – because you have no control, you suck everything up; because actually, it's not like you're *listening* to a thousand different broadcasts. It's like you're *living* them.'

The sky had lightened further now, threads of cream laced among the grey. Somewhere in the forest, a blackbird started singing. Moments later, a chaffinch added its voice.

Mallory cocked her head. 'Are you fucking with me?'

Obe massaged the side of his neck, looked over. 'No fucking intended.'

'What you're describing,' she replied. 'It sounds like hell.'

He took another drag, exhaled. 'You see why I can't be around people.'

'I don't even like most of the thoughts rattling around in my *own* head. Let alone having to tune into the bile spewed out by strangers.'

Obe studied her. 'You have a pretty low impression of other people.'

'I have a pretty *realistic* impression of other people.'

He shook his head. 'You're wrong about that, and you're also missing the point. It's not the *quality* I can't handle, it's the sheer quantity. It drowns me out. I can't hear myself; I become something I'm not. An echo, or a shadow. It's . . .' He rolled his tongue around his teeth. 'If you don't find a way to escape it, it floods you. Washes you away a little at a time.'

Mallory said, 'And that's why you smoke.'

'Smoke, drink. Whatever it takes.'

'It can't be doing you any good.'

'Like I said, I never expected to live long.'

'Have you tried medication?'

'As a teenager, I was prescribed every antipsychotic known to man – a walking chemistry experiment. Chlorpromazine, haloperidol, amisulpride, clozapine, quetiapine, risperidone.

Some of that stuff turned me into an extra from *The Walking Dead*, some of it into a suicide waiting to happen. The clozapine was about the only thing that drowned everything out, but after two months it started messing with my bone marrow and I had to come off it. I smoked my first joint at thirteen. After that . . .' He shrugged. 'Every year I'm using more of this stuff, just to keep still. At some point, I guess it'll stop working completely.'

'What'll you do then?'

He smiled. 'Pick up a surfboard. Paddle out.'

Mallory knew that he meant it to be a one-way trip. 'You don't seem particularly worried at the prospect.'

'There's a lot of beauty in the world. I've already seen more than my fair share.'

'You don't actually believe that bullshit, do you?'

He laughed. 'Of course.'

'What beauty?'

'Are you fucking with me?'

'No fucking intended.'

He sat in silence for a while. Then he nodded through the windscreen. 'Look out there.'

'I am.'

'What do you see?'

'I see a Frankenstein dog that looks like it used a Bic to shave its own head.'

'OK, I'll give you that – he's kind of hard to appreciate at first. But I'm not talking about Yoda.'

'The trees?'

'The trees, yeah. But more than that, the forest. What's beyond it; what's above it.'

'You've lost me.'

'Life,' Obe said. 'Creation.'

'Creation?'

'All of this beauty,' he told her. 'You, me, Yoda. The trees. The birdsong. The stars. The dawn. What's there, what isn't.

Every blade of grass. Every insect. Every human being. Every stone, every mountain, every river. Every little hope, every little dream.'

'I thought you couldn't handle the hopes and dreams.'

He stared at her, grinned. 'You *are* fucking with me.'

Mallory looked out of the driver's side window, and suddenly her throat grew tight. Because she *wasn't* fucking with him, not at all. The quiet reverence in his voice as he described the world around him was so incomprehensible that she couldn't begin to relate. It made her unbearably sad.

'I'm sorry,' he muttered. 'I didn't mean to upset you.'

Angry at herself, she continued to stare through the window. 'Can you read *my* thoughts?'

In the glass, Obe's reflection shrugged. 'Sure,' he said. 'I mean, if I wasn't stoned. It's as—'

'*Don't*,' she hissed, twisting around. 'Don't you dare *ever* do that.'

'It's not really something I can turn—'

She grabbed a fistful of his jacket, pinning him against the door. 'I mean it, Obe. If I ever catch you roaming around inside my head – if I ever *suspect* that you've even *tried* – this is *over*, do you understand me?'

He blinked, stared at her. 'This?'

Mallory held his gaze a moment longer than she intended, her anger growing white-hot. Fearing that she would punch him for the second time in a day, she released his jacket and scrabbled at the door. She clambered out and marched across the clearing, booting the propane stove against a tree. Twenty feet into the forest she came to a stop, scrunching her eyes shut, clenching and unclenching her fists.

*All of this beauty. You, me, Yoda. The trees. The birdsong. The stars. The dawn. What's there, what isn't. Every blade of grass. Every insect. Every human being. Every stone, every mountain, every river. Every little hope, every little dream.*

She'd never heard such bullshit.

When Mallory opened her eyes, a ghost of marijuana smoke sailed past her and drifted deeper into the forest.

# THIRTY-SEVEN

Obe watched from the passenger seat, bewildered and dismayed, wondering how anyone could harbour so much rage. When Mallory had woken him by grabbing a handful of his hair – he still hadn't learned why she'd done that – he'd spent the first few minutes trying not to vomit.

Ironic, really, that bile was what he'd sought to avoid, and yet had somehow managed to unleash. He'd kept out of Mallory's head, just about, while the smoke blanketed his overreaching mind, but he'd intruded on her once already, as he'd surfed the waves at Gwynver Beach. The experience had been so distressing that he'd nearly drowned. Never had he encountered such depths of cynicism or despair; until, of course, last night at the Mên-an-Tol Hotel, when he'd blundered upon thoughts so loaded with spite and loathing that they'd practically poisoned him.

In the east, the sky had blushed apricot. Birdsong filled his ears. His entire body ached; he'd been sitting in the car far too long. Opening the passenger door, he swung out his legs and stood. His arched back cracked like a dead twig. Digging in his pocket, he shook out a couple of co-codamol and swallowed them. On the back seat he saw a bag of supplies – presumably stuff that Mallory had picked up during the night. He grabbed a bottle of water and walked over to the propane stove. One of its fold-out legs was bent out of shape, but it looked salvageable. Carefully, he straightened it. Nearby lay an overturned kettle. It was hot, and still had some water sloshing around inside.

'There's coffee,' Mallory said, emerging from the forest with her arms folded. 'It's in my pack.'

'Coffee would be good.'

She moved past him to the car, returning with a mug and a small container, which she tossed down at his feet. He lit the stove and refilled the kettle. Once the water had boiled, he made himself a drink. Even with his senses dulled, he knew that Mallory wanted to clear the air and didn't know how. She observed him, awkward and stiff, transferring her weight from one leg to the other. In the car he'd seen a travel rug. He fetched it from the back seat and spread it on the ground. 'Want to sit?'

Mallory scowled, leaned against a tree.

Obe shrugged. After a moment's pause she unfolded her arms, crossed the clearing and sat on a corner of the rug. 'Want to share that coffee?'

'Sure.' He passed her the mug. 'Want to share something by return?'

'Depends.'

He looked at her. 'Those guys. Back at the sanctuary. Who were they?'

Mallory took a swig of coffee and grimaced. 'Something far worse than you'll come across in a comic book.'

'I figured that.'

'My mother's family called them *kötü*. It means "wicked" or "ungodly".' Mallory paused, looking around the clearing at the trees. '*They* wouldn't recognise that. They've called themselves many things, but the one that's endured the longest is Vasi. It translates as "guardian". An older interpretation is "purifier". Really, though, the meaning's irrelevant. What's important is this: for as long as the Arayıcı and Kusurlu have existed, the Vasi have been trying to destroy them.'

Obe frowned. 'How come?'

'In their eyes, humanity was God's perfect creation. Something to be protected from outside interference. Anyone with the potential to alter it unduly – or otherwise affect its course – was viewed as a corrupting influence, a threat.'

He stared at her, thinking again of the pockmarked stranger at the sanctuary: *Thing is, Obadiah, there's an impurity in you. A form of sickness, if you like.*

For the first time in a while, an image came to him from his childhood: his mother and father at the kitchen table; laid out before them, a knitting needle, a bottle of methadone, a filleting knife and a torch. He shivered, blinking the memory away. Yoda wandered over to the rug and collapsed down beside him. The dog's tail thumped twice against the ground.

Gently, Mallory took the mug, swallowed another sip of coffee and handed it back. 'We Arayıcı – we aren't devils, or succubi, or any other type of monster from folklore. We're not a cult or a coven. We don't drink blood or talk with the dead. Since the beginning, we've served as nothing more than an accelerator pedal for humanity's development. Over the centuries, thanks to the Kusurlu we've sought out, we've brought into the world individuals who have fundamentally changed it. As I said last night, society doesn't follow a linear path. It advances in fits and starts, unique individuals making huge contributions.'

'The beginnings of language,' Obe murmured. 'The invention of writing.'

'Those things were fundamental, yes. But there are more modern examples too. Arayıcı-Kusurlu children have been responsible for everything from evolutionary changes that improved life expectancy, to advances in medicine, science and the arts – even the founding of new belief systems and types of governance. Think of the world's great prophets, philosophers and astronomers; the groundbreaking scientists, artists and engineers. Investigate their backgrounds a little and in many cases – if you knew what to look for – you'd be surprised what you might dig up.'

Obe listened, silent. For the first time he heard something akin to passion in her voice, and it electrified him. He could not peel his eyes from her face. Fortunately, Mallory was too caught up in her monologue to notice.

'Despite the Vasi's successes, killing us off where they could, they saw what was happening – realised that mankind had drifted so far from their ideal that there was no way back. Unfortunately, instead of accepting that, they grew even more extreme. Eventually they convinced themselves that the only solution to Arayıcı-Kusurlu corruption was a modern-day Noah's Flood scenario, a grand reset – wipe out the entire human race and give God – or nature – the opportunity to start again. *Post violentiam, silentium*, as they're known to say.'

A prickle of sensation climbed the ladder of Obe's spine. 'They're a death cult,' he said.

'A global death cult – and one that's extremely well organised. Their resources are almost limitless and they're relentless, too. For the majority of human history there's been a symmetry between our successes and their own. But recently – I mean the last few hundred years or so – the balance has shifted. They've hunted down and killed far more Arayıcı than ever before. Not only that, they've begun to insinuate themselves into power structures the world over: political parties, law enforcement, private enterprise, the military. It's only a matter of time before they manage to unleash Armageddon. That is, unless some miraculous Arayıcı-Kusurlu intervention prevents it.'

Her hands, as she said that, dropped to her belly. Obe wondered if she'd noticed. 'What changed?' he asked. 'What allowed them to kill more of you than before?'

'They killed more of us because they *found* more of us,' Mallory said. 'Our survival's always depended on our ability to remain hidden. We're nomads by nature – there's no Arayıcı society as such. Although you could trace our origins to the Middle East, you'd find no clusters of population there. Our instinct is to wander, to seek out Kusurlu wherever they can be found, and we maintain only the loosest of links to those we leave behind.

'For all that, our Kusurlu interactions have always been incredibly rare. There aren't that many Arayıcı, and even fewer Kusurlu. Plus, they – you – have the unfortunate tendency to self-destruct quite young. Fortunately, most Arayıcı possess the ability to home in on those of us who've fallen pregnant with a Kusurlu child. When you look at the recorded histories of some of humanity's greatest contributors, you'll often find their births were attended by what historians believed were random visitors, unusual strangers; whereas in reality they were other Arayıcı, drawn there to protect the child from Vasi assassins.'

'Drawn there how?'

Mallory shrugged. 'I can't really explain it. Some believe it's divine guidance – God interacting directly with His creation. I don't go along with that. After all, birds migrate thousands of miles using the earth's magnetic field. Sharks can sniff out a single drop of blood in millions of gallons of water, and they say bears can track a scent across huge distances. I think it's something more like that – maybe a particular sensitivity to a hormone we haven't yet discovered. Point is, the moment I fell pregnant it was like firing a signal flare that'll take nine months to burn out. The Vasi can't track us that way, but once they learned of our ability it wasn't hard to exploit: abduct one of our number, break them through torture or brainwashing, and suddenly you've built yourself a low-maintenance Arayıcı bloodhound. I don't know how many of our own they've used against us over the years, but the impact has been brutal.'

The sky had grown even lighter now. Obe yearned for more sleep, and yet Mallory's story was so strange and so troubling that he knew, should he close his eyes, he'd see again the faces of those who had tried to kill him.

He thought of the acne-scarred man who had intercepted him in West Penwith:

*There's an impurity in you. A form of sickness.*

Obe shuddered. Climbed to his feet. Averted his eyes from the spread of dawn's pale fingers through the sky. 'You're telling me that for as long as this pregnancy continues,' he said, 'however far you run – wherever you try to hide . . .'

Mallory nodded. 'If I stay too long in the same place, they'll find me.'

# THIRTY-EIGHT

In the Mên-an-Tol Hotel's ground-floor office, Aylah İncesu watched Teke operate his laptop at a desk surrounded by potted plants. Under the archway that led to the reception desk, Murdina Tremethyk's corpse stared at the ceiling.

Guy Chevry leaned against a nearby wall. He'd found a bag of peanuts in the bar, and was passing the time by tossing them into the dead hotelier's open mouth. The carpet around her head was speckled with his failed attempts.

For twenty minutes they'd searched the headland for Mallory and Obadiah, but Aylah had known they'd stood little chance of finding the couple so soon after losing them. Because of her decision to maintain the Sennen Cove perimeter, most of her resources were further west. She'd believed that the boy was still contained, and yet somehow he and Mallory had hooked up. Aylah still didn't know how they'd managed that; when she found them, she'd take great pleasure in extracting the knowledge. And she *would* find them. In the meantime, she would redistribute her assets, monitor the intelligence and wait for them to make another mistake.

Thankfully, the lancing pain she'd experienced in the hotel bathroom had long since departed. She knew it had no physical source, but its arrival – coming almost immediately after her discovery of Mallory's discarded pregnancy kit – had distressed her greatly. She recalled the way her fingers had reached for her belly; and that inner voice, stricken with grief:

*It could have been you.*

Another peanut bounced off one of Murdina Tremethyk's teeth.

'Cut that out,' Aylah snapped.

Chevry looked up, and for a moment his expression was as blank as a mannequin's. Then, averting his eyes, he balled the bag and put it into his pocket.

'Wrap her up,' she told him. 'Put her in the car. And find that bullet casing.' She turned back to Teke. He'd stopped typing and was reading something on the screen. 'What've you got?'

With a hard-sounding scrape, Murdina Tremethyk slid towards the hotel lobby, hands trailing behind her. Her skirt rucked up, revealing tan nylon tights and sensible grey underwear.

Aylah went to the desk and leaned closer to the laptop. 'Well?'

Teke grunted, glancing around. 'Sorry. This is kind of fascinating.'

'What is it?'

'Obadiah Black. Remember he was classified as tier four by CAMH? I found a scan of the follow-up assessment, held at the hospital where he was first sectioned. It's written by a child psychiatrist – Dr Hillman.'

In the hall, Murdina Tremethyk's head bumped onto a rug. Her knuckles followed. Chevry dropped her ankles and flipped the rug's edge. He began to roll it up, encasing the dead woman like a sausage in a roll.

'Talk,' Aylah said, irritated.

'That news report you came across mentioned his parents' deaths, but not how they died. I hadn't got round to checking out what happened. This—'

'Are you deliberately trying to antagonise me?'

Teke shook his head. He tilted the screen towards her and

scrolled to the top of the page. 'Here,' he said. 'Read it for yourself.'

For a while, the only sound was the hiss of the hallway rug as Chevry dragged it towards the entrance.

Aylah whistled, long and low.

'Keep reading,' Teke said. 'That's nothing compared to what follows.'

The main hotel door banged open. Moments later came a series of dry thuds as Murdina Tremethyk's head, cossetted by the rug in which she'd been swaddled, bounced down the steps.

Inside the office, Aylah licked her lips with a tongue that was suddenly dry. This . . .' she whispered.

'Changes everything?'

When she turned to face him, she noticed how curiously hollow his eyes seemed. For a moment she wondered whether, if she plucked them out, she would reveal a stark black cavity inside his skull; not a brain but a void. The idea made her shiver.

'It's what we always feared,' she said. 'Someone with the potential to change everything. To undo all our work.'

Teke exhaled slowly, his chest settling. 'Strange to find him hiding all the way out here.'

'What was it Richard Dawkins said? "Islands are natural workshops of evolution."'

'Call this an evolution?'

'It's only evolution if it breeds,' she said.

'We need to put a bullet in this guy at the earliest opportunity.'

'No argument from me.'

'But we need to kill her first.'

'Again, no argument.'

Teke sat back in his chair. His eyes still looked like blank holes – windows into a lightless crypt. 'Your sister,' he said.

At that, Aylah felt an unpleasant flicker in her belly, as if a limbless creature, hairless and slick, had shifted in sleep.

Fifteen years had passed since Saul Manco had killed her

parents and offered her a chance to end the world's pain. She had despised him at first. Several times she'd even tried to kill him. But slowly, patiently, he had broken through, sharing with her the Vasi vision of a world relieved of humanity. No grief; no pain. An opportunity for God – or nature – to start again. Over time, the prospect grew too seductive to resist.

*After violence, silence.*

In the last ten years she'd done more to pursue that silence than the entire Vasi network combined; and yet despite her dedication, and the breadth of her achievements, she'd never shaken off the stigma of her Arayıcı roots. Only with her sister's death might she come close.

Standing at the desk, she offered Teke her hand. He kissed it, leaving the faintest gleam of saliva.

'I like you,' she told him. 'More than I should. But if you ever again call her that in my presence, I'll do to you what the little slut did to Levitan back in Clapham.'

Teke's eyes glimmered. A pulse jumped in his neck.

Carefully, she took a handful of his hair and eased back his head. With a fingernail, she exerted gentle pressure on the soft tissue of his throat. Leaning close, she breathed in his ear: 'There'd be so much blood.'

# THIRTY-NINE

In the back garden of his Trentino mountain home, high in the Dolomites near the border with Veneto, Matthais Gurvich beseeched his daughter with eyes that spilled over with sorrow, wretchedness and the most profound regret. In that frozen moment, watching from the trees, Mallory felt every ounce of his love for her – his hopes as well as his myriad terrors; a lifetime of feeling encapsulated in a single look.

'*Run*,' he urged.

Then the man with the slim black cane and long silver hair raised his gun and her father fell dead, his round metal spectacles tumbling into the snow.

A few feet away, in a heap, lay Laleh Gurvich. Mallory could see parts of her mother's head that should have for ever remained secret.

Even this far into the forest, she could smell the richness of *khoresh gheymeh* over the sharp scent of spruce. She wondered who would eat it now that her parents were dead; and then she flinched, shocked that such a ridiculous thought should surface. Even as she castigated herself, the monster she had mistaken for a woodland fairy turned and looked at her, and all thoughts of her mother's cooking bled away.

There was something spider-like about him, something scratchy and cold and altogether merciless. When he smiled,

Mallory felt an almost unbearable dread; it robbed her of strength, drained her of courage. Her life might have ended there, without her ever taking another step, but when his smile slid away and he stepped towards the trees she turned and ran, kicking her way through mounds of frozen needles.

As she raced past the fairy door, she caught herself moaning between snatched breaths: *Fairy friends, come to me, through this door upon this tree; grant my wish and you will see, a good companion I will be.*

Her heart knocked like a fist. This forest, she knew, stretched for many hundreds of miles. Venture too deeply into it and she would never walk out alive.

Behind her came sounds of pursuit.

How long she ran, and what distance she covered, Mallory would never remember. For a while her mind caged itself, operating on instinct rather than conscious thought. By the time she ran out of energy and collapsed to her knees, the sun had ladled its fire liberally over the western peaks. Beneath the trees, the forest was already dark.

It was not a place of silence. Platters of snow shuffled and slid from the upper boughs, landing with hollow-sounding booms. She heard the cries of animals she could not identify and wondered if the men had sent dogs to hunt her down. And then there were bears to think about. Her father had told her about them; brown bears, reintroduced to this forest from Slovenia a few years before she was born. The thought of being ripped apart by one energised her. Somehow, she found her feet and stumbled forwards. She made it only a few yards before she tripped over a tree root and crashed back down.

So cold.

She still wore her mittens – thanks to her father she'd left the house wearing her winter coat, and the mittens had been tucked into the pockets – but her feet, inside her boots, felt like lumps of frozen meat. Despite her woollen leggings, her legs chafed and burned.

Could she survive a night out here? The very idea filled her with terror, but it seemed increasingly likely that she must try. Before sunset, she'd known she was heading south, but she couldn't navigate by starlight.

For the first time since the Vasi had descended on her home, Mallory thought of her sister, and at last her composure dissolved. When she'd ventured downstairs earlier that day, arms clasped around the fairy door, Aylah had been lying on her bed, head cupped and heels knocking together as she flicked through one of her magazines. The girl had made a face, crossing her eyes and blowing out her cheeks. In response, Mallory had pushed her tongue beneath her lower lip and grinned like a bullfrog. They hadn't shared a word of parting, and now they never would.

Tears spilled down her cheeks. 'Oh,' she said. Her voice sounded strange; far older than it should. 'Oh, oh, oh.'

She started to shiver, and found that she could not stop, clutching herself around the shoulders and gasping. When her strength gave out completely, she fell onto her side and drew up her legs. Tucking down her chin, she closed her eyes and prayed for a quick death.

She woke a few hours later to find that her prayers had been ignored. She was colder, now, than she had ever thought possible. The forest was dark, busy with the sound of nocturnal creatures moving about. She could no longer feel her hands, and the thought of frostbite terrified her so much that she wriggled her arms out of her coat sleeves, eased off her mittens and trapped her fingers under her armpits. As they began to thaw they burned as if they'd caught fire, and she found herself in tears again: huge, wracking sobs that could not be contained.

It would have been so easy to have lain there, to have given up, but she realised, abruptly, that was exactly what the Vasi wanted. Somehow, she got a foot underneath her. Minutes later, another. Using every dirty word and filthy phrase she'd ever overheard, she pushed herself up.

Ahead, the moon was a white light between the trees. The air was so frigid that it seared her throat, pluming like steam when she exhaled. Her belly ached with hunger; her face felt as if a frozen brick had been pressed to it.

In the end, with nothing else to guide her, Mallory followed the moon. She tried to tune out the sounds of the forest: the hoots, the shrieks, the thump of falling snow. She tried, too, not to dwell on any of the dark stories she had read: of goblins, trolls, shape-shifters and worse. Her parents were dead. She was a child no longer.

A sister no longer.

She thought, again, of Aylah. Of the stupid face the girl had pulled, as if their encounter had been nothing special, a momentary interaction from many thousands to come. If Mallory had stepped into the bedroom and asked Aylah to come into the forest to plant the fairy door, would her sister have agreed? Would her life have been saved?

She saw herself again, standing on the threshold. This time, rather than pulling a face, she reached out a hand. On the bed, Aylah's face sagged. Flesh, as runny as egg yolk, slid off bone, revealing a cold white skull. The girl's blank eye sockets were accusatory, terrible.

'I'm sorry,' Mallory moaned. 'I'm so sorry.'

Believing that she could walk no longer, that the biting cold would swallow her up and the snow would smother her, she emerged, stumbling, from the trees and found that the moon, or perhaps her own primeval compass, had brought her full circle.

Before her stood the chalet she'd once called home. Its windows were black mirrors, liquid and aware. All the warmth the building had contained, all the safety it had offered, had leached away. The Vasi had left it standing, but had plundered it of something far more important than timber or stone.

The back door hung on one hinge like a broken jaw. In the centre of the lawn, on a patch of blackened grass from which the surrounding snow had receded, a leaning tepee of sticks sloughed off thin black cords of smoke.

Fingers trapped beneath her armpits, Mallory approached.

*Don't look. You'll never forget it if you do.*

But she had to look.

*Fairy friends, come to me, through this door upon this tree; grant my wish and you will see, a good companion I will be.*

A childish petition like that had no place here. Had no power here.

As Mallory neared the edge of the fire pit, she saw that the smoking bundle of sticks and ash had been people.

Her breath trailed out. She turned away and trudged towards the chalet, her nose filled with the stink. At the bottom step her strength gave out, forcing her to climb on all fours.

The kitchen still smelled of lime juice and stewing meat, but it couldn't mask the horrors outside.

'*Aylah?*' Mallory whispered, pulling herself to her feet. She cleared her voice and tried again. 'Aylah.'

The house breathed its silence.

Stepping deeper into the kitchen, she reached for the light switch. It would announce her presence to anyone watching the place, but right now the darkness felt like her most immediate enemy. She flicked the switch and the room blazed. Retreating to the broken door, she closed it as best she could.

From the kitchen she crept to the hall. Here, a wandering blood slick marred the wooden floor. Mallory fetched her father's coat from a peg, and was about to lay it over the stain when she caught his scent on the fabric. She wrapped herself in it instead, stepping over the blood.

In the living room she turned on more lights. Here, she found further evidence of struggle. No blood, this time, but an overturned chair and, on the floor, a copy of Homer's *Odyssey*, its dust jacket torn. Mallory picked up the book and laid it on a side table.

By the far wall stood the cast-iron stove, now cold. Opening the door, she loaded it with kindling, balled newspaper and three fat logs. With a match from the pot, she lit it. The orange flames spread quickly. The kindling began to crackle.

Trying to avoid thoughts of her parents, and the way the fire in the garden had consumed them, Mallory curled on the floor and swore to herself that she would survive.

When Obe woke, the sun had climbed above the trees. For a moment, his body stiff and numb, he thought he had slipped out of the chalet's living room and returned to the forested slopes of the Dolomites.

But the air, here, was warm enough; his breath didn't steam; his hands didn't burn. When he looked around he saw the Citroën, its tyres sunk deep into the soil. Mallory lay on the blanket beside him. She muttered something inside her dream, her forehead creasing.

Obe, fingers shaking, retrieved his tobacco tin and rolled himself a joint. The rasp of his lighter echoed among the trees. He took a long drag, studying Mallory more closely. This time he reached out, hovering his hand above her cheek, but after a moment he closed his fingers.

Inside his head, he saw again the horror of those blackened sticks, sloughing off smoke.

He stood up. Went to the car. Climbed behind the wheel and closed the door. Silent, he kept watch. His mind led him towards thoughts of his own father, his own mother.

As best he could, he steered it away.

# FORTY

Forty-eight hours after the incident at Godrevy Head, Aylah İncesu checked into the Peterson Court Hotel just outside Brecon.

Despite the earlier loss of her targets, it felt like she was growing ever closer to a successful interception. In Ealing, she had missed Mallory by minutes. In Cornwall, the couple had escaped after intuiting her arrival. Back then, it had seemed like mere bad luck. What she'd learned since, via the psychiatrist reports Teke had unearthed, suggested otherwise.

Earlier that morning she'd driven to Cheltenham, where she'd visited the Georgian townhouse home of Dr Harry J. Hillman, one of the many clinicians who had treated the young Obadiah Black. Hillman's reports had revealed a willingness to document the bizarre that most of his contemporaries had appeared to lack. Using forged credentials as cover, Aylah interviewed him in his first-floor living room. The white-haired and neatly goateed doctor was pensive and soft-spoken, pausing to choose his words precisely before he answered each question. He struck Aylah, even in his retirement, as unusually perceptive, and her dislike for him grew with every moment she spent in his company. Hillman waved away the disclosure order when she tried to present it, and appeared not the slightest bit interested when she quoted the

Terrorism Prevention and Investigation Measures Act.

'I don't care if you suspect Obadiah of stealing a nuclear weapon and threatening to detonate it,' he said, 'nor whatever godforsaken statute you're quoting. If I believe your questions are unwarranted, I'll protect my patient's confidentiality.'

'By telling me what I need to know,' Aylah said, 'you might help me protect him from himself.'

The doctor steepled his fingers. 'That would, of course, require me to believe you had his best interests at heart.'

'Or the interests of those he may seek to harm.'

Hillman collapsed the steeple and smoothed his immaculately groomed goatee. 'You'd have a hard time convincing me that Obadiah intends to harm anyone.'

Aylah wished, at that moment, that she'd brought Chevry along. Perhaps, with an electric iron pressed to his face, the doctor would have been less confrontational. Instead, she drew a sheaf of papers from her bag and laid them on the coffee table. 'In this brave new world of guns and bombs,' she told him, 'restricted information is far easier to procure than it once was. I've already read your reports. I just want to discuss some of the detail.'

Hillman sat up a little straighter at that. He put on a pair of gold-framed spectacles, his hawk eyes studying her more closely. 'What *exactly* is it that you hope to discover?'

'You called him Obadiah.'

'Yes.'

'Over the course of your career, how many patients have you treated?'

'I couldn't say. Hundreds, certainly. Far too many to count.'

'And yet, without any prompting whatsoever, you remember Obadiah Black: a patient you saw . . . what? Nearly a decade ago?'

Hillman stared at her, unblinking. His chest expanded a little as he breathed. 'Obadiah was what you might call a singular case.'

'How so?'

'You've read my reports.'

Aylah inclined her head. 'You were careful to avoid inflammatory language, even if you were a little more honest with your observations than your peers.'

'If I'd been any more honest, I'd have been a laughing stock.'

'Why? What you allege . . . if it actually occurred—'

'—which I assure you it did—'

'—would have made you famous, would have been one of the greatest ever discoveries of medical science.'

'Obadiah Black wasn't a *discovery*. He was a deeply traumatised boy who desperately needed my help. Admittedly, I documented our earliest sessions more honestly than was prudent, but that was because I had no idea, at first, of what he could do. In later sessions I deliberately played down the significance of what was happening.'

'You mean there was more?'

'By the time I became involved,' Hillman said, 'the boy was very unwell indeed. Further, he'd just lost both parents, in quite tragic and extraordinary circumstances. My role wasn't to bring him to the attention of the wider world. It was to help him convalesce.'

'And how did you do that?'

'Slowly. Very slowly. In the beginning, as I'm sure you're aware, Obadiah was hardly a willing patient. For him, understandably, confinement in a hospital was the most unimaginable torture. He wasn't just dealing with his own trauma; he was *living* the trauma of all those around him.'

'You might as well say it, Doctor. You believed the boy was telepathic.'

Hillman shook his head. 'Not in the classic sense. Obadiah never planted a thought in my mind, nor in anyone else's from what I could see. The traffic, if you like, appeared to be strictly one-way. He couldn't broadcast but he could receive. What's more, he had no filter; no ability to switch off that part of his mind, which is why interning him at the hospital – certainly one that was state-run and horribly over-capacity – was a quite monstrous mistake. I finally managed to get him moved to a smaller unit. After that, my involvement with the boy ended.'

'And your curiosity simply died?'

'By then I had something else to worry about, far closer to home.'

'What could compete with that?'

Hillman glanced through the window at the leafy square it overlooked. 'My wife,' he said. 'She was diagnosed with cancer at about the same time.'

Aylah nodded, suddenly noticing the room's dearth of photographs. There were no pictures of children; no images of Hillman, either in later life or as a young man. On his index finger he wore a gold wedding band.

When she looked up, he said, 'If we find love once in this life, we should count ourselves blessed.'

Somehow she managed not to tell him how empty she found those words. 'Talk to me about the boy's father. And everything you know about his death.'

Aylah remained with the doctor for another hour. Afterwards, she left his house as quickly as she could. That Hillman would choose to assist such an obvious abomination as Obadiah Black filled her with revulsion. The urge to fetch a knife and serve him justice had been overwhelming; only a monumental effort of self-restraint contained her.

Outside, sitting in her car, she drew the blade of her *qama* across her arm more than a dozen times before she could stop. After bandaging the wound, she put her Lexus into gear and was about to drive away when her phone rang. It was Teke.

'A Citroën Saxo was reported stolen from Godrevy Head last night,' he told her. 'ANPR picked it up on the M5 to Bristol. It stopped at a service station, and I've got a snap of the driver going inside to pay. It's definitely Mallory, even though she tried to hide her face. Afterwards she crossed the Severn Bridge into Wales and turned north towards the Brecon Beacons.'

'She's gone to ground.'

'Yeah. And in terms of manpower, the Beacons are far harder to lock down.'

Aylah mused on that. 'We've got time on our side, at least. She's Arayıcı and she's pregnant – if she holes up anywhere too long I'll be able to find her. Book me a room somewhere close. Somewhere with good road links.' Her fingers tightened on the wheel. 'We'll reel her in, Teke. I promise. And when we do we'll kill them both; stop this thing dead before it gets out of hand.'

Aylah switched on her satnav, programming it for Cardiff.

*We're coming for you, little sister,* she thought. *And the more difficult you make it, the longer you'll scream when I cut that maggot out of you.*

# FORTY-ONE

They remained in the forest for three days and nights. Thanks to the food Mallory had purchased they didn't go hungry, even if their diet was severely restricted. Yoda led them to a brook that supplemented their supplies of bottled water. In the boot of the Saxo they found a tarpaulin from which they made a simple shelter.

No one stumbled across their camp. Except for the occasional aircraft passing overhead, hardly any evidence of humanity intruded. Once, on the second day, they heard a 4x4 coming along the main forest road. Mallory snatched up her knife and Obe grabbed their packs, but the vehicle did not stop, and they never caught sight of it through the trees.

With little else to do, she listened to Obe talk. Much to her surprise, she sometimes found herself contributing. Their conversations never veered too closely towards dangerous topics – as if, independently, they'd reached the conclusion that this was a time for calm.

On the second day, Mallory took out the books she had rescued from her Clapham home. The first, authored by her grandfather, was a handwritten history that covered seventeen generations on her mother's side. Arayıcı families were matri-archal by nature, and Mallory's had been no different. Although the work had been written in Arabic, she had translated every page, inserting into each chapter a set of folded notes.

The second tome was by a Balliol College professor named Patrick Beckett. Beckett's academic field had been philology, but he'd possessed a passion for creation myths and associated folklore, and over the years his investigations had led him to stories of the Arayıcı, finding references to their history in sources thought for ever lost. While for Beckett the book was a work of folkloric reference, for Mallory it was a treatise on her wider ancestry.

As she busied herself outside, replacing the stove's gas canister and boiling water for coffee, Obe retreated to the Saxo's passenger seat and immersed himself. Several times, over the next few hours, she looked through the windscreen and saw only the top of his head as he bent over his reading.

Later that night, as they sat on their blanket, she asked him for his impressions.

For perhaps five minutes Obe didn't reply. Finally, he said, 'We think we know the world. And really we know nothing at all.'

It wasn't much of an answer but he wouldn't elucidate – and sat beside her for most of the night wearing a contemplative half-smile, his attention on the stars.

On the third day, with their rations reduced to a single packet of habanero moose jerky, they packed up their camp and drove the Saxo deeper into the forest, where they abandoned it. Mallory donned her Stetson and Obe donned his baseball cap, and with Yoda at their heels they emerged onto the main forest road and headed north, thumbs hunting for a ride.

Some hours later, a farmer they'd flagged down dropped them at a motorhome dealership just outside Builth Wells. Using most of Mallory's remaining cash, Obe haggled hard for a dilapidated Renault Trafic with two hundred thousand miles on the clock. While he possessed a unique advantage when it came to negotiation, his skill did not come without cost

– for the rest of that day a migraine-like pain crippled him.

The motorhome was thirty years old and smelled like the inside of a chicken coop, but it'd been fitted with a sink, a two-ring gas stove and a grill; its rear seats could be configured into a double bed or two singles. That first afternoon, they drove eighty miles west and checked into a campsite on the Pembrokeshire coast. After three days living in the woods, Mallory craved hot water and soap. 'Plus,' she told Obe, 'you stink. By that I don't just mean you smell unpleasant. What's rolling off you is biblical.'

They bought food in the campsite shop and, after scrubbing themselves raw in the shower block, retreated to the Renault where Mallory cooked a meal of canned hotdog sausages and burger buns. The food sent Yoda into paroxysms of ecstasy.

By then, Obe had started to look very ill indeed. The campsite wasn't full, but their pitch was surrounded by tents and other motorhomes. Mallory could see that he'd reached the limit of his defences. She returned to the shop and bought him a six-pack of Heineken, which he drank one after another until a little colour returned to his cheeks. Afterwards, they lay down on their individual beds and slept.

The next morning they left at first light. It took four hours to reach Birmingham, and from there they headed north towards the Peak District. That afternoon, passing through felted foothills that looked like they had been stitched together from the bolts of a seamstress's cloth, their road took them along the edge of a broad shelf of land. They crossed a bridge over a fast-flowing river, and when Mallory spotted a track winding down from the main road, she pulled onto it. The gradient was almost too steep for the Renault's brakes, but the vehicle slipped and skidded to the bottom without incident. There, the track surrendered to tufted grass. A hundred feet above them, the river spilled over a precipice in a white waterfall, crashing onto rocks before sliding away in a winding channel. The gorge walls protected the camper van from the wind and shielded it from the road.

As the sun began to set, the summer heather blazed. Mallory cooked more sausages, which they ate with the last of the buns. Afterwards, Obe angled two deckchairs in front of the falls and rolled himself a joint. He'd been smoking most of the day, Professor Beckett's book propped on his lap.

Returning from the riverbank with a flat stone, Mallory sat beside him and began to sharpen her knife. Yoda prowled the surrounding bushes, snarling at butterflies and thrusting his snout into anything that interested him.

'You think we're safe here?' Obe asked.

'You're the mind-reader.'

'Trying not to be.'

'How's that working?'

Watching the waterfall, he exhaled smoke. 'Place like this, with only you around, it's not so bad.'

She tensed at that, a coldness erupting along her spine. 'I told you, Obe. You'd better not be dig—'

'Hey,' he said, flicking the joint with his thumbnail and ejecting a cherry-red ember. 'Hang loose and serve chilled, right? You think I'm smoking this out of choice?'

She inspected his tobacco tin. 'What happens when you run out?'

Obe shrugged. 'I'll come up with something.'

'Are you always this optimistic?'

He laughed. 'The basis of optimism is sheer terror.'

'Is that another superhero quote?'

'Actually, I think it's Oscar Wilde.'

Mallory fell silent. For a while, the only sound between them was the soft roar of water and the steady scrape of steel against stone. 'Every time we stop for too long, they'll get a fix on me.'

'So we need to keep moving.'

She nodded. 'Money's growing tight.'

'I have savings.'

'No you don't.'

'Not a vast sum, admittedly, but I've—'

'Trust me,' Mallory said. 'Anything you had in the bank, you can forget it. The moment they worked out who you were, it was gone.' She paused. 'What've you got in your pockets?'

Obe pulled out his wallet and rifled through it. 'Five pounds. And a book token.'

'That, right there, is the sum of your buying power.'

He blinked. 'Man. How much do you have?'

Mallory pulled out her money clip and counted the notes. 'Three hundred and sixty pounds. On top of that I have a few credit cards in different names. Hopefully they aren't all compromised.' She ran her knife blade against the stone and thought about how much longer the money would last if she was alone.

In his deckchair, Obe shifted restlessly. 'Do you have to do that?'

'Do what?'

'The whole psycho-sharpening-her-knife act.'

'It's not an act.'

He raised an eyebrow. 'You're really a psycho?'

'I'm really sharpening my knife.' She lifted it, allowing the last traces of sunlight to wink off its blade. 'Want to feel how sharp?'

Obe grimaced. 'You *are* a psycho.'

Her barked laugh shocked them both. She reared away from him as if bitten.

'Whoa,' Obe said. 'Dude. What was *that*?'

Mallory jumped up so fast that her deckchair heeled away, clattering against the Renault's side panel. Blood rushed into her face. Embarrassed without understanding why, she marched away to the river. At the bank she sat down, trembling, and waited for her heart to slow. After a few minutes, Yoda slunk over. 'Get lost, you stinking damned beast,' she hissed, waving him off. Mallory remained beside the water, flinging stones into its depths, and as shadows crept from the gorge walls and lay flat upon the land, she began to realise why her laughter had so dismayed her: for the first time, she had caught herself relaxing into Obe's company. Now, more than any time in her life, she could not afford to lose her edge, nor the distance from others she had maintained for so long. Neither could she travel with him much longer. She didn't dislike his company; she'd surprised herself, over the last five days, with the extent of her tolerance. Never, in adulthood, had she spent such a prolonged period with another human being. She had even begun to feel a vague sense of responsibility for him. When the time to part arrived, she would do her best to leave him well-equipped. But that time had to be soon.

Yoda, as if sensing that the worst of her anger had dissipated, brushed against her arm. Mallory reached out and rubbed his hairless scalp, wrinkling her nose at his stench. She found a stick and played with him for a while before hurling it into the river. He dived in, swimming out to fetch it. She doubted he would smell much better when he returned, but it was worth a shot. When he emerged, stick clamped in his jaws, he shook himself dry all over her, and when she yelled with irritation she heard Obe chuckling in his chair, and that made her fume even more. She strode back to the van, boiled a kettle and made herself tea. With no milk, she drank it black, and didn't offer Obe a cup.

By the time she returned outside, he'd fallen asleep, and it struck her just how fragile he seemed. Five days earlier at Sennen Cove, he had practically fizzed with life; his muscles firm, his skin glossy and tanned, his eyes shining with humour and intelligence. Right now, he looked like he'd aged thirty years. His eye sockets were dark; his flesh sagged on his bones. Even his hair look tangled and dry. From the van, Mallory grabbed the rug they'd brought from Wales, tucking it around him before retiring to her bed. Lying on her back, she closed her eyes and rested her hands on her belly.

It was now June. By the time she gave birth – if she survived long enough – it would be February. Could she keep up this pace for eight months? Her reserves of cash wouldn't last more than a few weeks. At some point soon, she'd have to risk using the credit cards.

Outside, night fell. The stars descended, a silent audience. Somewhere out there, the Vasi were searching for her.

# FORTY-TWO

They camped beside the waterfall for another two nights. Sunday morning, they filled the Renault's fuel tank and meandered north along country roads. In the market town of Skipton they found a budget supermarket and stocked up on food, picking up a few clothes in the neighbouring shops. After that they headed north once again, chasing the river Wharfe.

Too stoned to drive, Obe sat in the passenger seat as Mallory piloted the van across the Yorkshire Dales. The countryside rolled and swelled around them, segmented by ancient hedgerows and crumbling stone walls. Vast oaks, their trunks clotted with dark ivy, spread their canopies across the road. At sunset, Mallory parked behind one of them and took Yoda for a walk. Cooped up for so long, the dog was desperate to run off his energy. He caught sticks, barked at rabbits, slobbered and bounded.

'He's a different dog,' she remarked.

Smiling, Obe nodded. 'We're the first real family he's had.'

That evening, after a simple meal of pasta and pesto, they sat outside and watched the stars. 'Going to have to ration myself,' he said, poking around in his tobacco tin. 'Otherwise I'll run out pretty soon.'

'What happens then?'

'Still working on that. I can't keep you out of my head for long without it.'

She looked at him sharply. 'I told you, Obe—'

'There's no off switch,' he replied, his voice low. 'I can't control it. If I could, do you really think I'd pry on you?' He shook his head, disappearing inside the van.

Alone, surrounded by the dark beauty of the Yorkshire sky, Mallory found herself wishing that she hadn't snapped at him.

They stayed in the Dales for another three days, tucking them-selves away wherever they could. Thursday evening, returning from another long walk with Yoda, Mallory said, 'We need to address the money situation.'

'What's our current total?'

'Do you still have that five pound note?'

He nodded, laughed.

'Combined, we have a grand total of two hundred and seventy-five pounds.' She took out her credit cards and cycled through the stack. 'Hopefully, the Vasi won't have traced all these, but we've got to assume that they have, which means they're strictly one-use. There're six cards, nearly all with five-hundred pound daily cash limits. That means we're looking at a haul of anywhere between zero and three thousand pounds.'

'Whoop,' Obe said. 'Travelling money.'

Mallory looked up at him, and wondered, for just a moment, how much better it would be to remain with him a while longer. It was a foolish thought, one she dismissed almost immediately. 'We haven't got it yet,' she told him. 'That's the hard part.'

'What's the plan?'

'I saw plenty of cashpoints back in Skipton. Plenty of CCTV cameras too. They already know what we look like, so getting snapped is hardly a problem, but we can't afford to let them connect us to the Renault. We'll go back tomorrow first thing, when you're not too stoned, and find somewhere to park. I'll go to the cashpoint, you'll stay in the van, ready to drive us out of there the moment I get back.'

'Bomb diggity.'

Mallory scowled, but her heart wasn't really in it.

That night, as a hunter's moon sailed overhead, the day's heat hung close to the land. They'd parked near to the river, and Obe used the opportunity to change into his board shorts and take a swim. He returned looking fresher than he had done in days. His skin had lost its ashen cast and his eyes were bright and clear. He went to his narrow bed and lay down on his stomach, turning his head to the window.

Mallory perched opposite, cradling a cup of tea. Her eyes, lingering on the muscles of Obe's back and shoulders, spotted something she hadn't noticed before: below his neck, a series of raised white circles spelled out the letter *B*. Beside the marks stood a small triangle of identical marks.

Water still dripped from his hair, creating a lazy river that trickled down his spine and formed a shallow lake in the hollow of his back. For ten minutes he lay unmoving, his breathing so slow and measured that she thought he was asleep. When he turned his head and looked at her, her cheeks burned with sudden heat.

'OK?' he asked, his voice thick.

Mallory swallowed. 'Uh-huh.'

'What's up?'

She shrugged, gripping her mug far too tightly. Peeling away a hand, she pointed at the scar tissue on his back. 'What's that? It almost looks like some kind of message.'

Obe glanced over his shoulder, nodded. 'I guess a message is exactly what it was.'

'Meaning?'

He flashed her a pained smile. 'My dad was having a bad day. I kind of got in the way of it.'

'He *did* that to you?'

'With a cigar. He was intending to write BAD, I think. Or

maybe BAD BOY. He managed to complete the B and most of the A before I got away.'

'You're . . .' She blinked, sat up straight. 'Are you kidding me?'

'Nope. The old man had style, though. He branded me with a Hoyo de Monterrey double corona, which I hear is a pretty fine Cuban smoke.' Obe turned onto his side, supporting his head with his hand. 'Dad was . . . he was like me, I guess. People got in his head. He drank pretty heavily to control it. Bit by bit, the drink stopped working.'

Mallory realised that she was holding her breath. She exhaled in a rush, filling her lungs with air that tasted sour. 'Is he still alive?'

'No.'

'What happened?'

'Bad stuff,' Obe said. 'Sad stuff.'

'Want to elaborate?'

'Not really. Not right now.' Turning away, he fell silent once more. Mallory didn't take her eyes off him, rolling his words around in her head.

The next morning they retraced their steps to Skipton. Obe parked on the outskirts while Mallory walked a roundabout route to the high street. Outside a branch of Barclays she inserted the first of her six credit cards into a machine, tapped in the PIN and glanced at her watch. She wondered if any of the electronic communications her actions had triggered were being monitored. If the Vasi had cracked her fake IDs, her location would be known within seconds.

In front of her, the machine chugged and whirred. She stared at the security camera's lens. An older woman, towing a two-wheeled shopping trolley, joined the queue behind her. The ATM's screen turned blue and a message appeared:

We are sorry we are unable to process your transaction at this time. Please contact your bank.

Mallory's skin prickled. Her stomach contracted; a sharp stone. She clicked her fingernails against the reader slot, waiting for the return of her card, but when the screen returned to its generic welcome message, she realised that the machine had swallowed it.

How they had uncovered the fake ID, she could not begin to guess. She knew that right now the machine's location was being flagged, certainly with a time-stamp, possibly with footage taken by its security camera. Quickly, she inserted her second card. This time the machine took longer to process the details, but the outcome was the same: a short message asking her to contact her bank.

Her third and fourth cards were swallowed. The fifth allowed her to withdraw five hundred pounds and the sixth disappeared without paying out. Mallory aimed her middle finger at the camera. Tucking the cash into her back pocket, she retraced her steps to the van. 'One out of six,' she muttered, climbing in and slamming the door.

'Better than nothing,' Obe replied, accelerating away.

'Do you have to be so fucking optimistic?'

'You know what they say—'

'No, I don't. And I don't want to.'

'Well, we've got around six hundred pounds. That's a lot more than we had this—'

'Obe, seriously. What's wrong with you?' She twisted around in her seat and stared at him. 'Do you *really* not get it? I'm six weeks pregnant. I've got another thirty-four weeks in front of me, with those lunatics trying to hunt me down. Thirty-four *weeks*, Obe, and all I've got in the world is six hundred pounds and a shitty, stinking camper van that sounds like its engine is about to blow up.'

'It's one hundred and six miles to the Lakes, we've got a full tank of gas, half a pack of cigarettes, it's light and we're not wearing sunglasses,' Obe said.

'I don't even know what that means.'

'Well, I changed some of it. It's from *The Blues Brothers*. The Dan Aykroyd speech. You're supposed to say, "Hit it."'

'I can't do this any more.'

'Do what?'

Mallory shook her head. Resting her elbows on her knees, cupping her head in her hands, she felt the hot sting of tears. That made her anger burn so fiercely that she almost made him stop the van so she could get out.

They drove in silence for the next ten minutes. Then, without warning, Obe yanked the vehicle over to the side of the road, barely bringing it to a stop before he flung open his door and jumped out. Mallory sat up straight, watching him lean over a dry-stone wall and begin to vomit.

She climbed from the van and walked over, arms folded. 'You need me to drive?'

Obe wiped his mouth, nodded.

'What's up?'

'I . . . I caught some of that.'

'What?'

He peered across the dry-stone wall, unable to meet her gaze. Taking out his tobacco tin, he began to roll a joint. 'Your anger . . .' He bent over, dry-retched, recovered himself. 'Some of it spilled over.'

Mallory watched, her heart thumping hard in her chest. 'My *anger* spilled over?'

With shaking hands, he sealed the joint and lit it, taking a drag and blowing blue smoke across the fields. 'I'm sorry.'

Stunned by his admission, she had no words, retreating to the Renault and climbing behind the wheel. She sat there, silent, while Obe finished his smoke. When he returned to the van, she started the engine and pulled back onto the road.

*Some of it spilled over.*

Were her emotions so toxic that Obe's experience of them had made him physically *sick*? If that were true it demanded scrutiny, even if she wouldn't like the answers.

★ ★ ★

For the rest of that morning, they travelled along the narrow, twisting roads strung between the hamlets that dotted the Dales. They ate lunch while driving – cheeseburgers from a roadside van. By early afternoon they reached the Lake District. As the sunlight began to fade, they found a campsite near Coniston Water and took turns to visit the showers.

That night, Mallory dreamed that unseen hands were restraining her while someone used the butt of a cigar to brand *BAD GIRL* into her back. She woke three times, always with the stink of burnt flesh in her nostrils. Every time she fell back asleep the dream found her again.

At dawn, she woke to rain drumming on the Renault's roof, and knew, without doubt, that the time to leave Obe had finally arrived.

# FORTY-THREE

Thursday morning, Aylah İncesu found herself across a desk from Gavin Duke inside a lopsided caravan that had been converted to a ramshackle office. Outside, above a ring of sad-looking vehicles around a gravelled track, a flapping canvas banner read: *DUKE'S MOTORHOMES AND CARAVAN SALES.*

'—couldn't believe it when I saw the paper,' Duke was saying. 'They seemed like nice folks. Young, really, to be buying a motorhome, but we get all sorts. These days, way things are, lot of people are cashing in their chips and doing something different. We've only got one life, after all.'

Aylah slid two photographs across the desk. 'And you're sure this is them?'

'Aye,' Duke said. 'Recognised them from the paper, I did. Is all that stuff true? About what they're saying they've done?'

'Yes,' Aylah replied. 'It's true.'

Two weeks had passed since the near-miss at Godrevy Head. They'd traced the stolen Citroën Saxo to a point just south of the Brecon Beacons, after which it had vanished. Aylah had remained in the region for three days before her Arayıcı instincts called her east.

Thanks to a subterfuge orchestrated by Teke, and implemented by Vasi converts in the police and intelligence services, detectives investigating the disappearance of Murdina Tremethyk were now seeking Mallory and Obadiah in connection. A few days earlier, a national media campaign had launched. Already, the couple's photographs were everywhere. By degrees, the noose was tightening.

'What did you sell them?' Aylah asked.

Duke opened a drawer, took out a sheaf of papers and handed them over. 'Cheapest thing I had – Renault Trafic I picked up last year in a part-exchange and couldn't shift. That boy of yours beat me down on it, even so. There was . . . something about him. Something about both of them, actually.'

The paperwork included an image of a cream-coloured motorhome with a flaking green strip along the side. Rust had sprouted from its wheel arches. 'Will this thing go?'

'Oh, aye. Might leave a slick of oil if it's parked up for more'n a few days, but it'll be around a while yet. Two hundred thousand on the clock, and it'll likely do that again before it packs up.' Duke rubbed his hands on his shirt, as if the paperwork had somehow tainted his skin. 'You think that woman in Cornwall's really dead?' he asked. 'Murdered? I mean, they hardly seemed capable of—'

'Her blood was all over the hotel carpet.'

'Still—'

'Pieces of her brain, too.'

Duke swallowed, his eyes widening. That part hadn't been on TV.

Back in the car, Aylah called Teke and supplied him with the Renault's details. 'Find it,' she said. 'And if you can't do that, make it famous.'

A day earlier, Mallory had attempted to extract cash from a machine in the Yorkshire Dales. Clearly the girl was using national parks as hiding places, moving on before Aylah could get a fix. So far, the strategy had worked.

No longer.

Teke phoned back within ten minutes. 'Everything points to the Lakes,' he said.

# FORTY-FOUR

Obe woke to silence. Not just inside the motorhome, but inside his head. He blinked, sat up straight, wincing as bright pain flared behind his eyes. His stomach flopped, greasy and loose.

The weather had turned overnight. Outside, rainclouds like immense grey warships slid low across the land, wetting everything they touched. Beyond the campsite's perimeter, Coniston Water had darkened to indigo. Wind chopped and diced its surface.

The temperature inside the van was noticeably chilly. Obe fumbled for his T-shirt and pulled it on. By the rear doors, Yoda stood with his front paws against the glass.

Mallory's bed was empty. Obe supposed she was taking a shower. Her towel was gone, along with her small collection of grooming products. He looked at his watch, surprised to see that it was past nine; he'd slept far later than usual. Odd, really, that Yoda hadn't woken him. Usually, by now, the dog was gnawing at his ankles, demanding to be let out for his toilet. Perhaps Mallory had attended to that. If so, he was grateful. In the last two weeks of close-living, his headaches and nausea had intensified. He'd dramatically upped his intake of cannabis to compensate. Last night, hoping to keep Mallory's dreams from intruding, he'd self-medicated with a half-litre bottle of vodka picked up from the campsite shop; right now, his mouth tasted like something had crawled into it and died.

In the driver's door cavity he found a can of Coke Zero, popped the tab and chugged it. His stomach gripped, but he managed – after a belch – to hold the drink down. Pulling on his trainers, he shrugged his arms into a hoodie. Had he eaten anything last night? He couldn't remember. Aside from the Coke, his stomach felt empty.

'What kind of mood was she in?' he asked.

Yoda glanced over at him.

'That bad, huh?'

Frowning, Obe noticed that Mallory's rucksack had gone. Almost immediately, he noticed something else: he couldn't see any of her stuff. Lots of the everyday items they'd bought since their escape from Godrevy Head had disappeared too.

On the stove, propped against the kettle, was a folded sheet of notepaper torn from a journal. His name was written on it, underlined in violent pen strokes.

A curious feeling came over him: as if a wall of water was rushing at his back. He tensed his shoulders, set his jaw. He knew what the note was going to say before he unfolded it: perhaps not the exact words, but the message.

> Obe,
>    I've gone. Wasn't an easy decision but it's the right one. If I can offer any advice – stay out of sight for as long as possible. In seven months, this'll be over. If I succeed they'll have no further interest in you.
>    Good luck.

Bizarrely, the discovery that she hadn't even signed her name hurt him more than the message's content. She'd excised him clinically, like a splinter from her flesh, making no reference to their two weeks together, nor any of the experiences they'd shared. Was she really that dispassionate? That *brutal*? He'd stayed out of her head as best he could – not merely because he'd promised but because of how disturbingly bleak he'd found the experience. She was, without doubt, the most isolated and fatalistic human being he'd ever met.

Beside the note, she'd placed the motorhome keys and a pile of money. Obe picked up the cash and counted it out. She'd left him exactly half their combined funds.

'You're crazy,' he muttered. 'Totally nuts.'

By the camper's rear doors, Yoda whined.

'Dude, not you.'

Obe balled up the note. He clapped his palms against his legs, filled his lungs.

Although Mallory had taken the toothpaste and the shampoo, she'd left him a dispenser bottle of liquid soap they'd lifted from a garage washroom a few days earlier. He picked it up, along with a towel. After locking Yoda inside the van, he slouched across the site to the shower block.

*I've gone. Wasn't an easy decision but it's the right one.*

He suspected that her decision had been a lot easier than she was letting on. Her single-mindedness – her refusal to bow to pressure or take the easy option – was unmatched. If she believed that leaving him was the right thing to do, she would. And she had.

In the shower stall, Obe was so focused on his predicament that for a while the thoughts of others who shared the facilities barely registered. Their emotions affected him, even so. As he stood beneath the shower head, massaging his scalp with liquid soap, he soaked them up like blotting paper: irritation, anxiety, sadness, disgust, envy, amusement, satisfaction, pride, hope. All those feelings could have been responses to his own situation, but among such noise it grew increasingly difficult to identify himself. Then, all too fast, streams of individual thought began to break through.

*—point-of-it-keeps-going-on-time-and-time-again—*
 *—fifty-no-forty-five-in-six-hours-and-that'll-crack—*
  *—tonight-as-soon-as-the-door's-shut-keeping-it-in-the-fr—*
   *—is it?-wAY-TO-GET-SOME—*
    *—LITTLE-BITCH-IS-GOING-TO-FEEL-*
      *WHEN—*
      *—ALWAYS-LIKE-IT-WAN**T-SOME-OF***
      ***THAT-AGAIN-HOW-MU—***

'Stop,' Obe moaned. 'Just stop.'

Like an orchestra responding to an aberrant conductor, their thoughts and emotions swelled in defiance of his plea. They filled him, overwhelmed him, pressed him down; and suddenly he wasn't standing beneath the shower head but curled in a ball on the cold tiles, shoulder clamped to one ear, hand pressed against the other. It made no difference, and he'd been a fool to think it would. He panted for breath, tried to focus on a single thought that would drown out all others.

*In seven months, this'll be over.*

He didn't have seven months. Not living like this. At the back of his throat he tasted last night's vodka. Poison, just like the slow accumulation of crap that was building in his lungs. For the first time in his life, he felt a sense of futility so crushing that it threatened to obliterate him. Despite the hot water and the steam, his teeth began to chatter. His body began to shake.

*Maybe I'm dying*, he thought. And found, with some surprise, that he did not much care.

By eight a.m., Mallory had walked six miles to Skelwith Bridge. From there she left the road and walked east, following the river Brathay towards Clappersgate, at the northernmost end of Windemere. It was a wet morning, and the air was heavy with moisture. The town stood a few miles south-east. From there she hoped to hitch a lift towards Keswick, and finally to the motorway that would take her north towards Scotland. With such meagre funds to sustain her, she would guard against every unnecessary expense. Despite the speckling rain, at least it was still midsummer. In her backpack she carried a lightweight sleeping bag and bivvy. They would serve her tolerably for a while.

Even as she thought it, she knew she deceived herself. By the end of September she'd be four and a half months pregnant. She needed a better plan than sleeping rough. By bequeathing the motorhome to Obe, she'd made her own task far more difficult; but she owed him something; felt duty-bound to give him the best chance she could.

Even though she'd left him only a few hours earlier, Mallory already missed him. All morning, she'd had only herself for company; the sudden contrast had made her realise just how tedious – and how joyless – that company could be. Usually, by now, Obe would have said at least a handful of things to amuse, irritate or confound her. Instead, her only distraction was bird-song. No left-field observations on life. No indecipherable sayings.

*Never wrestle a pig*, he'd told her a day earlier. *You both get dirty and the pig likes it.* At the time, she'd shaken her head and rolled her eyes. She still couldn't understand it. *The early bird gets the worm, but the second mouse gets the cheese.* At least that one had been a little more obvious.

Grimacing, Mallory adjusted the straps on her pack. The next seven months were beginning to look unbearably bleak. In Ambleside, on Church Street, she found a café and ordered a fried breakfast. Grabbing a newspaper from the counter, she slid into a window booth. Outside, a Land Rover rumbled past, towing a sleek white motor launch. The pavement bustled with hikers and tourists, most of them wrapped in bright waterproofs. Unfolding the newspaper, Mallory read the headline and saw two photographs: one of Obe, and one of herself.

Aylah İncesu reached the Lake District on Friday morning, checking into a hotel on Keswick's main street. Teke had chosen the place for its road links: the A591 south led straight to

Windermere; the A66 offered routes east and west.

It would take time to search the region's many campsites, and there was no guarantee that her targets would be found that way – the national park covered nine hundred square miles, offering plenty of places to hide a solitary motorhome. Still, thanks to the media campaign the couple would be taking a risk every time they tried to move; and if they holed up too long, Aylah would latch onto Mallory's trail as surely as a hound rooting out a fox.

That afternoon, Teke joined her at the hotel. In the evening, a larger contingent arrived: Saul Manco and his entourage, including Caleb Klein and the two men she'd taken to Obadiah's flat in Sennen Cove – Ali Irmak and Nik Pavri. There were twelve of them in total, and they took over eight different rooms, plugging in laptops and mobile phones and all kinds of other electronics. Under Manco's supervision, Caleb liaised with Vasi contacts in the police and the National Crime Agency. It was a snub to Aylah's authority noticeable by everyone who witnessed it; and it made her seethe with resentment even as it intensified her desire to locate Mallory and eviscerate her. Perhaps, she reflected early on Saturday morning, that had been Manco's aim. One thing she knew without doubt: she would never command the Vasi's full respect until her sister lay dead, severing the last links to her Arayıcı heritage.

At eight-thirty a.m., two hours after she woke, Teke burst into the room, mobile phone clamped to his ear. 'Got a sighting,' he said. 'Sounds like it's legit.'

# FORTY-FIVE

Twenty minutes after discovering the note, Obe was on the road.

Earlier, curled on the shower stall floor, he had felt that the journey was over – that his time with Mallory had ended and that he would never see her again – but somehow he'd managed to drag himself back to the Renault and climb behind the wheel. A horrific chorus of voices babbled in his head, growing more insistent with each minute that passed. What he needed was a joint, but he dared not allow himself that. If he stood any chance of finding her, he needed a clear mind. She'd given herself at least an hour's head start; she could be a hundred miles away already, at any point on the compass.

From Coniston Obe drove north-east, aiming for the main thoroughfare that bisected the Lakes. Traffic was heavy, and tourists were everywhere. Within ten minutes, his head was thumping so badly that his vision swam, the view through the windscreen becoming kaleidoscopic. From all around he caught bright snatches of thought, as dazzling as sunlight reflected off silver.

—*good-night-lAST-**NIGHT-WISH**-COLIn-would*—
—*if-we-don't-she-doeSN'T-**SAYS-SHE**-DOes-but-
she*—

*—find-it-iN-THE-MOR**NING-CAFÉ**-HAVEN't-been-*
   *or-have—*
   *—of-it-siCK-O**F-IT-SICK-**OF-IT-SIck-of—*
   *—pay-mE-**THAT**-IF-SHe—*
   *—if-I-call-or-ma**YBE-EMAIL-DON**'T-*
   *KNOW-can't—*

Those voices didn't relent, and for Obe, negotiating the
winding streets, it was like trying to calculate a complex formula
while strangers screamed out random numbers. He soaked up
not just thoughts but emotions, too, so many that his guts
twisted like a rubber band and his blood sang with adrenalin.
Several times he clipped the side of the van against a verge or
protruding stone wall. At a crossroads, he nearly mowed down
a pedestrian. At a roundabout, braking too late, he almost
ploughed into another vehicle. Through it all he hunted for any
evidence – any thought – of a grim-faced girl in a chocolate-
brown Stetson.

Rain spotted the windscreen, fat languorous drops that
promised an imminent downpour. Obe switched on the wipers
and immediately regretted it, watching as they smeared grease
and pollen across the glass. He swerved to avoid an oncoming
truck

   *—tWAT-**CAN'T-DRIVE**-WHAT-IS-he-do—*

   and his left-side wheels bumped up onto the pavement

   *—the-PUS**HCHAIR-OH-MY GOD-H**E'S-GOIng-*
   *to—*

before crashing back down. He hunched forward, saw that the
inside of the glass was fogging up too, daren't take his eyes off
the road to put on the heater, and used his sleeve to polish a
clean circle through which he could peer.

In front, a black van slowed to let some walkers cross the road.

Obe braked violently, foot jammed against the pedal. The front tyres shrieked, the motorhome yo-yoing on its suspension. He wiped sweat from his forehead, dried his hand on his jeans. The black van pulled away. Yoda swung his head around, giving Obe a long look.

'I know, buddy. I know.'

He accelerated, his vision skittering so acutely that it felt like he was looking at a zoetrope. When he turned his head he saw five dogs sitting beside him, rotating around a sixth. All of them looked anxious.

The village surrendered to hedgerows flanked by trees. The green foliage was so vivid that it stung his brain. A tractor trundled towards him, taking up more than half the road.

Obe slowed to walking speed, eyes fixed

*—sure-like-the-radio-said-diRTY-OLD-RENAULT-TRAFIC-THE-**COUPLE-IN-THE-PAPER-MUST-BE-LIKE**-FOR-THEM-WONDER-IF-ALI-HAS-FINished-cutting-the—*

on the farmer as he squeezed past. He wanted to pull over and throw up, find a river or lake and plunge his head beneath the surface. The clamour inside his head had become unbearable, but he couldn't stop. Mallory might think that she was better off without him but it wasn't true.

Mallory.

Mallory. Mallory.

Her name elongated in his head. Pealed like a bell. Dissolved into a chant devoid of context or meaning. Ahead, the road swung abruptly right, passing over a squat stone bridge with just enough room for two cars. Obe tried to think of where he could be. He passed a manicured green and a row of stone townhouses. When the road narrowed to a single lane, traffic began to slow. Shops appeared, interspersed by restaurants and hotels. People were everywhere, jostling and dodging past each other on the pavement.

> —running-out-agAIN-**BUT**-ENough-to-last-the-week-if—
> —nice-dress-but-I-COU**LDN'T**-GET-Away-with-that—
> —Jesus-Christ-those-lEG**S-LEGS**-LEgs-skirt-barely-covers-her—
> —last-that-loNG-IF-ON**LY-HE-**COULD-don't-think-Obe-would—
> —asking-directions-aS-IF-**HE**-KNows-what-he's talking—
> —mummY-UNFAIR-**ALWAYS-I-**WANTED-IT-She-nev—

As if a string had been pulled taut inside his spine, he sat up straight, tried to backtrack. Among the images and thoughts, he'd sensed a colour that felt different to the rest.

Obe braked hard, or thought he did; somehow his foot slammed down on the accelerator instead. The Renault lurched forwards, its engine rattling, and when Obe saw that he was about to plough through a group of cyclists he whipped the wheel to the left. The front tyre burst as it hit the kerb. The van bounced up, directly towards a cast-iron pillar box. With a hollow bang and a crunch of glass, the front grille folded, throwing Obe forwards in his seat. Beside him, in a scrabble of claws, Yoda struck the dash and rebounded. All around them, tourists slowed and stared.

> —guy-DOING-**HE-LO**OKS-Like-shit-Jesus-kind-of-id—
> —too-fast-enough-sPAC**E-T**HEY-Should-really-ban—
> —my-hand-because-it'**S-BUSY-AND-**SHE'S-going-to—

—looks-liKE-THE-**SAME-AS-T**HE-ONE-On-the-
news-this—
—call-THE-POL**ICE-BE**CAUSE-THat-guy-looks
just-like—

Obe gripped the steering wheel. Panted for breath. The faces around him melted, becoming a liquid montage. He slammed his fists against the horn. It cut through the chatter, silencing the voices for a moment before they flooded back.

Opening the driver's door, he stumbled into road. '*Mallory!*' he yelled. '*MALLORY!*'

# FORTY-SIX

Driven by Guy Chevry at the head of a small convoy of vehicles, Aylah İncesu headed south. The sighting had been at a campsite on the west flank of Coniston Water – to reach it they would head for the northern tip of Windermere before veering south-west. They passed a long body of water, which Teke's tablet told her was Thirlmere. On the left the land rose steeply, colonised by thick forest. Slate-coloured clouds swarmed overhead. Raindrops cracked against the windscreen.

When they reached Grasmere the road bunched up, turning east and chasing the River Rothay to where it flowed into Rydal Water. Aylah braced herself as Chevry bumped across a mini roundabout without slowing.

'Local police are going to beat us to it,' Teke said. On an earpiece, he was listening to updates in real time. 'Once they're in custody, it won't be easy getting them out, even with Manco's contacts. Not after the story we've been seeding.'

'Let's concentrate on catching them first.'

They hit the one-way system and slowed to a crawl. Cars queued along the street, nose to bumper, pedestrians threading between them. 'Something's up,' Aylah said. 'This isn't just holiday traffic.'

Beside her, Chevry hammered the horn, generating hostile

looks from those streaming past. Aylah wound down the window and stuck out her head. They inched past a junction, where another snarl of traffic merged from the left. Directly ahead the road split, and she saw that the right-hand fork was causing the problems. Some distance along it, a decrepit-looking camper van had collided with a pillar box. A crowd was gathering around it. 'Stop the car,' she told Chevy. 'Now!'

Aylah dived out before the vehicle had fully braked, catching her clothing against the running board and almost dragging herself beneath the rear wheels. Finding her feet, she sprinted towards the crowd. Behind her she heard car doors opening, more Vasi joining the pursuit. As she ran she felt her side-holster chafing beneath her jacket, but there was no way she could risk using a firearm here.

She reached the back of the crowd and pushed into it.

Chevry flanked her. 'Out of the *way*!' he bellowed, shoving people aside when they didn't move fast enough. With his assistance, Aylah forced her way to the front. The vehicle – a Renault Trafic – sagged on its suspension as if drunk. Its front doors hung open.

'Where are they?' she shouted, scanning the crowd. 'Where did they go?'

Alarmed by her urgency, the nearest spectators flinched away.

Shaking with adrenalin, Aylah began to bark orders at her team.

When Mallory heard the horn blast and her name being called from outside, her first instinct was to duck down from the window. Along the café's far wall, a corridor offered access to the customer toilets, from which she could escape to the back alley that served this row of shops. She pulled her rucksack off the booth seat and slung her arms into it. When she heard her name called again, she recognised the voice – Obe's – and could hardly believe it.

Lifting her head, she saw the Renault Trafic bumped up onto the pavement, a line of traffic halted behind it. A group of walkers had clustered around the driver's door.

The café owner appeared, wiping his hands on his apron. 'What's going on, do you think?'

Mallory heard Yoda barking, heard Obe bellow her name a third time. His voice sounded wrong, not at all like the person she had known.

She turned her head, glancing at the route out before returning her attention to the Renault. 'You stupid, stubborn bastard,' she hissed.

The man beside her flinched. 'What'd I say?'

Ignoring him, Mallory jumped up. She could see Obe, now, hunched over in the road, his cherry-red cast braced against his chest. Yoda stood guard beside him, teeth bared and hackles raised, lunging at anyone who got close.

'Stupid, stubborn, reckless *bastard*,' Mallory repeated.

Unable to believe what she was doing, she went to the café's door, yanked it open and strode out into the street. Obe looked shocking, bloodshot eyes rolling in his head, skin as grey as ash. He seemed *stretched*, somehow, as if his flesh had lost its elasticity. It was so good to see him.

He bellowed her name again, and the desperation in his voice tightened her chest. 'I'm here,' she shouted, running towards him. 'I'm right here.'

On the Renault's passenger seat lay his rucksack. Mallory scooped it out. Then she pushed her way through the press of tourists to Obe's side and looped her hands beneath his armpits. 'You just don't get it,' she told him, hauling him up. 'The two of us – it's not going to work.'

'In my head,' he slurred. 'All of them. In here with me. Can't find myself. Don't know where to look.'

Putting her lips close to his ear, she said, 'Then stop trying. Hold onto me. Don't worry about anything else.' She slung his good arm across her shoulders, supporting him around the waist.

'You need some help?' someone asked.

Mallory shook her head. 'He's my boyfriend. I can look after him.'

Turning Obe around, she guided him in the direction she had come, along a row of cars waiting to pass. The first was an MPV driven by a sunburned guy in his forties, a woman beside him and three boys on the back seats. Behind that was a 4x4 towing a caravan. Mallory shuffled past, only half-listening to Obe's moans.

Behind the caravan was a Volkswagen Lupo GTi painted a lurid green. A teenage boy, with ginger hair and a Manchester United shirt, hung out of the window on the driver's side.

Mallory dragged Obe towards the car. 'My friend's in a bad way,' she said. 'Fifty quid if you get us out of here right now.'

The teenager's Adam's apple bobbed. His eyes flicked over Obe, then Yoda. 'That your dog?'

'Yeah.'

'He don't look friendly.'

'Eighty quid,' Mallory said.

The boy stroked his chin, as if the soft down that grew upon it was a luxuriant beard. He craned his head, examining the crowd still gathered around the wrecked Renault. 'Are you trouble?'

Mallory shook her head.

'Stick your boyfriend in the back with that wolf. Make sure it don't bite.' He tapped the seat beside him. 'You sit up here, with me.'

She opened the passenger door, cranked forward the seat and ushered Obe and Yoda into the back. Then she clambered in.

Beside her, the youth looped the steering wheel with the palm of his hand and performed a screeching three-point turn. 'She'll do nought to sixty in eight seconds,' he said. 'That's faster than a Golf.'

Mallory nodded. 'Excellent.'

The raindrops bursting against the windscreen became a sudden deluge. On either side of the street, tourists backed into doorways, throwing up hoods and umbrellas. The Volkswagen accelerated.

'Lance,' the boy said, winding up his window.

'Thanks for helping us out.'

'And you are?'

'Grateful.'

Lance locked eyes with her for a moment before returning his attention to the road. From the door cavity he retrieved a pack of Marlboro, pulling out a cigarette with his teeth. 'Smoke?'

'No. Thank you.' She paused, glanced out of the rear window, then examined him once again. 'You want to earn some real money?'

Aylah pushed her way through the crowd, wanting to draw her gun and knowing that she couldn't. With the wrecked camper blocking one half of the road, and the abandoned Vasi vehicles blocking the other, a long stream of traffic was already building in both directions.

'Clear the street!' she shouted, turning to her team. 'Get these damned cars moving!'

As she jogged past a line of stationary vehicles, a sunburned guy in a Ford S-Max waved her over. 'You looking for that dickhead and his girlfriend?' he asked.

# FORTY-SEVEN

An hour and a half later they reached Lancaster, avoiding the motorway in favour of less travelled roads. As Lance squeezed the Volkswagen into a parking spot near the station, Mallory unclipped her belt and twisted around. On the back seat, Obe lay with his cheek pressed against the window. His eyes were open, but when she waved her hand in front of them he didn't blink or flinch. Hauling his rucksack onto her lap, she dug through it for his tobacco tin. 'You know how to roll a joint?' she asked Lance.

'Sure.'

She handed him the tin. 'My boyfriend needs a smoke.'

Lance nodded. 'If you two ever split up,' he said, pulling a cigarette paper from its pack, 'I do a bit of DJing. At the Bootleggers over in Kendal. You can catch my set most Fridays.'

'Great. You have a phone on you?'

'Samsung Galaxy. Latest one. Top spec.'

'Mind if I use it? I'll be really quick.'

He handed it over and Mallory got out of the car. She made two brief calls, keeping an eye out for CCTV.

Inside the train station she bought two tickets, using nearly all of their remaining funds. Travelling so publicly was reckless, but they needed to go south, and fast. Right now, taking risks seemed like their only option. Earlier that morning she'd convinced herself that Obe could survive without her. Now, to her consternation, she admitted that he wouldn't. The sight of him hunched over in the road, so ill that he could barely see, knowing that despite her abandonment of him he'd refused to let her go, had affected her deeply, but she had no time to process the feelings he'd stirred.

When she returned to the car, Obe was sitting up in the passenger seat, smoking the joint Lance had rolled. His eyes were red, his expression hazy, but at least he looked human. 'How're you doing?' she asked.

He vented smoke. 'Better for seeing you.' After a pause, he added: 'You came back.'

'You didn't give me much choice.'

'Could've left me there. Made a clean break.'

Mallory wrinkled her nose. 'Yeah. But where's the fun in that?'

He shrugged. 'I guess we probably have a few things left to argue about.'

'I guess you're right.'

'Are we fucked?'

'Moderately fucked,' she told him.

'Do we have a plan?'

'A shitty plan. Destined for failure.'

'I can't wait to hear it.'

'Can you walk?'

'Like an old man.'

'How's your head?'

'Feels like mine again.'

'I'm not sure if that's a good thing.'

He smiled. 'Me neither.'

Mallory leaned into the car. She passed Lance a fold of money. 'There's more there than we agreed. I'm hoping it might convince you to forget about us.'

★ ★ ★

They took a Virgin train to Euston, arriving in London two and a half hours later. Mallory made Obe wear his baseball cap, and kept the brim of her Stetson angled low. To avoid the underground they took a cab to Waterloo, grabbing drinks and filled rolls from one of the concessions. At two p.m. they boarded their next train. This one was a stopping service; every time it pulled into a station Mallory checked the concourse for police. They rolled through Surrey and then Hampshire. A guard came into their carriage and checked their tickets, but he didn't make eye contact, and seemed keen to get away from Yoda as quickly as possible.

With Obe asleep beside her, Mallory used the time to check their finances. All they had left was enough for one night at a hotel and a good dinner, or a few weeks of groceries. She wouldn't waste the last of their cash on accommodation, especially after their encounter at Godrevy Head. Tonight they'd be sleeping outdoors for the first time since the Welsh forest. Nine days earlier the weather had been ideal, but right now it was far less accommodating. Beyond the window, the land looked sodden. Above it, dark clouds flickered with lightning.

Clanking and rattling, the train pulled into Weymouth. Mallory roused Obe, grabbed Yoda's lead and led them off the carriage.

Rain was sheeting down outside. They took shelter beneath the station's overhanging roof, but Mallory quickly began to grow uncomfortable. Nearby, several CCTV cameras monitored the entrance, and she'd already seen one police car loop around the roundabout.

'Well,' Obe said, 'there's always the pub.'

Despite their limited funds, it wasn't a bad idea. Five minutes later, in a low-ceilinged lounge bar surrounded by horse brasses and rough-hewn oak, they convened around a small table, nursing a couple of Coronas. Yoda lay on the carpet between them.

'They knew about the motorhome,' Obe said. 'I caught a

thought – random guy driving a tractor. He recognised it from the news.'

'Your face is everywhere,' Mallory told him. 'The picture they've got of me isn't great, but they've got a whole trove of images for you.'

Obe grimaced. 'The sanctuary website. I'm plastered all over it.'

She tilted her head, examining him critically. 'Beard's coming along, though. I don't think you should shave.'

'I won't.' He glanced towards the bar, where the landlord was flicking through the *Racing Post*. 'You think we're safe in here?'

'We're not safe anywhere, Obe. Not until this is done.'

By the time they ventured outside, the rain had reduced to a light drizzle. They walked along the esplanade, where they bought fish and chips before cutting back inland. It took them thirty minutes to reach Wyke Regis. From there they followed the beach road. With the light fading from the sky, they arrived at the eighteen-mile stretch of Chesil Beach. Obe crunched across the shingle, found a piece of driftwood and entertained Yoda with a game of fetch. 'Wish I had my board,' he said. 'Not that there's much surf.'

Mallory looked at the rain-speckled water. 'You miss it. Don't you?'

'Out there,' he told her, 'it's one big silence. Just me, the ocean, a few fish. Can't remember the last time I went so long without it.'

'You might have to abstain a while yet.'

'Yeah,' he said. 'I figured.'

Night fell. Shrouded by cloud, the moon cast no lantern upon the sea. Mallory dug inside her rucksack, retrieving her sleeping bag and bivvy. She put up a makeshift shelter, listening to the rain crackle off the nylon.

Westward, far out to sea, a solitary boat cut a white line across the water. Watching its prow bump against the incoming swell, she said, 'Where we're going, I can't protect you. I can't guarantee anything at all.'

'That's not why I'm here,' Obe replied.

As the boat grew closer she heard its engine, a faint thrumming that ebbed and flowed on the wind. 'Why *are* you here?'

He shrugged. 'Where else would I be?'

Out to sea, the vessel changed its heading, aiming directly towards the beach. A spotlight winked on, sweeping the beach. Within a few moments its beam found them.

Mallory stowed the sleeping bag and bivvy in her rucksack. Jumping up, she walked down the shingle to the water's edge. As its engine died, the boat glided towards the shore in silence. A man sat at the stern, wrapped in a bright yellow oilskin. In the darkness his dreadlocks looked like hanging snakes. 'Just like I told you,' he said, leaping over the side and wading through the surf. 'Interesting shit.'

'Hello, Gollum,' she replied.

# FORTY-eight

With Yoda crouched between his legs, Obe watched the lights of Dorset's coastline recede and begin wink out. A few miles from shore the swell was higher, pitching *The Heart of Gold* in a motion that was balletic, hypnotic. Towards the bow, Mallory lay asleep inside her bivvy.

At last the rain eased off. The clouds separated, revealing a black swathe of sky. Far off to the east, an oil tanker crept towards Southampton. Obe drank a coffee, poured for him by his friend. Afterwards he exchanged the empty mug for a joint and took a hit, exhaling a cloud of smoke that the wind whipped away.

'Dude,' Gollum said.

'I hear you.'

'You know what they're saying about you both?'

'Can't imagine it's good.'

'It's total bullshit, is what it is. You OK?'

'I guess. It's been kind of hairy.'

Gollum glanced at the sleeping bag in which Mallory huddled. 'You know what you're getting into?'

'Just about.'

'Is she worth it?'

Obe nodded. 'Totally.'

★ ★ ★

From Chesil Beach it was sixty miles to the French coast. At ten knots, allowing for drift, the crossing would take around six hours. They shared the task of piloting *The Heart of Gold*, regularly checking their progress on Gollum's marine GPS.

In the milk light of dawn, the sea grew calmer. As they drew close to land, they saw many more vessels carving its surface: cargo ships, passenger ferries, fishing trawlers and pleasure craft. Gollum steered a quiet path among them. He did not head for Cherbourg's port, source of most of the traffic. Instead he aimed for one of the sandy beaches further west. There, the land rose from the sea at a gentle gradient, the low tide exposing a myriad of rocky obstacles. Obe was grateful for the light: in darkness their route would have been treacherous.

He woke Mallory with a mug of coffee. She knuckled away her tiredness, eyes on the French coast as it hove into view. 'Didn't think I'd sleep.'

'I'm glad that you did.'

'Are you stoned?'

'Pretty much.'

'How's your head?'

'Mellow, I guess.'

She nodded, scrunching up her face as she examined him.

Gollum eased back on the throttle. Adjoined by flat farmland, the beach was deserted. The breakers were barely a foot in height, dissolving into lazy clatters of foam. When *The Heart of Gold* nudged against the sand, Obe jumped over the side, trainers around his neck. Yoda followed, splashing enthusiastically, then Mallory.

Gollum handed them their packs, heavy with all the items they had requested: a two-man tent, an extra sleeping bag, food, water, additional gas canisters, dog bowls. Last of all the man handed Mallory a leather wallet. 'Two thousand euros, as requested.'

She slipped it into her pocket. 'We'll get this back to you.'

'I'm easy either way.'

'What's your plan now?'

'Pick up some fuel, bag myself a hotel. I'll probably head back tomorrow.'

'Take care of yourself.'

Gollum winked. 'Hang loose and serve chilled.'

'No idea what that means.'

'Instructions for a happy life.'

'If you say so, surfer man.'

Obe stepped forward, feeling with sudden certainty that this was the last time he'd see his friend. They shared their old handshake, then embraced. 'Watch yourself, Sméagol.'

'Good luck, Obi-Wan.'

Bracing his feet, Obe shoved the boat back into the water. Gollum fired up the engine and swung the vessel around. With a final wave he chugged east towards Cherbourg's port.

'He'll be OK,' Mallory said. 'You don't need to worry.' She lifted her hand and for a moment he thought she intended to touch him. Instead, she tugged down on her rucksack's straps. 'Let's go.'

That day they walked twenty-two miles, finding a campsite near the Cap de Carteret, with views of the Channel Islands to the west. By the time they erected their tent they were too weary to talk, and after a meal of tinned ravioli and French bread they crawled into their bags and slept. In the morning, they stowed their gear and set off once again. All that week they headed south, following Normandy's western coast until it reached the Couesnon estuary. Half a mile out, upon salt flats flooded each tide, they saw the granite outcrop of Mont Saint-Michel, and the walled commune that perched precariously upon it.

A day later, three weeks after she'd hauled Obe from the surf on Gwynver Beach near the tip of Land's End, Mallory introduced him to Sal.

# FORTY-NINE

They met inside the eleventh-century abbey, three hundred feet above the surrounding sea. Earlier that morning, they'd kennelled Yoda at the tourist facilities before crossing the man-made causeway that linked the island to the mainland. Even at that time of day the thoroughfare was busy: shuttle buses packed with tourists zipped back and forth along its raised strip. The rain had returned, lending the medieval architecture a foreboding grimness.

Gollum had refilled Obe's tobacco tin with cannabis before he left them, but Mallory asked the boy to abstain until later in the day. As they pushed through the crowds she saw the effect of her request in the ashen cast of his skin.

Inside the commune walls, they wound up through narrow streets to the monastery, and from there climbed the many steps to the Benedictine abbey at the top.

They found Sal sitting on a pew in the nave, his attention on the vast Gothic choir lit by morning sun streaming through the stained-glass windows. Mallory felt a pang of emotion when she saw him but she steeled herself against it, anticipating his reaction should she display any weakness. With Obe at her side, she sat down directly behind her old mentor.

For a minute or more, Sal did nothing to acknowledge her presence. Finally, just as she was about to lean forward and touch his arm, he turned around and scowled.

Years had passed since their last meeting. She was unprepared for how old he looked. His hair – once oily and black – had dried out with age, receding from his temples and feathering to grey. His face had developed deep trenches. Out of it his nose blossomed like some immense fleshy gall, pitted with pores and mapped by broken capillaries. His Middle Eastern eyes, bracketed by waspish eyebrows that had grown together to form a single thatch, remained inscrutable.

Age had not robbed him of his strength. Under a sun-faded black blazer and starched black shirt, his arms bulged with muscle. He sat stiff and straight, and Mallory felt certain that he carried a weapon under his clothes: not his favoured *kilij* or *yatagan*, but perhaps a *kard* or even a revolver. He smelled of aniseed and tobacco, a combination that dragged her fifteen years into the past.

After a moment's examination he swivelled on his pew, his attention returning to the choir. '*Merhaba*,' he muttered. His voice rasped: the scrape of leather against stone.

'*Merhaba*?' Mallory repeated, staring at his back. 'After all this time, that's how you greet me?'

'You want me to dance a *kolbasti*? I'm here, aren't I? Mistakes you've made, you're lucky to be alive. Look at the fat on you. Like a staggering Damascus cow, full of cream.'

'Bullshit,' she snapped. 'I've put on barely two pounds since we parted.'

Sal twisted around once again, his expression sour. 'Better greet your uncle now, before you drop dead of a heart attack.'

'Uncle. Ugh. Don't call yourself that.'

Mallory stared at him and he stared back. Finally his eyes narrowed and he laughed, a guttural bark. In response she leaned over the pew and kissed him, his cheek rough against her lips. Then, unable to help herself, she wrapped her arms around his neck and pulled him close, only half swallowing the sob that rose in her throat.

Sal tensed. He patted her arm, squeezed it. 'Show some spine,' he muttered, in a gentler tone than she had expected. 'I taught you to be strong.'

'I *am* strong.'

'You'll need to be.'

'This is Obe,' she said, pulling away. 'Obe, this is Salih Sabahattin Hazinedar.'

Sal peered at the boy, his eyebrows bunching. 'You're sure he's Kusurlu? He looks . . . unremarkable.' After a moment, he added, 'I don't mean any offence.'

'None taken,' Obe muttered.

Mallory looked around the nave. 'A hill-top monastery in a fortified town, with only one way in or out. Interesting choice of venue.'

Sal grunted. 'You gave me about a minute to suggest a meeting place we could both find, talking in a code I could barely understand. What did you expect? I've never even been to France. You're lucky I could name a single north-coast location.' He stood up abruptly, knees popping like champagne corks. 'I wasn't followed. You're safe, the pair of you, at least until you step back onto the mainland. So stop complaining and let's go and have some lunch.'

They ate at the hotel La Mère Poulard, where Sal had booked rooms. Over omelettes and red wine, he recounted news of his village in the Köroğlu Mountains, near the Turkish province of Bolu. It was the place Mallory had gone after her parents' deaths, and though her memories of it were bleak, she listened with fondness to his stories.

Once the plates had been cleared, and glasses of pastis had been ordered, Sal dispensed with the small talk. 'What's special about him?' he asked, thrusting his jaw towards Obe. 'What makes this more than just a drunken humping that got out of hand?'

Mallory glowered. 'I should slap you for saying that.'

'Instead, tell me how you met.'

With flushed cheeks, she explained how she'd left Clapham on one of her random excursions, arriving in Plymouth on the same day as Obe's visit and ending up, later that night, in the same bed.

Sal listened without comment. Then he threw back his head and laughed.

'All your life, you swore this wouldn't happen. Said you'd keep your legs closed and ignore your Arayıcı blood, that you'd defy the call when it came. That you wouldn't seek out—'

'I *didn't* seek anyone out.'

'Oh, really? These trips you mention – this desire, every month or so, to drop everything and travel halfway across the country. You think that was what – your artistic temperament? That's what Arayıcı men and women have been doing for thousands of years.' He grunted. 'Of course, only a fraction of them ever found someone worth more than half a cup of dog shit.' His attention turned to Obe. 'Which brings me to you. She seems to think you're Kusurlu. I have my doubts.'

Mallory filled her lungs, let out a breath. 'Show him,' she said.

Sal frowned. He picked up his wine glass and drained it. 'Show me what?'

Beside her, Obe placed his elbows on the table. He blinked rapidly, massaging his temples. Finally, he raised his head. 'You're cross with her because she worries you, and you don't like feeling powerless,' he said. 'You struggle to show your emotions, or even admit that you love her. You call yourself uncle but you're not. She's not your niece, certainly not your daughter, yet that's how you've come to think of her.'

'What is this?' Sal hissed, placing his fists on the tablecloth.

'I remind you of Osman, before he died,' Obe said, and winced. 'The boy from Antalya with his head in the clouds. You think the pair of us have less than one chance in five of surviving the coming year. You wonder if you'll see the baby.

You wonder if the omelette you just ate will give you indigestion. *Orospu çocuğu.* I don't know what that means.' Obe paused. 'Ah. "Son of a bitch." Of course.' He continued, a stream-of-consciousness commentary on everything spilling from Sal's head.

Finally, the man held up a shaking hand. 'Enough,' he growled. '*Enough.*'

Obe reached for an empty glass, knocked it over. Sal picked it up and refilled it, watching as the boy drank the wine in one long swallow. He refilled it again, and Obe drank that down too. Frowning, he switched his attention to Mallory. 'Is he alcoholic?'

She shook her head. 'The alcohol dampens it. Drugs, too. I don't know how much they help. I suspect not as much as he makes out.'

'Dampens it? Why would he want to do that?'

'Because it's killing him,' she replied, pouring herself a glass of wine. 'He can't control it.'

Sal was quiet for a while. 'How many weeks pregnant are you?'

'Six or seven.'

'Should you be drinking that?'

She gulped down a mouthful. 'Probably not.'

'This talent of his. If it's passed on – if it's *magnified* – think of what the child might offer the world. We won't know its true potential until it's born, but just consider the possibilities. Imagine the impact if . . . if it found a way to *share* that gift.'

Mallory felt her palms grow damp. 'Share it?'

'I'm speculating, of course I am,' Sal said, hunching over the table. 'But what if Obe's talent is latent in all of us? What if he's simply the first one to unlock it? What if this thing – whatever it is – could be taught?' He stared at her, his eyes more intense than she'd ever seen them. 'The consequences for humanity would be transformative.'

For nearly a minute, nobody spoke. Mallory's hands dropped

beneath the table and touched her belly. Until now, she had hardly considered the deeper implications of her pregnancy, or what might happen should she carry the child to term.

*What if this thing – whatever it is – could be taught? The consequences for humanity would be transformative.*

Abruptly, Sal's expression changed. 'These next months are crucial. You'll have to stay moving, the pair of you. For as long as you can. At least you're out of England. You're better off with a whole continent to get lost in.' He paused, leaning back in his seat. 'No doubt you came here expecting a reprimand for all your mistakes. But the fact that you're even sitting there means you've done better than expected. In the last fifty years, most Arayıcı women have been killed within a month of falling pregnant. It should be easier now. At least for a while. You have a new motorhome, for a start. It's waiting on the mainland.'

Mallory reached across the table and gripped Sal's hand. 'Thank you.'

He squeezed her fingers, motioning for the waiter to bring more wine. 'You'll stay here, tonight, in this hotel. You might only be six weeks' pregnant but you're going to have to start taking better care of yourself. I've booked you both a room beside mine. Try not to punch the headboard through the wall with all your exertions. I might not be your uncle, but I don't need to hear that.'

Again, Mallory felt the colour rising on her cheeks. 'You don't have to worry. It was a moment of weakness. Strictly a one-off.'

'Thanks,' Obe muttered.

Sal frowned, examining her more critically. 'Looking back,' he said, 'I never showed you much affection. I wanted to prepare you – to ready you for whatever might come your way. I see, now, that there are things I should've done differently.'

'You raised me to be a survivor.'

'Yes, but now you'll be a mother.'

'I can't be both?'

'Of course. And you *must* be both. My point is that I prepared you for one role to the exclusion of the other.'

They retired to their hotel rooms. After a week of sleeping outdoors, the bed looked luxurious enough for royalty. Obe rolled himself a joint, hanging halfway out of the window to smoke it while Mallory took a shower. When she emerged, wrapped in a towel to hunt for a hair drier, she found him lying on the bed with his hands folded behind his head.

'That business about a Damascus cow,' he said. 'He didn't mean it.'

'I know. It's just his way.'

'He's not as fierce as he makes out. I like him.'

'He sacrificed a lot to bring me up.'

'Will you tell me? About how you ended up with him?'

Mallory hesitated. Then she perched on a corner of the bed. She began to talk, haltingly at first, recounting her life in Trentino, how the Vasi had slaughtered her family and how she had stumbled from the forest to find their corpses smouldering on a bonfire.

Vincenti Vecchi, a fellow Arayıcı, discovered her two days later curled around the chalet's wood burner. He hid Mallory in his cellar for three months, making careful enquiries of the scattered Arayıcı network. Connections were re-established, messages were carried back and forth. Finally, Salih Sabahattin Hazinedar arrived at Vecchi's cabin. He was gruff and uncommunicative, addressing Mallory – who had barely uttered a word since her parents' deaths – with no concession to her age.

Within six weeks they reached the Köroğlu Mountains, where her education began. Sal offered her no physical affection, no comfort for her loss; but he fed her, clothed her, taught her history, languages and mathematics. By the age of ten she could hunt most animals for meat. Blood didn't bother her, nor the visceral realities of killing.

He sparred with her endlessly, inflicting bruises, cuts, even fracturing bones. Over time, her terror of him diminished; as she improved, and the beatings grew less frequent, her hostility graduated into respect. At seventeen, she left. This was the first time she'd seen him since.

Reaching the end of her story, Mallory realised that most of the light had leached from the sky and that she was reclining on the bed beside Obe, her hair still wet, wearing nothing but a towel. As the awareness struck her, she saw a flicker of something in his eyes and wondered if he had read her thoughts. Flustered, suddenly feeling so vulnerable that she might as well have been wearing no towel at all, she leaped off the bed and snatched up her rucksack. Back inside the bathroom she dressed quickly, trying to ignore the thump of her heart.

That night, they reconvened in the hotel bar for what turned out to be one of the most enjoyable evenings of her life. Despite their myriad differences, Obe and Sal quickly found common areas of interest. Within a few hours, and several more bottles of Anjou wine, they were laughing like old friends. Towards the end of the night, with Obe's arm trailed across the back of her chair, Mallory found herself leaning into him and flinched abruptly away. Her companions were so inebriated that neither seemed to notice, but later she felt Sal's eyes on her and knew he had seen her momentary loss of control.

They toasted her parents, and toasted the pregnancy, and Sal called down curses upon those who wished them harm. Afterwards, they sought out their rooms. Mallory guided Obe into bed, turned off the light and slipped beneath the covers.

The next morning, they liberated Yoda from the kennels. In the tourist car park, Sal handed over the keys to a brand new four-berth Morello motorhome.

'Man,' Obe said, looking around the interior, an oasis of cream leather and polished wood. 'Running in fear of our lives might suck, but at least we'll do it in style.'

Sal had other gifts for them, too. He'd filled the Morello's cupboards with clothes, including maternity wear in several different sizes. There were pregnancy books and maps of Europe, a well-stocked fridge and freezer, and, in one of the storage bays, a twelve-gauge shotgun with several boxes of ammunition. The motorhome boasted a large TV and sound system, a media player filled with movies, and all manner of other luxuries that would make the next seven months more bearable. Finally, Sal furnished them with a clutch of new credit cards, and detailed a secure method of contacting him should they need his help again.

With nothing more to discuss, Mallory embraced him tightly, kissing both his cheeks. Sal took her face in his hands and pressed his lips to her forehead. 'Grow big, but don't grow soft,' he counselled. To Obe, he added, 'Keep your guard up, and watch how much you smoke. Treat that gift of yours well and it might just save you both.'

Mallory climbed behind the Morello's wheel and twisted the keys in the ignition. Putting the vehicle in gear, she pulled out of the car park onto the open road.

# FIFTY

That first month, keen to exploit their new-found anonymity, they spent every night somewhere new. From Mont Saint-Michel they travelled east, following a zigzagging route towards Troyes, and from there on towards Germany.

One night, in an isolated part of the Black Forest far from any official campsites, Mallory asked Obe about his parents. They were sitting outside, Yoda poking around in the undergrowth. Obe had opened a bottle of wine and was halfway through it. He tilted back in his chair, and for a while his eyes lost their focus. 'Dad was a musician,' he said. 'Dude could pretty much pick up any instrument you could imagine and play it competently within a few days. Guitar was his passion, but sit him at a piano and he could make you cry just as easily. His gift was extraordinary – one of those talents that comes along a handful of times in a generation.'

Mallory recalled the first letters of *BAD BOY* that the man had branded into his son's flesh, and tried to square that image with Obe's description.

'Music was about the only thing that ever tamed him,' he continued. 'While he was playing, everything was right with the world. When he stopped . . . I guess that's when things went downhill.'

'Your mother?'

'Good-hearted, if a little flaky. They met at a concert in the early nineties. Dad was working as a session guitarist for some band. Mum talked herself backstage and they hooked up. Spent most of the night snorting lines of coke off each other's bodies, from what I gather. Amazing, really, that they managed to have sex. When she found out she was pregnant she booked herself an abortion, but for whatever reason she lost her nerve.'

Mallory thought of the night she'd confirmed her own pregnancy, and how, hours later, she'd obtained abortion pills from Dr Fabian Pataki. Touching her belly, she felt a sudden prick of shame. 'She told you that? That she tried to have you aborted?'

'I guess she blamed me a little, for tying her down. She never wanted kids.'

'They stayed together?'

Obe nodded. 'I don't know why. They didn't love each other, and neither of them felt any kind of pressure to stick together because of me. As I said before, Dad was . . . we were similar, I guess.'

Mallory frowned. 'Similar how?'

'He always knew what people were going to say before they said it. Always knew who was at the door when the bell rang. When he looked at you, you saw your thoughts in his face. It's why he took so many drugs – coke, pills, anything he could get. I don't know if it delayed the inevitable or hastened it along. He'd come out of his room and you wouldn't know if he was going to kiss you or try to strangle you. *I* wouldn't even know.'

'He tried that?'

'More than once,' Obe said. 'But it wasn't his fault. I know that sounds lame, but I also know how badly he was suffering. Towards the end, he just wanted a way out. For himself. For all of us.'

'What happened?'

'He learned of my ability. I don't know how – maybe I said something one day to spark his suspicion. What I do remember is the night he called Mum and me into the kitchen, barricaded the door and sat us down at the table. He was the soberest I'd ever seen him. He started talking in this super-calm voice, about how the voices in his head had damaged him, and how he wasn't going to let that happen to me; that what he needed to do might sound extreme, but it was for the best and we should support him in it.'

The surrounding forest smelled of pine sap but the air, as it entered Mallory's lungs, tasted fusty and dark.

'Dad put on the table a bottle of methadone, a knitting needle, a filleting knife and a torch. Said he'd identified the part of the brain responsible for all our problems and intended to cut it out of me before I got any older. Then he asked Mum to hold me down.'

Obe paused. He took a long pull of his joint, exhaling smoke through his teeth. 'There was a kind of logic to his idea, when you think about it.'

Mallory stared at him, confounded. 'He wanted to insert a knitting needle into your ear, scrape out a little piece of your brain, and you think there was a *logic* to it?'

'Well, an insane kind of logic.'

'What happened?'

'Mum just sort of stared at him for a bit. Then she started yelling. From there it escalated pretty quickly. There was . . . a struggle. Between the two of them. Dad was stronger, but Mum was quicker. She grabbed the knife and stabbed him, twice in the gut and once in the chest. Things got so intense that for a while I was in both their heads simultaneously – in Mum's as she stabbed him, in Dad's as the blade did its work. By then he was so crazy he didn't even realise he was meant to be dead. Amount of damage she inflicted, he never should've had the strength to snap her neck, but that's what happened.'

'They killed each other.'

Obe dropped his joint, crushing it beneath his heel. 'I like to think that even in his madness, he was trying to save me. What he cooked up was ten different flavours of batshit, but I don't blame him for that.'

Aside from Yoda's quiet snuffling, the forest around them was quiet. Mallory stared, at a loss for how to respond.

'Kind of a conversation killer,' Obe muttered.

She went over to him, put a hand on his shoulder and squeezed. It was one of the first times she'd touched him in their two months together, and the contact surprised them both. Flushing, she retreated to the motorhome, undressing in darkness and slipping under the covers of their shared bed. If Obe had followed her then she could not have said what would have happened, but the next morning she found him asleep in his deckchair outside, head resting awkwardly on his shoulder. She brewed coffee, brought him a cup. Afterwards, in silent partnership, they struck their camp, climbed into the Morello and drove.

# FIFTY-ONE

In the last week of September, Aylah found herself in Porthcurno on the Cornish coast, two and a half miles south-west of Land's End.

After her visit to the peninsula three months earlier she hadn't expected to return, but following the interception of Mallory and Obadiah's wrecked camper van in Ambleside, the trail had cooled. Although Teke had unearthed CCTV footage of the couple in Weymouth and at various train stations en route, the information had arrived far too late to be of use.

Still, the pair couldn't remain hidden indefinitely. One mistake, one momentary lapse, and the entire Vasi network would descend upon them. In the meantime, Aylah intended to discover as much of Obadiah's past as she could.

It was raining when she arrived in Porthcurno. The village, comprising scattered whitewashed homes and subtropical gardens, was strung along a wooded valley that opened onto a pale sand beach. Lynette Burgess's bungalow occupied a grassy acreage on the beach's rocky southern headland, with views across the bay to the sea. Aylah reached it via a winding drive flanked by palm trees and geraniums. Dogs began barking before she had even climbed from her car, only relenting when Lynette – late sixties, red-faced and overweight, wearing a crocheted tunic and mud-stained leggings – locked them in the kitchen with bowls of food. 'Silly old sods,' the older woman said, leading Aylah into a conservatory that smelled of wet fur. 'Don't know what's got into them.'

'How many do you have?'

'At the moment, five. Probably six before the week's out. We've been having a little trouble at the sanctuary since . . . what happened.'

'Must've been a shock. Learning about the maniac in your midst.'

'Oh, I don't believe that nonsense on TV.'

'The evidence is indisputable.'

Lynette waved dismissively. 'Wherever you find good-hearted people, you'll find bad ones trying to discredit them.'

'Have you spoken to Obadiah? Had contact with him in any way?'

'Not since he left.'

'Any ideas where he might have gone?'

'None.' The woman gazed through the conservatory windows at the foaming sea. 'I'd like to think he's on a beach somewhere, paddling out.'

'He's a surfer?'

'Best I ever saw. Always dreaming of the next wave, always talking about the beaches he wanted to visit. That boy, he was something special. Everyone who ever met him said the same.'

'With the possible exception of those he killed.'

Lynette shrugged. 'The truth'll come out soon enough. Was there something specific you wanted to discuss?'

Although Aylah questioned the woman for an hour, the information she gleaned was almost entirely useless. Towards the end, provoked by nonstop endorsements of Obadiah Macintosh's character, she'd developed almost as much animosity for Lynette Burgess as for her target. Somehow, she managed to remain calm; simple animosity was no excuse for a loss of control.

As she walked to the front entrance, the dogs recommenced

their racket, scratching at the kitchen door. 'The beaches he wanted to visit,' Aylah said, keeping her tone light. 'Can you name any?'

'Not off the top of my head.'

'Would you tell me if you could?'

'I doubt it.'

Grimacing, Aylah reached for the door latch and twisted it.

'You remind me of her,' the woman said. 'First thing I thought when you walked in.'

The latch turned greasy in Aylah's fingers. 'Remind you of who?'

'That girl. The one Obe is travelling with. I saw her photo on the news.'

Carefully, Aylah eased the latch back into its groove and turned around.

At the end of the hall, Lynette Burgess touched a hand to her throat, where a vein now flickered. 'You're not police,' she said. 'So who are you?'

# FIFTY-TWO

In November, they reached the Spanish border. Knowing their images were still in circulation, Mallory changed the style of her hair, cutting it into a ragged bob. Few would recognise her from the photographs the media had run. Obe's beard grew out, suiting him better than she had expected. He looked older, wiser. Sometimes she found herself forgetting just how young he was.

Her belly, by now, had swollen to such an extent that it had started to restrict her movements. She'd always kept herself in shape, and wasn't used to getting about so ponderously. At night she struggled to find a comfortable position, keeping herself awake with thoughts of her eventual labour. She felt the child moving regularly, and often saw the bulge of a foot or an elbow when it shifted position.

Her leg muscles began to cramp, especially in the evenings. Obe took over the driving from mid-morning to mid-afternoon, a period when he was stoned enough to ignore the thoughts of others, but not so baked that he risked careering off the road. Mallory supplied him with strong coffee, retreating to the back of the motorhome to avoid his smoke.

In the twenty-seventh week of her pregnancy, they reached the Portuguese coast and travelled along it to the resort of Nazaré. The town's sandy beach was renowned for producing some of the biggest waves on the planet. Mallory guessed that their arrival was no coincidence, suddenly understanding why Obe had been keeping such a close eye on the weather.

The skies were heavy with cloud as they parked on the Avenue Manuel Remígio. A strong westerly rocked the Morello on its springs. When Mallory saw the ocean, her heart rose into her throat. The water was dark and oily, simmering with violence. Waves gathered slowly. Their marbled faces flickered with black shapes, as if the mounting energy had spawned a congregation of webbed devils below the surface, ready to snatch anyone foolish enough to challenge their power. As wind whipped spray from their crests, the waves peeled themselves open in thunderous explosions of white water. Only a few surfers were out there, and all of them looked scared. A few guys zipped back and forth on jet skis, but whether they were lifeguards or simply spectators, Mallory could not tell.

'Man,' Obe muttered, hunched over the steering wheel. 'That's real. That's *insane*.'

She glanced across at him, and for once could not guess what he was thinking. In his eyes she saw reflections of the bursting sea. 'You're going out there?'

When he turned to face her, the ocean fled from his expression. 'This,' he said, 'it's what I wanted, ever since I was a kid.'

'Last time you went surfing, I had to pull you from the water.'

Looking down, Obe flexed the fingers of his right hand. He'd cut off the cherry-red cast some months ago. 'This is different.'

'Yeah. Those waves are about five times as big.'

He nodded, studying them once again. Yoda rose up from the floor, putting his paws on the central console. He gazed through the windscreen at the rising sea and yawned.

While Obe went into the bedroom to change, Mallory filled a thermos with coffee. Outside, she traipsed across the sand and unfolded a blanket. Yoda slumped down beside her. 'You'd better hope he doesn't do anything dumb,' she told the dog. 'Because I'm not wading into *that* to rescue him.'

Within a few minutes, Obe negotiated the loan of a board from a group of surfers who had retreated from the sea. He walked down the beach to the water's edge and flashed Mallory a shaka, thumb and little finger extended.

She tugged the dog onto her lap and watched him paddle out. A monster wave began to build. Obe paddled harder, the tail of his board leaving a white wake. As the water started to slope, he leaned forward and dived through it. The growing wave obstructed her view, and she couldn't see if he had emerged cleanly. Then it broke, a bass thump that rolled up the beach and vibrated inside her chest. When the spray died down she saw him, much further out, diving through another black wall of water.

At last, Obe got beyond the break line and sat up straight, studying the sea. He let a score of waves roll under him, scouting the incoming swell. Then he saw his ride. Frantically, he began to paddle. The water built beneath him, lifting him forty feet, tilting his board until it pointed almost perpendicular to the trough. Somehow, popping up, he locked his feet beneath him. The wave was breaking from right to left, and Obe dropped like a stone down its face before his rails took hold. He angled left, away from the whitewater, fins carving a bright slash.

Mallory had never seen anything more graceful. She no longer noticed the wind against her face, nor the sharp speckles of rain.

The wave began to barrel, trapping Obe within. Moments later he shot from its depths like a darting fish. He cutback once, twice, extending the ride. Finally, with water exploding all around him, he dived into broken glass. White spray leapt heavenward. The sea became a battlefield of foam.

Her spine twinging with the effort, Mallory lurched to her

feet. She could not see Obe, nor his board. Further along the beach, the group of surfers visored their eyes and scanned the whitewater.

Her teeth ground together. Her eyes roved the sea. Already, half a minute had passed since he'd dived beneath the surface. Now, another breaker hit, this one almost as large as the one he had ridden. Two of the surfers ran to the water's edge. A jet ski cruised past, its rider peering into the depths. The sea surged and boiled.

Then Mallory spotted him.

Obe was already beyond the nearest breaker, paddling back towards deeper water. 'Lunatic,' she whispered, breath rushing out with her voice. For the first time she realised just how closely their lives had become entwined. Six months they had been together. They had fought, had argued, had nearly driven each other mad. She couldn't imagine how she'd feel if she lost him.

Right then, Mallory felt the baby kick inside her belly. Hands cradled around her bump, chin raised against the wind, she watched Obe catch wave after wave.

He emerged from the water an hour later, returning the board to its owner and trudging back across the sand. When she saw his expression, she could not help but smile.

That night, it would have been the easiest thing in the world to have sought him out; but Obe, seduced by the sea, fell asleep almost instantly, waking the next morning with the same dreamy expression he had worn to bed. Later that day, they packed up the Morello and retreated from the coast.

They drove back through Spain into France, spending Christmas Eve in the forest above Lake Annecy, with snow falling white around them. That evening, Mallory stepped out of the motorhome to watch the moonlight floating on the water, and caught Obe staring into the sky. Up there, stars glittered on a satin backdrop. 'Don't tell me,' she said. 'You still believe in Father Christmas.'

He turned towards her and grinned. 'On a night like this, tell me you don't.'

Shaking her head, she followed his gaze and found herself bewitched. The temperature had dropped below freezing, but she couldn't bring herself to go inside. Obe fetched her a coat, plus a mug of coffee flavoured with a single shot of amaretto. He rubbed her back companionably while she drank it, and she didn't pull away. The next morning he surprised her with a stocking filled with presents that turned out to be almost universally awful: a graphic novel featuring a female superhero whose dialogue was printed in French; a slinky spring; an aerosol spray of geranium-scented water with which she could spritz her face during labour; a USB coffee cup warmer; and a glow-in-the-dark planetarium that could be strung from the motorhome's roof.

The last gift, however, ambushed her completely. When she unwrapped it her heart gave a startled thump; because there, nestled inside the torn paper, was a white cotton baby-gro.

Staring at it, their situation was suddenly impossible to avoid: in ten weeks, if all went to plan, the garment would be occupied by a living, breathing human being.

'I wasn't sure if it was appropriate,' Obe said, watching her reaction. 'But we're getting close, aren't we? Might be time we started thinking about this stuff.'

'You're right,' she said. 'It is.'

'There's something else in there, too.'

Mallory searched the wrapping and lifted out a red cotton bib. Across it, in a comic-book font, big yellow letters proclaimed: *THESE FOOLS PUT MY CAPE ON BACK-WARDS*. 'The obligatory superhero reference,' she said, laughing despite herself.

On Boxing Day they packed up their camp and headed east, crawling along snowy mountain roads towards Chamonix. All around them the Alps threw their weight heavenward, a stupefying landscape of jagged arêtes and white slopes.

They celebrated New Year's Eve in the shadow of Mont Blanc, the mountain lit by a round moon that hung like a lantern among the stars. From there they continued east, threading their way through the Pennine Alps, which winter had frozen like a jewel. At Chiasso they crossed the Italian border, arriving at the southern end of Lake Como and following a meandering path to Brescia.

Since Nazaré, Mallory had assumed navigational duties, but only as she directed Obe up the eastern shore of Lake Garda did she realise with some surprise that their seemingly haphazard wandering was leading them to a very specific destination. She spent long hours debating the wisdom of it, but the time was fast approaching when they must retire from the road and find somewhere to hole up. The thought of *that* made her skin crawl.

The weather, by now, had sharpened considerably. The higher they climbed into the mountains, the further the temperature plunged. Due to heavy snowfall, not all the roads were open, and they found themselves doubling back as often as they managed to forge a way through.

On the first day of February, as Mallory entered her thirty-sixth week of pregnancy, they turned off the main pass, fixed snow chains to the Morello's tyres and coaxed it up a single-lane road untouched by ploughs.

'Got a weird feeling about this,' Obe said, but he didn't explain his comment. Mallory watched him, disquieted. Despite the frigid conditions – the Morello's dashboard computer was registering an outside temperature of minus eight degrees – sweat speckled his forehead. His eyes were red-tinged and dull.

Halfway up, she called a halt so that he could smoke a joint. Afterwards, he put the motorhome back into gear and continued. The chains provided some traction on the frozen road surface, but it was slow going. Slabs of snow fell from over-hanging trees and burst across the windscreen; Obe ran the wipers constantly. After a mile they passed an abandoned hunter's cabin, reduced to rotting timbers that emerged like blackened teeth from white gums.

Finally the track reached the top of its gradient, emerging into a clearing that offered an extraordinary view of the valley below. Obe eased their vehicle to a stop and switched off the engine. He blinked, stared. His Adam's apple bobbed in his throat. 'I know this place,' he whispered. 'I've seen it before.'

# FIFTY-THREE

Once darkness had fallen, Aylah İncesu climbed from her Lexus and stole into the trees. All day, the sky had been absent of cloud. Now, with a bowl of stars glimmering overhead, the temperature had plummeted. Her breath sailed ahead of her in white streamers.

Snow had brought silence to the forest: no cries of night predators; no furtive rustlings of prey. As she trudged through the darkness, *qama* swinging at her waist, it was almost possible to believe that she was the only one out here; but of course such a thought would have been false, because there were dead folk hiding among these trees – they simply did not know it.

Seven months had passed since she'd discovered Mallory and Obadiah's crashed Renault. There'd been a possible sighting in France, followed by another a few weeks later in northern Spain. In Nazaré, Portugal, she'd missed the couple by no more than half an hour. The surfers she'd interviewed on the beach maintained the pair were heading to Biarritz, but that lead seemed to have been a deliberate deception; and thanks to Mallory's continuous movement, Aylah's Arayıcı sense – through which she could home in on her pregnant sister's location – had been largely frustrated.

Then, three weeks ago, she'd experienced once again that familiar heaviness in her head, as if a part of it had been magnetised and was subtly beginning to pull. Steadily it had led her here, to this frozen forest under this dark and silent sky.

Strange, really, how Arayıcı women always chose such remote locations in which to give birth. With no potential witnesses, it made the challenge of killing them almost pedestrian. If roles had been reversed, and Aylah had found herself in the early stages of labour, she would have forced her way onto a long-haul flight, delivering the baby thirty thousand feet above the earth with four hundred cheering passengers obfuscating the efforts of any attendant Vasi.

How strange, to consider what might have happened if fate had dealt a different hand all those years ago: if the Vasi had captured Mallory and Aylah had been the one to escape. Would she have found Obadiah Macintosh and slept with him? Would it have been *her* hiding in these woods, ignorant of the calamity that now approached?

It was only as Aylah came upon the clearing that she noticed her left hand had slunk into the pocket of her mountain jacket and was absently caressing her belly. Hissing in dismay, she drew up short; violently shook her head. Saul Manco had shown her the truth of the world, and there was no way back from her enlightenment. Humanity was a pathogen. The Arayıcı acted as a mutagen, increasing its virulence. Aylah – in concert with the Vasi – comprised the cure. Retrieving her Glock from its holster, she curled her hand around the pistol's grip.

*After violence, silence.*

Ahead stood the cabin: a clapboard structure with little to recommend it except a stout tin roof. Black smoke chugged from the chimney. Only the slimmest ribbon of light escaped through the shuttered windows. Those inside would have no warning of what was coming.

Aylah stepped from the cover of the trees. All around her the moon had sown diamonds upon the snow. As she closed on the cabin, violet shadows filled the holes sunk by her boots. It wasn't until she reached the building's near wall, pistol braced against her chest, that a dog started barking. Moments later, that slim ribbon of light leaking from the shutters winked out.

Aylah felt her heart begin to knock. In her right ear she heard a scratch of static. *'You need back up?'*

'No.'

Keeping low, she circled the cabin and identified its main entry points: the front entrance at ground level, the rear entrance up a flight of steps. She chose the former, pausing beside it and taking three breaths to steady herself before she pivoted and kicked.

The door was of flimsy construction, crashing open with such force that its hinges tore loose. Aylah sidestepped just in time to avoid a muscular black mass that surged out. She fired three rounds, dropping the creature before it reached her. Its chest heaved once and grew still. She retreated, hurrying around the cabin to the back door. From past experience, she knew that those inside would focus on the entrance that had most recently been breached. Climbing the steps to the back door, she kicked it open too.

Her pulse, by now, was jumping like a wind-up toy. She could smell the richness of the forest; could sense the huge sky bearing down. Curious, really, that only in the presence of death did she ever feel truly alive.

'Police!' she shouted. 'Stay where you are and don't shoot.'

It was an old Vasi trick, one that she'd dismissed as absurd until the first time she saw it deliver. Retracing her steps, she came again to the front entrance. The dead dog lay in the snow, steam rising from the holes in its flesh.

Aylah switched on a torch, lifting it in alignment with her gun.

Now, the greatest danger; the point at which her own enduring silence was closest. Like the Vasi she emulated but would never truly become, she did not flinch from it. Instead, knocking snow from her boots, she slipped inside the cabin.

Colours bloomed in the torchlight. Shadows swung like horses on a carousel.

She saw bare floorboards, peeling walls.

In one corner, flames danced inside a cast-iron woodstove. The heat was fierce, a stark contrast to the frigid forest.

Aylah kept low, angling her weapon left and right. She noticed a rough-hewn dining table; a half-empty water glass and the remains of a meal. On the floor lay a pair of moccasins. Along one wall was a stockpile of food, water and supplies. Among the inventory she saw neatly folded piles of baby clothes.

An open doorway stood opposite. Aylah shone her torch through it, revealing a basic kitchenette. Beyond that, the back door hung open, the frame a mess of splintered wood.

To her right, a narrow staircase ascended into darkness. Gritting her teeth, she began to climb.

No pictures on the wall. No carpet beneath her feet. At the top of the flight she came to a tiny landing and another two doors. One opened into a squalid bathroom. The other was closed.

Aylah's skin prickled. Was that movement she heard? Or merely sounds of combustion from the wood stove downstairs? Her fingers tightened on the gun. Nothing to lose, here, but her life.

*After violence, silence.*

Kicking open the door, Aylah surged inside.

Her torch beam flitted, delivering clarity from darkness.

Wardrobe; dressing table; empty bed.

Clothes on the floor; rucksack lying open; discarded duvet in the far corner.

The window was shuttered, locked from the inside.

Aylah closed the door and switched on the light. For a minute she didn't move or speak, watching the king-sized duvet in the corner as – almost imperceptibly – it rose and fell.

'I'm guessing you have a gun under there,' she said.

In an instant that tiny movement ceased, but it could not be stilled indefinitely; by degrees, she watched it return.

'If it's a revolver,' Aylah said, 'then you've probably got six shots. If it's a pistol, you've a lot more. Thing is, *orospu*, while you might have a pretty good fix on my voice, if you miss with your first shot you won't get a second, and then you'll die, pissing yourself under a moth-eaten duvet in this shithole cabin in the woods. Hardly the most dignified of endings.'

She waited, counting off the seconds. At thirty, a flap of the duvet unfolded, revealing a pale face.

'I'm going to die anyway,' the girl whispered.

Aylah filled her lungs. She pocketed the torch and took out her *qama*. 'What's your name?'

A pause. A shudder. 'Damla. Damla Gültekin.'

'Where're you from?'

'Originally . . . Ankara.'

'Arayıcı.'

The girl swallowed.

'Do you have a weapon under there, Damla?'

'I . . .'

'Put it down. Slide it away from you.'

'What are you going to—'

'Put it down,' she repeated. 'Slide it away from you.'

Some seconds later, a gun that looked as if it might date from the Second World War nudged out from beneath the duvet. Aylah was about to pick it up when she realised that the girl might have another. 'Get up.'

A pulse began to tick in Damla's throat. She opened her mouth to speak, before appearing to decide against it. With some difficulty, she climbed to her feet. The duvet fell away, exposing her grubby nightdress; beneath it, her hugely distended belly.

'Go to the bed,' Aylah said. 'Sit.'

The girl obeyed, tears spilling from her cheeks.

'How far gone?'

'Thirty-seven weeks,' she said miserably. 'I couldn't travel any further. Had to find somewhere safe to hole up.'

'Pity you didn't manage it. You're alone?'

'There was Mikey. I guess you killed him.'

'The dog?'

Damla nodded.

'You're right, he's dead.' Aylah gestured with her *qama*. 'It's a Kusurlu child?'

Another nod.

'Where's the father?'

'Gone.'

'He left you?'

'No.' The girl paused. Sniffed. 'He killed himself.'

'What was his gift?'

'I never found out. Before we could have the conversation, he . . .' A sob wracked her. She covered her face with her hands. 'You're *her*, aren't you? The one they use against us. The one they call *Şeytan*.'

Aylah holstered her Glock, came over to the bed and sat. 'Since when did they start calling me that?'

'Since you started murdering us,' Damla whispered.

The girl was so heavy with child that she could only sit with her knees splayed. Her belly button had popped outwards, pressing through her nightdress like a hard bean. Aylah found herself transfixed by the sheer horror of it. 'What's it like?' she asked. 'Being pregnant, I mean. Having a life growing inside you.'

Damla looked up, her pupils so large that her eyes seemed almost entirely black. Her throat bobbed, the smooth muscles of her pharynx contracting and relaxing. 'This child,' she said, 'knowing that it's Kusurlu . . . knowing that, had it lived, it might . . .'

A spasm of grief rocked her. She wrapped her arms around herself and grew still.

Aylah caught a flicker of movement in her peripheral vision.

She glanced down in time to see a lump bulge out from the girl's belly, moving three inches across it before disappearing. She gasped, amazed, and suddenly she was reaching out, laying her palm flat against the girl's nightdress. Beneath, the flesh was hard, hot. She felt something press briefly against her hand: a tiny foot, or perhaps a shoulder.

'What did they do?' Damla whispered, her head still bowed. 'What could they possibly have done to turn you against your own?'

'They opened my eyes,' Aylah said, perturbed at how mechanical she sounded.

'To what?'

'An end to pain.'

'You're Arayıcı. You're one of us.'

Aylah took away her hand, wiped her fingers on the mattress. 'Not any more.'

'What happens now?' the girl asked. 'How does this end?'

# FIFTY-FOUR

Twenty yards away, empty and yet immutable, stood a mausoleum to childhood memories. Mallory had expected the sight of her old home to affect her, but not like this: she couldn't breathe, couldn't blink, couldn't turn her eyes away. When the last air trickled from her lungs, for a while she did not know how to fill them.

Although the surrounding forest had changed markedly in the fifteen years since she'd left, the chalet looked much the same; but it did not *feel* the same, and that was perhaps what shocked her – it was like a much-loved painting from which all the colour had been drained. The chalet's stone chimney climbed like a crooked finger. Above it, a solitary hawk circled in a perfect blue sky. When Mallory turned towards the patch of snow where her parents had died, she felt a coldness settle over her.

*Why did you come back? What did you hope to find, except old wounds and rotten memories?*

'Maybe you just wanted to be close to them,' Obe said. 'This place holds good memories as well as bad.'

Mallory felt so numb that it was a while before she realised he had touched her hand. 'I asked you to stay out of my head,' she said. 'You promised me.'

Obe filled his lungs. 'I've tried my best. But I can't control my dreams. Nor yours.' His eyes slid over the chalet's walls and its snow-covered garden. 'Some memories – some *emotions* – are too powerful to avoid. You're shouting, Mallory. Shouting just about as loudly as a person can.' Breaking out his tobacco tin, he began to roll a joint.

She should have been furious, and yet somehow she couldn't work up the necessary rage. 'You're right,' she told him. 'I miss them. It's been fifteen years, and I still . . .'

Her throat closed up. She couldn't swallow. Obe pulled her into an embrace and for a while she clung to him.

Back in Normandy, Sal had explained that Vincenti Vecchi, the Arayıcı hermit who had discovered her after her parents' deaths, still lived in the area. The old man visited the cabin regularly to ensure that the place endured.

They found the door key in a tin can, buried a few feet from the front step. Inside, the chalet smelled nothing like Mallory's recollections – no rich aromas of Iranian cuisine, no faint tang of woodsmoke – but she recognised plenty of other things. In the living room, her father's chair still stood beside the fire. On a side table lay one of his pipes. Books still lined the shelves, although the work of fifteen winters had left them warped and discoloured. In the kitchen, her mother's pans hung from the rack. Everywhere she saw trinkets and keepsakes – a hundred little things that had faded from her memory and now pricked at her, bittersweet.

She couldn't venture upstairs to her old room. Not yet. The girl who had lived up there would be the most difficult memory to confront. Instead, she built a fire in the wood burner and listened to the building come alive, creaking and popping as it thawed.

That first night, the prospect of sleeping in the chalet was too much, so they retreated to the Morello. The next morning, dressed in every scrap of winter gear they owned, they took a walk through the forest. Twenty yards into the trees, beneath a canopy so thick that hardly any snow intruded, Mallory saw something that astonished her. At the base of a huge spruce, tucked between two roots that looked like the tentacles of some enormous sea creature, stood a rotting wooden arch built from scavenged timber. The paint had long ago fallen away, but Mallory recognised its shape: the fairy door she had installed on the day of her parents' slaughter. She passed it without pause – and, just like her journey the previous day, it wasn't until she reached her destination that she realised where she had been heading all along.

Fifteen years earlier she had lost herself in these woods, emerging the next morning after hours of aimless wandering. This time, benefiting from both a compass and a clear Alpine day, she found what she'd been seeking within an hour of setting out.

Stepping into a clearing she saw, across the valley, the extra-ordinary chipped teeth of the Cristallo massif: Monte Cristallo, Cima di Mezzo, Piz Popena and Cristallino d'Ampezzo.

Nearby, Vincenti Vecchi's log cabin looked smaller than she remembered. The stone-built ground floor was partially recessed into the mountainside, providing a solid foundation for an upper level timbered in seasoned spruce. A wooden staircase rose to a balcony protected by an overhanging slate-tiled roof. Black smoke chugged from the chimney. A cherry-red Mitsubishi truck stood outside.

Sal had assured Mallory that the man still lived here, although he must have reached a ripe age by now. Holding tight to the guardrail, she climbed the steps to the balcony. At the top, she hammered on the door, but nobody answered.

'Maybe he went out,' Obe said, cupping his fingers around a glass bezel in the door.

'Maybe he didn't,' growled a voice behind them. They turned to find a bent old man at the bottom of the steps, aiming a rifle.

Vincenti Vecchi had always been striking, but old age had

warped his features so dramatically that he looked like an effigy from a Black Forest clock: lumpen chin, flapping ears, hooked and mushroomed nose. His eyebrows had grown so tufted that they almost obscured his eyes. '*Perché sei qui?*' he demanded. Then, in English: 'What do you want?'

Mallory raised her hands, careful to keep her movements slow. 'You don't recognise me, Vincenti? Even after all this time, I'd hoped that you might.'

The old man scowled. 'Do I know you?'

'You did. But you knew my parents better.'

Vecchi's eyebrows twitched. Condensation plumed from his mouth. 'It can't be.'

'It is.'

'A . . . a letter came,' he stammered. 'From Salih. I hardly thought it could be true.' Abruptly, he swung the barrel of his rifle away. '*Uffa*! What am I doing? Brains of a mountain goat taken by an eagle.' He lurched forwards, shouldering the gun, and scuffed up the steps to the balcony. Placing his hands on Mallory's shoulders, he examined her. '*Bellisimo*,' he muttered. 'Your father's eyes, your mother's bones.' His gaze dropped to her eight-month bump and he sighed out a breath. 'So, it *is* true. An Arayıcı child. The first time in . . . I don't know how long.' He patted her shoulders. Then his attention turned to Obe. 'This is the father?'

'His name's Obe. Obadiah.'

Vincenti Vecchi dragged the boy into an embrace. 'Obadiah,' he said. 'Servant of God. Were your parents religious?'

'No, sir.'

'But they named you well, I think. Come. I have a fire going. Food and drink.'

The décor inside Vecchi's home had not changed in the fifteen years since Mallory had last seen it. Animal skins covered the floor. The sofas were draped with knitted throws. A collection of bleached skulls lined the windows overlooking the valley.

Shelves and cupboards were stuffed with books and old maps. In one corner, a cast-iron stove hissed with burning logs.

'It won't be long, I think,' Vecchi said, eyeing Mallory as she peeled off her coat.

'Three weeks, give or take.'

'Maybe even sooner. Have you had any problems?'

'Nothing worth mentioning.'

'You feel it kicking?'

'Not as much as I did. It's getting fairly cramped in there.'

'Has anyone examined you?'

She shook her head. 'I never wanted to risk it.'

'Mind if I do? See what's going on?'

'Not at all.' She stood in front of his armchair, unbuttoning her shirt while he took out a pair of spectacles and perched them on his nose.

Vecchi rubbed his palms together before placing them directly onto her belly. After a moment's pause he began to apply gentle pressure, working from the front to the sides. The old man's brow furrowed deeply as he concentrated, but it was impossible to guess his thoughts. At last, he removed his hands. 'The head's engaged,' he said. 'So there's no danger of a breech birth. Have you had any contractions? Any bleeding or pain?'

She shook her head.

'It was a good plan, I think – returning to these mountains. Your parents' chalet is probably the last place they'd think to look. You've timed it just about perfectly, too. Early enough to get settled. Late enough that those Vasi maggots will struggle to sniff you out.' He nodded, clapping his hands together. 'Now, I want to hear more about this boy, and discover whether everything Salih wrote about was true.'

They spent the rest of that day with Vecchi. Obe demonstrated the ability he had revealed in Normandy some months earlier, and the old man seemed profoundly affected. He questioned the boy closely, scribbled down notes on a spiral-bound pad and jumped up frequently to fetch well-thumbed Arayıcı texts, through which he leafed, muttering and twitching.

'I have to concur with Salih,' he said, much later. 'We Arayıcı – some say we're like guides in the darkness, lighting the way ahead. But we've only ever revealed the truth of what was possible in all of us: language, writing, science, art. This gift of Obadiah's, this new ability to communicate – he might be the first to unlock it, but I suspect it's inherent in everyone.'

'I'm not,' Obe said. 'Not the first to unlock it, I mean.' And for the next ten minutes he told the old man the story of his childhood.

Mallory listened in silence, and though she had heard the tale before, it affected her no less deeply. She marvelled at how he could talk so matter-of-factly about his experience at the hands of his father. Strange to think that once she had considered him weak.

Vincenti Vecchi nodded, his eyes like coal chips beneath his tufted brows. 'Hearing that, it's a miracle you're here at all. Not just that you survived what happened, but the fact that you were even born. Most Kusurlu become overwhelmed by their gift far in advance of having children.'

The old man paused, bringing his palms together in his lap. 'Which brings us to this child. Every Arayıcı-Kusurlu birth is an event, a catalyst for humanity's development. But this . . .' He blew out his breath, indicating Mallory's belly. 'If your child works out a way to share this gift, to *teach* it . . .'

Perhaps he caught something in Obe's expression, because he added: 'Are you worried? About the baby?'

'I don't want anyone else to go through what I did. This thing – this gift, as you call it – it's been killing me. *Is* killing me. I've contained it so far, but sooner or later it'll win out.'

Vecchi tapped the boy's knee. 'That might be true, and it might not. We don't know God's plans for us. We can only try to please Him as best we can.'

'I'm not sure I—'

He brought you to the Arayıcı, don't you see? I, myself, am convinced of it. You're a blessing to be shared, Obadiah, even if the journey has been difficult. Even if the future, right now, probably looks bleak.'

Hours later, with the moon lambent in a violet sky, Vecchi offered to drive them back up the mountainside, but Mallory refused, determined to find her way back unassisted. The following afternoon, the old man drove over to see them, his truck crammed with supplies. After they'd unpacked, he led them through the forest to a small clearing. At its heart, standing proud of the snow, stood a polished granite gravestone.

'You won't remember this,' Vecchi said. 'But before Sal came for you, I gathered up your family's remains and buried them here. A few years later I installed the headstone.'

To discover, after all this time, that her parents' bones had been preserved, and that they lay here beneath this very soil, was initially too much to process. Mallory stumbled through the snow to the gravesite, and with some difficulty sank down onto her knees. Pulling off her gloves, she placed one hand against the frozen stone. 'Abba,' she said, her voice husky. 'Mama.' She did not cry. For fifteen years she had refused to concede any power to those who had caused her pain. She was not about to start now.

That afternoon, back at the chalet, she climbed the stairs and investigated the upper floor. In her old room she came across stuffed toys and treasures that she had long ago forgotten. But of everything she saw up there, it was Aylah's room that affected her most acutely. Despite the four-year age gap, Mallory had idolised her older sister. They had played together, plotted together, had confided and laughed as if they were twins. Of the two, she had been the more cerebral, losing herself in books and make-believe. Aylah, by contrast, had thrived on physical challenges: skiing, climbing trees, hunting deer with her father. Her room contained no books, but its surfaces were plastered with drawings: eagles, foxes, bears; all the predators that roamed these mountains.

Standing there, surrounded by her sister's old artworks, recalling the girl's hopes and dreams, Mallory could not help but wonder what would have happened if their roles had been reversed, and *she* had been slaughtered by the Vasi that day. Would Aylah have been the one to seek out Obe? Would she be standing here now, days away from her labour? One thing was certain: Aylah would have handled the last eight months – and likely the last fifteen years – far better than her younger sibling had managed.

With the upstairs rooms conquered, Mallory's uneasiness about sleeping in the chalet faded. Downstairs, with logs crackling in the wood burner, she asked Obe to fetch the Morello's mattress and make up a bed in one corner. Not only would they sleep here from now on – if all went to plan, she would give birth here too.

Seven days later, at the end of the first week of February, that plan began to unravel.

# FIFTY-FIVE

*What did they do? What could they possibly have done to turn you against your own? You're Arayıcı. You're one of us.*

Aylah stumbled through the forest, Damla Gültekin's words ringing in her head. '*Orospu*,' she spat. '*Budala*.'

She would never be one of them, would never squeeze out a Kusurlu rat into a world already suffering the defilements of humanity.

As she ran, the frozen night burned in her throat. She would find her sister, and she would tear the girl limb from limb, wreaking such carnage that no one would doubt her allegiance, or her conviction.

*You're her, aren't you? The one they use against us. The one they call Şeytan.*

Memories flitted from the forest like bats. Aylah screamed, pawing them away. Crashing against a tree, she tumbled into the snow. Rolled to her feet. Pushed on.

*Dripping water. Whispering voices. An excrement-streaked cage.*

Oh, the agony of that cage. The torments she'd endured within; torments that had taught her the true depravity of humanity. She regressed even further, recalled her parents lying dead in the snow. Saw their bodies prepared for burning – nothing, now, but slumped meat. Then she was back in the cage, the cage, the cage. With the drip of water. The voices.

The unbearable expectation of fresh pain.

And, out of all that, a light; Saul Manco's alligator eyes; his steady, patient voice: *'There's a way to end this, Aylah, if only you'll open your eyes. A way to end your torment, a way to end all the world's torment. Would you like me to tell you about it? Would you like me to show you the true path towards silence?'*

She'd spat in his face, had tried to claw out his eyes.

'*Post violentiam, silentium,*' Aylah moaned. '*Post violentiam, silentium.*'

She stumbled on, putting the cabin and its secrets far behind, running with one hand held as a shield to low-hanging branches, her face tilted towards the moon.

'*Aylah?*' The voice came through the bud still screwed into her ear. '*Aylah, what's your status?*'

She quickened her pace, feeling the cold weight of the Glock knocking against her ribs as she ran. In her right hand she gripped her *qama*, released from its sheath. No way she would relinquish it. Not out here. Not in these deathly woods.

'*Aylah, talk to me. What's happening?*'

At last she burst out of the trees and stumbled onto the road. There was her Lexus. Teke paced back and forth beside it. When he spotted her his eyes flared.

'*Bok,*' he spat, marching over. 'You went silent. Was it her? Was it Mallory?'

He tried to take her arm. She shrugged him off, staggering towards the car.

'Talk to me, Aylah. Is she dead?'

'It wasn't her.'

She opened the car door. The interior light came on.

Teke's jaw dropped. 'You're covered in blood. What happened back there? Who did you find?

'Get in,' Aylah hissed. 'And stop asking questions.' She grabbed a cloth from the door cavity, wiped her *qama* clean.

*You're her, aren't you? The one they use against us. The one they call* Şeytan.

Aylah started the Lexus, found first gear. She spoke through gritted teeth, unable to control the tremor in her voice. 'Mallory's got to stop soon. When she does, we'll find her. And when we find her, you'll see what I'll do. You all will.'

# FIFTY-SIX

Mallory was the first to fall sick. The cabin's running water was fed by a pump that took its supply from a five-hundred-gallon tank buried outside. Rain and meltwater, pouring into the gutters of a tool shed further up the slope, fed the tank. Years earlier a complex filtration system had ensured that the water was potable, but it no longer worked and neither of them knew how to fix it. They'd brought plenty of bottled water, so they used the chalet's pumped supply purely for showering and for flushing the toilet.

Then, one night, Mallory made an evening meal of grilled sardines and pasta salad, and in a momentary lapse of concentration she dumped the cooked pasta into a colander and rinsed it under the cold tap. They ate at the dining table by the window, and afterwards Obe went outside for a smoke. On his return he loaded the wood burner with fresh logs before climbing into bed. Mallory woke in the early hours, her stomach feeling like someone had buried a knife in it. She just managed to reach the upstairs bathroom before she vomited.

Obe discovered her on the floor, arms clasped around the toilet and head resting on the lid. She was shivering uncontrollably. Beads of sweat glistened like jewels on her brow. Somehow, he managed to get her back downstairs without jolting her too severely, but before he could get a bowl from the kitchen she was sick all over their bed. The vomit stank; not the normal reek of partly digested food but something immeasurably more foul. Obe carried the contaminated bed-clothes outside and dumped them in the snow. Then he gave Mallory some bottled water and checked the pregnancy books for advice. Before he reached any conclusions, her bowels began to loosen, and he only dragged her halfway up the stairs before she soiled herself, a thin black stream of faeces that stuck to her legs like glue. Obe got her onto the toilet before it happened again, but such was her shame at what he'd witnessed that she began to sob and wouldn't stop. With a bucket of bleach, he scrubbed the wooden stairs and stuffed her nightwear into a refuse sack. After that, he helped her into the shower and thoroughly rinsed her down.

By now, the combination of cold air, hot water, nausea and wretchedness had drained her of almost all her energy. Some-how, Obe managed to get her back into bed, remaking it with blankets and rugs. Mallory vomited again, this time into a bowl he'd placed beside her – agonised retching that brought up nothing but bile. 'Pasta,' she moaned. 'Pasta.'

When he asked her to explain, a violent blast of thought hit him

—*STUPID-STUPID-HURTS-SO-BAD-WHAT-WAS-I-DOING-HURTS-NEVER-USED-THE-TAP-WATER-THE-WATER-LIKE-BEING-RIPPED-OPEN-THE-BABY-I'VE-DONE-WHAT-HAVE-I-DONE-BABY-THE-PAIN-OH-WHAT-IF-I-HARMED-THE-WHAT-ABOUT-OBE-WHAT-IF-WE—*

along with an image of the pasta-filled colander as water gushed over it from the kitchen tap.

He was still woozy from his last joint, but Mallory's anguish was so savagely intense that it blasted past his defences and filled his head with fire. Overcome, he staggered outside, crashing down the steps and collapsing into the snow. If he'd passed out then, hypothermia would have claimed him before he woke, but Yoda bounded after him, barking and snapping, until he climbed to his feet and found his way back inside.

Mallory, meanwhile, had lapsed into a state halfway between unconsciousness and sleep. Obe dared not leave her unattended for fear that she might vomit again and choke, so he spent the rest of the night by her side, teeth clenched against a headache so brutal that at times he could not help but cry out.

When dawn arrived, Mallory woke and needed the toilet again. This time they didn't even attempt the stairs; instead, she squatted in a bucket beside the bed, sobbing while Obe tried to reassure her. She managed to drink a little water, but she couldn't keep it down. Already, the entire chalet reeked of vomit and excrement. Cossetting her in blankets, he built up the fire and opened a window to let in some air. For the rest of the morning, assailed by stomach cramps, Mallory threw up whatever she tried to swallow, whether fluids or simple food.

Before sunset, Obe dressed in his warmest winter gear and went up to the tool shed, from which the underground water tank was filled via a system of guttering. Before it disappeared into the ground, a cutaway section of downpipe allowed the water to pass over a gauze filter that prevented leaves and other detritus from getting into the system. Right now, that filter was buried beneath a six-inch crust of snow. When Obe broke through it, he revealed the stiff carcass of a rodent, its claws tangled in the mesh. It had decayed so badly that it was impossible to tell whether it was a rat, a squirrel or some other creature; clearly it had been there for some time, which meant that much of the water pouring down the pipe had flowed over it. Its flesh had turned green in places. It stank worse than anything he had ever smelled. Obe felt his own guts churn as he examined it, but whether the cause was the same sickness as Mallory's or simple revulsion, he did not know. Tossing the carcass deep into the forest, he traipsed back to the chalet and scrubbed his hands until they were raw and red.

That afternoon, helping her on and off the bucket, urging her to drink and supporting her head whenever she vomited, he washed the soiled bedding and placed it near the fire to dry. He opened a tin of dog food for Yoda and a tin of beans for himself. As he ate, he searched the pregnancy books for advice, but all of them counselled against the use of diarrhoea medicines in favour of juices or broths.

The second night was even worse than the first. Mallory thrashed on the mattress, consumed with pain. To keep her out of his head, Obe smoked constantly, complementing the cannabis with half a bottle of vodka. He thought about hiking to Vecchi's cabin, but inebriated as he was, he did not trust himself to navigate the route.

The third day, things deteriorated further. By now, Mallory's risk of dehydration was acute, and after stumbling through the pregnancy books yet again – this time too wooden-headed to retain much of anything he read – Obe decided to dose her with Imodium. It wouldn't fight whatever bacteria assailed her, but it might just settle her stomach long enough to take on fluids. Unfortunately, Mallory couldn't even keep that down; minutes later he was rinsing the medicine out of the bowl they kept beside the bed. During the short hours of daylight he thought again about making the trip down the mountainside to rouse Vecchi, but by now he dared not leave Mallory alone for fear of what might happen.

That evening, the clutching pains he had experienced at the tool shed returned, and this time they did not abate. In the upstairs toilet, his bowels loosened horribly, and not long after that he began to vomit. Unlike Mallory, he faced no restrictions on the drugs that he could take, but although he loaded up on Imodium and aspirin, what they both needed was antibiotics, and of those they had none.

So hard did Obe's sickness hammer him over the next few

days that he had no need of cannabis or alcohol; the silence inside his head was that of a cathedral, as if the part of him that intruded on others had shrivelled, perhaps as a way of conserving his energy. He lay beside Mallory on the mattress, too ill, even, to stoke the fire. Outside, the snow fell steadily.

On the fourth day, with the wood stove cold and dead, the temperature in the chalet plummeted. Obe crawled to the kitchen, his throat a blister, and found a bottle of water. He managed to drink a little of it, and carried what remained back to Mallory. Her skin felt as hot and dry as an oven. 'The baby,' she croaked. 'I think it may have died.'

Obe did not know how to comfort her, but he did know that they'd reached the limits of their endurance. Outside, ten inches of snow now covered the ground. He had nowhere near enough strength to hike through it to Vecchi's cabin. In desperation, he pulled on boots and coat and fought his way through the snow to the Morello. Inside, he switched on the heater before succumbing to a fit of shakes so violent that he thought he must be having a seizure. Curled in a ball, head knocking against the carpet, he hardly retained enough control of his movements to breathe.

He must have passed out for a while, because when he opened his eyes the temperature inside the motorhome had risen considerably. Sweat sheeted down his face. His clothes clung to his body, slimy and wet. He could smell himself, too: a graveyard stink, sweet and rich, reminiscent of the rodent carcass he'd found at the tool shed.

Obe pulled himself up. Clumsily, he searched the cupboards until he found what he was looking for: the mobile phone Mallory had left in the Mên-an-Tol Hotel's bathroom, along with the battery he assumed must power it. That night, eight months ago, he'd stuffed it into his backpack before waking her. Now, if he could get a signal, perhaps he could arrange a medical evacuation, by helicopter if not by road. He took the phone to a bench seat and reassembled it, but his attempts to activate it failed. Assuming that the battery had discharged, he resumed his search, this time unearthing a USB lead and an adaptor that worked with the Morello's sockets. After plugging in the phone, the white outline of a battery appeared on screen. He'd expected the device to power up almost immediately, but a minute later it still hadn't absorbed enough charge to bring up a welcome screen.

While he waited, Obe stared through the windscreen at the falling snow. His stomach bubbled and he belched, grimacing at the foul taste. Moments later the chalet door banged open and Mallory appeared, propping herself up against the frame. Her jaw hung slack, her eyes unfocused. 'Obe!' she shouted, head swinging as if drunk. 'The baby. The *baby!*'

# FIFTY-SEVEN

As he scrambled from his seat, Obe nearly faltered beneath the weight of panic that pressed down on him. He threw open the Morello's door and sank into the snow. 'Stay there!' he shouted. 'Don't come outside!'

He waded through drifts to reach her, and when he saw her expression he could hardly bring himself to ask what was wrong; but in the end she answered for him: 'The baby,' she repeated, through clenched teeth. 'I think it's coming.'

Her words sluiced the sickness from him faster than any medicine. His head still felt barricaded, but the broken glass in his stomach drained away like sand. 'Let's get you back to bed,' he said, but Mallory shook her head.

'Not yet. I need to stand.'

'I thought . . . I thought you were going to tell me th—'

'Don't. Don't even say it.'

He ushered her back inside, shutting the door behind them. 'How're you feeling?'

She swallowed. 'Like I'm in the worst possible state to give birth.'

'I'll get you to a hospital. Make sure you have the right—'

Violently, Mallory shook her head. 'It'd be a death sentence, for all three of us. The Vasi know that I'm due. They'll be waiting for exactly that. I'm having this baby here, Obe. For better or worse.'

He nodded, felt a powerful rush of love for her. 'Mallory,' he began, and couldn't fathom a way to express himself.

She touched his arm. 'Better get things organised. This place is a freezer.'

'I'll bring in some wood.'

'As much as you can. I don't think we'll be leaving any time soon.'

'Have you drunk anything?'

'A little water.'

'You're having contractions?'

'Yeah. But not too bad. Not yet.'

'How far apart?'

'I don't know.'

'We'll get through this.'

She nodded, offered him a tight smile. 'That's why you're here, Obe. To provide a stream of useless platitudes.'

'Well, you know what they say—'

'If it's a superhero quote, save it until I need to punch you.'

He took a breath, tried to slow his heart. 'Is it painful?'

'I've punched you before. Don't you remember?'

'I meant the contractions.'

'I wouldn't recommend them.'

'Right.'

'How about that firewood?'

He nodded, looked at the door, tried to take a step towards it. For some reason he was finding it difficult to leave her side. 'We'll get through this.'

'You already said.'

'I did?'

Hissing with pain, she braced herself against the kitchen counter.

'Mallory?' he asked. 'What can I do?'

'Firewood, Obe.' Through clenched teeth she added, 'It looks like tree, except all chopped up. You'll find a shitload of it stacked outside.'

He spent the next ten minutes ferrying armfuls of logs from the covered store, amazed at how his sickness – temporarily, at least – seemed to have diminished. He started a fresh fire in the wood stove, tending it until it threw out a fierce heat. After that he lit a score of candles, placing them on shelves and side tables, hoping to burn away the stench of sickness. Mallory couldn't sit, and she couldn't lie down. Instead she paced the chalet's ground floor, dosing herself with paracetamol and blotting away her sweat.

Lying forgotten inside the Morello, the mobile phone blinked on and began to search for a signal. It was registered to a UK network, and when it failed to connect it locked onto a TIM radio transmission from Telecom Italia. After an automated authentication process lasting around three minutes, two of the five reception circles on the device's screen filled with white. Then the GPS sent out a ping.

# FIFTY-EIGHT

Aylah İncesu was checking into the Grand Hotel Continental in Bucharest when the call came through. Signing a register at the front desk, she didn't retrieve her phone fast enough to answer it, but the device fell silent for only a moment before it began to trill again. Dumping her bag on the counter, she took out the phone and answered it. 'Whatever it is,' she snapped, 'make it quick.'

'I'll think you'll want to hear the detail on this one.'

'Don't irritate me, Teke. Get to the point.'

'Remember that phone we were tracking, eight months ago back in Cornwall? The night we nearly snatched Mallory at the hotel? Guess what?'

'You just got a hit.'

Teke made a sound like a TV gameshow rewarding a correct answer. 'Got a location, too.'

'Where?'

When he told her, she could hardly believe it. 'The bitch crawled home.'

'Seems that way.'

Aylah drummed her fingernails against the reception desk. 'She's not stupid. To use that phone now, after we tracked her through it before – she wouldn't have considered it unless she was desperate. Something must have gone wrong. Badly wrong. Where are you?'

'About to fly out. You?'

'I can be at Ferenc Liszt in thirty minutes. Get me on a flight. Find Chevry too, plus whoever else that's close. *Our* guys, not Caleb's. There's nothing useful he can add. I know those mountains. I grew up there.'

'What about Manco?'

Picking up her bag, Aylah strode across the lobby. 'If we do this right, the first he'll know of it is when he see pictures of their dead bodies.'

She heard his breathing escalate, knew that she aroused him with those words. 'I'm going to gut her, Teke,' she hissed. 'I'm going to cut her into so many pieces of wet meat that it'll take Manco an hour to figure out what he's looking at.'

# FIFTY-NINE

As night fell, with logs crackling in the stove and water boiling on the hob, the chalet's windows grew misty with steam. The outside world melted away and the entirety of creation shrank to the dimensions of their single low-ceilinged room.

Mallory stood at the window, gazing out at the night, and Obe found, strangely, that he could look at her only in snatches, lest the intensity of his emotions overwhelm him. He could not say that he was proud of her, because that would have implied some level of ownership, but his admiration of her was boundless, and he was heartened, more than he could possibly have anticipated, that she would trust him enough to keep him close at the point when she was most vulnerable.

For comfort she wore a loose-fitting nightshirt and sheepskin boots. A simple black band kept the hair from her face. Every so often she braced a hand against the wall. Her mouth tightened, and her breath caught in her throat. Obe waited until the contraction was over, timing the interval until the next.

'Nine minutes,' he said, when this one came to an end; he'd learned, early on, not to bother her with information during them.

Mallory nodded, took a lungful of air. Outside, an owl began to call, a series of haunting, low-pitched hoots. Looking through the window, she said, 'I haven't heard one of those since we arrived.'

Unbidden, Yoda padded over. He placed his forelegs on the sill and peered across the valley. Then he swung his head around, looking at Obe with fire-brightened eyes.

'What is it, buddy?'

The dog sneezed, shook his head, returned his attention to the night.

By eleven p.m., the intervals between Mallory's contractions hadn't reduced. Two hours later, they were arriving every six minutes. Obe brewed coffee and persuaded her to eat some dry toast. She didn't complain about the pain, but he could tell it was intensifying. Her skin was greasy with sweat.

Days earlier, before the sickness struck them, Obe had discovered an old radio in a box of her father's things. The batteries inside it had corroded, but when he removed them, sanded down the contacts and loaded fresh ones, he managed to stir it into life. Now, he tried to tune it to something calming, but the only station he could find was broadcasting Europop. 'Well, that sucks.'

'Leave it on,' Mallory told him, through clenched teeth. 'I don't care if it's shit.'

'When I was born, the song playing on the radio was "I'd Like to Teach the World to Sing", by The New Seekers.'

Hearing that, she barked with laughter.

Obe grinned. 'What's funny?'

'It's just so . . . *you*,' she gasped, as a new contraction began to grip.

Yoda turned in circles between them, trying to figure out the source of their amusement. Then his head snapped towards the window and he began to growl.

Outside, a sound such as Obe had never heard, except in a few movies of apocalypse or war, broke through the mountain stillness and climbed the slope towards them, filling the chalet with urgency and horror.

Aylah İncesu's flight landed in Innsbruck, Austria, three and a half hours after she received the call from Teke. From there, a helicopter should have flown her to the tiny airport at Bolzano in the Alpine province of South Tyrol, where she was due to rendezvous with the rest of the strike team, but thanks to whatever failures of Italian efficiency, she found no aircraft waiting. In frustration she hired an SUV and made the trip overland. Fortunately, an army of snow ploughs had been working to keep the main toll route open; despite the severe weather, Aylah completed the journey in just over two hours. She stayed in contact with Teke throughout, and when she learned that the others – Guy Chevry, Ali Irmak, Nik Pavri, Elias Hunt and Talaal Safi – had already assembled, she sent most of them on ahead, anxious not to lose more time.

At the airport, Teke commandeered a Bell Jet Ranger. Guy Chevry, a licensed pilot, would fly it. Aylah strapped herself in one of the passenger seats, laying her *qama* beside three suppressor-equipped Heckler and Koch MP5s. As well as the sub-machine guns, Teke had brought along two Beretta semi-automatic pistols, but the firearms would only be used as a last resort: if all went to plan, Aylah anticipated a few hours of heavy knife-work.

Mallory had been shrewd to choose the family home as a final retreat. Not only was it difficult to reach, but it was also one of the last places Aylah would have thought to look; everything she'd learned in the intervening years suggested that her sister remained indelibly scarred by the events in Trentino fifteen years earlier.

The Jet Ranger's turbine increased in pitch. Aylah felt a lightness in her stomach as the uplift pulled them into the sky. Leaning her forehead against the window, she watched the sparkling lights below. The world was a beautiful place, but it had become infected with humanity; defiled. The Arayıcı, as they had done since the beginning, offered nothing but a means of spreading that contagion. Far better to experience the serenity that came from understanding truth and accepting it.

Mankind would endure for some generations yet. But one day, years or decades into the future, human chatter would cease, human structures would crumble. The planet would reclaim its forests and its climate. The oceans would once more teem with life.

*After violence, silence.*

As the Jet Ranger's rotor blades chopped apart the surrounding air, Aylah felt her heartbeat begin to slow.

She heard Teke's voice, tinny in her headphones. *'Just had word from Safi. Amount of snow on the ground, the road up to the chalet's impassable. They got within a mile before they had to stop. They're continuing up on foot – one team from the south-east, one from the south-west. Safi has eyes on the place already. Says it's lit up like a Christmas bauble. Irmak's a few minutes behind.'*

Aylah thought of Damla Gültekin back in Sweden, of all the other Arayıcı who had cowered inside their bolt-holes long after they should have fled. She wondered if Mallory would be any different.

*'ETA two minutes,'* Teke said.

# SIXTY

On nights as clear as this, for as many years as he cared to remember, Vincenti Vecchi liked to look at the stars. A short distance from his cabin stood his observatory. Inside, there was just enough space for his telescope, a catalytic heater and a table on which to place a thermos and a plate of *tortelli di zucca*. Decades earlier, he'd built the hut to help him answer some of his questions about the universe; these days he was content simply to observe the beauty of the heavens.

During the early years of his obsession he had used a Cave Astrola scope, eventually graduating to a Celestron Eight. Currently he employed a Meade twelve-inch refractor, balanced on a motorised equatorial mount. It had taken him to faraway places that he'd never expected to see.

Tonight, however, he had postponed his usual tour of deep sky objects so that he might reacquaint himself with a few close neighbours. For the first hour, he explored the mountains and plains of the lunar surface. From there he hopped to the ice caps of Mars. Afterwards, it was a short leap to Jupiter's moons and onwards to Saturn's rings.

Eventually, Vecchi felt himself drawn deeper, to more mysterious skies. He was programming the GOTO mount to seek out M13, the globular cluster in Hercules, when he heard the sound of an engine some distance away.

On a different night he might have ignored it, losing himself in the spectacle of God's creation. Not tonight. Taking his eye from the scope, he switched off the heater and held his breath.

Definitely an engine. From the sound of it, a diesel.

Rolling back his sleeve, Vecchi peered at his wristwatch: three-twenty a.m. It was unusual enough to hear a vehicle in these mountains so late. With weather conditions this severe – he'd waded through an eighteen-inch snow drift to reach the observatory – it was unprecedented. Immediately his thoughts turned to the couple further up the slope. A week had passed since he'd last seen them. Despite his concern for their well-being, he had left them in peace.

Had something gone wrong? Perhaps a medical emergency, for which they now sought aid? If they were trying to make their way down the mountain tonight, they were desperate indeed. Even with snow chains, they stood little chance of successfully negotiating roads untouched by ploughs. If they lost traction, smashing through one of the barriers that wrapped the many hairpin turns, they'd have long seconds of freefall to rue their mistake.

Rising from his seat, his spine crackling like bubble wrap, Vecchi pulled on hat and gloves, threw open the observatory door and crashed outside. The cold punched him like a fist but he lifted his chin in defiance, ignoring the frozen air that slipped over his collar and sank down onto his chest.

Definitely a diesel engine: he could hear it more clearly now. It was still some distance away, fading and growing, its location difficult to assess. These peaks did funny things to sound, flinging it, distorting it and sometimes swallowing it.

Zipping his coat to his throat, he concentrated.

The engine sounded like it was straining, which meant that the vehicle was ascending, not descending . . . and yet that made no sense.

Vecchi blinked away tears. When he rubbed his face on his coat sleeve, he felt the crunch of ice crystals in his nose.

Definitely ascending.

Which meant . . . which meant . . . what, exactly?

Perhaps Obe had descended into the valley earlier that day, and was only now returning.

Perhaps it was Sal, on his way to attend the birth.

Then the sound of that single diesel engine split in two and Vecchi realised that there was more than one vehicle climbing the slope towards the chalet, and that the girl, the boy and the dog were in more trouble than they could possibly have known.

Moments later, the engines died. Silence returned to the slopes.

Vecchi felt his skin begin to itch, as if he'd rolled naked in a patch of nettles. The thick forest around the chalet would have smothered the sound of those engines. The couple would have no warning of the approaching danger.

Lurching through the snow, following the path he had cut earlier that evening, Vecchi hurried to his cabin. Inside, he clattered up the stairs. Twice his boots slipped from under him and he had to snatch at the rail to keep himself upright. He owned no mobile phone, and while he still maintained the short-wave radio he'd operated during his youth, the couple had no way of receiving him. His truck would make it halfway there, but he wouldn't arrive in advance of those he had heard.

On the first-floor landing, he used a broom to drop the loft hatch and unhook the ladder. Up he went. The unheated space was cluttered with a lifetime's collection of junk: old engineering projects, half-forgotten restorations – the manifold distractions of a solitary life. Shuffling forwards, he pulled off his gloves and felt for what he sought. Within seconds his hands began to stiffen, but he persevered, and moments later found what he needed, wrestling it free of its neighbouring junk. It was a task to get back down the ladder without dropping it. Somehow, he managed.

Careful not to slip on the melting snow he had tracked up the stairs, he made it outside to his truck.

The air-raid siren – an electric dual-tone model built in 1940 – had originally been used during London's Blitz. After the war it had turned up in Italy's South Tyrol region, where it had been used for some years to warn of avalanches and other extreme weather events. Vecchi had rescued it from a municipal dump; he had restored it, grown bored with it and eventually archived it.

Dropping the truck's tailgate, he dumped the device onto the cargo bed and hurried back to his cabin. Next, he wheeled out a portable four-stroke generator, bumping it down the steps and hefting it over the tailgate. When he pressed its electric start, the pistons hopped once and caught. The exhaust chugged smoke.

Vecchi gave it a few moments to stabilise. Then he hooked up the air-raid siren and switched it on. Inside the main housing, an impeller began to spin inside two separate drums. Within seconds, those drums began to emit their characteristic two-tone whine. As the motor accelerated, the siren's pitch rose. Slamming the tailgate, Vecchi disappeared back inside the cabin for his final trip. He emerged with a hunting rifle and a few magazines preloaded with ammunition. Climbing into the cab, he started the truck's engine and accelerated into the night.

# SIXTY-ONE

Obe's first reaction was to go to the window, but Mallory grabbed his arm and dragged him back. He frowned, listening to that two-tone warble floating up from the valley. It was a sound to wake the dead and terrify the living, a harbinger of something wicked: of imminent calamity. 'What *is* that?'

'Sounds like an air-raid siren,' Mallory said. Bent over, still gripping his arm, she waited until her contraction had passed. Then she went to the corner, picked up the shotgun Sal had given them and broke it. The brass heads of its chambered rounds glimmered in the firelight. She snapped the gun shut, a sound like a breaking neck. 'Whatever it is, it's meant for us. We've got to go. Now.'

Obe stared. 'You're in *labour*, Mallory. Where the hell are we—'

'Damnit, get the rucksacks! You can stay here and greet them or come with me.'

He blinked, unable to process what she was saying. Their mountain hideaway had seemed so safe and anonymous that it was hard to accept the approach of something monstrous.

Near the door, Yoda began to whine, ears flattened against his skull.

Obe pushed out his mind, trying to sense the presence of anyone lurking beyond the chalet walls, but he couldn't even sense Mallory standing right beside him – with his sickness still raging, he was deaf to the wider world.

By the time he'd fetched their rucksacks from the kitchen, she had shrugged on her coat, wrapped a scarf around her neck and pulled on hat and gloves. Obe slung his arms through the straps of his pack, watching with horror as she filled her pockets with shotgun cartridges she'd shaken from a cardboard box. 'It's freezing outside,' he said, lifting her rucksack and wearing it across his chest.

Mallory's eyes, when she glanced up at him, were large and scared. Her chest rose and fell. 'I know.'

Outside, the siren's two-tone wail was a mountain banshee climbing the slope towards them. Obe looked around the room, wondering what else to take. On the bed lay two woollen blankets. He rolled them up as quickly as he could. 'What else?' he murmured. 'What else?'

Mallory looked at the boy upon whom she'd come to depend and realised, in a single shocking instant, just how deeply she cared for him. The discovery made a washtub of her insides. She knew that blood would be spilt in these mountains before the night was through. The thought that it might be *his* blood made her physically sick.

For nearly eight months she had fretted about the prospect of childbirth; but never, even in her worst-case scenario, had she considered that her labour would coincide with the very moment that the Vasi found her.

She still burned with fever. Obe, too, looked horribly sick; his skin appeared bloodless, his eyes ringed by dark circles. The rucksacks so encumbered him that he could barely hold himself upright.

When he asked 'What else?' she shook her head. There *was* nothing else. Nothing else to do except flee into the frozen night and trust to dumb luck that they could survive whatever violence pursued them. Even if they avoided their would-be executioners, the mountain would likely extract its price.

She pushed Obe in front of her, through the living room and into the kitchen. A memory slunk into her head: Laleh Gurvich crashing down the back steps to the garden, a perfect Valentine's carnation blossoming in the centre of her chest.

Mallory shoved the image away. Could the same tragedy strike twice? She considered, just for a moment, going through the door ahead of Obe, but however much she wished to keep him safe, she knew her first responsibility was to the baby.

Funny, that after all this time, her Arayıcı blood should compel her so forcibly. But perhaps it wasn't her heritage at all; perhaps it was nothing more remarkable than a mother's instinct – if such a thing could ever be described as unremarkable.

Cringing, she followed Obe down the steps to the garden. The cold air slammed her, tearing the warmth from her flesh. Ahead, Obe stumbled in the snow before pulling himself upright. Yoda surged past them both. They were halfway to the trees when they heard the whine of a turbine and the brutal clatter of rotor blades.

'Go!' Obe shouted, kicking through the drifts.

Mallory tried to match his pace, but just then she felt a terrible, clutching pain in her belly, and staggered to a halt in the middle of the clearing.

Noise, all around. Then, something far worse: the white beam of a spotlight, lancing down from the sky and crawling up the slope.

Obe reached the treeline, turned and saw her stranded in the snow, beset by the agony of her labour. She had never seen him look so forlorn.

Before that white finger of light even found her, gunfire rang out.

As the Bell Jet Ranger dove out of the sky towards the clearing, Aylah İncesu saw, for the first time in fifteen years, the chalet she'd once called home. The sight triggered a panoply of emotions far too complicated to unravel. For so many years it had seemed that her memories of the place had ceased to exist; but now they came crashing back, and her head sagged with the effort of containing them. She saw her parents – not as they had been when Saul Manco carried her, kicking and screaming, from the house, but as they had lived; joyful, defiant, full of hope.

Aylah curled her lip, gripped by an almost all-consuming desire to inflict pain. She glanced at the *qama* on the seat beside her; imagined, for a thrilling instant, how it would feel to plunge it through the back of Guy Chevry's seat, opening him up and sending the Jet Ranger tumbling from the sky.

*You're her, aren't you? The one they use against us. The one they call* Şeytan.

A muscle twitched in her cheek.

Aylah's ground teams had been instructed to open fire on the chalet windows the moment they heard the helicopter: controlled bursts, aimed high, intended to subdue the occupants and dissuade them from fleeing.

As the Jet Ranger arced towards the clearing, she saw intermittent white flashes from the trees to the south-east and south-west, and even though she couldn't hear the clatter of automatic weapons, she knew that her subordinates had done as instructed.

'Down!' she screamed, gripping her headphone mic. 'Put us on the ground!'

Up front, Chevry pushed forwards on the stick.

# SIXTY-TWO

When Obe reached the treeline and turned his head, he expected to find Mallory right behind him. Instead, to his dismay, he saw her in the middle of the clearing, face creased in agony.

The pulse of the helicopter's rotor blades was a pressure in his chest. Even as he broke from cover, retracing his steps through the path he'd kicked through the snow, a chorus of gunfire erupted all around. Glass exploded. Bullets struck wood. White fire sprouted from the surrounding trees. Reaching Mallory's side, he threw his arm around her. 'Go!' he yelled. 'We have to go *now*!'

Tears streaming down her face, she shuffled forwards. The helicopter swung in from the east, its rotor blades raising a blizzard of flakes.

Eyes closed, cheeks stinging, Obe battled through the snow, one hand gripping Mallory's arm. They had seconds, now. No more.

Somehow, she found a little extra speed. At their back, gunfire crashed again, this new assault even more furious than the first.

Obe risked a glance behind him. Immediately, his shoulder slammed against a tree, spinning him around. He released Mallory as he fell, frightened that he'd pull her down with him.

When he tried to stand, pain raced up his leg and burst like a firework in his head.

He heard shouts, now, from the other side of the clearing. Men's voices: excited, jubilant.

Back on his feet, clutching Mallory once again, Obe stumbled forwards. Beneath him, the snow surrendered to frozen forest mulch. A few more yards and the maelstrom whipped up by the helicopter's rotor blades began to subside. He heard the turbine winding down. Knew that the Vasi had found a place to land.

'Slow,' Mallory hissed, through clenched teeth. 'Got to slow down.'

'We can't,' he said, gripping her arm.

'Go to stop. Go to sit.'

'They're too close.' He yanked her after him, cringing at her short, hard scream.

'The baby's coming,' she moaned. 'The *baby's* coming.'

Nothing he could say to that, nothing he could do. He couldn't carry Mallory without dumping the rucksacks, and if he abandoned their supplies they were as good as dead. Ahead, the land began to rise at a far steeper gradient. With peril at their backs, their only option was to climb higher, into a landscape even more extreme, and temperatures even more inhospitable. Mallory's voice had degenerated into a wordless keening. When the tree canopy receded enough to permit a shard of moon, Obe saw that the sweat beading her face had begun to freeze. Driving her on felt like the most unconscionable cruelty, but what option did he have? Death behind, death up ahead. No choice at all. For days, sickness had suppressed his ability to hear her thoughts but now, perhaps as a reaction to their plight, that awareness returned; although they were not Mallory's thoughts he heard this time

*—find-her-stake-her-cut-the-mutant-out-of-hER-KEEP-*
*HER-ALIVE-WHILE-YOU-DO-IT-THE-BOY-TOO-*

*PULL-THE-DIRTY-THING-TO-**PIECES-WHILE-**
**THEY-WATCH-TEAR-IT-APART-RED-**
**AND-WET**—*

but those of another.

Obe collapsed to his knees, pressing his hands to his head.

'What is it?' Mallory screamed. 'What's happening?'

Behind him, a single shot rang out.

He turned, unbearably frightened at what he might see.

Aylah İncesu leaped from the Jet Ranger the moment its skids touched the ground, emerging into a world whipped white by the downdraught. She waded through the snow until she realised that in such poor visibility her own men might mistake her for their target. Crouching, she waited for the blizzard to dissipate.

As the helicopter's turbine wound down, a new sound intruded, rolling out of the forest further down the slope. Aylah canted her head. The two-tone wail was a sound to augur Armageddon, igniting in her an animal excitement, an over-whelming hunger for bloodshed.

Finally, her surroundings coalesced; and there, in a clearing of snow ringed by dark trees, stood the Alpine chalet of her childhood. Hardly a scrap of glass remained in the windows that faced south across the valley. The outer walls bore hundreds of scars from the fusillade they had endured. Woodsmoke belched from the chimney. Inside, the ground-floor rooms flickered with firelight. Clear signs, if any were needed, of habitation.

She prayed that its occupants had not been harmed; that they were cowering on the floor, helplessly awaiting her arrival. How good it would feel to put an end to them, how immeasur-ably cathartic. With Mallory dead, the last fragment of Aylah's history would be eradicated. Nothing to link her to the past, nothing to bind her to the future. She would exist in the moment, for as long as the moment lasted. And humanity would have taken another small step towards its doom.

*After violence, silence.*

On the chalet's top step, Talaal Safi appeared. Alarmed, Aylah rose to her feet. Were her targets already dead? Had Safi ignored his orders, just like Korec and Levitan eight months ago?

'What's happening?' she shouted, wading through snow to reach him. 'Are they here? Are they alive?' She thundered up the steps and pushed past him, through the kitchen and into the living room.

Memories, black and toxic, seeped from the walls. Unprepared for their intensity, Aylah put out a hand to steady herself. She heard a clatter of footsteps and a dark shape burst into the room, not much higher than her waist. When it turned towards her, face as blank as the night, she yelled and batted it away, even as she recognised its silhouette: her sister, nine years old, flesh blackened and smoking on her bones.

Her father walked in, turning a hollowed-out face towards her. Aylah fell to the floor. As she kicked away from his apparition she saw her mother appear behind him. The woman's eyes were black holes, accusatory.

Abruptly the images vanished, leaving Aylah gasping for breath.

*After violence, silence. After violence, silence.*

'What is it?' Safi asked, appearing in the doorway. 'What did you see?'

Aylah dragged herself up. She owed this Vasi foot soldier no explanation for her behaviour. Recovering her breath, she gazed around the room, seeing it as it was, rather than how it had been.

A double mattress lay at its heart, heaped with blankets and pillows. A pile of pregnancy books rested on a side table. Among the general clutter she saw medical supplies, packs of bottled water, an old radio she recognised as her father's. Logs burned in the wood stove. A large reserve had been stacked beside it. 'Did you check upstairs?'

Safi nodded.

Aylah strode to the front door and threw it open. Near the treeline she noticed a large modern motorhome, heavily encrusted with snow. She saw no tracks from other vehicles. If the couple had fled on foot, they'd be dead from hypothermia in a few hours.

That eerie two-tone wail still sang out. Clearly it was some kind of early-warning system. She wondered what had triggered it. Leaping down the steps, wading to the middle of the clearing, she tried to get a fix on its source.

Teke appeared around the side of the chalet, his weapon drawn, Guy Chevry and Elias Hunt behind him. 'They aren't inside,' Aylah said. 'But they didn't leave by car.'

'Is that an *air-raid* siren?'

'That or something similar. Seems it gave them a head start.' She turned to Hunt. 'Where's Irmak and Pavri?'

'Haven't seen them. We came in from different directions, like you instructed.'

'You haven't *seen* them?'

'No, as I said, we—'

'Have you spoken to them?'

'Sure. Just before you flew in.'

'Not since?'

'No. I—'

He would have said more, but just then something smacked against the front of his chest. Hunt flinched, eyes widening, and as he dropped to his knees a single gunshot rang out from the surrounding woods. Coughing up a dark splatter, he pitched forwards onto his face.

'Down!' Aylah shouted, grabbing Teke. 'They're *engaging* us!'

They dived into the snow as another bullet snapped through the air above their heads. The chalet's front door swung open and Talaal Safi appeared, silhouetted. Instead of shouting a warning, Aylah turned her attention to the treeline. An instant later she was rewarded with a flash of light in her peripheral vision, followed by the crack of a high-powered rifle.

Safi started screaming. She tuned him out, grateful for his sacrifice. Moments later another shot perforated the air right beside her position. This time she'd been looking in exactly the right direction, but when the muzzle flash revealed the shooter's face she discovered something she hadn't expected: not the boy, nor the girl, but an old man with a hooked and mushroomed nose, and eyebrows so tufted that they almost obscured his eyes. Coal-black and glinting, those eyes locked onto her, and in that instant Aylah recognised her parents' old friend.

As she raised the barrel of her MP5, Vincenti Vecchi drew back the bolt of his rifle. Even as he put the stock against his cheek, Aylah's sub-machine gun stitched a red line across his chest. The old man spun like a top, weapon tumbling from his fingers. Her second volley erupted across his back in a series of scarlet fountains. She walked towards him, gun trained. When his body relaxed, fingers opening like flowers, she saw that he would not rise again.

Ejecting the spent magazine, Aylah slapped in a spare and racked the bolt. Further down the slope, that cataclysmic wail still issued, rising and falling. Talaal Safi's screams, less forceful than before, offered a jarring counterpoint.

Dangerous to assume that the old man had acted alone; but there were so few Arayıcı left in the world that the chance of an accomplice was slim. Even so, Aylah did not present her back to the trees as she retraced her steps. When she rejoined Teke and Chevry, it took her a moment to process what she saw.

'Is he dead?' she asked finally. Her voice, over the siren's lament, sounded curiously wooden.

Chevry grunted. 'Half his skull is gone. No coming back from that.'

For the space of a breath it seemed as if something would tear inside her, and then the feeling passed.

Death had robbed Teke of the last vestiges of his humanity.

His eyes dull and off-kilter, the top of his skull a jagged crown, he looked monstrous. Aylah had known him seven years, had been intimate with him for over half that time. Fortunately, Manco had taught her the absurdity of grief. Death – even the death of one's closest associates – was cause for celebration not sadness, each tiny contraction of the human race a victory.

'Idiot should have kept his head down,' she said.

Chevry climbed to his feet, nodded.

'Anything from Irmak or Pavri?'

'Nothing. Got to assume that crazy fuck rinsed them before we landed. He must've taken out four of our guys before you slotted him. Pretty impressive.'

Realising that Talaal Safi's screams had faded, Aylah pushed through snow towards the chalet. When she climbed the steps she saw that Vincenti Vecchi's tally was closer to five. Safi lay halfway inside the entrance, curled around a spreading pool of blood. He was still breathing, just about – she could see the slow rise and fall of his shoulders. 'Sorry,' she told him. 'I had to let him shoot you. Otherwise I might not have spotted him.'

Hearing her voice, Safi twisted around.

'You're losing a lot of blood,' she added. 'And we can't afford to waste time getting you to a hospital. I expect that seems harsh but it's the reality. Even if I called for back-up, I doubt you'd survive until it arrived.' She wouldn't admit that she *couldn't* call for back-up – not until she brought this to a successful close. In her desire to take Mallory alone, she had defied Saul Manco once again. 'Want me to end it?' she asked, lifting the barrel of her gun.

Wild-eyed, Safi shook his head.

Chevry appeared, like a stalking wolf. From a belt sheath he drew a thick-handled blade. It looked to Aylah like a Yakut knife, designed for butchering meat. Licking his lips, he stared at the injured man. 'Sure?'

'*Sh* . . .' Safi croaked. '. . . *Sure.*'

Chevry frowned. 'Sure you want us to end it? Or sure that

you don't? If it's pain you're worried about, you'll hardly feel a thing. One thrust, up under your chin. It'll be over in a snap. Or I can open an artery. You're going to bleed out in an hour or so, anyway. No point prolonging it.'

Safi's right foot twitched. His legs scissored. Slowly, agonisingly, he began to snail along the hallway, leaving a slick so dark that it almost seemed like his heart pumped molasses.

Chevry stalked him, moonlight glimmering on saliva-streaked teeth. 'I'm trying to help you, here,' he said. 'Trying to do what's right. I've got to say that you're being a little selfish.'

Reaching the limit of his endurance, Safi's progress stalled. He rolled onto his back, began to gasp.

'Just do it,' Aylah snapped. 'And be quick. We don't have time for a big performance.'

Chevry slung a leg over Safi, straddling his chest as the man squirmed beneath him. Leaving them to it, Aylah retreated to the helicopter and collected her *qama* from the passenger cabin.

Teke was dead. He wasn't coming back. She would not grieve, but she *would* find Mallory, and she *would* get her revenge.

*After violence, silence.*

Rolling up the sleeve of her mountain jacket, pressing the *qama*'s blade to the meat of her forearm, she sliced a deep fissure into her flesh.

# SIXTY-THREE

For a while, as Mallory stumbled through the frozen forest, her face scratched by pine needles and her feet tripping over tree roots, her contractions stopped entirely, as if the baby inside her belly had intuited that the world awaiting it was unsafe, and chose to delay its arrival.

It did not mean that she was without pain. In the last four weeks she'd grown so heavy with pregnancy that moving even short distances left her breathless. Out here, in this violent cold, trudging steadily towards ever harsher terrain, she felt every complaint tenfold. The vertebrae in her lower spine shrieked; her hips, as they rotated, felt like glass had worked into the sockets. Her ankles produced an electric horror show of sensation every time she planted a foot. Each breath was a cold fire in her throat. Each exhalation stole more warmth from her core. She felt hoarfrost growing on her eyelashes and inside her nose. In her gloves, her fingers were so stiff that they felt as if they'd frozen around the shotgun; she doubted that she retained the dexterity to fire it.

Beside her – never in front, never behind – Obe walked in silence, struggling to bear the weight of their packs. She heard his breath rattling in his lungs; clear evidence that he hadn't recovered from the sickness that had assailed them both these last seven days. Every so often his chin dropped onto his chest, and inevitably a tree would appear in his path right then and he'd slam it with his shoulder. Mallory tried to keep an eye out, but beneath these boughs the forest was so dark that she rarely spotted an obstacle in time to warn him. Yoda ranged around them, ears pricked and nose raised.

Time seemed no longer a constant. Mallory could not have said whether ten minutes had passed since their flight from the chalet or an hour. They saw the moon rarely. Even when it appeared, its position seemed to swing back and forth in the sky.

Eventually, as if she had needed a further reminder of their plight, her contractions returned. The first one hit with little warning, stopping her in her tracks with an intensity that made her screech. It felt like powerful arms had wrapped around her, mashing her insides to paste. She couldn't breathe, couldn't see; had Obe not grabbed her shoulders she would have fallen. Somehow, still bearing that monstrous pain, she managed to shuffle through a drift of dead needles to a tree, dropping the shotgun so that she could hold onto the trunk.

Finally, the contraction receded and she could breathe again, great clouds of condensation billowing from her mouth. Obe, releasing her, put his hands on his hips. 'We should keep going,' he told her. 'In between contractions. For as far as you can.'

She wanted to scream at him for that, wanted to snatch up the shotgun and slam the stock against his head, but she knew the truth of his words, and that he was merely trying to save their lives. Tilting back her head, she gazed through a narrow shaft between the trees and saw starlight glimmering.

Mallory closed her eyes for the space of three breaths. Then she nodded, releasing the trunk. Obe picked up the shotgun and slotted it into her frozen fingers.

A few minutes later she stopped again as another fierce contraction gripped her. This one felt like it was never going to end, and at its peak she felt an almost uncontrollable urge to push, which frightened her very badly indeed. 'It's coming,' she moaned. 'There's nothing I can do to stop it.'

They'd reached a place where the trees grew sparsely, offering little protection from prying eyes. 'A bit further,' Obe insisted. 'We have to find somewhere better than this.'

He was right, she knew it, but her need to rest was irresistible, and when Obe saw that she couldn't be dissuaded, he lowered her gently to the ground. The frozen earth pressed through her clothes with a rawness that stole her breath, and when the next contraction hit she almost passed out for lack of air. It would have been a mercy of sorts, because this time the pain was so brutal as to be inhuman, a clutching agony that made her eyes feel like they might burst from the pressure. When finally it receded, and she saw just what an exposed mountain flank she'd chosen, she groaned in dismay, because if they used any kind of light out here they would be spotted with ease, and yet without a fire to chase away the cold she would likely die of exposure in the very act of labour.

'Get me up,' she hissed, lifting a hand towards Obe, and it was the hardest thing she'd ever said. Relieved, his eyes full of love, he raised her and helped her to shuffle forwards, taking the shotgun and adding it to his burden.

Their pace, now, was so agonisingly slow as to be almost worthless: a few steps, pause, a few steps more. Every other minute, a contraction wrenched her so mercilessly that she howled for mercy.

Inch by inch, yard by yard, they progressed. They put the open flank at their backs and climbed to a new swathe of forest where the ground was lumpen and fissured. There they ascended past grey pinnacles of stone, precursors to the huge rock monoliths that crowned these mountains; not that they would ever reach them – it was time, unquestionably, to stop.

Obe seemed to sense it even without asking, because for the first time he began to range ahead, scrambling onto bluffs, peering into ravines and hunting for the best spot to make their camp.

Behind him, Mallory came to a halt, supporting herself

against a tree as yet another contraction gripped her – and with it, that horrible compulsion, once again, to push. She felt a popping sensation between her legs, followed by a gush of fluid down her thighs, warming her skin for only an instant before it began to freeze. Pain engulfed her, so intense that she could think of nothing else. This was the most monstrous episode yet, leaving her gasping and moaning and utterly bereft. Raising her head, she found that both Obe and the dog had vanished from view.

The discovery triggered a wholly terrifying feeling of abandonment. Whichever direction she looked, she could see no signs of life except trees. To think that this was what the Vasi coveted – a world entirely absent of speech, of companionship, of human thought – overwhelmed her with anguish; overwhelmed her, too, with incredulity at how greatly, over these last nine months, she had changed. Before her pregnancy, before Obe, her beliefs had not been that dissimilar to those who wished her dead. She'd clothed herself in cynicism, existing in a vacuum of meaning or joy. Some of that had been a consequence of her experience and had served, tolerably, as a survival tool; but some of it hadn't.

Obe, by comparison, had suffered similar if not even more devastating hardships, and yet he had never allowed those misfortunes to poison his outlook, nor to diminish his appreciation for the grace he perceived all around him.

She thought again of his words, eight months earlier, in the Brecon forest where they'd sought sanctuary: *All of this beauty. You, me, Yoda. The trees. The birdsong. The stars. The dawn. What's there, what isn't. Every blade of grass. Every insect, every human being. Every stone, every mountain, every river. Every little hope, every little dream.*

At the time, she'd thought him deluded. Now, finally, she thought she understood. She'd never see the world in quite the same way that he did, but the fact that she could grasp even a fraction of what he'd described was cause for the greatest relief.

It made her want to survive the night, and not just for the sake of their child. It made her want to live.

A minute later Obe returned, and she was so pleased to see him – and so angry that he had left her – that she started crying. The cold, by now, had penetrated so deeply that she wasn't sure she could move again.

'I found a place,' he said, wiping a slush of frozen mucus from his upper lip. 'It's not perfect, but it's the best we'll find.' He bent over, bracing his hands on his legs. 'Can you make it?'

Swallowing her distress at the thought of walking a single step further, Mallory worked up enough saliva to speak. 'Is it far?'

'A minute's walk. Maybe two.'

Pitiable, really, that such a short distance should seem so utterly unfeasible. Lacking the energy to talk further, she held out a hand and allowed Obe to peel her from her tree. The journey took far longer than his two-minute promise, because halfway there another savage contraction assailed her, and she screamed wildly in its throes. 'Quickly,' she panted, when it passed. 'This baby's coming, one way or another.'

Obe nodded, his face grave. He half-guided her, half-dragged her, their boots slipping on arrowheads of stone that pushed up through the thinning soil. When he led her to the right, a protuberance of rock began to flank them, growing into a sheer granite wall that blocked their view back down the mountain. Its angle was so acute that Mallory doubted it was traversable from the other side. Along its ridge, far above their heads, a line of trees stood silhouetted against an indigo sky.

Opposite, in the direction they'd been climbing, she could see the peaks that crowned this part of the Alps. They rose above the forest like a row of jagged teeth.

'Here,' she gasped. 'It's got to be here.' She didn't know if they'd travelled far enough, only that she could do no more.

Obe cast down the rucksacks, dumping the blankets and shotgun nearby. Free of the weight, he arched his back and clapped his gloved hands together to enliven them. 'We need a fire.'

'Yeah.'

'I don't know if we can risk it.'

'Have to.' Her words, now, were thick in her mouth. She suspected she was hypothermic. 'Have to, otherwise we'll freeze. The baby, too.'

Obe nodded, eyes apprehensive as he watched her. Spreading out the blankets at the base of a tree, he helped her down onto them, dragged over the rucksacks and rifled through their contents. Pulling out her old propane stove, he set it up beside her. Fortunately, it was fitted with a Piezo ignition; she doubted either of them retained enough feeling in their fingers to light it any other way. From a single click, a ring of blue flames appeared, accompanied by a roar of combusting gas. The heat that sloughed off it was a miracle; the most wonderful sensation she had felt.

Using her teeth, Mallory pulled off her gloves and held out her hands to the flames. Obe joined her. For several minutes they stayed like that, flexing their fingers and encouraging the warmed blood to flow.

'I'll get some wood,' he said. 'Won't be more than a few yards away.'

She nodded, biting back a cry as another contraction hit. 'Shotgun,' she gasped. 'Leave me the shotgun.'

Placing it down, he disappeared into the trees. Mallory sat with her knees splayed, panting through her agony, feeling that if her abdomen tightened any further her heart and lungs would be forced into her throat.

Yoda collapsed next to her, his torso pressed close. When he twisted his head and met her eyes he whined miserably, as if sensing her torment.

Minutes later, Obe returned with an armful of wood. A few feet from Mallory's blankets, he built a tepee of twigs and small boughs, around which he stacked larger logs. From the rucksack he retrieved a notebook and tore out its pages, screwing them into balls and pushing them through the tepee's gaps. He lit the paper with a match, and when the twigs began to crackle, he got down on his knees and breathed life into his creation.

The kindling took quickly. Soon, red flames were leaping heavenwards. Smoke spiralled up but there wasn't much of it; despite the snow, the air at this altitude was almost completely free of moisture, which meant that the fuel Obe had scavenged was tinder dry. Mallory was more concerned about noise. The logs popped like gunshots as they burned, releasing flurries of yellow sparks. Sap hissed and spat. But nothing could abrade her relief at being warm again. Kicking off her boots, she held her frozen toes as close to the flames as she dared. Within minutes, rivulets of sweat began to run down her head.

Obe switched off the primus stove and folded it away. He filled an aluminium kettle with snow and placed it on a flat stone near the fire. Retrieving a water bottle from one of the packs, he encouraged her to drink. 'I'll make some tea,' he said.

Mallory nodded, her teeth grinding as another contraction emptied her mind of thought. They were coming so frequently now that she could barely find any pause between them. She said, 'I need you to take off my leggings.'

He nodded, eyes larger than they had been, and when she raised her buttocks he peeled the leggings down her thighs.

'Underwear too,' she muttered, and it was difficult to look at him then; difficult to grant him such intimacy, even if they'd shared some once, a lifetime ago.

Obe stripped off her knickers, tossing them on top of the discarded leggings. 'It's going to be OK,' he told her. 'I know you won't give up. You never do, even if sometimes you wish you could.'

She nodded, her awkwardness forgotten when that familiar pain began to grip again. Through the blankets she grabbed fistfuls of frozen earth, squeezing with the same intensity as the contractions that were brutalising her. She planted her feet wider, arched her back. 'How is it?' she hissed. 'What can you see?'

Obe's throat bobbed. In the firelight he looked frightened but determined; and so incredibly young. He leaned between her legs, face as pale as the moon. When she noticed the pinched lines across his forehead, and just how fast he was breathing, she wondered whether he had intuited something, a problem she could not sense.

'I see . . .' he began. 'I see . . .'

The next contraction hit. It felt as if her spine had shattered, a pain so monstrous and merciless that her scream bounced off the flat stone wall and up into the night, until every molecule of breath had escaped from her lungs. Filling her chest, she cried, 'You see what? You see *what*?'

'It's . . . I . . . it's coming, Mallory,' Obe stammered, taking hold of her leg. A moment later he released her, delving into his rucksack and dragging out a wad of spare clothes. He laid a clean T-shirt between her legs, stripped off his coat. Retreating to the fire, he grabbed the kettle and poured hot water over his fingers, wincing at the heat. Then he took out her switchblade and doused that too.

'Come back here!' she cried. 'Obe, get *back* here right now!'

He dropped the kettle, rushed over to her blanket. Crouched between her legs. 'OK,' he said. 'OK, OK. I'm here. I'm ready. I think you are too.' He wiped his forehead on his sleeve and took a great lungful of breath. 'I think, on the next one – on the next contraction – I think you should push.'

'Can you see the head?'

He swallowed. 'I think—'

'Can you fucking see the *head*?'

'I think yes!' he shouted. 'That's what I think. I think yes – a head. Definitely a head. The baby – the baby's head, I'm sure of it.'

Mallory began to say something and almost immediately

abandoned it; because she could feel the next contraction building, could hardly hold herself still in anticipation of it, could feel her legs shaking, her chin beginning to tremble, as if she were strapped to the rails of a train track and felt the zinging, buzzing announcement of a high-speed locomotive tearing down the line. 'Ah shit,' she whispered. 'Ah *shit*.'

'You're doing this,' he told her. 'You're *doing* this. Who would have thought it? Halfway up a mountain. Middle of winter. Under the stars with a big fire going.'

'Shut up, Obe. Shut the fuck up.'

He reached out to her, and despite herself she grabbed onto him, because he was all she had, and she was unlikely to need anything more.

Mallory twisted in agony, knocked her head against the tree, closed her eyes and opened them again, looked up past that endless grey wall of stone, up to the indigo night and the platinum stars it cradled, and even in her torment she found herself thinking of her mother, and her father, and Aylah and Salih and old man Vecchi; and then, when the pain grew too extraordinary to hold them in her head any longer, with her heart labouring in her chest, tendons straining in her neck, and with a bellow so raw that it shredded her throat as it tore loose from her, a cry not of a woman at all but a savage, a wild animal, Mallory pushed, pushed despite pain now so deep and grotesque that she thought her insides must be haemorrhaging, pain from which she could not retreat, and through it she heard Obe shouting too, unintelligible words of encouragement, and somehow she sucked in another breath, releasing it like a steam whistle, and this time she felt something different, a new sensation just about discernible through the agony, a breaching, a release of sorts, and then Obe was busy between her legs and she could distinguish his words once more.

'*Again!*' he insisted. 'I've got the head, Mallory! I'm supporting it! Again! *Again!*'

His voice was so charged with passion that she did as she was asked without question, blowing hard, sucking in a breath and bellowing once more.

And then, suddenly, it was over.

That terrible pressure dissipated. The night brightened around her. When she heard Obe sigh, she opened her eyes. He was hunkered down between her legs, his face obscured, his movements delicate and slow.

Mallory listened for the sound of a baby's cries, trying to lift her head, but those final moments of labour had sapped the last reserves of her strength. She felt hollowed out; an absence where there should be weight.

'Is it . . .' she began, and found that she was unable to complete her question for fear of the answer.

Obe looked up, and although she could not have described what she saw in his expression, she would never forget it. With infinite care, he lifted his hands and presented her child.

He'd wrapped it in one of his T-shirts, and after that in a green hoody. She saw a tiny hand, the fingers moving; saw, too, a face scrunching up, as if the crackling fire and the forest chill were too much stimulus to bear.

'Hey, kiddo,' Obe breathed, immersed in that tiny bundle of life. 'I think there's someone here who wants to say hello.'

He lowered the child onto Mallory's chest and she wrapped her arms around it.

No words for this. Nothing could have prepared her. She found herself falling into eyes so deep that they seemed un-worldly. Such was her fascination that it was a matter of minutes before it even occurred to her to find out anything more. Easing open a gap in the makeshift wrap, she changed the angle of her arms and took a peek. 'A boy,' she said.

Obe nodded.

'He doesn't even cry.'

'Maybe it's too cold,' he replied.

'Maybe.'

'He's beautiful, Mallory. You're both . . .' He paused, wrinkled his nose.

'You did well,' she told him. 'Back there.'

'Don't think I'll make a career out of it.'

'I mean it, Obe. Thank you. It couldn't have been anyone else.'

He looked abashed at that. His gaze dropped from her face and his expression changed. 'Oh. We're not done yet.'

Her heart lurched. For a moment she thought he referred to a second child, but he only meant the placenta, which she discovered soon enough.

Once she had delivered it, Obe looked at her and said, 'You know, there's a—'

'I don't want to hear any disgusting stories about how I should eat it. Or turn it into a smoothie. Or any other damned thing.'

'I heard that the Romans—'

'Seriously. Take it over there somewhere and bury it.'

He did as she instructed. Yoda rose onto all fours and came forward. 'You can have a look,' she told him. 'But I promise that if you even attempt to lick him with that stinking doggy tongue, you'll regret it.'

Yoda woofed, rubbing his pink scalp against her elbow. Then he sank back down and yawned.

Obe returned, laden with wood. He scanned the sky before building up the fire. 'We haven't heard that helicopter since,' he said. 'If it comes back, we'll have to kick this out pretty fast.'

His words poured cold water on her tranquillity, reminding her that this – the silent forest, the stars, the child in her arms – was an illusory peace. Soon they would have to move again, before those already on the mountain caught up. Once they left the warmth of the fire, the cold would creep back, this time far deadlier than before. They'd have little time to descend to a lower elevation before it overcame them.

Disquieted, Mallory realised that giving birth might not be

the hardest challenge she faced this night. Still, she had a little time, yet. Making some space on the blanket, she said, 'Come and sit down.'

Obe squeezed up close, resting his back against the tree. She laid her head against his shoulder, and it felt good. When he put his arm around her and drew her close, that felt good too.

'He'll need a name,' she said, as they looked at the child they'd created.

'That's true.'

'Do you have any ideas?'

'You want my opinion?'

'I'd prefer not to refer to him simply as "The Kid".'

'I always thought you'd pull rank on that.'

'You're the father,' she pointed out. 'You should have a say.'

'Well . . . thanks.'

She rolled her eyes. 'You don't have to get all funny about it.'

'I was just expressing my gratitude.'

'And you can forget Clark, while you're at it. Or Bruce, or Peter, or whatever. He's not going to be named after a Marvel Comics character.'

'Those first two are DC.'

Mallory sighed. Near their feet, the fire popped. One of the logs collapsed into ash.

'How about Spock?' Obe asked.

'Forget it.'

He kissed her hair. Together they watched their son, and their son watched them back.

They sat that way for twenty minutes before Obe disentangled himself. 'We should patch you up,' he said, climbing to his feet. 'Get you dressed.' Grabbing a clean T-shirt and wetting it with hot water, he washed her legs of blood before carefully dabbing them dry. 'You know,' he said. 'For the first time in days, I'm actually kind of hungry.'

'Inappropriate, Obe. Especially while you're doing that.'

He flinched. 'I only meant—'

'Relax. I'm just goading you.' She pulled her rucksack closer, and with one hand began to rummage through it. 'We've got dehydrated stuff, but you'd have to boil another kettle. Not much in the way of snacks.' She felt something lurking at the bottom. When she pulled it out, she found herself transported back to the June night eight months earlier when she'd hitched a ride with Joos Lagerweij, the Dutch trucker who had presented her with his Stetson. 'There's some habanero moose jerky.'

'Oddly,' Obe said, 'that was going to be my first request.'

'If you don't want it, fine.'

'I have to say, that of all the things you could have brought along, I'm a bit sur—'

She threw the bag at him.

Obe caught it, broke it open. He scooped out a handful of dried meat and began to chew. After a few seconds, his eyes widened.

'Don't blame me.'

Obe shook his head, coughed. 'It's actually pretty good.'

'Must be the habaneros.'

'To be honest,' he replied, 'I think it might be the moose.' Tossing the empty bag into the fire, he found some clean underwear, padded it with sterile dressings and eased her into it. Then he helped her into a fresh pair of leggings. 'How's the pain?'

'Bearable. But the thought of walking makes me nauseous.'

He checked the sky again. 'You want to rest a while longer?'

'Yes. But we shouldn't. We can't.'

As if sensing her disquiet, Yoda rose to his feet. Whined.

Obe began to dismantle their camp, packing away the clothes, the primus stove, the bottled water and the kettle. He leaned the rucksacks against the stone escarpment on the far side of the fire, carried over the shotgun and laid that down on top. From somewhere in the forest came a sudden flapping of wings; birds, disturbed from their overnight roosts.

Then the world changed.

# SIXTY-FOUR

From mountain stillness to violent movement; from cathedral quiet to clamorous noise; from the peace that followed childbirth to plumbless terror; the transformation of their secluded forest glade was as sudden as it was shocking.

So hard did Mallory's heart slam inside her chest, so tightly did her jaw clench, so quickly did her head snap up and her hands tighten around her newborn child that it was impossible, initially, to make any meaning of the chaos that had intruded.

The firelight magnified her disorientation, throwing trenchant shadows against the rock wall that cavorted across its surface like devils joined in dance, mocking not merely those who made this their camp but the malevolence of flesh and blood that had burst upon it.

Yoda leaped in front of Mallory, anchoring himself with hind legs tensed and forelegs splayed. Beyond the dog, she heard a loutish rasp of breath, a snarl and then a rumble, and saw at last through squinted eyes that their intruder was not one of the Vasi assassins she had feared but something far worse, something she had never expected to see in these mountains despite the stories she had heard in her youth: a brown bear, fully grown.

It loped around their campfire, flanks shuddering and eyes wild. It seemed distressed – twisting about, pulling up, bellowing as if in agony. Mallory watched, horrified, her breath frozen in her throat. She knew that brown bears were aggressive. This one looked like it weighed six hundred pounds. Right now it should have been hibernating, living off its reserves of fat.

The bear lumbered to a stop beside the fire, dodging away when a log detonated in a burst of sparks. Yoda backed up, muscles trembling.

Then, the little bundle of life in Mallory's arms began to cry. The sounds were not loud or grating, but the surrounding silence seemed to magnify them, heightening their urgency. Desperate, she gently rocked her arms, but her efforts seemed to encourage her son rather than pacify him. His cries grew more intense.

Beside the fire, the bear rose up on hind legs. Its black lips rolled back, exposing canines as long as Mallory's thumbs. From its throat came an agitated rasping.

Mallory did not want to take her eyes off the animal, convinced that it would charge towards her the moment she did. But now she risked a glance across the clearing.

Obe stood beside the rucksacks, as inanimate as the rock wall at his back, the shotgun's stock jammed against his shoulder. In his eyes she saw the firelight dancing.

'Obe,' she croaked, fearful to speak, even more fearful to remain silent. 'Shoot it.'

He didn't blink, didn't look over. The shotgun barrels hovered in the air.

Beside the fire, the bear began to blow, releasing great gouts of condensation. It clacked its teeth and dropped onto all fours, turning full circle. Then it eyed the newborn and took an uncertain forwards step, clacking its teeth once again.

Mallory drew up her legs, trying to angle her body away, but the huge animal sidestepped.

'Obe,' she moaned. '*Please*.'

He had a clear shot. Two clear shots. She could not understand why he hadn't taken them. She knew how deeply he loved animals, knew that he had dedicated most of his life to their care; but she could not believe that he weighed this creature's worth equally to their child's.

The bear lumbered closer, positioning itself between her and the fire. Its shadow fell over her, and almost immediately she fell a coldness seep out of the forest at her back. Her world reduced: the thump of her heart; the bear's breath, like forge bellows gradually filled.

In the dimness she could no longer see its eyes. It glanced away as if disinterested. Then it swung back its head.

'*Coward*,' Mallory hissed at Obe. 'Fucking *traitor*.'

During the course of her pregnancy, during the time she had spent with him, she had noticed changes in herself far more profound than the developing shape of her body. Anger, hatred, bitterness – those emotions had ebbed from her gradually, leaving her a little more purified each day.

But nine months was no recuperation from a lifetime of bad feeling, and now, in her despair, it came flooding back, aimed not at the bear but at the person on whom she had come to depend.

Tears fell hot on her cheeks.

'Why?' she moaned, through clenched teeth. '*Why?*'

The bear shuffled forwards. It put one enormous paw on Mallory's leg. Transferred some of its weight.

An almost unbearable sadness filled her. She was prey, now, nothing more, held in place until the creature summoned its courage. She could feel the tips of its four-inch claws breaking her skin. There was no pain, as if pure adrenalin had wicked it away.

'Mallory,' Obe said. She could no longer see him, but she could tell from the direction of his voice that he hadn't moved. 'I can't.'

She hated him then. Given the chance she would have beaten him, pulverised him for standing there like a useless, pacifist shit and allowing this to happen. 'We're going to die,' she said. 'And you're going to stand there and watch.'

In her arms, her son's cries intensified.

The bear swiped at the air, its claws coming within an inch of the child.

Death, swinging past like a sharpened pendulum.

She could smell the animal now, a musk in her nose and throat. It lifted its snout towards her and she felt a blast of warm, damp air against her face.

She wanted to close her eyes. Wouldn't.

Wanted to turn away. Couldn't.

Half the bear's weight was on her leg, pinning her. It opened its mouth wide. She saw the pale glint of those monstrous yellow teeth.

Another blast of breath across her face.

In her arms, a tiny struggle of limbs.

Putting its snout to the swaddling, the bear tilted its head and nudged.

Mallory held herself as still as she could.

The bear nudged the bundle of clothes again, using the soft tip of its snout. And suddenly, in Mallory's arms, the child fell silent.

A change seemed to settle over the clearing.

The bear looked over its shoulder. Then it turned back to the newborn. Raising its paw, it raked its claws against the swaddling, but the movement was gentle, controlled; of an elegance that belied the creature's size. Mallory's breath came in rapid bursts. She watched the bear paw the material again, this time dislodging a flap. Intuiting that she was caught up in something infinitely more extraordinary than she had first imagined, she allowed the animal to tug away the swaddling, exposing the tiny, wrinkled baby beneath. Its jaw hinged wide. Then, accompanied by those slow and forceful expulsions of air, a pink tongue emerged and began to lick the child's skin – its arms and torso, the back of its head, its feet – cleaning away the last remnants of blood and fluid.

Mallory's heart fluttered like a bird.

The bear lifted its snout, examined her; a moment later it submitted her to the same attention, that rough, peculiar tongue sliding over her cheeks, her eyelids, her forehead. She bore it as best she could – knowing, then, that somehow they were no longer in jeopardy: that the predator was no longer a threat.

A moment later, the bear took its paw off her leg. It turned sharply about and shambled back into the forest.

Recovering her breath, Mallory readjusted the swaddling as quickly as she could. In the firelight, she could see large gashes in her leggings where the bear's claws had punctured the fabric.

Overhead, a curtain of cloud crawled across the sky.

Obe lowered the shotgun. He came around the fire and halted a few feet away. 'Mall—'

'Don't speak to me,' she said. 'Don't even *look* at me. You know what you did. What you didn't.' She set her jaw. 'A bear, Obe. And you just watched.' She struggled up, and when he tried to help her she snarled and shook him off. Standing unassisted almost defeated her, but the thought of him touching her was worse.

From one of the rucksacks he took a sweatshirt. Cheeks darkening, he proffered it. 'For the baby,' he said, and when she didn't move, he added: 'Please, Mallory. Once we're—'

She snatched it from his hand, wrapping the child even tighter.

Obe extinguished the fire, kicking the burning logs into the snow where they fizzled and hissed, releasing great clouds of steam.

Mallory took a last look around the camp; at the blackened circle where the fire had burned; at the sodden blankets on which she'd given birth. She glanced up at the sky, trying to orientate herself via the stars that remained visible. Holding her baby close, steeling herself against a wave of exhaustion and dizziness, she stepped into the forest and began to walk.

# SIXTY-FIVE

Obe watched her depart, and knew, with a heaviness in his gut, that if he didn't follow she wouldn't wait, and that however far ahead she walked she would never look back.

He did not regret his decision at the camp, but the bitterness in Mallory's voice, and the speed at which she had denounced him – had stung him far deeper than he had anticipated.

Only minutes before the bear's arrival, in the peace that had followed the birth, they had seemed to share a connection that was transcendent. Mallory had called him to her, and together they had sat beneath the tree and marvelled at the life they had created.

And he had felt something. Not from Mallory – although he could sense her satisfaction like a vague purring inside his head – but from their son. It was a sensation he had experienced before once or twice, these last few weeks; although only ever fleetingly, and never as clearly as this. It was not a thought, as such, and it maintained no particular structure. Rather, it manifested as a clean pulse of energy – the promise of something good. He sensed it more surely than anything he had previously experienced, and despite the vast potential of its power, it caused him no ill effects. The corridors of his mind, and the chambers of his heart, felt like they'd been strengthened, fortified; swept clean.

Yet however transformative that contact had been, Mallory's reaction to him back at their camp – her brisk and unflinching dismissal – had robbed him of much of his joy. Theirs had always been an uneasy partnership, but during these last eight months they had steadily dismantled the barriers between them, achieving an equilibrium; or so he had thought.

Since that cleansing experience beside the campfire his awareness had returned, as acute as before his sickness diminished it. Now, as well as the steady pulse of energy emanating from the child, he sensed Mallory. Exhausted by childbirth, consumed by cold and the stultifying journey through snow, she formed few conscious thoughts, but her mind sloughed off a complicated cocktail of emotions even so: fear; determination; anger; hope; disgust; unadulterated love. It wasn't difficult to attribute their causes.

Below them, the forest surrendered to steep Alpine meadow layered with crystalline snow. Cloud now obscured half the sky, but the moon still shone unimpeded. The landscape glowed with a spectral luminescence, jewelled flakes sparkling in beds of palest lavender.

Mallory paused at the treeline, her breath drifting in white threads. She lifted her chin, surveying the meadow for the easiest path. In her arms she clutched her child, but the tightly wrapped clothes wouldn't keep him warm for long. They had to drop down to a lower elevation as quickly as possible.

Suddenly, like nails inside his head, Obe sensed something lurking in that meadow, something so sour and unpalatable that he nearly stumbled. Ahead, the child started crying. The steady pressure it had been producing began to pulse.

Too late, Obe realised that the interloper – whose lizard-like touch he recognised, now, from a night long ago – came not from the meadow but from the darkness

*—have-it-now-can-watch-her-do-it-watch-her-kill-it-open-it-up-make-the-blood-steam-do*N'*T-LET-IT-TRICK-YOU-*

*PUT-A-BULLET-IN-IT-SOMEWHERE-SOFT-THE-
GIRL-FOR-THE-GIRL-BUT-IT-HAS-A-BABY-THE-
BABY-IS-MINE-PROMISED-ME-THINGS-I-CAN-
DO-WHAT-I-WANT-WHAT-I-WANT-WITH-IT-
WHAT-I-WANT—*

to the right of Mallory's
position, at the point where forest met snow.

Out of the murk a stranger appeared and raised a black pistol,
the ugliest piece of metal Obe had seen. Dwarfish in appearance,
mildly overweight, the man wore a down-filled mountain
jacket so glossy and voluminous that it lent him the appearance
of a beetle. His eyes, dark inside their sockets, broadcast hungry
expressions of his intent.

Mallory pulled up sharply. The breath gushed out of her.
She stood motionless, child hugged tight to her chest. Then she
squared her shoulders and thrust out her jaw.

With his gun, the man beckoned her forwards, out of the
forest and into the snow.

She submitted in silence, as if aware that appeals for clemency
would be greeted by mockery. Her movements, as she stepped
from the trees and waded through the drifts, were slow and
deliberate.

Never in his life had Obe harmed a living thing. Never in
his life had he considered that he would. Now, he braced the
shotgun's stock against his shoulder almost without thinking,
leaning on his forward foot and lining up the barrels. The man
must have seen a glint of metal through the trees, because his
expression changed and their eyes met.

Before either had a chance to speak, the gun kicked against
Obe's shoulder, an echo of the power he'd just unleashed. The
air unzipped with a clatter-crack of departing energy that
slapped off the surrounding peaks. In front of him, Mallory fell
to her knees and toppled to her side, the breath bursting from
her lungs as if she'd been punched. Ahead of her, the stranger

lifted his own weapon, and when Obe saw the rising muzzle, the adrenalin fizzing in his blood seized control, and in the frozen instant before what came next, he saw that his initial aim had been awry, and although he was about to take a Vasi bullet he still had one more round in the shotgun, and all he had to do was pull the trigger a second time, which, as he realigned the barrels, he did.

Their weapons fired in tandem, the twin reports producing a shocking cannonade of sound.

Adrenalin had insulated Obe against sensation so far, but now, even with such stimulus, the energy drained from him like water from a tap. Barrels smoking, the shotgun tumbled from his grip. He took a forward step to steady himself, but his leg wouldn't support his weight, and he crashed down on one knee. He felt a flickering behind his eyes, as if a cage of thrashing spiders had been loosed inside his head. Mallory lay prone, arms still wrapped around her child, subject of a vast globe of moon. A few yards away, the stranger who intended to kill her sat propped up in the snow.

If Obe's shot had killed him it would have been a mercy of sorts, but the twelve-gauge had been loaded with bird-shot, designed for hunting game. The man's eyes were gone, and most of his teeth. Blood sheeted down his face in steady pulses. His windpipe had been perforated, causing his breath to shriek in his throat. At least one of the shotgun round's steel bearings appeared to have cleaved a path through his brain, because some vital part of it had clearly been damaged; his feet pedalled slowly, rhythmically, and his fingers snapped open and closed at his sides. It was a horror show – a spectacle of the grotesque from which there was no reprieve.

In Mallory's arms, the bundle began to shriek. Obe had never heard a more desperate sound. Even before he could bring himself to look, he heard another crash of movement in the undergrowth, and saw the forest release another monster. He had experienced this one before, and recognised its shape.

Shambling across the snow, the brown bear fell upon the wounded Vasi with a savagery that was hard to watch. Amidst the slash of claws and the snap of teeth, interspersed by grunts and blasts of breath, there came a sound of liquid protest, of half-formed screams.

The spider-like skittering in Obe's head intensified. And then, with an abruptness that left him hollow, the sensation vanished. The bear raised its head, roared. Turning about, it lumbered back into the forest. Within moments, the screening trees reduced the sounds of its departure to silence.

Obe climbed to his feet. Stepping over the discarded shotgun, he waded through the snow to where Mallory lay.

Perhaps that vacuum in his head, brought about by the stranger's violent ending, had robbed him of his ability to sense her thoughts. He prayed that was true.

She had fallen with her back to him, and although her coat had not been shredded by the shotgun round that went astray, her head was tucked down, out of sight. 'Mallory?' he whispered, his voice husky.

She rolled onto her back and blinked up at him.

So much passed between them in that look. A history, and perhaps a future. He sank to his knees, put his arms around her and the child. Hugged them close.

'We should get going,' she said, and he nodded. Her eyes swung over to the stranger's ragged remains. The bear had eviscerated him so thoroughly that his flesh steamed on the night air. 'Help me up.'

Silent, he pulled her to her feet. She rearranged the bundle of clothes and cradled the child closer to her chest.

'You shot him.'

Obe swallowed, expecting a weight of remorse, but when he looked over at the corpse he felt nothing. 'He was going to kill you,' he said. He could have finished there – could have closed his mouth and left things unsaid. Instead, he took a steadying breath. 'Back at the camp,' he began. 'What happened.'

Mallory's expression tightened. 'Obe—'

'Please, hear me out. Let me explain.' When she didn't protest, he added, 'By the time I'd figured out what was going on, that bear was a few inches from your face. I didn't shoot it, and I know you think that makes me a coward. A traitor, you said.'

He swallowed; even repeating those words gave him pain. 'Do you think if I'd unloaded a couple of rounds into its backside I would have improved the situation? You saw the size of that thing. One swipe, it would've killed our son. One more, and it would've killed you too. It was powerful, yes, but more than that it was *fast*. The shotgun wouldn't have dropped it – just would've made it mad.'

He saw how intently she was watching him, and struggled on. 'Even . . . even if I'd could've killed it cleanly . . . that bear was *drawn* there, don't you see?' He pointed at the bundle she cradled. 'Drawn there by *him*. Then, afterwards . . . you saw what happened.'

He saw, in her eyes, that she believed him. Not just believed him but felt bowed by shame at her earlier reaction.

'Obe—'

'It's OK.'

Her eyes filled with tears. 'Ah shit. No, it's not. It's not at all.'

'It makes no difference. None. All that matters is you, and him. That you're both safe. That you continue to be safe.' He glanced away from her, studying the snow-covered slope. 'We should go.'

'Obe, I'm—'

'Dude. It's forgotten.'

He went back into the trees, picked up the shotgun and loaded it with fresh rounds. Together, they wound their way down through the meadow: Obe, Mallory, newborn and dog.

From the wide curtain of cloud that had drifted across the sky, snow began to fall, silently filling their tracks. They descended slowly, carefully. When Obe saw lights in the valley below – not the lights of search parties but of dwellings, of civilisation – he thought, just maybe, that they might find sanctuary.

# Two Weeks Later

Salih Sabahattin Hazinedar arrived in Salzburg, Austria, three days after leaving Istanbul, making the eleven hundred mile trip by car because he couldn't bring with him what he needed on an aeroplane.

The situation in Italy was still far from clear, but by studying the news reports, Salih had surmised a little of what had happened. Vincenti Vecchi was dead, that much was certain. The old man's bullet-riddled corpse had been discovered in woods near Mallory's old home. He hadn't died alone. A few hundred yards away, police had discovered the body of a heavily armed man, who'd died from a single knife thrust to the neck. Close by, a third victim had suffered a similar fate. A fourth had been found in the clearing outside the property, and a fifth inside. Both had been shot, although the latter had crawled halfway through the chalet before someone had slit his throat.

So far, the authorities had released few details of their investigation, but they *had* revealed that the chalet showed signs of recent habitation: supplies of food and drink, as well as a number of items relating to childbirth. Some miles away, at an even higher elevation, a seventh man's body had been discovered. This one had puzzled investigators most of all – the dead man appeared to have been shot in the face, then mauled by a bear.

Every day, Salih braced himself for news of further fatalities:

Mallory; Obe; their child. He fasted, he prayed, and perhaps a little of that did some good, because a week later there had been no further announcements. Eventually, he dared to believe that the three of them had got away.

She wouldn't contact him, he knew that; certainly not until the current furore died down. Even then, he wasn't sure if he'd hear from her again. Relying on intelligence alone, the Vasi would find it far more difficult to find her once she'd given birth, but they wouldn't give up.

It was because of that he had travelled to Salzburg. Six days earlier, an Arayıcı contact who covertly monitored Vasi channels had alerted him to something important about to occur in the Austrian city's outskirts. Within forty-eight hours, Salih had verified the source. Twenty-four hours later he loaded up his car and hit the road. Now, with his satnav indicating that he was within two miles of his destination, he stopped the vehicle at the side of the road and climbed out.

Aylah İncesu arrived at the Villa Ilimani on the banks of the Salzach River shortly before noon. A marvel of Baroque architecture, the building's façade featured towering pilasters that flanked a grand central portal, over which hung balconies protected by ornate stone balustrades. Bas reliefs depicted military scenes from Greek mythology.

It was an edifice designed to communicate power, and Aylah knew that was exactly why Saul Manco had chosen it.

She parked beside a stone fountain populated by green statuary. Before leaving the car, she retrieved her *qama* and carved a furrow into the flesh of her left thumb. The blade bit deeper than she had intended, spilling blood onto the leather seat and forcing her to bind the wound with surgical tape.

A man she didn't recognise greeted her at the villa entrance. Silent, he led her through a hall clad in Carrara marble. In the far wall, a Roman arch admitted her into a vestibule whose doors were guarded by two bronze lions perched on stone pillars. She passed through them into a grandly appointed room.

Overhead, the ceiling had been painted with a *trompe-l'œil* mural of such colour and splendour that its effect was disorientating. Stuccoed turquoise walls supported it. In the centre of the room stood a giltwood console table topped with a polished slab of *verde antico*. Beyond it, Saul Manco leaned on his cane and gazed through the tall windows that overlooked the river. He must have heard the echo of Aylah's heels as she crossed the floor, but he did not turn to greet her.

The air was cooler here than outside. She felt the skin on her forearms pucker into goosebumps.

'Why do we do what we do?' Manco asked, at length. His tone was soft, ruminative, almost as if he asked the question of himself. He continued to study the view.

'I have a hunch about where they'll go next,' Aylah said. 'I doubt they'll try to stay an—'

'I've always believed,' Manco continued, as if she hadn't spoken, 'that the curse of the human race – one of its many curses, in fact – is ego.' At last he turned to face her, and when she saw his dispassionate, reptilian eyes she felt a complex mix of emotions.

'I don't mean in the Freudian sense,' the man said. 'I suppose what I'm really talking about is ego*tism*.'

'Saul, please. I want that bitch and her child dead just as keenly as—'

'Do you?' He walked towards the table, his cane's silver tip cracking against the floor. '*Do* . . . you?'

'What happened, in Italy. It's what I came here to explain. There was . . .'

When Manco began to shake his head, her words ran dry.

'You came here, Aylah, because I summoned you.'

It hadn't been a question, so she didn't respond, waiting with her heels pressed together and her hands clasped behind her back.

'Your orders were clear, were they not?'

'Yes.'

'You were told to liaise with Caleb and his people. To work *with* them, to share intelligence, and – above all else – to keep me informed. Yet somehow, aware of those instructions, you ignored them.' He paused, shook his head. 'Ego, Aylah. Your downfall, too.'

She knew, from his tone, that nothing she said would make a difference. Better to face this with dignity and return to the field. She glanced at his cane, her flesh tightening.

In the wall to her left, a door opened. Aylah turned her head, surprised to see a number of high-ranking Vasi begin to file through. Caleb Klein was among them. She nodded, in acknowledgement not of his presence but the significance; this time, it seemed, Manco intended to humiliate her publicly.

The Vasi principal waited for her peers to form a loose circle before continuing. 'You were thirteen when I took you out of the Dolomites,' he said. 'Back then, many believed that I was being reckless, that of all the Arayıcı we'd recruited, *you* would prove too difficult to tame. It won't surprise you to learn that many of those people stand here today. They were wrong, of course – there are few things I've lived to regret, and you're certainly not one of them. In the last five years, you've done more to realise Vasi goals than anyone, which is exactly why I chose you as my right hand over others who may have felt they had a claim.' He paused, his alligator eyes unreadable. 'Please. Lift up that hand. I want everyone to see it.'

Aylah felt her cheeks darken, aggrieved that he would enlist her in this pantomime. Sweeping her gaze over the gathered Vasi, she raised her right hand above her head. Let them see it if they wished.

'I'm not in the habit of quoting religious texts,' Manco said, addressing her directly. 'Certainly not from that body of work the Christians call the Synoptic Gospels. But there's a passage in one of them that today strikes me as appropriate.' He paused, and when he spoke next his voice had changed in tone. '"If your right eye causes you to sin, gouge it out and throw it away. It is better for you to lose one part of your body than for your whole body to be thrown into hell."'

Aylah listened, a muscle beginning to tick in her neck.

Saul Manco approached the table. When he halted in front of it, someone stepped out of the circle and handed him a *yatagan*, an Ottoman weapon with which she had trained often. This one was ivory-handled, its forward-curving blade forged from two feet of heavy steel.

'The passage continues thus,' Manco said: "'And if your right hand causes you to sin, cut it off and throw it away."'

The *yatagan* he cradled seemed to exert a gravity all of its own. Aylah could not lift her eyes from it.

Drawn to the spectacle, the audience edged closer.

'The writer – Matthew, I believe it was – makes a rather pertinent point, does he not?'

'Saul—'

'Place your right hand on the table, Aylah.'

She blinked, replaying his words. Her diaphragm spasmed. Suddenly she could find no air in her lungs.

'Place your right hand on the table,' Manco repeated. 'Spread your fingers.'

Somehow, she managed to regain control of her breathing. With her gaze fixed firmly on her mentor's face, she approached the table and placed her palm on its surface, splaying her fingers as directed.

Manco considered her for well over a minute. Then, reversing his grip on the *yatagan*, he laid the blade upon his forearm and offered it to Caleb. 'It's only appropriate,' he told her. 'One hand replaces the other.'

'I can *find* her, Saul.'

With sickening deference, Caleb accepted the weapon. He made a pretence of inspecting its workmanship: the winged pommel, the heavily engraved steel. He swung it once, parting the air, before raising its tip to twelve o'clock.

'I made a mistake,' Aylah said, her voice husky. 'And yes, ego was a part of it. But she's my *sister*. It was *my right*. What you said just now, it's true – nobody here has done more to further the Vasi's aims. *Nobody*. If you look around this room, which of these pale sycophants would you choose instead of me? Which?'

Manco's eyes, as he watched her, were lifeless.

Aylah screamed as the steel blade whistled down. It bit into the marble table top, cracking it into pieces. Fine white debris jumped into the air.

The pain, when it came, was extraordinary. Had she not spent her adult life increasing her tolerance, she would have fainted, or snatched her hand away.

Caleb had done a poor job. Half her little finger had gone, along with one third of her ring finger and the tip of her middle finger just below the cuticle. The severed pieces, lying in the marble fragments, looked like slugs of painted wax. Around the stumps, dark blood was spreading.

Averting her eyes from Saul Manco, Aylah stared at the man who had mutilated her and bared her teeth. 'After all your empty rhetoric,' she spat, 'all your pretensions of power – and this is the first Arayıcı blood you've spilled.'

Caleb's eyes flared, filled with hate. He lifted the *yatagan* high above his head, bringing it down with savage force. More shattered marble sprayed from the table top.

This time, the blade hacked off what remained of her little finger and reduced her ring finger to a chunky protuberance below the second knuckle. Her middle finger had been short-ened further.

Aylah's eyelids flickered. She clenched her teeth, refusing to pass out. 'I can't hold myself any stiller, Caleb. Let's hope you never have to face someone who fights back.'

Snarling, he raised the weapon a third time, but this time Manco intervened. '*Enough!*' he hissed. 'This isn't a restaurant. You're not making *sujuk*.'

He stepped forward and offered Aylah a white cloth. Swaying on her feet, she bound her injuries as tightly as she could bear. Indignant at his reprimand, Caleb tossed the *yatagan* onto the table. Without a word he strode from the room. The others filed out after him.

Saul Manco considered Aylah a moment longer. Then he turned away, his eyes moving to the river. 'Our session is concluded.'

Incredulous, she stared at the wrinkled patch of skin between his collar and his hairline. Despite the tightness of her binding, she could feel blood steadily pulsing from her stumps. She wondered if she should retrieve the pieces of finger that lay on the table top, but even if she found a surgeon competent enough to reattach them, what use would she get from digits that had not just been amputated but diced?

Her gaze moved to the *yatagan*, its etched steel smeared with her blood. How cathartic, to pick up that sabre and swing it; the heavy blade could separate a man's head from his shoulders with no difficulty at all. But Aylah could not wield the weapon with her left hand, and Caleb had destroyed her right.

'Goodbye, Saul,' she said.

'We still have work to do.'

She blinked, hesitated. 'Meaning?'

'I still have use of you. Perhaps not in your previous capacity, but there's a role, should you wish to maintain one.' He paused. 'Give it some thought.'

She felt a curious fluttering behind her eyes. Suddenly the colours in here were too vivid, too sharp.

*You're her, aren't you? The one they use against us. The one they call* Şeytan.

Turning from her mentor, Aylah fled through the vestibule into the grand hall, and from there down the front steps. When the morning air filled her lungs she thought she might be sick, but she reached her car without disgrace. Inside, she found a stash of painkillers and tore open the box with her teeth. After chewing two pills from the plastic packaging, she leaned back against the headrest and watched a gardener in cloth hat and boots emerge from an outbuilding and push a barrow past her car.

Aylah crunched the analgesics into a bitter paste, swallowed. She closed her eyes, saw again the *yatagan*'s blade as it cut through the air, and hastily opened them.

*I still have use of you. Perhaps not in your previous capacity, but there's a role, should you wish to maintain one.*

How close she had been in the Dolomites. How tantalisingly close. She thought of Teke, lying dead in the snow; of Guy Chevry, stalking Talaal Safi through the chalet's ground floor; and, days earlier, of Damla Gültekin, frightened and alone in her forest hideaway.

So much bloodshed. So much pain.

She watched the gardener push his barrow towards the front gates. His back was to her now, but she'd glimpsed him in profile: salt-and-pepper hair, a nose that looked like it had been crudely modelled in clay. She hadn't seen him in fifteen years, which was why she hadn't recognised him at first: Salih Sabahattin Hazinedar. An Arayıcı long suspected of active resistance, the man had spent years on the Vasi's kill list.

Aylah glanced at the main building, thinking of all the people assembled inside. She recalled a key tenet of Vasi doctrine, as explained by Saul Manco: death – even the death of one's closest associates – was a cause for celebration, not sadness, every tiny contraction of the human race a victory.

Starting the car, she drove slowly around the fountain, the Villa Illimani looming large in her rear-view mirror.

*There's a role, should you wish to maintain one.*

*Give it some thought.*

Ahead, Salih Sabahattin Hazinedar reached the end of the drive. Aylah pressed gently on the accelerator. Fortunate that the rental agency in Salzburg had leased her an automatic. No way she could have changed gear in a left-hand drive car.

Behind her, the Villa Illimani's ground-floor windows blew out in a glorious eruption of yellow flame and grey smoke. The pressure wave rolled across the lawn, driven by a blast of such violence that all Aylah could hear in its wake was a bell-like ringing. Chunks of stone and grit rained down all around. The grey smoke boiling from the wreckage turned black.

'I thought about it,' Aylah said. 'Goodbye, Saul.'

Ahead, Salih Sabahattin Hazinedar reached the end of the drive. He pushed his barrow between the front gates and disappeared from view.

If anyone could lead her to Mallory, and the vengeance she still sought, he could. The pain in her mutilated hand muted, Aylah licked her lips and followed.

# EPILOGUE

They called the boy Jacob, and he brought them much joy. After a period of travelling, they settled – two adults, a child and a dog – in the commune of Eaux-Bonnes in the French Pyrenees. There they rented a simple, stone-built house on the road towards Gourette, fully plumbed and supplied with electricity and gas.

That summer, Obe found work with a local cabinetmaker, Clément Kléber. Before Jacob, such a thing would have been impossible, but during that night of horror and wonder in the Dolomites, Obe had looked into the eyes of his newborn child and felt a cleansing pulse of energy inside his mind, as if the petals of some perfect flower had unfurled to release a healing scent. It was both a restoration and an awakening; in the coming days he discovered something transformative: no longer, in the presence of others, did his head ring with their thoughts. He threw away his tobacco tin and enjoyed the most prolonged sobriety of his adult life.

Despite such relief, Obe might have felt the merest pinch of sadness at the contraction of his sensory world; but to his astonishment he found that his ability remained as potent as before. He was simply its master, now, rather than its slave.

In truth, it was rare that he wished to intrude on those around him. He was no voyeur, and he'd never gained satisfaction from rooting through private hopes and fears. Still, the capacity to sense complex emotions, even if experienced without context, allowed him a level of empathy that seemed to benefit everyone he met. It made him all the more keen to see how the gift would manifest in his son: for *gift*, after all these years, was finally how he chose to describe the phenomenon that for so long had seemed a blight.

Mallory adapted to motherhood the way she adapted to all new things: with determination and resourcefulness, interspersed with bouts of bad temper. At night she slept in the master bedroom beside Jacob's cot. Obe slept across the hall. In October, as temperatures in the Pyrenees began to fall, Mallory suggested that he join them.

Jacob grew at a healthy rate. He graduated from breast milk to puréed meals, and from there to simple finger foods. He adored melon, eating it by the bowlful. Alone in his cot, he babbled a constant stream of nonsense sounds, but in company he was quieter than other babies his age.

One Saturday just before Christmas, Mallory went into the town and left him with his father. For lunch Obe grilled some chicken, cutting it into strips and serving it with steamed broccoli. Sitting in his highchair, Jacob peered inside his bowl and immediately upended it. Obe collected the spilled food and presented it a second time, only for Jacob to upend it once more. As the stand-off intensified, the boy began to cry.

Admitting defeat, Obe unclipped him from the seat and took him over to the window. They watched the birds pecking at the grass, and after a while Jacob began to calm down. Then a funny thing happened. Eyes still wet from tears, the boy looked up and Obe's mouth flooded with the taste of melon. Then, suddenly, he *saw* a melon in his head, so vivid and yellow and sharply defined that it seemed almost cartoonish. Jewels of dew glimmered on its skin. It looked ripe enough to burst.

'OK,' he said, laughing hard. 'I get it. You're not a fan of *le poulet*.'

When Mallory returned from her shopping trip, she found Jacob in his highchair, tucking into a bowl of melon chunks. Obe, unable to contain his excitement, explained what had happened: he hadn't been intruding on the boy's thoughts; rather, Jacob had planted the melon, and its associated taste, in his father's head.

As Mallory listened, her eyes narrowed. 'Where's the grilled chicken?' she demanded.

'Back in the fridge. I—'

'Go and get it.'

'Huh?'

She folded her arms. 'Think about this, Obe. Just for a damned second. What're you going to do when he turns up his nose at mashed swede and fills your mouth with the taste of doughnuts? Grab your jacket and rush off to the bakery? What are you going to do when he tosses his milk over the wall and makes you burp up a cherry Coke? What about when he puts an image of a puppy in your head? Or a goldfish? Or a trampoline? Are you going to run out and get him those things too, just because he *asked* for them? We're not raising some kind of Frankenkid here. We're raising our *son*. Shit like this – it needs management.'

'You're right,' he said. 'Of course you're right.'

'Get me the grilled chicken.'

Chastened, Obe fetched the bowl and handed it over.

Mallory marched across the room, snatched up the melon chunks and replaced them with the chicken.

Jacob, as expected, turned a mottled red and flung the bowl across the room.

Lips pressed tightly together, she retrieved the chicken strips from the floor, returned them to the bowl, and slammed the bowl back down in front of him. '*Eat*,' she said.

Jacob thrust forward his chin, glowered.

Mallory lowered her face until it was inches from his own. 'Just try me.'

For a moment, the boy's eyes lost their focus. Then, abruptly, the colour fled from his skin. He began to tremble. Reaching out, he took a piece of chicken and put it into his mouth.

Obe looked at Mallory. 'What did you do?'

'That's another thing we need to teach him,' she said, rising to her feet. 'Don't go poking around in other people's heads without permission. Otherwise you might get burned.'

'Tell me it wasn't something bad.'

'He's eating his chicken,' she pointed out. 'So I guess it worked.'

'He's ten months old. A bit young for his first neurosis, don't you think?'

'*You* survived.'

'Yeah. Luckily I hadn't met you at that point.'

She rolled her eyes. Going to the fridge, she took out a wedge of melon and sank her teeth into it.

That spring, Obe cleaned out the stone outbuilding beside the main property and converted it into a workshop, fitting it with benches and sawhorses, and stocking it with tools he purchased second-hand, or that Clément Kléber donated. During the long evenings of summer, he spent hours crafting new furniture for the house. The pieces featured few of the creative flourishes evident in Kléber's work, but they were sturdy, built to last. Sometimes, as he worked, Mallory would come out to watch him.

In December, they celebrated their second family Christmas. Jacob began to string together his first two-word sentences. The images he placed in their heads, along with the different tastes and smells that he conjured, began to develop into a language all of its own. And while they couldn't have explained their intuition, they knew there was more to be revealed.

The child still needed boundaries, and Mallory proved adept at setting them. Under her supervision, the boy seemed at no risk of turning into the Frankenkid that she had feared. Eight months after his second birthday, she approached Obe with an idea she'd been mulling. He listened as she talked, and agreed with her conclusions. They contacted Sal a few days later, using the secure method her old mentor had outlined during their meeting at Mont Saint-Michel.

Within a week, they received a response: Sal was overjoyed to hear from them; yes, he would like to visit the child, but it would take careful planning; the Vasi's ability to find them had been severely abraded, but with Jacob's arrival the family was more vulnerable than ever.

Sal sent a single news article with his reply. It covered an explosion at a private Salzburg residence two weeks after their son's birth, from which the bodies of twenty-four men and women had been recovered. Mallory knew, the moment she read the piece, that the dead had been Vasi, and that the pool of people wishing Jacob harm had contracted significantly; knew, too, that she had Sal to thank for that.

His trip was arranged for the following summer. One morning in August, she climbed into her beaten-up Fiat and made the three-hour drive to Toulouse, where his flight was due to land. She was completely unprepared for her upwelling of emotion when he walked through the arrival gates. She flung her arms around him, crying and laughing and not caring a bit about how he perceived such flamboyance.

'I see you've been living too long among the French,' he growled, but he hugged her just as tightly, and when she released him she saw that his eyes were a little glossier than they had been.

Back at the house, Mallory introduced him to Jacob, and when Sal saw the boy he wept openly and without shame. Afterwards, he got down on all fours and acted more like a benevolent grandfather than the grizzled fighter she had known.

He had brought gifts, too. Among them was a steel-strung *bağlama*, an olivewood *tavla* board and a bone-handled *kard* complete with a silver repoussé sheath. Mallory put the instrument and the knife out of reach, but she let Jacob play with the *tavla* set for a while, until he tried to feed one of the marble playing pieces to Yoda.

Sal stayed for three weeks, and Mallory wished it could have been longer, but the house was too small to offer much privacy, and he was unaccustomed to such close living. She drove him to the airport and they shared an emotional goodbye. He promised to visit again, yet Mallory could not help feeling that this was the last time she would see him. Driving back to Eaux-Bonnes with an ache in her heart that was bittersweet, she pulled into the driveway and knew, immediately, that something was wrong.

For a start she heard no customary barking from Yoda, acknowledging her return. Obe could have taken him for a walk with Jacob, but it was more than that: the stones of the old house seemed darker, somehow, as if they had absorbed something poisonous that now roamed the interior.

Such was her sense of foreboding that as she opened the car door and stepped onto the gravel her flesh felt as if it were rejecting her bones, peeling away like old paint. She felt light, ephemeral. Had there been a breath of wind, it might have carried her away.

Three years and seven months they had lived as a family: an unconventional one, perhaps, but a family nonetheless. So many experiences they had crammed into that short time; so much joy. But three years and seven months was no time at all. She wanted so much more.

Mallory discovered Yoda at the rear of the property, a few yards from the back step. The foam around his nose and lips suggested that he had been poisoned. When she crouched down to stroke him, she found that his flanks were cold. In death, he'd achieved a grace he had never seemed to possess in life. She hoped that his last moments had not been filled with pain.

It was an effort to stand. The back door hung ajar, revealing a narrow view of the kitchen. Looking at it made her eyes water so fiercely that she could barely see. Blinking away her disorientation, she glanced through the living-room window, but sunlight was reflecting off the glass.

Taking shallows breaths, Mallory edged to the door.

They had prepared for this; had always known that the Vasi might catch them. Sal's ruthlessness in Salzburg had reduced the likelihood but Mallory had still taken precautions. Weapons – which could be accessed quickly and without fanfare – had been secreted in numerous places around the property. From behind a planter filled with blue-flowering gentiana she retrieved an extendable steel baton. From a neighbouring planter she removed a can of pepper spray.

The guns were in the house: a shotgun and a hunting rifle.

Slipping the pepper spray into her back pocket, Mallory touched a finger to the door and pushed. It rolled open without a sound. She was certain, even so, that her presence was already known; certain, too, that the three and a half years of joy she had found in Eaux-Bonnes had come to a tragic and terrible end. Perhaps Obe and Jacob were already dead. If that were the case, she had no wish to survive the day.

Mallory stepped into the house. On the nearest wall, a clock counted off the seconds. She swept the kitchen with her gaze, taking in the countertops, the cupboards, the wheeled butcher's trolley Obe had built during the first few months of his apprenticeship. Her eyes fell to the floor tiles, but she saw no slicks of blood, no evidence of struggle.

Past the clock stood the door to the living room. Usually, a cast-iron doorstop propped it open. Now it was closed. The door itself was an ancient slab of panelled oak. Mallory paused beside it, listening, but she could hear nothing from the room beyond. The ticking of the wall clock was loud in her ears.

Her eyes flickered to the fridge, where a magnet held a piece of paper to the door. On it were two tiny handprints in bright red paint. Until today, she had always thought it a cheery image.

Now, those prints looked blood-dipped and grim. On the countertop stood a Donald Duck sippy cup. Beside it, her son's red superhero bib with its legend: *THESE FOOLS PUT MY CAPE ON BACKWARDS.*

Mallory doubled over as if she'd been gut-punched. The floor rocked beneath her feet. Clenching her teeth, she somehow summoned her old rage.

Coached from a spark, it burned with cold white fire.

Padding to the countertop, she rolled open the cutlery drawer, selected a filleting knife and pocketed it. Then she took a carving knife, gripping it in her right hand.

With finger and thumb, she touched the living-room door handle. There was a chance, she knew, that those inside would not even wait for her to enter. The oak door was thick, but it wouldn't stop a high velocity round. She might die in this kitchen without even seeing what lay beyond. In some ways, that might be a mercy; which was why she felt confident that it wouldn't be her fate.

The clock ticked. Mallory grimaced, levered the handle downwards and pushed. The door rolled open on well-oiled hinges, coming to a stop as it reached its maximum arc.

She stepped through.

It was darker in here. Drapes had been pulled across one of the windows. To her right stood the rectory table where they usually ate; beyond it, the sofa where they sat at night. To the right of the fireplace was a low bookcase that held their modest collection.

Jacob, and the man Mallory had come to think of as her partner — even if they'd consummated their relationship only once, briefly, a long time ago — had been placed in separate corners at the room's far end.

When she took a breath, it caught in her throat like a death rattle.

Her son sat facing her. The boy was alive, at least. He watched her with eyes so large and solemn that his comprehension of the unfolding horror was undeniable. He held his hands together in front of him, fingers interweaving as if he washed them beneath an imaginary tap. When Mallory saw that, she felt her heart shrivel.

It was no use trying to reassure the boy. Already she could feel his probing, like the tick of an insect's wings inside her head.

*Mummy loves you*, she thought.

*Mummy loves you. Mummy loves you. Mummy loves you.*

She concentrated on an image from happier times: the boy on her lap, her arms around him.

Jacob blinked. His fingers churned in his lap. Then he looked across the room at his father.

Obe stood with his back against the wall, hands cuffed by plastic ties. Blood leaked down his face from a cut above his right eye.

*I'm sorry*, he mouthed.

Mallory shook her head. No need for that. Finally, she switched her attention to the woman who stood between her son and the man she thought she might love.

Dark hair, pulled into a no-nonsense knot. Hard eyes, devoid of mercy. The face was a mask. Behind it lurked an absence of humanity.

The Vasi's warped doctrines had mangled more than just the woman's mind. Her right hand was a misshapen lump that comprised only a thumb, a forefinger and a stub of middle finger; she held it at her side, as if ashamed of its deformity. In her left hand she clutched a semi-automatic. Lifting it, she trained the muzzle on Mallory.

'If you let us,' Mallory began, 'if you give us a single chance to change your mind, we can show you something that will—'

The woman barked a laugh. 'You think this brat of yours makes a difference to me? You think the fact that you rolled in the sack with some broken-minded freak and squeezed out its offering *changes* anything?'

'Not at first, I didn't,' she replied. 'Now I do.'

'It's been costly, this. Costly for us both. But it ends here. Today.'

Sweat had begun to slicken the handle of the carving knife Mallory clutched. 'If only you'd give us—'

'You don't even recognise me, do you?' the woman asked, lifting her chin. 'Even this Kusurlu freak of yours was quicker to work it out. Look carefully, Mallory. It's important that you fully understand what's happening here.'

Mallory glanced across at Obe. She saw the anguish in his eyes and wondered what it meant.

'I'm sorry,' he muttered. 'I'm so sorry.'

Behind her, she could hear the steady tick of the wall clock. 'Sorry for what?'

His shoulders dropped. 'That night, in Cornwall. That night we escaped from the hotel. If I'd been thinking more clearly, I'd have figured it out. The pieces were all there. I just wasn't able to arrange them.'

The tick of the wall clock was a pressure in Mallory's ears. She felt herself teetering on the edge of a revelation too monstrous to consider. 'What are you talking about? Figured out what?'

In answer, his eyes drifted to the woman who separated them. 'Figured out who they were using against you.'

Mallory stared at him a moment longer.

Three heartbeats, and then she understood.

Her knees sagged. The carving knife slipped from her fingers, clattering against the floor. The steel baton bounced once and rolled under the table.

It couldn't be.

A flash of light and she was back in the forest near her old home, beside the giant spruce where she'd planted her fairy door. She looked through the trees and saw the man with the slim black cane. Moments later, the chalet's back door banged open. Laleh Gurvich appeared. The mountains crashed, a red carnation bloomed.

'Eureka,' Aylah said.

Shadows seeped from the walls. Mallory felt the floor begin to tip, as if she stood on the prow of a sailing ship tossed by a storm. 'I thought . . .' she began. Her words were thick in her throat. Her head felt packed with sand. 'I thought you . . .'

'Dead?' Aylah asked. 'Is that the word you're looking for? If it is, then you're right. That girl – that sister of yours – she's as dead as the two deceivers that kept us prisoner in that house.'

Mallory stared. Felt her breath rush in and out of her lungs. She thought of all the years she had wasted, believing that she was alone in the world. All the bitterness she had hoarded; all the grief.

Of everyone she had lost in the Dolomites that day, the death of her wise and beautiful sister had been the hardest to bear. She'd guarded her last memory of Aylah – the girl lying on her bed, legs swinging as she flicked though a magazine – more jealously than any other. And now it had been replaced by this: a thing so damaged and so reduced that she could hardly recognise a single fragment of the person it had been. With that discovery, Mallory understood that the Vasi had robbed more from her that day than she could ever have possibly anticipated. 'When I found my way back to the house, it was empty. I . . . I thought they'd killed you too.'

'They *rescued* me,' Aylah hissed. 'Liberated me from all that twisted Arayıcı propaganda our parents loved to spin.'

Mallory shook her head, unwilling to believe what she was hearing. Her sister's face was so twisted with hate that it was difficult to behold, but for the sake of everyone she loved – Aylah's memory included – she persevered. 'If . . . if I'd known you were still alive . . .' she began. 'If I'd known where you were being held . . .'

She shrugged, helpless, as her words petered out. She'd been nine years old that day, no more than a child. There wasn't anything she could have done to influence those events. 'What happened, Aylah?' she asked. 'What did they do to you? What could they possibly have done to—'

'They opened my eyes. They showed me the truth.'

'*Truth?* What truth?'

'What you've done, what you've produced. It's degenerate – a perfect example of the contagion destroying this planet.' With her mangled hand she gestured at Jacob. 'You think one life is going to make a difference? A *positive* difference? You think it's going to *change* anything?'

'It's changed things before,' Mallory said. 'All throughout history. One life is all it's ever taken.'

Aylah sneered. 'You don't believe that.'

'Please. Please don't do this. Whatever you have planned, please don't. I'm so sorry that we were separated, and for whatever it was that they did. I can't imagine it was anything other than brutal. Inhuman, even. But that little boy in the corner. He's your nephew, Aylah. Your flesh and blood. As for Obe' – her words caught in her throat as she mentioned him – 'you could spend a hundred years searching, and you still wouldn't find anyone to—'

'You don't have to tell me,' Aylah said. 'I know *exactly* what he is.'

In the silence, only the ticking clock.

Mallory glanced at the boy she'd come to love, and saw that his eyes, focused with such intensity on her sister, had glazed. She recognised that look – knew that right now he was only partly inside his own head. The paleness of his skin was stark evidence of what he had learned. When his eyes regained their clarity, his back straightened and his muscles tensed.

If he threw himself at Aylah, hands still tied, he'd have no way of defending himself. Mallory knew that wouldn't stop him. Nor could she – or would she – attempt to change his mind. People were going to die in this room. By working together, as mother and father, they might just save their son. 'You could have killed them already,' she said, sweat breaking out across her forehead. 'You could have shot them before I arrived. But you didn't.'

'Not yet.'

'Is that because—'

'I've killed before,' Aylah said. 'I enjoy it.'

'Never your own family, though. Never someone who loves you. This — what's happening here — this is different. I know that you see that.'

Mallory talked, not because she believed in the truth of her words, nor because she retained any hope that her sister could be persuaded, but because through dialogue she hoped to distract Aylah from whatever course of action Obe hoped to take.

*That girl — that sister of yours — she's as dead as the two deceivers that kept us prisoner in that house.*

Their parents hadn't deceived them, and neither had they ever kept them prisoner, but Matthais and Laleh Gurvich's eldest daughter was unquestionably dead. That fact should have been hard to accept — a raw and unexpected new source of grief — but here, now, Mallory learned that there were only two people in this room that she truly cared about.

'I kept them alive,' Aylah said. 'Because I wanted you to choose.'

'Choose?'

'Between them. Don't get excited — none of you walk out of here alive today. But I *am* granting you the power to decide one thing. Say a name, and that one dies first, cleanly and without pain. No trauma. No mess. I reserve the right to take my time with whoever's left, but it's a choice, at least. An opportunity for you to grant a little mercy.'

'You're insane.'

'Actually, I'm merely intrigued. Who do you choose, Mallory? Your son or your lover? I know it's an unreasonable question, but I'm convinced you already know the answer.' Aylah angled the gun away from Mallory, pointing the barrel at Obe's temple. 'Do you choose him?' she asked, her eyes hard. Abruptly she swung the gun around in an arc, aiming it at Jacob.

'Or do you choose—' at which point Obe lunged out of his corner towards her.

Even as Mallory ripped the pepper spray from her back pocket, she saw that although Obe had judged, correctly, that Aylah's attention had shifted away from him, he hadn't counted on her speed. Before he managed to close the distance between them, she twisted around and shot him in the chest.

The report crashed off the walls, ringing so hard in Mallory's ears that she barely heard her own scream. She charged forwards, but there was far too much space to cover, and Aylah brought the gun around even as Mallory unleashed a jet of red foam into her face.

The pistol spat fire.

The bullet passed within a few inches of Mallory's head, blasting a chunk of plaster from the wall.

Contaminant dripped from Aylah's face like the bloody froth from a lung-shot deer. She staggered backwards, clawing it from her eyes with her deformed hand. Crashing against the wood burner, coughing, choking, gagging, she swung the gun wildly before her. 'Get back!' she screamed. '*GET BACK!*'

Mallory froze, watching the barrel pass back and forth in front of her face.

In the corner, Jacob cowered, tears glimmering on his cheeks. Once more his hands were an agonised blur of movement, tiny fingers weaving and clasping, weaving and clasping.

*Mummy loves you, Jacob. Mummy loves you. I'm so sorry. I'm so sorry.*

As if reacting to some minute change in air pressure, Aylah lurched forwards, unleashing four shots in quick succession. One of the rounds passed to the right of Mallory's head, three to the left.

Reaching behind her, Aylah brushed her mutilated fingers against the bookcase. She seemed to recognise what she touched, using it to orient herself. This time, when she pointed the gun, her aim was lower, towards the floor where Obe had fallen.

'*No*,' Mallory cried, but before she could intervene another gunshot rang out. Obe grunted as the bullet tore into his thigh. Already, the barrel was swinging back. Mallory ducked low, saw a flash of fire and felt the air unzip beside her right cheek. An instant later she slammed into Aylah and punched her against the bookcase. They rebounded in a tangle, and Mallory dragged her sister down on top of her, trapping the arm that held the pistol beneath her spine.

Red foam dripped from Aylah's chin, revealing skin that was blistered and red. When the gun fired again, Mallory felt a searing pain across her right shoulder, as if a heated poker had been dragged along her flesh. She mashed her forehead into Aylah's nose, knocking her sister to one side. Rolling onto her front, she inadvertently released the gun. If the pepper spray hadn't done its work, Mallory would have been killed at that moment, but when the weapon fired its aim was off yet again, the round blasting another lump of plaster from the wall.

She snatched at the pistol, tried to wrestle it away. Aylah fought back, scratching and clawing. Finally, Mallory's two good hands won out. Reversing her grip, she smashed the butt into her sister's face. Aylah fought on as if the pain hadn't registered.

Winding back her arm, calling on all her strength, Mallory delivered a monstrous blow. This time the woman's head snapped to the left, rolling back loosely. The breath huffed out of her and she grew still.

Silence in the room, pierced by Jacob's quiet weeping.

'It's OK,' Mallory whispered, though her words were clearly a lie. 'It's OK.'

'Dada,' the boy said.

*Mummy loves you, Jacob. Mummy loves you. I'm so sorry. I'm so sorry.*

Her strength deserted her. She inched across the floor, sliding the bloodied pistol before her and dragging her legs behind.

Obe lay on his back, his eyes wide open. Aylah's first bullet had smashed through his sternum. Mallory did not know what kind of round it had been, but the devastation it had wreaked was clear. Blood pooled around a centimetre-wide entry hole in the front of his T-shirt. The rest of the fabric was black with it. When he took a breath, bubbles formed and burst. She saw more blood creeping out from beneath him, creating a widening circle.

When he turned his face towards her he looked like he'd aged thirty years, but his eyes were just as bright. 'Dude,' he said.

Mallory felt a pressure in her throat so intense that she could barely speak. 'I told you about that,' she replied, gently chiding him.

'Oh.' Obe nodded. 'I forgot. Not meant to call you dude.'

'I'll forgive you. Just this once.' She edged closer, blinking away tears. Dropping the pistol, she took his hand.

'Is it bad?' he asked.

Mallory clenched her jaw. Tightly, she nodded. When she regained control of her voice, she said, 'You've shown me so much light.'

'We all need a little of that,' Obe said. 'Good for the bones.'

'I should have stopped her. I should have been better prepared.'

He shook his head. Blood ran from his mouth. 'Jacob . . .'

'Is alive. Thanks to you he's alive. You saved him. Me too.'

'Ah, it was nothing.'

She laughed. Squeezed his fingers. 'Is that right?'

Obe blinked, took a breath. 'You'll be fine,' he said, and then his chest stilled.

Mallory shuddered. She closed her eyes, allowing herself ten seconds of silence. Then, fearing what such raw and terrible grief might do to the mind of a child, she tried to clear her head.

Releasing Obe's hand was difficult, but she managed it. She

retrieved the pistol and, after slipping it into the waistband of her jeans, crawled over to Jacob and drew him close.

'Dada,' he said.

'I know,' she whispered. 'I know.'

*Mummy loves you. Daddy loves you. We both love you so much.*

'Gone,' the boy remarked.

In her head, Mallory formed a picture of all three of them, an image from happier times. She didn't know if it was the right thing to do or the wrong thing. She did it anyway. For a moment or two the image trembled. With Jacob's assistance, it grew firm.

They stayed that way for a while, Mallory rocking her son in her arms and making pictures for him in her mind.

*Mummy loves you. Daddy loves you. We both love you so much.*

Across the room, Obe lay with his arms outstretched and his fingers uncurled.

Some time later – Mallory could not have said how long – Aylah began to stir. Her back arched and she took a heaving breath. Her fists came up, knuckling away what remained of the pepper foam from her eyes. Rolling onto her side, she spat onto the floor.

Mallory watched, stroking Jacob's head, concentrating hard on the picture she'd created.

At last, Aylah angled her head and saw her sister. Angled it further. Saw Obe.

*Mummy loves you. Daddy loves you. We both love you so much.*

Gently, Mallory unfolded her arms from her son. 'I'm going to leave you alone,' she said. 'Just for a little while.'

The boy's eyes widened. He shook his head.

'Yes,' Mallory insisted. 'Just for a while. You're safe, now. Safe in here with Daddy.'

'He'll never be safe,' Aylah whispered.

Maintaining that soporific image was a feat of concentration that nearly eluded her, but somehow Mallory managed it. Lifting Jacob away, she said, 'Close your eyes.'

He did as he was asked.

Mallory pulled the gun from her waistband and stood.

*Mummy loves you. Daddy loves you. We both love you so much.*

She went over to Aylah. 'Get up.'

'If you think—'

Reaching down, she grabbed a handful of her sister's hair and towed her to the kitchen. Aylah kicked and thrashed, but her feet found no purchase. Mallory closed the door behind them. 'I can drag you like this,' she said. 'Or you can walk.'

'*Fuck* you.'

Nodding, Mallory hauled her outside.

'I'll walk,' she hissed. 'I'll *walk.*'

Abruptly, Mallory released her grip. Aylah's head cracked against the concrete path. Sliding her feet beneath her, she stood.

'Walk.'

'Where to?'

'Straight ahead. Into the trees.'

'No chance.'

Mallory pressed the pistol to the base of Aylah's skull. Saw the woman flinch at that cold press of steel. 'Walk straight. Into the trees.'

They passed the hut where Obe kept his tools. Mallory couldn't look at it. They passed the wooden bird table he'd built. She couldn't look at that, either.

Inside the treeline, fifty yards from the house, they came to a halt.

'Turn around,' Mallory said.

It was hard to meet Aylah's eyes and witness, once again, that terrible absence of humanity. But she forced herself. With the pistol trained, she said, 'I don't want to kill you.'

Aylah's lips curled back. 'Then you're either a liar or a fool.'

'A year ago, before Obe, I wouldn't have hesitated. Sister or not, I'd have taken you out here and put a bullet in you without listening to a word you had to say.'

'I'm pleased he had such a transformational effect.'

'Don't. Don't do that. Don't mock him.'

Aylah wiped blood from her nose. She spat a red streamer into the snow.

'If we left you here, today,' Mallory said. 'What would you do?'

'I'd find you. I'd kill you.'

'Why?'

'I'd kill your son first. So that you could watch. Open him up, a little at a time. Peel him like a onion, each layer revealing its secrets. Your precious brat would—'

The pistol jumped in Mallory's right hand, surprising her with its recoil. The report chased among the foothills.

Aylah fell backwards. Her heels twitched, digging furrows. Mallory lowered the gun and fired twice more.

She turned her face away. Looked back at the house. Wondered if fifty yards of distance was enough to prevent Jacob from witnessing what had happened.

*Mummy loves you. Daddy loves you. We both love you so much.*

She wouldn't cry. Not yet.

Lifting her head, Mallory retraced her steps to the little boy that awaited her.

# EIGHTEEN MONTHS LATER

They settled, after a prolonged period of travelling, in the Tabernas Desert – known to some as The Badlands – in the Spanish province of Almería. The carven sandstone landscape, riven with dusty arroyos, had once been the bed of a saltwater lake. It reminded Mallory, in some ways, of the moon. But here, unlike the lunar surface, the temperature in summer could approach fifty degrees.

Despite its starkness, the desert hosted a resilient ecosystem. They saw ladder snakes and wall lizards, along with the eagles and falcons that hunted them. In areas with a source of water, olive trees grew abundantly.

They did not settle in the town of Tabernas to the southeast, but in the heart of the desert itself, far from the dust-caked highway that cut through it. There they found a community of like-minded souls; exiles, castaways and those who had chosen a different kind of existence. The locals called it Alto Paraíso, which translated, loosely, as High Haven. It contained no structures of any real permanence, comprising an eclectic mix of motorhomes, buses and marquees, arranged in a protective circle like the Wild West wagon trains of old.

There was no plumbed water, no gas. Two rows of solar panels provided a paucity of electricity. The sculpted rock formations blocked mobile phone coverage, and internet access was only possible via a satellite terminal owned by one of the residents; even then, the service worked at speeds that seemed Palaeolithic. Once a week, a rostered volunteer drove the community's aging bowser into town and brought it back slopping with water.

The day Mallory arrived with Jacob, Alto Paraíso comprised twenty-three souls. When the desert winds blew, the flags of many different nations fluttered from the poles around the ring: not just from Europe but all over: Canada, the US, Japan, Iraq, South Africa, India, New Zealand. She had heard about the settlement during a chance encounter outside Huércal-Overa, an hour and a half's drive north-east. Her beaten-up Fiat had overheated, and a passing Alto Paraíso resident had pulled over to offer assistance. While they waited for the engine to cool, they talked. Afterwards, Mallory pointed her vehicle towards the desert and followed the woman's directions.

When they rolled up to the site, towing a white streamer of dust, the caravans and trailers emptied of curious folk. Mallory watched through the windscreen as they began to converge. Then she turned to the boy.

*What do you think?*

Jacob, perched on a cushion beside her, peered over the dashboard, examining the rusting vehicles, the wind-sculpted sandstone towers, the snapping flags, the people.

He grinned. *Cool.*

Mallory tasted doughnuts on her tongue. Caught, in her nostrils, the gunpowder whiff of fireworks. Jacob had only ever seen fireworks once, on Bastille Day; they'd made a lasting impression.

*We go slowly here*, she insisted. *OK? Until we know if we can trust them.*

The boy continued to peer through the windscreen. *We can.*

Mallory's skin tingled, as if she were sliding into a warm bath. She shook herself free of the sensation. *I mean it, Jacob. It's my decision.*

*Yes, Mummy. I'll be good.*

Her heart melted a little when he said that. Unclipping her seatbelt, she opened the car door.

First to welcome them was Rosario Magdalena Delgado, a sensuous grey-haired woman in her late sixties, and one of the community's earliest residents. Although no formal hierarchy of authority existed at Alto Paraíso, Rosario functioned as the community's unofficial spokesperson. Most people, Mallory would learn later, simply called her Madre.

They met others with far less conventional names. Many had gravitated here to forget their former lives, and often that began with the shedding of old monikers. Madre introduced, among others, Niamh Desert Lizard, Bijoy Disco Mahadevhi, Chili Smurf, Mimi La Bombe, Caecilius II, Stormy Angelique and Notte Stellata. That last name, Mallory discovered, was Italian for 'Starry Night', and belonged to a strikingly beautiful Hawaiian woman from Waimea Bay on the North Shore.

They all had their quirks, their scars and their ghosts. Chili Smurf, a wiry old Philadelphian whose near-translucent skin seemed impervious to the desert sun, was a former Wall Street banker whose marriage had collapsed during the economic crash. Niamh Desert Lizard had fled here from Syria. Caecilius II, a retired Latin teacher from Johannesburg, insisted that he was the reincarnation of a Pompeian banker – Lucius Caecilius Incundus – who had lived during the reign of Augustus and had perished in the eruption of Vesuvius.

For the first few days, while Mallory checked out the settlement, she had planned to sleep in the Fiat with Jacob. In the end that proved unnecessary; Madre lent them the use of a trailer that was currently being used as the communal library. They stayed in it for two weeks before driving back to Tabernas, where Mallory sold her car for scrap and used half of her remaining funds to buy a motorhome of her own. It was not a tenth as luxurious as the Morello in which she had travelled around Europe with Obe, but it was an improvement on the rusting Renault Trafic they had bought in Builth Wells after their three-day stay in the Brecon Beacons.

Mallory thought about Obe often, and his memory regularly brought her tears. But the dry desert, its sandstone monuments and its startling blue sky, offered a respite of sorts. She refused to think about her sister.

Using text books from the community library, supplemented by those she picked up in Tabernas, she educated Jacob as best she could. She wasn't a patient teacher, but her son was a natural student, and he benefited, too, from an entire community of willing tutors. Caecilius II taught him Latin; Bijoy taught him about faith; Chili Smurf showed him how to cook. When the desert sky darkened each night, Notte Stellata took him on tours of the heavens.

*How do you like this place?* Mallory asked, at the end of their second month at Alto Paraíso.

In response, the boy flooded her senses with the aroma of strawberries, the taste of chocolate and the musk of old books, worn leather and comfortable shoes.

*Home,* he said, and she had to agree.

She spent much of her time with Madre, helping to cultivate a plot of irrigated land in one of the arroyos, or sitting beneath the awning of the old woman's trailer while they watched Jacob play.

In March, a few weeks after the boy's fifth birthday, they were standing in the mobile library, cataloguing the books, when Madre said, 'He's different from other children.'

Mallory glanced up to see her friend's eyes on her. 'What do you mean?'

It was a minute or so before the woman continued. 'You never talk about your *before*,' she said at last. 'And that's OK – a lot of people here don't, and I've never been one to ask. But you and Jacob. You're different. You come from something else.' She snorted. 'Tell me to zip my mouth and I'll zip it. I'd never normally intrude. I hope you know that.'

Swallowing, Mallory nodded. 'It's OK. Really.'

After another pause, the older woman said, 'He's . . . *different* isn't sufficient. Not really. There's a kind of . . .' She took a breath, laughed. Dumping a handful of books onto a shelf, she wiped her hands against her tunic. 'You know – when he's near, I'm always tasting coconuts. Isn't that funny?'

Coconut lassi, Mallory knew, was Madre's favourite drink.

'Caecilius always says it's limes,' the woman continued. 'Notte says she gets taro root. Chili Smurf says it's a bunch of different things, but that old rascal's tongue is so burnt out on spice that I wouldn't trust a thing he says.' She glanced out of the window, narrowing her eyes against the glare. 'It's not just that. Jacob always seems to understand what I'm *thinking*. He answers my questions before I've managed to ask them. Sometimes before I've even thought of them. I'm not the only one. The others have noticed it too.'

Mallory stiffened. 'Why are you telling me this? What do you want?'

'What do I *want*? I don't want a thing. Except for you to be happy, that is. Happy and safe and fulfilled. The boy too. Especially the boy. I'm telling you simply because I thought you'd want to know.'

Realising it was the truth, Mallory bowed her head. For so long her instinct had been to run or fight; she still dealt poorly with compassion when she encountered it. 'Madre, I'm sorry. I mean it. I—'

The older woman held up her hands, shushed her. 'I've no need of apologies and you have no cause to make them. You're a mother, protecting your child. What could be purer than that? Me, I'm just a nosy old *entrometido* with a brain fried by too much sun.'

'You're not,' Mallory told her. 'You're kind-hearted. Full of patience and love. I'm just not used to it. And sometimes, because of that, I bite.'

Madre cackled. Then her face grew serious. 'Recently,' she said, 'your son spoke to me.' Lifting a wrinkled brown finger, she tapped her forehead. 'Up here.'

Suddenly, it seemed far too hot inside the mobile library. A bead of sweat zigzagged down Mallory's spine.

'You know about that,' Madre said. 'Don't you? Know what he can do. I'm not pressing for an explanation. Really. I just want to know that I'm not completely mad.'

After a minute of silence, Mallory said, 'You're not mad.'

'There,' the woman replied. 'That's all I wanted to say. If you ever want to talk about it, I'll gladly listen. If you don't, I won't raise it again.'

Mallory spoke to Jacob that night, but she didn't castigate him. Over the last year, the residents of Alto Paraíso had become his family; she could hardly expect him to communicate with them with one of his senses leashed. She counselled caution, even so, asking him to limit himself to those he'd known the longest and trusted the fullest.

A few weeks later, as she watered a row of olive saplings in the arroyo, Bijoy Disco Mahadevhi paid her a visit. He talked in wide-eyed wonder, stumbling over his words as he recounted a similar tale to Madre's.

A few days after that, Chili Smurf sought her out, followed by Niamh Desert Lizard. Mimi La Bombe, Stormy Angelique and Notte Stellata arrived as a trio.

Madre was good to her word, refusing to probe Mallory for information, and treating the boy exactly as before, but it was easy to see that a change had come over the community, and while it was an enlivening one – benign rather than malignant, unifying rather than divisive – Mallory saw that soon the situation would need to be addressed.

One Friday afternoon, as black vultures circled in a breathless sky, and with the sun so hot that the desert rocks shimmered with heat, she sat in Madre's gazebo, drinking a San Miguel and watching Chili Smurf barbecue halloumi kebabs and marinated tempeh. 'They're curious, aren't they?' she said. 'They want to know more about Jacob. About what's happening here.'

'Naturally.'

Mallory clinked the bottle against her teeth. 'They're being very good about it.'

'They don't want to frighten you away. You're loved, the pair of you. You're dear to us all.'

'I know that.'

'You can trust everyone here,' Madre said. 'You may not have noticed, but we haven't taken in any new settlers for a while. We decided, unanimously, to stop mentioning this place to those who might choose to join us. Just until we figure this thing out.'

'I noticed there hadn't been anyone new. I didn't realise it was deliberate.' Mallory took another swig of beer. 'Can I tell you our story?'

'Child, you can tell me anything.'

So she did. She talked, first, about her parents, and all those who had come before them. But mostly she talked about Obe, and when she relived her memories of him she began to cry.

Her ears, as she recounted the story of how she had found him that morning on Gwynver Beach, crashed with the sound of the sea. Ocean salt bloomed in her nose. Madre lifted her head as she listened, almost as if she could hear the same waves, and smell the same brine.

Mallory talked of their eight-month journey across Europe, culminating in the night upon the mountain when she gave birth. She talked, too, about family life in Eaux-Bonnes, how it had ended in tragedy, and how she had travelled with Jacob for months before discovering Alto Paraíso.

*It must have been so hard for you.*

'Losing Obe,' Mallory said, watching the smoke rising from Chili Smurf's barbecue. '*That* was the hardest thing. The worst thing. We were so close to getting away. So close. He was such a great dad, Madre. Jacob would have learned so much from him.' *And I wouldn't have been alone.*

'You're *not* alone,' the woman replied.

It was a moment before either of them realised what had happened. They turned their heads. Stared at each other in silent incredulity.

Mallory replayed their conversation. 'Did you . . .' she began.

Madre's face had lost some of its colour. 'I think I might have done. But I don't know.' She chugged from her beer, spilling a little of it onto her blouse. 'Don't stop,' she said. 'Don't make a thing of it. Carry on.'

Heart thumping, Mallory did as she was instructed. Returning to her story, she explained more about Obe's gift, how the boy had suffered with it and what had happened with his father. Then she began to talk about Jacob. 'Obe was the first to notice,' she said. 'I was out of the house at the time, and he'd made grilled chicken for lunch. But Jacob wanted—'

*melon*

'—yeah, and when Obe wouldn't give it to him—'

*the boy made him taste it*

'Exactly.'

Suddenly, it felt as if the desert sun had sucked the breath from Mallory's throat. In the centre of the clearing, framed by the circle of rusting vehicles and the bright flags stirred by not a lick of wind, Jacob played football with Bijoy Disco Mahadevhi, Niamh Desert Lizard and Stormy Angelique. Between them they kicked up great clouds of white dust.

'Think about something,' Mallory said softly. 'A single, simple image. Anything you like.'

Licking her lips, Madre nodded. She closed her eyes and concentrated.

Mallory flinched. Then she barked a laugh, her tension releasing like a spring. 'An erect penis.'

The older woman sniggered, slapping her knee. *Try me.*

Closing her eyes, Mallory concentrated.

A few moments later, Madre roared with laughter. 'OK, that was *far* too dirty.'

*You started it.*

'True. OK, let me try something else. Ready?'

'Ready.'

Abruptly, the taste of beer vanished from Mallory's tongue, replaced by something she didn't recognise, and wasn't entirely pleasant.

*I don't know what that is.*

*Then you've lived a very sheltered life, chiquita.*

Mallory blushed, suspecting that there was a degree of truth to the woman's words.

Madre might have been the first to be touched by Jacob's gift, but she wasn't the last. Chili Smurf was next. After that, Caecilius II and Bijoy Disco Mahadevhi. By late summer, the entire community – now numbering twenty-seven souls – had undergone the transformation. For a while, as they adapted to their new reality, things became chaotic. At times, Mallory experienced such sensory overload that she began to understand what it must have been like for Obe. Initially, those with Jacob's gift could not help but shout; nor could they direct their thoughts with any degree of accuracy, or corral their emotions with any hope of success. Walking among the caravans and trailers, her mouth would flood with the taste of caramel, mint, ginger, chilli, pecans, margaritas or salted pork. She would hear church bells ringing, birdsong, wind chimes, a sitar's plucked strings. She felt grief for the passing of people she hadn't met, guilt for transgressions she hadn't committed; but mostly she felt love, and she felt hope, and a burning sense of what could be.

For a while it was almost too much, but they persevered, working hard and long at refining their talents: sharing without intruding, talking without shouting, and gradually intuiting the ethics and etiquette appropriate for such powerful new gifts.

That autumn, by general consent, they lifted the moratorium on recruitment. Steadily, a second ring of dwellings grew up around the first. More motorhomes arrived. More trailers and more tents. Flags fluttered on the desert wind.

By the start of the following year a third ring had grown, and the number of souls at Alto Paraíso had swelled to two hundred and eight. They raised a huge canvas marquee. Inside, the community's old-timers helped to instruct the newest arrivals.

As before, there was no hierarchy, none of the traditional structures of power.

Ideas were shared and debated. With the honesty that resulted from such powerfully empathetic bonds, consensus was surprisingly easy to achieve.

*We need to decide what comes next*, Mallory ventured one day, as they gathered beneath the canvas to escape the midday heat. She heard a silent chorus of agreement.

There were, she added, many communities such as theirs spread across the world, where honest folk had gathered in peace to dictate the pace of their lives. She pointed out that the settlement of Alto Paraíso was well represented internationally; its members hailed from every continent.

That spring, after months of preparation, the big marquee was dismantled, the tents were packed up and the gathered vehicles – those that could still move – were filled with fuel. Tyres were inflated, batteries were charged. Soon after, a long convoy of motorhomes, cars, buses, trucks and motorbikes pulled onto the desert road and made its way east to Tabernas. There, items of value were sold. Bank accounts were emptied. Money was pooled and spent.

Mallory did not need to say goodbye to Madre, because the grey-haired matriarch was one of twenty-three Alto Paraíso residents assigned to communities in Europe. They had calculated numbers based on population density: thirty-two others would fly to Africa; fifteen to North America; twelve to

South America. The majority would go to Asia.

At the airport, after bidding farewell to those flying out, Mallory put her arm around Jacob and walked the boy towards one of five rust-speckled motorhomes that would carry the twenty-three to their various European destinations.

*Ready?* she asked.

He filled her head with the scent of wild flowers. *Ready.*

*I love you, kiddo.*

*Love you too, Mummy.*

*I wish your dad was here to see this.*

*I do, too.*

*He was the best, you know.*

*I know.*

*The very best, at everything he did.*

Jacob grinned. *You didn't like his jokes.*

*I LOVED his jokes.*

In her head, a trombone played a glissando. When her son looked up at her and laughed, Mallory's heart filled.

Together, they climbed aboard Madre's old bus, closed the door behind them and took their seats.

# ACKNOWLEDGEMENTS

Huge thanks to my editors on this book, Emily Griffin and Sara Adams, and to Esen Yıldız for answering all my Turkish language queries.

# THE
# DISCIPLE

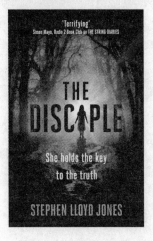

*They are coming . . .*

On a storm-battered road at the edge of the Devil's kitchen, a woman survives a fatal accident and gives birth to a girl who should never have lived.

The child's protection lies in the hands of Edward Schwinn – a loner who must draw himself out of darkness to keep her safe – and her arrival will trigger a chain of terrifying events that no one can explain.

She is a child like no other, being hunted by an evil beyond measure.

For if the potential within her is realised, nothing will be the same. Not for Edward. Not for any who live to see it.

**HEADLINE**

# WRITTEN
## IN THE
# BLOOD

FEAR THE TRUTH, IT'S...

WRITTEN
IN THE
BLOOD

STEPHEN LLOYD JONES

**High in the mountains of the Swiss Alps Leah Wilde is about to gamble her life to bring a powerful man an offer. A promise.**

Leah has heard the dark stories about him and knows she is walking into the lion's den. But her options are running out. Her rare lineage, kept secret for years, is under terrible threat. That is, unless Leah and her mother Hannah are prepared to join up with their once deadly enemies.

Should the prey trust the predator?

Is hope for future generations ever enough to wash away the sins of the past?

With a new and chilling danger stalking them all, and the survival of their society at stake, they may have little choice . . .

**HEADLINE**

# THE STRING DIARIES

**He has a face you love. A voice you trust.**
**To survive you must kill him.**

The rules of survival are handed from mother to daughter.
Inherited, like the curse that has stalked Hannah and her family across centuries.

He changes his appearance at will, speaks with a stolen voice and hides behind the face of a beloved, waiting to strike.

Generation after generation, he has destroyed them.
And all they could do was to run.
Until now.
Now, it is time for Hannah to turn and fight.